Something you should know

MELISSA HILL

D0489221

POOLBEG

This novel is entirely a work of fiction. The names, characters and incidents portrayed in it are the work of the author's imagination. Any resemblance to actual persons, living or dead, events or localities is entirely coincidental.

Published 2003
by Poolbeg Press Ltd
123 Grange Hill, Baldoyle
Dublin 13, Ireland
E-mail: poolbeg@poolbeg.com

© Melissa Hill 2003

The moral right of the author has been asserted.

Typesetting, layout, design © Poolbeg Press Ltd.

3 5 7 9 10 8 6 4

A catalogue record for this book is available from the British Library.

ISBN 1-84223-161-8

Typeset by Patricia Hope in Palatino 9.6/13.5
Printed by
Nørhaven Paperback, Denmark

www.poolbeg.com

About the Author

Melissa Hill is originally from Cahir in Co. Tipperary, and now lives with her husband (and their dog Homer) in Ashford. She has worked in retail, banking and computers and presently works full-time in the family business in Wicklow.

Something You Should Know is her first novel. Her bestselling novels, *Not What You Think* and *Never Say Never* are also published by Poolbeg.

Also by Melissa Hill

Not What You Think
Never Say Never

Acknowledgements

I'm pretty certain that the majority of first-time writers, like myself, compose this bit feeling equal measures of excitement and terror. After all, if you get to the stage where you're thanking the people who helped with your novel, then chances are you're getting published!

So here goes:

First and foremost, a huge thanks to my brilliant husband Kevin for your love and continuing support. You may not have played the part of the typical coffee-bringing writer's hubby, but you never once gave up on me, and we both know that this is as much yours as it is mine.

To my family, particularly my mother Nell, who is responsible for all of this by getting me addicted to books when I was small and using them as bribes to get me in to the dentist! Thanks, Mam, not just for the books (and looking after my teeth!) but for your unending support and faith in me.

To my dad Noel, who for this novel gave me the low-down on life as a hero fireman, and who to me is, and always has been, a true 'hero' in every sense of the word.

A massive thanks to my fantastic sister, Amanda, who was the very first person to read my scribblings and, luckily for me, kept asking to read more. If it wasn't for her, I might never have shown it to anyone else.

To my baby sister Sharon, an absolute legend for passing her driving test first time and who swore she wouldn't read this until it was 'a proper book' – no excuses now, Shar!

To my oldest and closest friends, Fiona Noonan and Marie Costigan, who are almost as excited about this as I am – and Marie, if I ever need a publicist, I know where to look! Thank you for all your support and encouragement, not just now, but throughout our long friendship – I don't think you have any idea how much it means to me.

To great friends – Lisa Hamilton, who read the story,

loved it, and insisted I give it a go, Sarah and the Cahir gang, Breda Barrett, Aine Smyth, Laura Doyle, Mick and all the lads, who have been hugely supportive of me and my writing – when they aren't slagging me off about it! We'll all make it to Las Vegas one of these days – I promise!

To Andy, Kay and the Hills who have been a tremendous support, particularly my sister-in-law Janet, one of the very first to lend her encouragement to *Something You Should Know*.

To Pat, Sue and Emma Fitz, who I know will be flying the flag for me across the water!

A colossal thank-you to my brilliant agent Ger Nichol for putting her faith in me, and also for her great advice, boundless enthusiasm and support for my writing. Ger, you are a true lady.

To the Poolbeg team, an incredibly dedicated group of professionals who deserve so much credit for the truly amazing work they do for their authors. Thank you all, especially the fantastic Paula Campbell, for giving me and my book a chance. To Gaye Shortland, whose good humour and tireless patience ensured the editing process was a pleasure.

Without schoolteachers, it's doubtful most of us could write a single sentence – let alone a novel – so thank you all, but a special mention to Jo O'Neill who instilled in me a real love of writing.

To everyone in my home-town of Cahir and my adopted Wicklow who has taken the time to wish me well and express support in the run-up to publication. I've been completely overwhelmed by the encouragement and it really means a lot – again, thank you.

Most importantly, a million thanks to the readers who spent their hard-earned cash on this book. I really appreciate it and very much hope that you enjoy *Something You Should Know*. I'd love to see what you think, so, if you can, visit me at www.melissahill.info

Praise for Melissa Hill

"Hill has managed to combine elements of romance with the page-turning benefits of a thriller. One to read" *U Magazine*

"An excellent book by first-time novelist Melissa Hill – a welcome new kid on the block" *Ireland on Sunday*

"Well-written . . . An enjoyable read" *Evening Herald*

"A refreshing read from a fresh new talent" *The Evening Echo*

"Be warned – you won't put it down!" *Sunday World*

"It's a gem! Another very good read and a worthy successor to *Something You Should Know*" *Evening Herald*

"A great book" *Woman's Way*

"Well done to Melissa for providing us with another excellent read" *Sunday Life*

"Sharp . . . fast-paced and unpredictable" *Kilkenny People*

"Another great read featuring Melissa's unique style of fiction with its unusual twists and turns" *Wicklow People*

Dedicated with much love to my husband, Kevin

&

In Loving Memory of
Jerry & Bridie Ryan and Josie & Fitzie FitzGerald
who I know would have been thrilled . . .

Chapter 1

The weighing-scales lay menacingly on the bathroom floor, daring Jenny to put herself out of her misery. She stepped on the scales, and felt her throat go dry watching the tiny needle come to a standstill after what seemed like minutes of bobbing back and forth. Eleven and a half stone. Eleven and a *half* stone! Where had the bloody half-stone come from?

She had been using her Slendertone and her Air-Glider all week. OK, maybe not *all* week, she admitted, but certainly for most of it and she specifically remembered missing *Coronation Street* on Monday night because she had spent longer than expected on her 'exercise routine'.

And despite her efforts she hadn't lost a single pound – in fact, she had *gained* half a stone. How had that happened when her horoscope for the month clearly predicted that she would lose all the weight for the wedding?

The self-sacrifices you make between now and August will

1

eventually result in the conclusion of a lengthy struggle you have had with yourself.

Wasn't it plain for all to see that 'self-sacrifices' meant giving up chocolate and garlic chips and the 'lengthy struggle' was obviously her lifelong battle with her weight?

So why the extra half-stone then?

Suddenly the thought hit her. Water retention – it was probably just water retention. Her friend Karen was as thin as a lath and she sometimes complained that she couldn't fit into her clothes as a result of water retention. That was it, Jenny consoled herself. She hadn't gained weight at all. It *had* to be water retention.

She heard Mike whistle from downstairs in the kitchen. She couldn't understand how her fiancé could be so sprightly in the mornings. He never seemed to want to pull the covers over his head and drift back to glorious sleep, shutting out the rest of the world. Jenny would have loved to stay in bed just a little longer and, if Mike hadn't persisted in getting her up, she might very well have stayed there until midday and that would be a total waste of the day.

What a pity the exam was so soon, she sighed, rinsing the conditioner out of her hair. She would need to get a lot of work done today and the earlier she got started the better. There was no way she would be promoted to Mortgage Officer at Alliance Trust Bank if she didn't pass this exam. At this stage, she would have to make up for lost time and hope against hope that what she did today would be enough. And Mike had gone out of his way to ensure that she had a quiet day to herself – for once.

She wrapped a towel around her head before joining Mike downstairs in the kitchen.

He put a steaming mug of tea and a plate of warm buttered toast on the table in front of her and kissed her lightly on the forehead.

"Awake now, Goldilocks?" he teased.

Jenny made a face at him.

"My darling, I know now why I decided to marry you – you have the nicest scowl. It just brightens up my day."

Jenny took a bite of her toast, grimaced and then spat it back out onto the plate.

"*Arggh!* What's that?"

"What's what?" Mike looked perplexed.

"The toast – what did you put on the toast?"

"Kerrygold," he answered nonchalantly. "Why?"

"Kerrygold . . ." Jenny trailed off in amazement. "Mike, you know I'm eating Low-Low these days. You *can't* put real butter on my toast or on anything else when I'm on a diet. You know that!"

"Low-Low, huh?" he said, his eyes twinkling with amusement. "And I suppose Leo Burdock's deep-fry their chips in Low-Low these days, do they?"

Jenny stuck her tongue out. "That's different. What I eat at weekends doesn't really count, not yet anyway."

"Oh," Mike said, struggling to keep a straight face. "Anyway, Jen, you don't have to kill yourself dieting – you know that I think you're perfect the way you are."

He reached across the breakfast bar and planted a kiss on the top of her head.

Jenny gave him a petulant look. "Mike, I've been wearing size sixteen clothes for most of my adult life and up to now it hasn't really bothered me, but this time I'm determined, *really* determined to fit into that size twelve wedding dress sitting in my wardrobe."

"Really determined, huh?"

"Absolutely."

"Right. So where's the Low-Low then?"

"What?"

"You're still eating the toast I buttered for you."

"I know. But that's because – because I'm in a bit of hurry, what with everything I have to do today and I don't really have time to wait for fresh toast and – stop laughing at me!"

Despite herself Jenny chuckled and then remembered what lay ahead for her.

"Oh, I dread hitting those books, and look – it's such a nice day out today."

She looked wistfully towards the window and out at the cloudless February sky.

"You'll be fine once you've started, you know that." Mike pushed his plate away and refilled his teacup. "Anyway it will be all over this time two weeks and then you can forget about it."

"That's the problem though," she moaned. "It's only two weeks away! Oh why oh why didn't I spend more time on this earlier? I'm an absolute idiot to have left it this long."

She picked up one of the study manuals that lay on the table and stared at it, willing the information to somehow transport itself from the pages onto her memory.

A copy of *Hello* magazine lying underneath her books distracted her momentarily. There was a picture of Liz Hurley arriving at some movie premiere or another in one

4

of her trademark figure-hugging, cleavage-boosting, split-to-the-thigh dresses. Jenny stared at Liz's midriff. There was no way anyone's stomach could be that flat. It was impossible – what with water retention and all that. In order to look like that the woman *had* to be wearing a pair of those hold-me-in knickers.

"Jen, you'll be fine," Mike soothed. "You're probably already familiar with most of the material for this exam. Haven't you been working alongside Conor for a few months now? You're bound to have picked up on the important things."

"I know, but I haven't put much effort into learning the heavy stuff – Legal Title, Land Registry and the like. If I don't know about those, I can't possibly qualify as an adviser. I could be granting mortgages left right and centre without researching properly. Imagine?" She bit her lip.

Mike smiled at her encouragingly and took one of her hands in his.

"Don't worry about it, Hamilton. I know you're well able for it. There is no one better for the job and you know that it's good as yours as far as the Bank are concerned. Just use today's peace and quiet to study hard and then tomorrow night we'll go out for a few drinks and relax. What do you think?"

Jenny nodded and they shook on it. Mike was right. There was no point in fretting about the exam. She would get stuck in today. It was just the thought of all that studying that was putting her off. And she should really make the most of a day to herself.

"I was just thinking," Mike said. "If you don't mind, I might ask our new guy along tomorrow night with his partner – if he has one. I haven't had a chance to get to know him socially yet – what do you think?"

Jenny helped herself to another piece of toast.

"No problem here," she said. "I'm anxious to meet this new whiz kid anyway. What's he like?"

Mike shook his head in wonder. "He's terrific, Jenny, and I think he's going to be a real asset to InTech. He's had plenty of marketing experience, especially whilst working in the States and you know how useless I am at that."

Jenny smiled knowingly. Mike was an excellent programmer but, while he had designed software for some of Ireland's biggest firms, he was no salesman. With the growing number of Information Technology companies setting up in the country, and particularly in Dublin, her fiancé's company needed the right person to promote their products within what was becoming a rapidly saturated market.

Mike and his partners had been trying for quite some time to find someone who knew the industry from the inside out. This new guy, it seemed, was a rare breed: he was a highly proficient programmer and equally adept at Marketing and Sales.

"He's no fool either," Mike said. "It took us some time to hammer out a decent contract with him. He didn't want to come in on ground level and commission bonuses like the rest of them. Stephen thought he was a cocky little git."

Jenny rolled her eyes. "Stephen would. I'll bet he was disappointed that you weren't employing some ravishing redhead with a cleavage and figure to die for."

Mike laughed at Jenny's all too accurate assessment of his business partner's character.

"Seriously though, this guy is a tough nut to crack. He's already had a few run-ins with Frank. Poor oul Frank kept calling him Ronan last week – he couldn't get the hang of his name and your man wouldn't stand for it. 'There is no "n" in my name. It's Roan, not Ro-n-an," Mike mimicked exaggeratedly.

Jenny's toast stopped halfway to her mouth and her heart hammered in her chest.

"What did you say his name was?"

"I know. It's unusual, isn't it? Roan – I've never come across the name before. I think he's from Kildare somewhere – Monasterevin, he said."

She had to use all her strength to try and stay calm. Her mouth went dry and for a second she didn't think she would be able to breathe. My God! It couldn't be him, could it?

"I knew a guy called Roan a few years ago, when I lived with Karen," she said, trying to keep her voice light, although her hands were shaking. "Roan Williams – I wonder is it the same guy?"

Mike didn't seem to notice her discomfort. "Yeah, Williams, that's his surname. Isn't that funny? It's true what they say about it being a small world but it's especially true in this country. Did you know him well?"

Jenny smiled falsely as she tried to swallow her toast. It felt like lead in her mouth. "Not that well," she answered automatically, her mind racing. She couldn't believe it. Roan Williams was back in Ireland. How could she face him? Should she tell Mike about him? No, not yet. She needed some time to think about this, to establish what to do next.

Mike's voice interrupted her thoughts. "Jen, did you hear me? I said that maybe we should go into town tomorrow night – what do you think?"

She looked at him blankly.

Mike got up and ruffled her damp curls. "You're not with it, hon. I thought you'd be well awake by now."

Jenny fixed him with a sharp look.

"OK, OK!" He held his hands up "You're obviously in great form today so I think I'll leave you to it. I'm off now to battle the Dublin traffic and when I get home this evening, I'll pretend to be a first-time buyer and you can tell me everything there is to know about securing the house of my dreams, right?" He drained his cup and put it in the sink, then gave Jenny a light kiss on the nose.

Jenny instantly felt like a heel. Pulling Mike towards her she kissed him soundly on the lips. "Sorry, love, I'm like a bear with a sore head. I don't know how you put up with me."

Mike adopted a serious tone. "Jennifer, I don't know how I put up with you either, but as of next August, I'll be stuck with you for good so I suppose I'll just have to make the best of it."

"Get out, you brat, while you still have the legs to carry you!" Jenny swung at him and Mike ducked out the door, laughing as he went.

"Oh, by the way," he said, putting his head around the door. "I'll be home a little bit later this evening, remember, so don't make dinner too early."

"Are you sure you don't want me to go to Rachel's?" she asked distractedly.

Mike waved the suggestion away. "It's all organised.

I'm leaving work at four so that I can get across town early – hopefully before the worst of the traffic. I wish my little sister would get herself a pad on this side of the city and save me a journey. Anyway, we'll see you later."

Jenny nodded and forced a smile but it was a relief to see him leave.

She sat at the kitchen table for a long time after she heard the front door close.

How would she feel if she saw Roan again? *When* she saw him, she corrected herself. She and Mike went out with the guys in InTech all the time – their paths were bound to cross sooner or later.

It had to happen, didn't it? Just when everything was going so well for them – Roan Williams had to come back into her life – *their* lives.

With a heavy heart Jenny got up, cleared the table and put the dirty dishes in the sink. She opened the fridge door and looked inside. She stared blankly at the shelves for a moment and then closed the door again, forgetting why she had opened it in the first place. She filled the kettle with water and switched it on, then poured washing-up liquid on the dishes and put the bottle back in the cupboard.

She went over to the kitchen window and looked out towards the small back garden. Then, leaning her head against the window, Jenny finally surrendered to her tears.

Chapter 2

Karen Cassidy checked her watch and quickened her pace as she strode down Grafton Street, cursing under her breath when she read the time. She'd be late for her appointment if she didn't hurry. It was almost nine o'clock and she still had to find the place. Pushing her dark hair away from her face, she stopped suddenly as an outfit caught her eye in the window of Pamela Scott's. That pink and purple halter-neck dress would be stunning for Jenny's wedding. What a pity that she already had her outfit! Well, she might buy it anyway, Karen decided. With everything that was happening lately, she deserved a treat.

She continued quickly towards College Green and just as she reached the pedestrian crossing at Trinity College, she heard the tinkle of the Irish National Anthem come from inside her handbag.

The lights went green and she struggled to find her mobile whilst crossing the road. Blasted things! Why was it that the inside of every handbag was always black and you could never find anything when you needed it? It would make a lot more sense, Karen thought irritably, if they made the inside of the bag a lighter colour than the rest of it. Wouldn't it be a lot easier to find everything instead of struggling like she was now, trying to find the bloody mobile phone? But *they* never seemed to have an ounce of cop-on.

"Ah, here we are," she said out loud to herself, unaware of the curious looks she was getting from her fellow-pedestrians.

She stepped into the doorway of the huge Bank of Ireland building to take the call and the ringing promptly stopped.

"Shit!" she exclaimed, glaring at a passer-by who stared at her with undisguised amusement. She was about to replace the phone in her handbag when it beeped loudly. She read the text message from Jenny. *PLEASE RING ME BACK AT HOME AS SOON AS YOU GET THIS.*

Jenny would have to wait, Karen thought, putting the phone back in her bag and continuing up Dame St. She was definitely late now. She raced up the street trying to find the address she had written on her hand. Eventually she stopped in front of a building with the name Stevenson & Donnelly Solicitors inscribed on a large brass plaque beside the doorway

She had found it – finally. Karen pushed the intercom and seconds later she was inside the building.

The receptionist smiled at her. "Miss Cassidy?"

Karen nodded.

"Mr Donnelly will see you now." She gestured to one of the doorways behind the reception area. "Would you like some coffee?"

"I'd love a cup, thanks." Karen smiled back as she removed her coat and knocked on the heavy wooden door.

"Come in, please."

Karen opened the door and was greeted with a nod from a serious-looking, older man. He was seated behind a large oak desk, which had heavy books and sheets of paper strewn all over it. *I thought I was untidy,* Karen thought to herself. A typical solicitor's practice. Luckily, over the phone John Donnelly sounded like he knew what he was doing

"Karen, how are you? It's nice to finally meet you face to face. Please – sit down."

He gestured to the comfortable-looking leather armchair in front of his desk and Karen obliged.

"I'm very sorry I'm late, Mr Donnelly. I had a little trouble finding the place."

He waved that away. "That's no trouble at all, dear. Did Linda offer you some coffee?"

At that very moment Linda appeared with a tray and Karen gratefully accepted a mug of what smelt like very strong coffee and a Rich Tea biscuit.

"Thank you, Linda." Donnelly smiled at the receptionist and then sat back in his chair. "Now, Karen, we should get down to business. I know we've discussed the case in detail over the phone but I just want to run through everything with you one more time, just to make sure I understand things perfectly. The property is where – Harold's Cross, I believe?"

Karen nodded. "22a Harold's Cross Crescent. It's a two-bedroomed townhouse and we bought it just under three years ago."

"And there is a mortgage on the property?"

"Yes. The mortgage is basically the root of the problem. I'm unsure of my rights – legally I mean, because the mortgage was never in my name. I just didn't see any need – at the time."

"I see. The mortgage was solely in Mr Quinn's name then?"

"That's right," Karen answered quietly.

"But you have contributed financially throughout the duration of the mortgage?"

"Oh, absolutely – we each had separate accounts but we keep – I mean we kept – a joint account for electricity bills, heating and the mortgage repayments."

"Well, that's a start certainly. I assume you have bank statements that verify your contributions to the account from which the mortgage payments were made? And Mr Quinn does not dispute the fact that you made these contributions, does he?"

"Not as far as I know, he doesn't. It's just –' Karen was nervous. "It was always Shane's house, wasn't it – legally I mean? What I paid means nothing?"

"Mr Quinn's name may have been on the mortgage but the building society, in truth, hold the title deeds to the property until the mortgage is repaid in full. While you both contributed, and while the mortgage was solely in Mr Quinn's name, no one has full legal title until the loan is repaid. However, Karen, I should warn you that the judge is likely to rule in favour of Mr Quinn."

God, he was so dispassionate about it all! Did he not realise how hard it was for her to come here and discuss all of this with a perfect stranger? Still, these things meant nothing at all to him, she supposed. He was just doing his job. Sympathy didn't come into it. She had asked for his advice and here he was advising her. What did she expect? A big hug, soothing words and a box of Kleenex?

"You see," she told him, "I have nowhere else to live at present so I'm still living there. Mr Quinn has asked – " *Asked?* That was an understatement. "that I move out so that it can be sold. But I don't want to move out. That's why I'm determined to bring this to court, to see if I have any right to stay there. It's been my home for the last few years and I don't want to go back to rented accommodation again, not now, after . . . everything."

She noticed that Donnelly was writing all of this down on a notepad as she spoke. At least she *thought* he was. Maybe he was just doodling; maybe he was bored by her predicament. He was probably used to more exciting cases, like people falling over and suing the Corporation for breaking an ankle and the like. Or divorce cases. There must be loads of those about, seeing as it was legal to get divorced in Ireland these days. This must be dead boring for him.

Donnelly said nothing for a long while, then he asked, "I assume you have spoken at length about this with Mr Quinn?"

"We've spoken a few times but only through our respective solicitors. My solicitor – the one I had before you I mean – hoped that we might be able to come to some arrangement between ourselves. But, Mr Quinn and I have quite an acrimonious relationship now. He won't agree that I'm entitled to anything. Which is why I am here with you today."

Karen was amazed at how civil she made it sound. If only he knew!

"I see," Donnelly said. "Well, as things stand at the moment, you may have no option but to go to the courts. You are quite fortunate that Mr Quinn has let you stay on so far. However, I would imagine – if things are as you say – that he will be anxious to move on and bring matters to a satisfactory conclusion."

Karen was fuming. Why was he taking *his* side? Anxious to move on indeed! He made it sound like she was nothing – just a temporary inconvenience. What about her feelings? She wanted this sorted out so she could begin to move on too. But she'd be damned if she was going to just roll over and play dead with this one. There was no way he was going to throw her out on the streets. She had paid her dues too; hadn't Donnelly himself admitted that earlier?

The solicitor noticed her expression and smiled kindly. "Karen, please don't take any of this the wrong way. I understand that you have been through a lot in the last year or so and for that I sympathise. I know nothing of your relationship with Mr Quinn and, in truth, that relationship has no bearing on this situation. I'm merely discussing your options with you, but one thing you have to remember is that the sooner this matter is sorted out the better, for both yourself *and* Mr Quinn. You have to consider that he may put some serious pressure on you to bring the matter to a close even before the case comes before a court."

Karen nodded. This was awful! At least, in a marriage, you knew your legal rights. But in situations like this, when you weren't married, well, everything was a lot more muddled. How did it ever come to this, she wondered. Shane had loved that house so much and the two of them had such fun at the beginning, picking out different bits and pieces in Woodies and Atlantic DIY. Stop it, she told herself. Don't start getting maudlin about it now; just concentrate on the task in hand.

She brightened a little. "I understand that you need to look at it from every angle, Mr Donnelly, and I'm sorry if I seem a little –" she searched for the right word, "edgy. But I've never been through anything like this before and I find it all a little bit daunting to tell the truth." Her head lowered and she looked up at him through dark eyelashes. "I suppose I never considered that something like this could possibly happen."

She felt a lump form in her throat.

"Karen, I know all of this must be very difficult for you," he said kindly, "but now you must examine your options very carefully. Please think some more about an agreement with Mr Quinn before you go to court. Because you were never married, and the house was never in your name, then I'm afraid you don't have much of a case.

As for the contents of the property, well, this is something that you will have to iron out between you. Unless you have retained receipts for every individual purchase for the house, it is very difficult to ascertain the legal ownership of fixtures, furniture etc."

Karen nodded.

Donnelly leaned forward and regarded Karen thoughtfully.

"Are you absolutely sure that you want to follow

through on this, Karen? You know I have an obligation to tell you that I don't think you can retain even part-ownership of the property. The law is against you on this one."

Karen wasn't fazed. "You're not the first person or indeed the first solicitor to have told me that, Mr Donnelly. But I owe it to myself to follow through and I'm determined that nobody will take the house from me – not without a fight."

Donnelly set down his pen. "All right then. Hopefully we can get it sorted out sooner rather than later. I'll press ahead with Mr Quinn's solicitor and I'll be in touch in with you as soon as a court date is confirmed."

Karen stood up and went to shake his hand "Thank you. And thank you for taking the case. This means a lot to me. I haven't had much luck with solicitors over the last few months."

"You're very welcome, Karen, and I promise that I'll do my best for you. My late partner, Mr Stephenson, was a good friend of your father's so I'd better not let you down." He smiled and shook her hand warmly. "You have my card – if you need advice about anything else, please give me a call."

"I will, thanks again."

As Karen left, Donnelly noticed the steely determination in her dark eyes.

He shook his head as he sat back down behind his desk. It was becoming a common occurrence these days. So many couples were buying houses together before marriage without giving a second thought to their individual legal rights should anything happen. Poor girl, she was obviously determined to go as far as she could with this. And despite his intricate knowledge of the law and the hopelessness of such a case, the solicitor hoped that somehow Karen Cassidy might win.

Chapter 3

Shane's sister Barbara looked around the small kitchen and wrinkled her nose in disgust.

"Not much of a housekeeper, is she?" she said, eyeing the used teabags on the table, the smear of butter and scattering of crumbs on the worktop, dried spaghetti on the wall above the cooker, and a pile of dirty dishes in the sink.

"No, tidiness was never Karen's forte," her brother agreed, opening the fridge and stepping back quickly as a strong whiff of some unrecognisable mouldy food filled his nostrils.

"I wish the estate agent would hurry up. What if she comes back?" Barbara didn't want to stay here any longer than was necessary. She was sorry she had come actually, sorry that her curiosity about this place had got the better of her. It was an absolute dive.

"Relax, Babs, she won't be back from work until at least after five. And her office is a good forty-minute walk or fifteen-minute bus ride from here." He looked around the room and frowned. "It *is* an awful mess, isn't it? I suppose I'd better go upstairs to the bedrooms and see if they look any better."

"Don't be long, will you? It's nearly lunch-time and I fancy going into town for a while after we're finished here."

Barbara went into the living-room and flopped onto the small two-seater couch between the brightly coloured scatter-cushions. This was a nice room, actually. The bay window was a lovely feature and seemed to make the place look a lot bigger than it actually was. Despite the mismatched furniture and that awful rug. If she had a house like this she would replace the cheap pine floorboards with pure oak and have the walls repainted a decent colour, anything but that vulgar orange it was at the moment. And purple cushions on a cornflower-yellow couch? That girl hadn't an ounce of taste! Barbara picked up a magazine from the coffee table and began to flick idly through it. She was studying a page from the fashion section so intently that she didn't hear the key turn in the front door. She did however hear the door shut and, startled, jumped up from the couch.

"Hello," Jenny said, surprised at seeing this blonde girl that she didn't recognise. "I didn't realise there was anyone else here." She offered her hand. "I'm Jenny Hamilton – a friend of Karen's. She's on her way back – she just stopped off at the shop for a few things. I hope I didn't surprise you too much? She gave me the keys." Jenny held the keys up apologetically.

"He's just upstairs. I'll get him," Barbara said, starting up the stairs.

But he was on his way down.

"Hello, Jenny, how are you? I haven't seen you since –"

"I'm fine, thanks," Jenny cut him off as he appeared at the foot of the stairs. "I didn't realise that you would be here today." Then she added pointedly, "I don't think Karen did either."

"Well," he said, "we needed to check out a few things." He nodded at his sister. "You remember Barbara, don't you?"

Jenny turned and studied the older woman with undisguised surprise. Barbara, Shane's sister – she hadn't recognised her at all. She was certain that the girl's hair had been dark the last time she had seen her. Today she looked completely different.

"Can we go now, please?" Barbara asked, ignoring Jenny. "I don't think I can stand the smell in here any longer and my skirt's ruined just from sitting on that couch. Those cushion-covers have obviously never been washed."

Jenny examined the other woman's cream-coloured skirt for signs of spoilage but couldn't see a thing. The cheek of it – Karen would be livid. She was sure that her friend had no idea he was here at the house. And bringing that one along too! If Jenny had known who Barbara was she wouldn't have been so pleasant when she came in and found her lazing on the couch. How dare they?

He looked at his watch. "I suppose we'd better go. It was nice seeing you again, Jenny."

"I'm sure Karen would like to see you both before you go," Jenny said, enjoying the sight of them squirming.

"Ah no, sure we'll head away – we have to be somewhere else anyway. Tell her I said – "

The door slammed and they heard a voice call out

from the hallway. "You can tell me yourself, you ignorant pig!"

Karen bustled past them, her arms laden down with shopping. She dropped the shopping bags in the centre of the room and, turning, put her hands on her hips.

"What the hell is going on? And how did you get in here?" she snarled.

"Now hang on just a minute, Karen," he began. "It's our house. We have as much right to be here as you do – more actually, as you well know."

"Well, I've got news for you, Quinn. According to my *solicitor*, you have nothing over me with regard to this house. I've paid my dues too. That means," she added, eyes blazing, "that I have every right to tell you to get the hell out of here!"

It was a lie but Karen was pleased to see his eyes widen at the mention of the solicitor.

"Why did you have to go behind my back?" she continued. "Why didn't you just tell me you were bringing her over for a look? But that's not your style, is it? You can't be straight up about anything; you never could. Sly and sneaky – that's your way, isn't it?"

"I think you'd both better leave," Jenny said quietly, feeling that she needed to say something to defuse the situation. She stole a glance at Barbara. She couldn't be certain, but the girl looked as though she was really enjoying the confrontation.

But just then she rounded on Karen. "You little madam! How dare you speak to him like that? You're lucky that he's let you stay here for as long as he has. If it was up to me . . ." she trailed off, glaring at Karen. "At least now that we're going to court, it won't be long before we're rid of you – finally."

She glared at Karen as though she was a piece of doggy-doo stuck to the bottom of her Dunnes shoes. Jenny knew that her shoes were Dunnes because she had a pair herself and the heels hurt like crazy.

"Give it up, Karen," Barbara said. "You know you haven't a hope in hell."

Jenny knew that Karen was using every ounce of restraint she possessed not to attack the other woman physically. But she was better than that.

"Barbara, you learned how to put a sentence together – good girl!" Karen said, her voice high and dripping with sarcasm. "Has your brother been teaching you some new words? You must have been practising that speech for ages!"

"Karen, look, there's no need to upset her – we're going now," he said, going into the hallway and taking his coat from where it hung on the coatstand.

Just then the doorbell rang and Jenny noticed Barbara look decidedly nervous as Karen opened the door.

"Hello, I'm Patrick Ryan from Ryan, Mitchell & Associates," said the affable-looking man standing in the doorway. "I'm here to meet with Mr Quinn – for the valuation?"

"Valuation!" Karen whirled around to face them. "You organised a valuation on my house without my permission! How dare you? How dare you try and sell this house from under me, you gutless bastard?"

The estate agent looked as though he hoped a group of aliens would land, take him to their spaceship and carry him off to Mars – anywhere else but there.

"Erm, maybe now is not the best time . . . " he began.

"You're damned right it's not the best time," Karen growled. "I'm very sorry but it seems that Mr Quinn has wasted your time. There will be no valuation of this property today and not for as long as I'm here!"

"We'll see how much longer that will be," Barbara hissed, easing out the door past the white-faced estate agent who now stood well back from the door, unsure what to do next. Eventually he retreated to the safety of his Volvo parked a little way down the road. When the others were safely out of the house, Jenny closed the door behind them and went back into the living-room.

Karen was sitting on the couch and hugging one of the purple and gold Sari cushions she was so fond of, tears streaming down her face.

"The stupid bastard," she said as Jenny sat down and put her arms around her. "How dare he come in here behind my back? I would never have known if I wasn't off work today. And you know, it mightn't have been the first time – he could have been here lots of times that I didn't know about." Enraged, she threw a cushion across the room. "Why did he have to go behind my back and why did he bring that anorexic, dyslexic, bleached-blondee bimbo with him?"

In spite of her tears, Karen grinned, seeing Jenny trying to hide a smile at her description of Barbara.

"I don't know why I'm crying over the bastard. I've done enough of that – it was just such a shock to see them standing there when I came in." She sat up and wiped her eyes, determined to get rid of the tears.

"I can't believe I didn't recognise her,' said Jenny. "I

came in the door and introduced myself, thinking she was a friend of yours from work. I should have known who she was when she was so unfriendly. And I couldn't believe it when you slagged her off about being slow."

Karen face broke into a broad grin. "Yeah, did you see the look on her face? Serves her right for thinking she could have a go at me."

"Well, no better woman than yourself to put her in her place, Cassidy!"

"I wonder were they here long?" Karen asked, wiping her eyes with her sweater. "And sure enough the place would have to be in an awful state. I was late for my appointment in town this morning so I didn't get a chance to do the washing-up."

She snorted. "Typical! The one day he decided to pay a visit. God, I need a cigarette!"

"*He* had a cheek coming in here without telling you, don't forget."

"I know that, Jen. It's just that I don't want to give him any more excuses to get me out of here." She sniffed. "But John Donnelly, the solicitor I met with this morning, reckons that he'll take the case to the courts with me. Remember I told you I spoke with him on the phone about it?"

Jenny nodded. "I had forgotten that you were seeing him today. What else did he say?"

"I'll tell you over a cup of tea and a chocolate-chip muffin." Karen stood up from the couch, picked up her shopping and went into the kitchen. She emptied the bags, put the contents in the cupboards and then filled the kettle while at the same time absently removing a piece of dried spaghetti that had somehow ended up on the wall above the cooker.

She called to Jenny. "But you tell *me* why you sounded so anxious on the phone earlier and why you are here now, instead of at home studying like you're supposed to."

Jenny's heart sank as she joined her friend in the kitchen. She had almost forgotten about her own problems what with all the commotion a few minutes ago. Now that she was here, she didn't know if she could bring herself to tell Karen. She tried to brush her off.

"Look, it's nothing really. You've enough on your plate. Tell me what the solicitor told you about the house."

"Don't start with me, Jenny Hamilton! I know there's something up. Did you and Mike have a fight?"

Karen picked a chocolate chip from one of the muffins and popped it into her mouth. "Don't mind me. I don't want to waste another second discussing that lowlife. Go on, out with it!"

"The thing is . . ." Jenny sat down at the untidy kitchen table and absently began playing with the sugar bowl. "The thing is, Karen, I think Roan Williams is back."

Karen immediately stopped picking at her muffin.

"Back? Back in Ireland – back in *Dublin*, you mean?"

Jenny nodded, her eyes firmly fixed on the table in front of her.

"But how do you know that?" Karen asked carefully. "Have you seen him? Have you heard from him? What do you mean you *think* he's back?"

"He's back in Dublin and he's taken a job at InTech."

Seeing the look of utter disbelief on her friend's face Jenny continued. "Mike told me his name this morning –

you know the way they've been looking for someone new to take over the sales and marketing end of things? Well, apparently good old Roan is the man of the moment."

"But are you sure? I mean, how do you know it's actually him? Oh shit," she said, as a thought crossed her mind. "Mike doesn't know who he is, does he? Roan didn't say anything to him, did he?"

"No, no, of course not. I don't think Roan would know that Mike had any connection with me. Anyway," she looked away, her eyes brimming with tears, "I doubt that he has given me a second thought since he left."

"Jenny, are you absolutely certain that it's the same Roan? I know 'Roan' is an unusual name but must be more people in Dublin with the same name."

"With the same surname and from Kildare?"

Karen grimaced. "OK, it's definitely him then." She poured boiling water into a teapot and stirred it. Then she looked at Jenny and hesitated a second before speaking. "Look, I don't mean to sound harsh, but you and Roan . . . well, that was a long time ago. His coming home shouldn't mean that much to you. It's been years."

The tears were by now streaming down Jenny's face and Karen noticed that she was shaking. She went to put a comforting arm around her friend's shoulders.

"Come on, Jenny! You're not still carrying a torch for Roan, surely? You've got Mike now and he's one of the nicest guys you could meet! You're getting married in a few months' time and –"

"It's not what you think, Karen, and . . . oh, I *know* I should have told you this before. To be honest, I don't really know where to start but . . ."

"Go on," Karen said, sitting down beside Jenny, disturbed by her over-the-top reaction to her old flame's homecoming.

Jenny took a mouthful of steaming tea and looked her friend squarely in the eye. The hot liquid burned her throat as she swallowed but she didn't care.

"It's just . . . it's just . . . Karen, I think I've ruined everything. About Roan and me . . . well, there's something you should know – something I should have told you a long time ago."

Chapter 4

Four Years Earlier

Karen groaned when she saw the long line of people sitting on the steps in front of the house. "Blast it, anyway!" she said in disgust. "It's the same old story everywhere we go! How do they all get here so fast?"

Jenny took the newspaper from her bag, and examined the page that they had earlier defaced with red ink whilst circling the ads for Flats to Let.

"It says here that viewing is from five o'clock to seven o'clock and it's only – what?" She checked her watch. "It's only four now – another hour before the landlord even gets here! This is hopeless, Karen. Look at all those people ahead of us – one of them is bound to take it before we even get a chance to see it."

"But, what else can we do? We have to live somewhere – here, give me a look at the newspaper again."

Jenny handed her the well-crumpled evening newspaper, which was the ultimate bible for flat-hunters in Dublin – particularly in Rathmines, where they were at the moment. It didn't look good, she thought. They had been waiting for ages outside another flat in Ranelagh, and when the landlord finally did turn up, he told the eagerly awaiting group of potential tenants that the flat had already been let to somebody else.

It was such a waste of time – they could spend days doing this. And she had to get the bus back home to Kilkenny later. It looked as though Karen would be staying on her friend Gerry's couch for a little while longer, after yet another luckless flat-hunting session today. They had already been through the same situation this time last week, and time would be running out for them soon.

She had hoped that she and Karen would be able to find a place without too much bother. She certainly hadn't expected it be this difficult. Since her return from Australia a few weeks earlier, she had been anxious to get settled in Dublin.

The Personnel Department at Alliance Trust Bank had been happy to allow her return to the bank assistant's job she had left to spend a year backpacking in Australia. Jenny and her then boyfriend Paul had ended up staying for nearly eighteen months – well over their working visas. Jenny returned to Ireland after she and Paul broke up. The bank told her that they couldn't take her at the Alliance Trust branch at home in Kilkenny and that she would need to take a post in one of the Dublin branches. Jenny didn't mind. If anything she welcomed the change. It would be difficult to return home to live and work in the small Kilkenny town in which she and Karen had grown up. She had been delighted when Karen suggested they get a flat together somewhere in Dublin. Karen had been living in a house-share with three others, but apparently one of them, Gerry, was moving in with his girlfriend, and Karen didn't get along with the other girls.

"I'd rather live in an igloo than stay in a house on my own with those control freaks!" she had told Jenny, "They're so bloody tidy. If I leave so much as a wet teabag in the sink, they make me feel like I've committed a mortal sin! And you'd swear that the dirty dishes would up and disappear forever if they didn't get washed right away."

Jenny and Karen had never lost touch and since her return the bond between them was even stronger. Now that she was back, she was anxious to get going with her new life and forget all about Australia - and Paul. She was to begin work in the Dun Laoghaire branch of Alliance Trust in three weeks' time, and she hoped that they would find a flat before then.

Karen worked as the Assistant Personnel Manager for Acorn Fidelity, one of the larger insurance companies in Ireland, and was based in Rathmines near Portobello Bridge. Until she and Jenny found a place, she was staying with her ex-housemate, Gerry, in his new flat. Jenny had thought it a curious arrangement at first, but apparently she and Gerry's girlfriend, Tessa, were also very good friends.

"Hold on a second, here's one we haven't circled," Karen said. "It's only a phone number, but by the looks of it I'd say the number is from around here somewhere – look, it starts with '496' – that's a Rathmines number, isn't it?"

"There's a phone box at the end of the road," Jenny

said. "Why don't we ring and find out? There's no point in staying here." She looked back at the growing number of bored-looking flat-hunters gathered outside the flat, all clutching the obligatory newspaper. The phone box was unoccupied, and Jenny called the number out to Karen as she dialled expectantly.

"Hello, I'm enquiring about the flat advertised in the paper?" Karen said. There was a short pause "It is?" She smiled and gave a thumbs-up signal to Jenny. "Leinster Square? Yes, I know where that is."

Jenny felt a tingle of anticipation. It sounded good.

"We'll be there in a few minutes. Thanks a million!" Karen hung up. "Guess what? It's here in Rathmines, and it was in the paper today by mistake. The landlord isn't due to show it until next week because it's being redecorated, but he's there now and he says if we call within the next quarter of an hour he'll let us have a look."

The girls got in a taxi and were outside the house in Leinster Square within five minutes. Karen pressed the buzzer expectantly.

"It doesn't look bad at all," Jenny said, examining the freshly-weeded and obviously well-attended flowerbeds on either side of the path. "And the fact that he's decorating is a good sign too."

Impatient, Karen pressed the buzzer a second time and had just released her finger from the bell when a large heavyset man answered the door with a smile.

"Hello, you're the girl I was speaking to on the phone just now, is that right?"

"Yes, that's me," Karen said eagerly.

At least he was friendly, which, Jenny thought, made a

change from all the other landlords they had met so far –
all surly individuals who weren't exactly great
conversationalists. Karen had tried her best to engage in
chat with some of them and she had got the odd grunt in
reply, if she was lucky. This man, however, with his thinning
hair and alarmingly bright blue eyes, had a very friendly
face.

"Is that a country accent I hear?" he asked, as they
walked through the hall and upstairs towards the top
floor.

"That's right. I'm Karen, and this is Jenny. We're both
from the same area in Kilkenny."

"Ah, sure wouldn't you know it, we're practically
neighbours! I'm from Waterford, not far from ye at all."

The landlord opened a dark-blue door on the top floor
of the building. "This is the flat. As you can see, the
furniture is all over the place while it's being painted, but
I'm sure you get the general idea. One of the bedrooms is
through there, and the other is just over that way, beside
the bathroom. Have a good look around now, don't mind
me." He made his way downstairs, leaving the two girls
alone in the living-room.

Jenny and Karen looked at one other excitedly.

"Karen, this is miles better than anything we've seen
so far – and a bedroom each! I thought we'd have to
share." Jenny went into the tiny bathroom, which was
brightly tiled in blue and green.

"The place is very clean, isn't it?" Karen said, opening
the kitchen cupboards and examining the workspace. The
kitchen and living-room were one and the same, but there
was plenty of space.

"I really think we should just take it. It's a little over our budget, but I'm sure we could manage. What do you think?" Jenny felt slightly guilty. Maybe Karen would be happier sharing a bedroom if the rent was cheaper. Before returning home from Australia, Jenny had shared a grotty room with three other girls in Sydney, and she was desperate for some privacy.

Karen grinned. "Of course we should take it! I'll go downstairs and ask him when we can move in."

"Brilliant!" Jenny clapped her hands with delight as she looked around the living-room. It would be gorgeous once they got going on it. They could get some plants and maybe a rug for the middle of the room. That wonderful Ayers Rock print she had brought back from Australia would be perfect on the far wall, and she could fill the place with some of the other knick-knacks from her travels.

Karen and the landlord came back into the living-room.

"Ye can move in next weekend, if that suits," said the landlord, who they learnt was called Frank. "There's a bit of painting to be done in the bedrooms, but I should get that finished at the weekend. I'll be putting a new carpet in the front bedroom too, so the place should be spick 'n' span by the time ye move in."

"Thanks a million for letting us see it first – we really appreciate that," Karen said. "It's just so hard to find a decent place these days."

"Well, to be honest, I'm glad to find some nice respectable girls like yourselves for it. The last crowd I had in here wrecked the place altogether – a crowd of lads they were. Not that they're all bad," he added. "I have a few fellas in the flat downstairs that have been there for a few years now, and they've never given me a bit of trouble."

The girls paid a deposit, and made arrangements to collect the keys from Frank the following week.

"It's a lovely flat, isn't it?" Jenny said elatedly, walking back out onto the street.

"Perfect! And it's so close to everything," Karen agreed. "The shopping centre is just across the road, and we're within walking distance of my local, which, incidentally, is where we're going now for a celebratory pint!"

She linked Jenny's arm, and the two girls walked up Rathmines Road, thrilled with themselves.

"How come you didn't move in with Shane?" Jenny asked, when they were comfortably seated in Boland's pub. She was hoping that Karen didn't regret suggesting that they share a flat together, instead of moving in with her boyfriend of eleven months.

Karen shrugged. "It was never an issue. Shane is happy enough where he is – he shares a flat with a crowd just up the road from here in Rathgar – and anyway, I think we'd end up killing one another. Unfortunately, Shane is the kind of guy who washes your teacup right after you've taken your last drop of tea. So, you can imagine what the two of us would be like together. Anyway, why do you ask?"

"I suppose I was afraid that you might regret asking me so soon. After all, it was a spur-of-the-moment decision."

"Not for me," Karen said, opening a packet of dry-roasted peanuts. "I was delighted when you told me you were coming to work in Dublin. It was perfect timing. Thank goodness Tessa and Gerry let me stay with them until we found a place of our own. I'll tell you what," she said wide-eyed with excitement. "Why don't you stay with us tonight, instead of getting the bus back home?"

"But I couldn't . . . " Jenny began.

"Sure you could. They wouldn't mind a bit." Karen was feeling especially magnanimous after her third bottle of Budweiser. "Tessa told me lots of times that you should stay over, instead of travelling all the way home. Nothing fancy – you'd have to sleep on the couch, but she and Gerry would be fine about it. Anyway, she's dying to meet you."

"Are you sure it'd be OK?" Jenny asked, enjoying the drinks and the excitement of finding the flat. She wasn't at all looking forward to the bus journey back to Kilkenny. If anything, she was anxious to celebrate the beginning of her new life in Rathmines.

"It won't be a problem, I promise you," Karen said. She checked her watch. "Tessa is a nurse and her shift ends mid-afternoon this week, so she should be home by now."

Tessa *was* at home when they called, and Jenny knew – as soon as she saw the girl's friendly smile welcoming them into the clean and cosy flat – that she was going to like Tessa. Despite the fact that the girl was the skinniest person besides Kate Moss that Jenny had ever seen. She wore a pair of blue denims and a bright pink hooded top that were so tiny, she couldn't have bought them anywhere other than Baby Gap. Barefoot, and standing no taller than five feet, Tessa looked minuscule beside her – a dainty little shrub to Jenny's awkward oak tree.

"Come in and sit down, the two of ye – Jenny how are you? Lovely to meet you finally," Tessa said in her West Cork brogue. She blushed and ran a hand through her short blonde crop. "Don't mind the state of me. Karen, why didn't you tell me you were bringing Jenny? Then I would have changed into something that didn't make me look like a scruffy old slob."

Jenny smiled. She couldn't imagine someone like Tessa ever looking anything other than effortlessly stylish, but the girl's genuine self-deprecation made her like her even more.

"I hope you don't mind me turning up on your doorstep like this –" she began.

"Not at all," Tessa waved her away. "I don't know how many times I said to Karen, 'Don't be sending the poor crature home when she can stay here for as long as she likes'. And," she added, winking at Jenny, "after putting up with the likes of this one for these last few weeks, I think I could put up with anyone."

Karen put her hands on her hips in mock consternation.

"Well, that's just lovely, isn't it? OK, Tessa, if you feel that way, I think I'll keep the chocolate I bought you all for myself!"

"Oh, Galaxy Caramel!" Tessa squealed. "Quick, give it here!"

"*And* we found a flat, so I'll be out of your hair soon and you can have Gerry all to yourself," Karen added, hiding the chocolate bar behind her back.

"You found a place! That's brilliant," Tessa said.

"Where? What's it like? I'll put on the kettle and the two of you can tell me all about it."

They followed Tessa into the tiny kitchenette, situated to the right of the living-room.

"Don't mind the state of the place, Jenny. It's not always like this. I was just about to get dinner organised."

Jenny laughed. "I've just spent nearly two years living in and out of grotty hostels and overcrowded flats. Believe me, this place is an absolute palace!"

"Oh, that's right, you were in Australia. What's it like? I'd love to go myself but Gerry has no interest."

"No interest in what?" said a deep voice from the doorway.

Jenny looked up to see a smiling six-footer enter the kitchen. He went up to Tessa and gave her a peck on the cheek. Jenny gasped. He was so handsome! With his fair hair and darkly tanned skin, he could easily give the likes of Brad Pitt a run for his money. Apart from the fact that he looked a million times more sophisticated, dressed as he was in a navy suit, turquoise tie, and horn-rimmed glasses.

"Gerry, I didn't hear you come in. This is Jenny – she and Karen found a new flat today."

"So you're the poor misfortune that'll be stuck with Cassidy," Gerry grinned, extending a hand. "I hope you know what you're letting yourself in for."

"I have a fair idea," Jenny gave a sideline glance towards Karen. "I've known the girl since we were both in nappies."

He chuckled. "Then you probably know that you'll be wasting your time trying to keep the place tidy once Cyclone Karen is around."

Karen made a face but she had no argument. "What's for dinner?" she asked Tessa, changing the subject.

"Chicken gruel," Gerry said before Tessa could answer. He rolled his eyes at Jenny. "You might have been all over Australia, but I can guarantee that you've never eaten anything like this."

"Don't mind him," Tessa grunted, trying to swipe at Gerry with a tea towel. "The chicken gruel he's talking about is actually my speciality – creamy chicken and mushroom tagliatelle. Of course, this big man from the northside of Dublin was raised on spuds and cabbage and wouldn't be at all used to 'foreign dishes'."

"Oh, so they feed them Italian food in the wilds of Cork, do they?" Gerry countered.

This time Tessa hit him square on the nose, and Gerry yelped in pain, retreating into the living-room.

Tessa put her hands on her hips. "That'll sort him out, and hopefully shut him up for a while. Now, Jenny, will you set the table and, Karen, you open that bottle of wine. Hopefully, that'll disguise the taste of the dinner."

Jenny smiled as Tessa pointed out the cutlery drawer. If Karen's friends were anything to go by, life in Dublin should be very interesting.

* * *

The following week, the girls collected the keys from the landlord, and Jenny's mother helped move her things from home.

"Now remember, madam," lectured Eileen Hamilton, "you were very lucky that the Bank was generous enough to take you back on. You've been given a second chance, so make the most of it and don't be gallivanting out on the town every night."

"Mam, I'm twenty-eight years old and I'm not stupid. Naturally we won't be out *every* night – just most nights." Jenny grinned, her blue eyes glowing with mischief.

"Don't worry, Mrs Hamilton. I'll make sure she keeps her feet on the ground. It'll be fine. I'll look after her," Karen soothed, with an almost imperceptible wink at Jenny.

"I know, Karen. I'm glad it's yourself she'll be living with. You were always great at calming her down. She can be a bit – excitable, to say the least."

"Mam, I'm not a child. I do have some sense, you know!" Jenny said incredulously.

"I know you do, love. That's why you left a perfectly good job and went gadding off to Australia after that Lyons eejit." She sniffed disapprovingly.

Jenny looked at Karen and rolled her eyes in frustration.

Karen smiled at her friend but felt a faint ache inside. At least Jenny could say that her parents cared about what happened to her. Her own parents, Clara and Jonathan, lived in Tenerife where they ran a business organising corporate golf tours. While they retained their home in Kilkenny, they rarely came back to Ireland, and Karen only saw them when she took it upon herself to visit them at their villa over Christmas, and maybe once or twice during the summer. As an only child, and with a life of her own in Dublin, the Cassidys had been long since released from their parental obligations towards Karen.

"Do you need to go for a shower before we go out?" Karen asked, as she brushed her long dark hair in front of the mirror over the mantelpiece. Jenny's mother had left for home a few hours earlier, and most of the girls' belongings were put away.

"You mean go out – tonight?" Jenny replied absently. She was engrossed in a particularly hilarious episode of *Father Ted*.

"Well, it's our first night here, and Shane is coming over soon. We have to go out and celebrate."

"OK then!" Jenny jumped up from the couch and went into her bedroom.

Half an hour later and right on time, Shane arrived at the flat.

"Very nice," he said, taking a good look around the comfy living-room, which the girls planned to decorate over the coming days. "It's quite roomy, isn't it?" He took in the large three-seater couch and armchair in front of the fireplace. A long breakfast bar divided the kitchen area from the rest of the room. The landlord had replaced some of the existing appliances and the girls now had a brand-new fridge and a silver chrome kettle. A row of formica cupboards lined the wall above the cooker.

"I take it that these are souvenirs from Oz?" Shane indicated the *Kangaroos Crossing – Next 200km* sign hanging on the wall and Jenny's Ayers Rock print.

Karen nodded. "Jenny loves that one. It reminds her of her backpacking days. She's not long out of the shower – she should be ready soon."

"I'm looking forward to meeting her –" Then he frowned. "*What* is that racket coming from next door?"

Karen giggled. "That racket is Jenny playing her *Disco Hits* CD while she's getting ready to go out."

Shane rolled his eyes. "Oh no – not another disco freak! I'll bet she and Tessa will get on like a house on fire."

Karen chuckled. "She's also a bit of a Joe Dolan fan, which thrilled Tessa no end. The two of them are already trying to rope us all in to go a show next time he's in Dublin." Tessa was an avid fan of the Irish showband singer and never missed an opportunity to see him play, much to her boyfriend's chagrin.

Karen finished applying her lipstick in front of the mirror.

"Hey, you look nice," Shane said approvingly, noticing Karen's appearance for the first time. She was wearing black leather trousers with a deep-red slash-neck top. A pair of small silver hoop earrings completed the outfit and, set against Karen's shoulder-length dark hair, the effect was casual but sexy.

"Going clubbing tonight, are we?" Shane teased, pulling her close to him.

"I hope so," she said, giving him a quick kiss. "I know Jenny will be expecting a good time on her first Saturday night in Dublin."

"Ah, speak of the devil," Shane said, as Jenny entered the room wearing an outfit that immediately made Karen feel frumpy and boring.

Jenny's blonde tresses were piled high above her head with a few tendrils framing her strikingly pretty face, and emphasising her full lips and large almond-shaped eyes. She wore a purple shirt with an intertwined cerise and gold pattern along the front, over a pair of rich black velour trousers. A pair of gold drop-earrings dangled

attractively from each ear. Karen thought her friend looked
sensational – effortlessly exotic. Jenny had a definite knack
for wearing clothes that made people look twice at her.

Shane extended a hand. "How are you, Jen? I'm Shane
Quinn, the fine thing that I'm sure Karen has been raving
about."

"Pleased to meet you." Jenny laughed as they shook
hands. It was obvious that Shane was a lovely guy, but he
was far from a fine thing. Dressed in combats and a baggy
striped rugby top, his lanky frame towered over Karen,
and his dark hair was tightly cropped, ostensibly to
disguise a slightly thinning hairline on his forehead.

But Jenny could easily understand why Karen had
been attracted to him. For some reason the sprinkling of
freckles across his cheeks, sharp green eyes and devilish
grin made him terribly appealing.

The night was great craic.

Karen, Jenny and Shane had met Tessa and Gerry in
Rody Boland's and Shane's friend and housemate, Aidan,
joined them later that evening. Karen was afraid that
Jenny might find the group quite daunting but she had
chatted happily with everyone and had won them over
with her bubbly and infectious chit-chat. It was good to
see Jenny out and about and enjoying herself. Her
confidence must surely have taken a battering after the
break-up with Paul.

Karen had discovered quite by accident the reason
Jenny had split from her ex. Her friend had hardly
mentioned him since her return, and considering that
Jenny and Paul had been a couple for some time, Karen
had naturally been curious. She had mentioned it in

passing one afternoon and Jenny had been quite frank about it.

"He wanted to stay and I wanted to leave – simple as that," she had said. "We had a big bust-up during a trip to Cairns, and I decided to head back to Sydney before returning home."

"Didn't Tasha visit you in Cairns?" Karen said, referring to a mutual friend from their hometown who had met up with Jenny earlier that same year.

Jenny nodded, but didn't elaborate.

"So, she went back to Sydney with you then?"

"No, she stayed with Paul," Jenny said flatly.

"What? Why would she stay with Paul?"

Jenny smiled. "I mean she *stayed* with Paul."

Karen sat upright in her chair. "The little wagon! I was wondering why I hadn't heard a thing from her! Who does she think she is? And as for Paul Lyons – well, he'd better not come near me in a hurry, or he'll be half a man by the time I've finished with him!"

Jenny chuckled at her friend's reaction. "Thanks, but it's OK –I don't really mind, actually. Paul and I were growing apart long before then, and Tasha was the final nail in the coffin, so to speak. Anyway, it gave me the incentive to stop drifting, so I came back to Dublin to 'think about my future', as Mam would say."

"So, you're not bothered about Paul at all then?"

"Nope. Anyway, I went to my fortune-teller not long after I came home – you know, just to see what life had in store for me, and all that. Karen, she was just brilliant! She knew all about Paul and the break-up, and she knew that I had been away and –"

"Let me guess – she told you that you had experienced a tough time recently, but that things would improve and you'd be going on a journey," Karen said sardonically. She could never understand how Jenny, a supposedly intelligent twenty-something was always so gullible when it came to these fortune-tellers. Then again, she had always been the same – over the years the same fortune-teller had supposedly predicted Jenny's Leaving Cert results, her mother's shingles and her dog Lucy's pregnancy. The fact that this so-called fortune-teller lived in the same town, and was well aware of Jenny's studious tendencies, her mother's repeated public discussions on her health and Lucy's (a pedigree King Charles) unmitigated escape from the Hamilton household one weekend, hadn't at all tarnished Jenny's high opinion of Mrs Crowley's so-called 'predictions'.

Jenny made a face. "It's not like that. She was very particular this time, strangely so."

"Jenny, she *knew* you had gone backpacking with Paul and had come home without him. It doesn't take a genius to put two and two together and come up with a 'surprising revelation'."

Jenny folded her arms sulkily across her chest. "Karen, just because you have a naturally cynical and suspicious nature doesn't mean that the rest of us shouldn't have faith in her."

Karen sighed and put both hands up in defeat. "OK then, tell me about Madam Crowley's amazing predictions this time."

"Well, OK, she wasn't *that* specific but – "

There's a surprise, Karen thought.

"She told me that I will meet someone special before the end of the year, and this guy – she said he had hair of 'a similar colour to my own'– would be the one. Can you believe it, Karen? She actually said he would be The One!"

"Really?" Karen drawled.

"This is exactly how she put it. She said that I will meet him after 'a moment of lapsed concentration' and we will have 'upheavals' throughout the relationship, but we'll be able to fend off everything that gets thrown at us, until eventually nothing will keep us apart."

Karen couldn't help but snigger.

"Think about it, Karen. What if it really happens?" Jenny asked, her blue eyes widening with excitement. "What if he's here now – in Dublin? And it's heading towards the end of the year, so I must be about to meet him soon!"

Chapter 5

"Are you nervous?" Karen asked, watching Jenny try to smooth down her unruly curls for about the tenth time that morning. She had to admit, her friend looked very smart, dressed in a mulberry-coloured jacket and matching ankle-length skirt, the rich colour setting off Jenny's features beautifully.

"I suppose I am a little bit," Jenny said, deciding finally to clip her hair back from her face. She frowned at her reflection. "I don't know – do I look a bit untidy? Oh, I wish I had straight hair!"

Karen laughed through a mouthful of cornflakes. "Do you realise that women all over the world pay a fortune getting in curls like that on a regular basis? Seriously, Jenny, I've never seen you look like that before. I love that suit – the executive look is really you, you know."

So it should be, Jenny thought. It had cost an absolute fortune in Jigsaw. But while she might look it, she certainly didn't *feel* professional. The butterflies in her stomach would start pouring out of her mouth soon – there were so many of them. She wished she could just get the first day over with, and then hopefully things would be easier. Jenny knew that the Dun Laoghaire branch of Alliance Trust Bank was very big and very busy. Hopefully, her future colleagues wouldn't be too busy to get to know the newest member of staff. She took a deep breath.

"Right then, I'm off! Wish me luck!"

Karen got up from her chair and gave her a reassuring hug.

"You'll be fine, Jen. It's not as though you haven't done the work before, and I'm sure it'll all come back to you once you get going. You worked at a bank in Sydney for a while too, didn't you?"

"I know, I know, but I'm just dying to get the first day over with, then I'm sure I'll be fine." She picked up her handbag, and took one last look in the mirror, before leaving to catch a bus into the city centre. From there she would get a DART train out to Dun Laoghaire.

Karen left the flat about twenty minutes later and set off on the short walk to the Acorn Fidelity building.

She hugged her trench coat tightly around her midriff, as the chilly morning breeze blustered against her. It was early September, but Karen could already feel the weather getting colder with each passing day. She'd have to start taking the bus to work soon. That would give Shane a laugh. He worked for Viking Engineering, a civil engineering company located on the northside, and had to take two buses a day to get to work, whereas Acorn Fidelity was luckily within walking distance for her. She wished he'd hurry up and get that car he was always talking about. It would make getting around Dublin much easier, but then again – Karen thought, reminding herself of the merciless city traffic – maybe not.

Karen reached for her identity card, which gave her access to her building, and walked through the plush reception of Acorn Fidelity.

Pamela, the receptionist, waylaid her as she walked past. "Catherine Mitchell is out sick today. She's got three interviews this morning, so you'll have to take them. The first one is waiting for you outside your office."

Great, Karen thought to herself. So much for an easy Monday morning at the office!

She shouldn't have to take the Personnel Manager's candidates – she had enough work of her own to do and those interviews should have been rearranged. But obviously Little Miss Efficiency had it all worked out. She and Pamela had detested one another since Karen's first day at Acorn Fidelity nearly three years before, and for no discernible reason. Catherine Mitchell, Karen's boss, called it 'a distinct clash of all too similar personalities'.

Karen didn't agree.

"Fine," she said to Pamela shortly. "Anything else, while you're at it?"

"Why, yes actually,"Pamela beamed, pleased at Karen's irritation. "I have eight telephone messages for you, and another thirteen for Catherine. I suppose you can deal with those when you're finished with the interviewees?"

"Yes," Karen said, through gritted teeth, "I suppose I can."

* * *

Later, back at the flat, Jenny blustered in the door with

such commotion that Karen looked up in bewilderment.

"What a shower of absolute bitches!" she said, throwing her keys onto the breakfast bar.

Jenny rarely used bad language, so Karen deduced that it must have been a particularly bad first day. "What happened?" she said, taking in her friend's wretched appearance. "You look awful." Jenny was drenched in sweat, her hair had spilled loose from its clip and her curls were matted against her forehead. She looked completely different to the supposedly calm professional that had left the flat earlier that morning.

"She's just been mugged."

It was only then that Karen noticed the broad, attractive guy standing behind Jenny. He wore a dark pinstripe suit, and was carrying a nylon laptop-holder under his left arm. His dark hair was short and tightly-cropped and his eyes were also dark, a deep chocolate brown – striking against his honey-coloured complexion. There was a hint of dark stubble on his chin – he seemed to Karen like the kind of man who always had stubble, no matter how often he shaved.

"She got off at the bus stop in front of the shopping centre, when a gang of gurriers grabbed her bag and ran off," said the Attractive One. "I saw it happen, and we both ran after them, but it was too late. I nearly caught them, but they hid in the flats up the road – she's very upset." He regarded Jenny with a concerned look.

"Jen, you poor thing," Karen said, absorbing what he had said. "Did they get that much money? Have you cancelled your credit cards?"

"I didn't take any cards with me, and there wasn't that

much cash in my purse. But that new cherry lipstick I bought last week – you know the one that's supposed to stay on for ages, even if you do nothing but drink coffee all day? Well, that was in my handbag and it cost me a fortune." She added glumly, "So did the bag."

"Look, sit down there on the couch and relax. Will you both have tea? I've just made a fresh pot."

They both nodded and Karen poured mugs of strong tea for Jenny and her saviour. As she handed them the tea, she shook her head in disgust. "Maybe you should ring the gardai – they might be able to at least get the bag back."

"It would probably be a waste of time," Jenny said despondently. "The gardai won't be able to do anything. I'm sure it's a regular occurrence, and as there wasn't much in the bag, they won't really bother."

The so-far anonymous one chuckled. "I doubt the gardai would grasp the importance of stay-on lipstick either."

Jenny flashed him a bashful smile.

"But they shouldn't be allowed to get away with that carry-on," Karen exclaimed, her hands on her hips. "It's a bloody disgrace! I tell you, if I got near any of them –"

Jenny interrupted her. "Calm down, Karen. There's no point in getting upset. At least they didn't draw a knife on me or anything – it's only a handbag. I think the shock of it was the worst."

She took a sip from her tea and then suddenly remembered her manners.

"Oh, I'm so sorry – I forgot to introduce you two," she spluttered, waving an arm in the air. "Karen, meet Roan Williams – Sir Galahad in disguise."

Roan flashed her a brilliant white smile and, as they

shook hands, Karen noticed that his front teeth were slightly crooked.

Jenny gazed at Roan. "I really appreciate you helping me out like that," she said sweetly. "You didn't have to get involved at all."

"Of course I had to get involved," he said with a smile. "I think it's terrible that no one seems to bat an eyelid when these things happen any more."

Karen watched the exchange between the two of them with interest. It was obvious that, saviour or no saviour, her friend was smitten with this guy.

Roan took a gulp of tea from his mug and looked around the room. "This is a nice flat, much nicer than where I'm living now."

"And where might that be?" Karen enquired, for Jenny's benefit.

"Along the canal, near Ranelagh. I share a house with three guys that tell me they're from Monaghan somewhere, but with the way they carry on you'd think they were raised in the orang-utan's enclosure at Dublin zoo. Last week I found a plate of something resembling spaghetti bolognese under one of the armchairs. I'd say it must have been there for weeks."

"I'm trying to place your accent," Jenny said thoughtfully. "You're not from Dublin, are you?"

Roan laughed. "No, but you're not far off. I'm actually from Kildare, but I've been living in Dublin for a long time now, what with college and work." He pointed towards the laptop, which lay at his feet.

"Roan, will you have another cuppa?" Karen asked, refilling the kettle.

"I won't, thanks. I was actually on my way to get a takeaway, when I was waylaid by this damsel in distress." He winked at Jenny. "Are you sure you're all right now?"

Jenny looked up at him through thickly mascara'd eyelashes. "I'm fine. It was the shock that got to me more than anything else. I think that if I had been concentrating properly I . . . " she trailed off, as if suddenly remembering something, then collected herself, "if I had been concentrating properly, I would have kept a firm hold on my bag, and it wouldn't have happened in the first place. Thanks again. I appreciate it."

"No problem," he said, giving both girls a repeat of his earlier dazzling – but crooked – smile on his way out the door. "Hopefully we might run into one another again some time."

When Jenny was sure he was safely out of the house and onto the street, she let out a shriek of excitement.

"Karen, it must be him!" she cried, clapping her hands together with delight. "He *has* to be the guy the fortune-teller predicted for me! Remember we were supposed to meet after 'a moment of lapsed concentration'? Well, I was in a world of my own getting off that bus, and my getting mugged and his helping me out is how we met."

Karen did nothing to hide her scepticism. "Jenny, please don't tell me that you actually believed that rubbish. Anyway, I thought his hair was supposed to be 'of similar colour to your own'. Your man's hair colour there was darker than an undertaker's suit!"

"Well, she can't get everything right," Jenny said huffily. "Anyway, it might be same colour as my hair eventually – I mean, I could always decide to darken my hair, couldn't I?"

"Jenny Hamilton, you are just incorrigible," Karen said, with a smile and a shake of the head. "You can't go around trying to fit this so-called prediction against every man you meet between now and Christmas. That's not the way life works."

"We'll see," Jenny said confidently. "But a girl can dream and I think that if destiny brought us together today, then destiny will make sure that we meet again. After all, we haven't exchanged phone numbers or anything. And, Karen, even *you* have to admit that he's drop-dead gorgeous."

Karen picked up a knife and began slicing a carrot into thin slices. Drop-dead gorgeous he might be, she thought worriedly, but could you really trust a man who looked that good?

* * *

The following Wednesday evening, Boland's was packed to capacity. Jenny saw Gerry wave from the back of the pub and she and Karen struggled through the crowds and made their way towards him.

"Hiya, Jen!" Tessa motioned for Jenny to sit down beside her. "Shane was telling us what happened to you the other day. How are you feeling after it all?"

Jenny smiled ruefully at her. "Not too bad now – it was a bit of a shock at the time. Luckily they didn't take much." She took off her coat and nodded hello at the others.

"The brats," Tessa exclaimed. "There you are coming home from your first day at work, and a shower of layabouts that won't get up off their lazy backsides get away with robbing you like that – it would make you sick."

"Did you call the gardai?" Gerry asked.

"I reported it, but I don't think it'll make a blind bit of difference." She nodded her thanks as Karen handed her a bottle of Budweiser.

"Did you tell her about your knight in shining armour?" Karen asked with a grin.

Jenny grinned and excitedly relayed the circumstances of her meeting with Roan to Tessa. "He was the sexiest man I've ever seen outside television," she said in conclusion.

"I wonder if you *will* see him again?" Tessa asked. She turned her chair around to get a good view of the television screen situated on the wall. "Oh good, the match has started."

"Who's playing?" Karen asked, following her gaze.

Shane slapped a hand to his head in exasperation. "'Who's playing?' she says. Karen, do you see those lads running around wearing green jerseys and white shorts? Well, believe it or not, that's actually the *Irish soccer team*."

"Oh, good for them," Karen shrugged nonchalantly and went back to her Budweiser.

"Jenny, how's work going for you?" Tessa asked, keeping one eye on the television. "Have you settled back into it OK?"

"It's been fine – much better than I expected actually."

On her first day at Alliance Trust in Dun Laoghaire, the personnel manager, Marion, had told Jenny that for the first few weeks she should re-familiarise herself with the day-to-day running of the Bank, while working with the

Accounts office away from the main floor. She had introduced her to Olivia, the friendly and easygoing PA to the Branch Manager. Olivia had taken Jenny under her wing, and in turn introduced her to the rest of the staff, giving her advanced – and much appreciated – warnings about their various idiosyncrasies. So far, Jenny had found most of her colleagues to be pleasant, chatty, and interested in hearing about her experiences in Australia – not that she wanted to bore them rigid about it.

Gerry bought another round of drinks and some crisps, and handed them round the table. Karen groaned, but couldn't resist opening a packet of salt 'n' vinegar. "I really need to go on a diet soon – the waistband of these trousers keeps digging into me."

"Well, if you need to go on a diet, *I* need my jaws wired shut," Jenny laughed.

Tessa took up the theme. "Girls – don't mind all these faddish Dr Atkins-type high-fat and high-protein diets. I've tried them all, but nothing is as good as my very own White Trouser Diet."

"Your *what*?" Jenny asked, with interest.

"Go on, tell her about your famous White Trouser Diet," Karen drawled.

"Well, it's as simple as this," Tessa began. "I have a pair of white trousers that fit me perfectly. I try them on at different times of the month, but at least once a month – or after a particularly heavy munching session – and if there's a slight bulge, anywhere at all, it's thirty minutes a day on the treadmill and not a square of chocolate until they fit me perfectly again."

Gerry guffawed loudly behind her. "You liar, Tessa

Sullivan – you've never been able to give up chocolate."

Tessa tut-tutted and ignored her boyfriend. "Don't mind him, Jen! If you try it, you'll find that it really works."

"That's all very well if you can fit nicely into a pair of white trousers, or can manage thirty minutes on a treadmill in the first place," Karen laughed. "Anyway, I couldn't give up chocolate. I think we're all biologically programmed to constantly crave Dairymilks and Fruit & Nut."

"True," Jenny agreed. "My father told me once that when he was a young lad his mother used to scold him for stuffing his face with sweets, when he was a teenager he was afraid to eat junk food because he'd get spots, and now that he's older he can't eat what he wants for fear of cholesterol. He reckons it's a battle that none of us can win, so why bother? We might as well just forget dieting and enjoy our food while we can."

"Maybe so," Tessa said, with a grin. "But I'll bet your dad never had to try and fit into a pair of white trousers!" With that, she turned her attention back to the television. "Oh, referee, that was a blatant two-footed tackle! Send him off!"

Shane laughed and shook his head. "Tessa, for a girlie-girl who wears flouncy dresses and glitter on her eyelids, the fact that you can manage a convincing argument about Michael Owen's left foot never ceases to amaze me."

"Shane, for a supposedly intelligent guy, the fact that you can get away with a sexist comment like that, never ceases to amaze *me*," Tessa said, impatiently lighting a cigarette. "The way you lot go on about football you'd swear it was some kind of rocket science. And when was the last time you saw me in a flouncy dress?"

"Oh, please – I don't have to break up yet another slanging match between you two, do I?" Karen said, with a slow shake of the head. "Shane, leave her alone, will you?"

Her plea was drowned in a chorus of yells, as just then the Irish team were awarded a penalty kick. All conversation halted as a member of the team stepped up to take the kick. When the ball hit the back of the net, the pub erupted in a perfectly synchronised roar of cheers and applause.

Jenny was in mid-celebration when she felt a tap on her shoulder. Her heart leapt as she saw Roan Williams crouch down beside her stool. He smiled, and Jenny noticed for the first time the tiny dimples on either side of his mouth.

"Hello again," he said. "I've just come in, and when I saw you guys sitting up here, I said I'd better make sure my damsel was no longer in distress but functioning normally."

"Well, hello yourself," Jenny beamed at him. "Pull up a stool and sit down."

She patted the space beside her eagerly. Dressed casually in jeans, white T-shirt, Timberland boots, and a soft brown leather jacket, she thought that tonight he looked even sexier than he had the other day.

He nodded a greeting at Karen, and Jenny briefly introduced him to the others sitting at the table. As Roan shook hands with Aidan, the other man looked at him curiously.

"Mate, you look very familiar – I think I've met you before," he said.

Roan shrugged. "Well, I drink in here regularly – you probably just know my face."

Aidan frowned and shook his head. "I don't think so. I'm nearly positive I know you from somewhere else – were you in UCD, maybe?"

"'Fraid not – and I don't think I know you. You're probably just mixing me up with someone else. I have that kind of face." He gave a short laugh.

"Maybe." Aidan shrugged, and returned to his pint.

Roan quickly turned his attention back to Jenny. "So how are you after your big adventure the other day – and, more importantly, did you manage to replace the magic lipstick?"

Jenny laughed. "Not yet! But thanks again for helping me out. I don't know what I would've done otherwise."

"Not a problem. Listen, Jenny, I'm with a crowd down the front, so I'd better head back to them. I might see you later?"

Her heart sank. Of course – he was probably with someone – someone *female*. A man that good-looking would almost certainly be in a relationship.

"OK, see you later, and thanks again," Jenny said, a smile disguising her disappointment.

"Wow – he *is* cute," Tessa exclaimed, watching Roan as he disappeared through the crowds. "Nice firm backside on him too."

"Hey, I heard that," Gerry said in a warning tone.

"Sorry, but you know full well that nobody could beat yours. My Gerry's is the backside of all backsides!"

Shane nudged Gerry. "And that's all thanks to White Trouser Diet, I suppose?"

Tessa giggled.

The match ended with a convincing win for the Irish team, which prompted another round of celebration in the pub. A DJ was promptly installed, and within minutes he had cranked up the music, sustaining the already lively atmosphere.

"I feel a bit woozy already," Jenny said, after her fifth Budweiser. "And it's early yet."

Aidan drained his pint and slapped the empty glass on the table with a flourish. "I'd love to stay on for a while longer, but I'm on duty early tomorrow morning. I'll see you guys later." He slipped on a jacket.

Jenny turned to Karen. "Duty? Is Aidan a doctor or something?"

"No – he's a fireman. He's based in Tallaght."

"A fireman – wow!" Jenny was impressed.

"Not another one!" Shane said, exasperated. "What is it about a bloody fireman that makes a woman go weak at the knees? That big, strong, hero thing is such a cliché. Jenny – my eighty-year-old grandfather has got more hunk in him than Aidan has."

"It's not just looks though, is it?" Jenny said dreamily. "It's the whole notion of somebody putting his own life at risk, to save other people's lives. I don't think it's the same for doctors or nurses – sorry, Tessa – because they don't have anything to lose. Firemen are just so courageous."

"Courageous, my foot! From what I can make out, Aidan spends most of his time playing poker at the fire station, if he's not coaxing tabby-cats down from trees!"

Karen gave him such a dig in the ribs that Shane had

to relent. "OK – OK! I made the last bit up – it's not like that at all. He's a hero, he's a hero!"

The others laughed.

"Right, who's on for a bit of boogying?" Tessa jumped up from her seat, and wiggled her hips in time to U2's latest. It wasn't long before Karen and Jenny followed suit and the three girls danced happily around the table, Gerry and Shane trying their best to fade into the background and ignore them.

A short time later, Jenny noticed Roan reappear at the table. He caught her eye and smiled.

"Hi," she said with a coy smile, the drink having long since taken effect. The dancing had given her a euphoric feeling, and she was ready for some serious flirting.

"Love the dance moves," Roan teased.

"Why don't you give it a try then?"

"Not me," he said, shaking his head with a smile. "I have a reputation to uphold."

"As what?" she laughed. "Boring old git?"

"No, downright cool dude."

They both laughed. Jenny found herself becoming more and more comfortable with him as they chatted. They talked about silly things at first, and then imparted bits and pieces of information about one another. Roan told her that he worked in Euramax, an IT company based in the city centre, and that he'd been living in Dublin for nearly five years.

"I should really think about buying a place of my own, instead of going out partying all the time but I love it here," he said, "and I'm not ready to commit myself to lifelong debt just yet. The job is fairly demanding, and I think I'd go crazy if I couldn't go out a couple of nights a week to relax. No chance of that if you've got a mortgage hanging over your head."

"I know what you mean," Jenny said. "I thought that the Cock and Bull in Sydney was mad, but it's nothing compared to this place."

"I've always wanted to go there – Australia, I mean – not the Cock and Bull. But I went straight into the job after I left college, and there never seemed to be any time to travel after that."

"It's exciting at first, and the lifestyle is completely different over there – a lot more laid back but I'm glad I came home."

"I'm glad too," he said softly, and Jenny knew from the way he was looking at her that there was real meaning behind his words. Suddenly his face seemed uncomfortably – or was it comfortably – close to hers? She shivered deliciously.

"Some game of football, eh, Roan?" Shane said suddenly, and the moment was lost.

While Shane and Roan lost themselves in a conversation about their favourite football teams, Jenny tried to work out what had just happened. If Shane hadn't interrupted, she was almost certain that Roan had been about to kiss her.

Coming back to the table, Karen groaned. "No more football talk tonight please, Shane! Anyway, I think it's time you and I called it a night. Don't forget we've got work in the morning. Are you coming, Jen – or do you want to stay on for a while?" Karen was waving goodbye to Tessa and Gerry, who were already heading towards the exit.

Jenny looked across at Roan and he smiled.

"You go ahead," she said. "I think I might stay on here for a little longer."

"Don't worry," Roan said. "I'll walk her home later."

The others left.

"I'll see if I can get another drink before the bar closes," he said. "Do you want one?"

"Why not?" she said, raising her glass to him and trying to prevent a threatening hiccup.

Roan came back with the drinks and set them on the table.

Three drinks later, they got up to leave.

On her way out, Jenny thanked each member of the bar staff personally and, supported by Roan and one of the bouncers, walked on unsteady legs out the front door.

"You're sooooo nice," she said to the stone-faced bouncer escorting her out. "I didn't expect people to be sooo nice in Dublin, but everyone is reeeeally nice."

"I'll look after her from here, mate – thanks a million," Roan smiled apologetically at the bouncer, as they came out onto the street.

"Right, Jenny, time to get you home – woah, you're all over the place!" He laughed as she stumbled against the wall, trying to walk down the road.

"I'm just so tired," Jenny yawned, as she continued walking. "I want my bed now."

"Hold on a second! Don't walk so fast," he said, putting his arm around her and trying his best to keep her steady.

"You're nice, Roan – did anyone ever tell you that?" she asked, slurring her words as she gazed up at him. "You have nice eyes, too. And nice hair. And you're very sexy – oops!" She put her hand to her mouth in mock embarrassment. "I shouldn't have said that! I don't want to give you a big head."

He smiled. "Jenny, you told that bouncer back there that he had a fine head of hair, and the poor man was a bald as an egg. I think I'll take what you say tonight with a pinch of salt."

She laughed and soon they reached Leinster Square.

"Here we are!" she announced loudly, as they reached the front door. "Are you coming in?" Standing above him on the step, her eyes were just below the level of his.

He hesitated for a minute. "No, I won't, Jenny, " he whispered. "Thanks all the same. It looks like everyone else has gone to bed, anyway. Will you be OK from here?"

"I'll be fine. Just hold on until I get my keys." She fumbled in her bag for the keys, before realising she already had them out. "Whoops – there they are!" Jenny grinned and dropped the keys as she tried to unlock the front door. Roan bent down to pick them up and, as he handed them to her, she grabbed him impulsively and kissed him firmly on the lips.

He immediately broke away and Jenny cringed with embarrassment as she realised what she had done.

"Oh God, Roan, I'm really sorry – I don't know what came over me, I –"

He silenced her by engulfing her in his arms and kissing her powerfully. She wrapped her arms tightly around him as he pushed her against the door and began to kiss her neck. She groaned as his hands quickly reached under her clothes and her breath caught in her throat as she felt him caress her with his tongue. She couldn't believe that she had kissed him like that! It was so unlike her! After all, she had only met him a couple of hours ago.

Then, suddenly, Roan stopped and again broke away from her

"Jenny, I'm sorry, I shouldn't be doing this." He ran both hands through his hair, and looked at her. "We've both had too much to drink – it isn't right."

Mortified, Jenny tried not to meet his eyes. She re-buttoned her jacket.

"You're right – it's my fault. I'm sorry." She turned quickly, and this time found the lock in the door with no effort.

"Jenny, wait, can we just . . . "

She didn't hear the rest of his words, as the door closed quickly behind her. How embarrassing! She hoped Karen was in bed. She couldn't tell her about this. What was the matter with her? Why did she have to make a fool of herself in front of him like that? Why did she have to get so drunk?

She tiptoed past Karen's bedroom, and made her way quietly towards the kitchen. As she gulped down a glass of water, she looked at her reflection in the living-room mirror. She looked an absolute state. Her hair was all over the place, her cheeks were flushed and her mascara had run. There was a black circle under each of her eyes. No wonder he had blown her off!

Jenny cleaned her face, got into bed, and cringed as she replayed events in her head. How could she ever face him again?

Chapter 6

It was a weary Jenny who arrived home the following evening after work. Her hangover was only just beginning to improve. She hadn't looked at food all day and was looking forward to a nice quiet evening slobbing on the couch. As she came in the door, she stepped back in surprise. Standing on the kitchen counter-top was the biggest bunch of red roses that she had ever seen.

"Welcome home," Karen grinned, from where she sat on the couch. "Somebody likes you – there are two dozen there."

"You mean those are for *me*?" Jenny screeched delightedly. "I thought Shane might have sent them to you."

"Are you mad? Shane Quinn doesn't even know what roses look like. Open the card, will you? I'm dying to see who they're from, although I have a fair guess."

Sorry about last night – I panicked. Will dinner tomorrow night make up for it? Pick you up at eight. Love Roan.

"Oh my God," Jenny said, putting a hand to her mouth,

"I can't believe it! He wants me to go to dinner with him tomorrow night."

"He sounds keen. What did you two get up to last night, then?"

Eagerly, Jenny relayed the previous evening's events to her. "And I thought I had blown it completely jumping on him like that."

"Obviously not," Karen said. "Saving you from muggers, sending you expensive flowers, taking you out for posh dinners – your Sir Galahad is turning out to be a right Mr Romantic, isn't he?"

* * *

The following evening, Roan rang the buzzer at eight o'clock on the dot.

"Do I look all right?" Jenny asked Karen, in a moment of anxiety about her clothes.

"You look terrific," Karen said, envying her friend's stylish flair.

That night, Jenny wore kitten heels, a lilac chiffon ruffle skirt and matching halter-top – a smattering of delicate sequins along its low neckline emphasising her generous cleavage. Karen thought the outfit was perfect for the occasion – not too overdressed or trashy. And Jenny always managed to carry her none-so-slim figure with perfect ease.

Roan didn't look too bad either, she thought, eyeing him as he came in. He wore black combats and a tan-coloured, linen, short-sleeve shirt.

Dinner was a lively affair. They went to a Chinese restaurant in the city centre, and from the minute they were seated, they chatted together like old friends meeting again after a long separation.

Jenny talked easily about her life, and told him about her family, her life as it had been in Kilkenny and her relationship with Karen. She learned that Roan's father was a doctor and had hoped his elder son would follow him into the profession. However, Roan wanted nothing to do with it. His younger brother Christian had instead taken up the mantle and was currently studying medicine at Trinity College. His mother, it seemed, stayed at home and made her own career out of looking after the three men in her life.

"I think she'd like me to move home eventually," he said, "but probably just so that she could keep an eye on me, or even try and get me married off. But I couldn't see myself moving back there again. There's so much more out there for me, you know?"

Jenny nodded. "Part of the reason I went to Australia in the first place was because my mother was so dead set against it. We have a strange relationship – sometimes we argue so much I can't believe that we're actually from the same gene pool. My dad though, he's a different story." She smiled fondly at the thought of Jim Hamilton. "He'd let me get away with murder – even help me commit it."

Roan chuckled. "Will we get dessert?" he asked, signalling to the waiter.

She nodded, relieved that he was the kind of guy who didn't stare in amazement at every morsel she put into her mouth. Her ex, Paul, who had known Jenny since childhood, and was aware that she had always struggled with her weight, used to make her feel like The Cookie Monster every time they went out for a meal.

'Jenny, don't get the sweet and sour, there's too much batter on it,' or 'Do you really need that much fried rice?' And he would never let her order dessert, yet was quite happy to sit in front of her with his banana fritters slathered in cream. Jenny didn't know why she had stayed with Paul for as long as she had.

She stole a glance across the table at Roan, who was studying the menu intently. He looked especially handsome tonight, she thought. He had such long, dark lashes and a masculine face with a very sexy mouth. She shivered, as she remembered what it was like to be kissed by that mouth. Jenny noticed that they had attracted looks from nearby tables as they entered the restaurant. Everyone was probably wondering what someone like him was doing with a plain-Jane like herself. She topped up her glass.

The desserts arrived soon after, and Jenny eagerly tucked into her pineapple sorbet, pleased to see Roan do the same. They ended the meal with tea, and the obligatory chocolate mints, and afterwards Roan asked for the bill.

"We'll split this one, will we?" he said easily. "After all, I think you ate nearly twice as much as I did."

Jenny was startled. She didn't quite know how to take that comment but hoped that he meant it as a joke. Wasn't he the one supposed to be taking *her* out to dinner? Then again, maybe it was only right. It was an expensive menu, and they had ordered every course. And in this day and age, women couldn't demand to be treated equally, and then expect to have it all their own way, could they? Jenny wasn't an extreme feminist – she liked a little bit of chivalry now and again. But Roan wasn't to know that, she supposed. Anyway, hadn't he already spent a fortune on the roses?

"No problem," she said, taking out her purse. "How much do I owe you?"

Afterwards, Roan managed to hail a precious taxi, and Jenny sat back beside him contentedly, pleased that she didn't have to walk all the way back to Rathmines in her kitten heels. She smiled when suddenly Roan's hand rested on her thigh.

"Are you coming home with me tonight?" he mumbled, his breath warm as he nuzzled her neck, making her body tingle from the tips of her toes upwards to the top of her head. He was so very sexy.

They reached his flat, and as she got out, Jenny practically threw the fare at the taxi driver, so anxious was she to get inside and be alone with Roan.

But, despite her excitement, she was astonished when she saw the state of the flat: the amount of dirty dishes, coffee mugs and empty food-cartons in the kitchen would put a teenager's bedroom to shame. There were various items of clothing strewn all over the sofa, so much so that she couldn't find any space to sit down.

"Sorry about the mess," Roan grimaced. "It's not normally like this, but one of my flatmates has his brother staying with us at the moment. He sleeps on the couch and there's not much room for his gear. We usually take it in turns to clean the kitchen but . . . " He trailed off, exasperated.

She knew exactly where he was coming from. Although she and Karen hadn't been sharing all that long, Jenny had soon realised that she and her friend had very different attitudes to housekeeping. Karen was woefully untidy – shoes and clothes strewn all over her bedroom, unused make-up bottles and face creams scattered all over the bathroom – but, despite her clutter, Karen somehow managed to stay organised. Considering the state of her bedroom, Jenny could never understand how her friend ever managed to get outside the door in a pair of matching *shoes*, not to mention matching socks. It seemed Roan shared her problem, she thought, remembering that he had mentioned his flatmates' untidiness that first day they met.

Then Roan flashed his gorgeous, sensual, deep-dimpled smile, and from then on, the appearance of the flat paled into insignificance. He reached across the room and took Jenny in his arms, pulling her close to him and kissing her – gently at first, but becoming more and more intense as his passion deepened.

Jenny immediately felt a massive rush of desire course through her. She kissed him back, unbuttoned his shirt and ran her hands across his broad chest, feeling the taut muscles underneath.

"Stay with me tonight," Roan said eagerly, when he eventually came up for air.

Jenny's breath caught in her throat as he began planting tiny kisses on her neck, right on the sensitive spot just below her ear.

She didn't need any more persuading.

* * *

Early the following morning, as she lay on the sofa watching breakfast television, Karen heard the key in the door. She looked up as a bedraggled but happy Jenny came in the door.

"Well, hello!" she teased. "Somebody had a good night last night!"

Jenny smiled bashfully and switched on the kettle. "We had a lovely time. The dinner was great – he's great."

Karen was pleased for her. "So are you seeing him again?"

She nodded. "He said he'd meet us in the pub tomorrow night. How did your night out with Shane go?"

Karen sniffed. "We had an argument – well, I should say, *I* had an argument. Shane usually just sits there, says nothing and pretends to listen, but eventually he just walks off on me."

"Nothing serious, I hope?"

Karen was nonchalant. "Nah, just a typical night out with Shane Quinn. Anyway, tell me what happened with Roan? It must have been pretty passionate last night – you're actually glowing!"

Jenny couldn't help but smile. Passionate? Karen was right. If she thought about it properly, yes, it had been passionate. Certainly, she had been a bit taken aback when things had been over so quickly, but shouldn't she take that as a compliment? After all, it was only their first time, and Roan had wanted her so much he probably couldn't help himself. And he was so lovely afterwards, so affectionate and gentle. Jenny loved the way he had snuggled up to her and held her close to him all night. Paul had *never* done that. No, she thought, the next time would be miles better. And more importantly, there would actually *be* a next time.

She poured herself a mug of tea and joined Karen on the sofa.

"So, if you're not going out with Roan again tonight, do you fancy watching a video with me?" Karen said.

"Good idea." Jenny said, the thoughts of a quiet night in appealing to her enormously. "What will we get?"

"Something along the lines of *Fatal Attraction*," Karen said, a wicked glint in her eye. "After the night I had last night, I'm in bunny-boiling mood!"

Chapter 7

Sitting in Boland's pub the following evening, Jenny couldn't figure out how the coarse, loud, redhead with the grating laugh, sitting across from her, could possibly be related to Shane's friend. Aidan was an absolute sweetheart, but his sister Lydia was so far removed from sweet that she could be related to a family of lemons.

Lydia had been rude and obnoxious from the very first second she arrived, dismissing Jenny's attempts at being friendly, and flirting openly with Aidan's friends – directly in front of their girlfriends. Jenny had known by Karen's glowering expression when Lydia joined the group, that there was no love lost between the two of them.

"Lydia and Shane had a bit of a fling a while back," Tessa explained to Jenny, when Lydia was out of earshot.

"It wasn't even a fling – it was just a one-night stand," Karen clarified, "but if that one even looks at him sideways, I'll level her."

Within seconds, Lydia had indeed turned her

attentions towards Shane and cheekily laid her hand on his knee, as she flirted shamelessly with him. Karen was trying her utmost to pretend she hadn't noticed, but Jenny knew it was only a matter of time before she exploded. Whether she would explode all over Lydia, or all over Shane, was a matter yet to be decided.

"I still can't figure out why Shane ever went near her," Karen explained to Jenny. "It was just before we started going out – just before we met, actually – but I don't think she's ever forgiven me for putting a spanner in the works. She seems to think that Shane would've been all hers, if I hadn't come along."

"Well – beauty is in the eye of the *beer*-holder, and I seem to remember Shane having more than a few the night he went home with Loathsome Lydia!" Tessa joked.

Jenny groaned inwardly. She hoped Lydia wouldn't start working her charms on Roan. She never knew how to handle things like that. It was all right for Karen – she and Shane had been together long enough for Karen not to be too much bothered about Lydia's blatant attention-seeking, but Jenny knew she wouldn't be able to stand it.

Still, things were going well so far. One evening, shortly after their first night out together, Roan had called to the flat with a shy smile and yet another huge bunch of roses. They had hardly spent a night apart since.

Their lovemaking was still a little 'intense', but Jenny believed that this was certainly no reflection on Roan. She hadn't slept with all that many people, what with her and Paul being together for so long. People were different, and it wasn't Roan's fault that he didn't seem to need that much foreplay to get in the mood. Nor was it his fault that it was always over very quickly. Jenny told herself that it was just a matter of getting used to the fact that not everyone would spend as much time on her as Paul had. And, after a while, things would surely improve, once she and Roan got to know one another's needs better.

Just then, Roan returned to the table with another round of drinks. He sat on a vacant stool beside Jenny, gave her another of his full-dimpled smiles, and rested a hand on her knee.

"*Roan Williams*!" Lydia screeched. "What are *you* doing here?"

Roan looked up sharply, and Jenny saw a faint blush appear on his face as he recognised the other girl.

"Hello, Lydia," he said quietly.

"Where's Siobhan?" Lydia asked, looking over his shoulder, as if the mysterious Siobhan might be hiding behind him. "I haven't seen her in ages. Have you two set a date yet?"

Jenny felt her heart thump loudly in her chest and her throat suddenly felt dry. *Set a date?*

"Um, we're not together any more," Roan said, looking decidedly uncomfortable.

Lydia's eyes widened with disbelief. "Really? I thought that was True Love. Remember the last time I met you together at the house? You had just proposed – after a weekend away, wasn't it? A romantic weekend in Paris."

Jenny could tell by her tone that Lydia was clearly enjoying imparting this information to the group, and equally delighted that Jenny had no clue as to who this Siobhan might be.

"That's it!" Aidan declared. "I *knew* I had seen you

someplace before. I met you that time I went to collect Lydia from her boyfriend's house – what was his name again?"He looked at Lydia for assistance, but then remembered. "Mark – that was it. You were the bloke going out with his sister."

Jenny tried her best to look nonchalant in front of them all, but her insides were churning. Was Roan already in a relationship with somebody else?

"We broke up shortly after that," Roan said quietly. "It turned out that neither of us were ready to get married. We're still friends though, no hard feelings."

"You let a stunner like Siobhan get away – after eight years?" Lydia was incredulous. "I can't believe I never heard anything about it."

"Well, it's finished anyway." Roan drained his pint in a single mouthful and stood up. "Anyone want another drink?"

He was obviously anxious to change the subject, Jenny thought. Well, she wouldn't blame him. If she had split up with someone after eight years, she wouldn't want to broadcast it either. No wonder he hadn't wanted to tell her. He must be still hurting.

"You should have seen Siobhan," she heard Lydia say. "She's absolutely stunning. She's a model, you know, always jetting off to London, Milan, and places like that. She has such a *fabulous* figure – size ten, I'm sure. Roan must be heartbroken over her."

"I'm sure he is," Jenny said, trying her utmost to lighten her tone.

"Especially after eight years," Lydia continued, warming to her subject. "They'd been together since school, apparently, and everyone thought they'd be together for good. Of course," she said conspiratorially, "Roan was always out for a good time, and I don't know how many times I've had to turn him down myself." She giggled coquettishly. "But there was no way I'd go near him – I couldn't do it to Siobhan. And, needless to say, I was going out with her brother at the time, so it would have been more than a little weird."

Jenny nearly choked on her drink. This girl was completely deluded!

"Jen, will you come with me to the ladies'?" Karen asked suddenly. "I need to borrow some more of that lipstick you gave me earlier."

Lydia looked disappointed to lose her audience when Jenny gratefully got up and followed her friend towards the end of the room.

"Phew, thanks, Karen – I thought she'd never shut up," she said airily, checking her reflection in the mirror.

Karen was silent.

Jenny looked at her. "You don't believe her, do you? You don't think that Roan was actually engaged?"

Karen shrugged her shoulders. "Lydia seems to know a lot about him – more than the rest of us do, and I remember that she *was* going out with some guy called Mark from Kildare, not so long ago."

"But why would he lie to me? Surely if the guy is engaged, he's not going to be making dates and sleeping with other women, is he?"

"Just be careful. That's all I'm saying."

"I don't think that *is* all you're saying, actually," Jenny said, realisation dawning, when Karen wouldn't meet her eyes. "You don't like him at all, do you? I noticed that you haven't exactly been falling all over him when he visits the flat."

Karen grimaced. "I don't know, Jen – I know you really like him, but there's just something about him that I can't quite put my finger on."

Jenny looked at her. "Well, thanks very much, Karen, but I think I'm a pretty good judge of character, and I *know* he's a decent guy. Then again, if I wanted your opinion, I would have asked for it, wouldn't I?" With this, Jenny picked up her handbag and flounced out the door, leaving Karen standing open-mouthed with bewilderment.

"Can we go now?" she asked Roan, eager to get away from the odious Lydia. Damn Karen and the lot of them, she thought. Roan was a lovely guy and if they didn't realise that, it was their loss.

Roan nodded and quickly finished his drink. He took her hand as they walked out of the pub. "I'm sorry you had to find out like that, Jenny," he said. "I was going to tell you – it's just, I didn't know how you'd take it. These things can be a big deal to some people and I suppose . . . I suppose I was afraid I might lose you."

Jenny's heart went out to him. Up until recently, she too had been in a long-term relationship, and she hadn't exactly been bending the ear off him about Paul, had she? Didn't everyone have some kind of a past? Anyway, she thought, with looks like his, it'd be a lot weirder if Roan *didn't* have a series of equally gorgeous exes.

"Forget it," she soothed. "It's not important. Don't feel as though you have to explain anything to me. Your past is entirely your own business."

Jenny held his hand tightly in hers, as they walked to the taxi rank across the road. She would be staying in his flat tonight. Karen could believe what she wanted, but as far as Jenny was concerned, Roan was telling the truth. Her friend just didn't know him as well as she did. That was all.

Chapter 8

Karen closed the file in front of her and sat back in her chair.

"So, Courtney, I've been asking the questions for the last half hour or so – do you have any questions for me about Acorn Fidelity?"

She hoped, for the sake of her growing migraine, that Courtney O'Connor, the pretty and seemingly mild-mannered school-leaver Karen was interviewing for a position at the Acorn Fidelity call centre, wouldn't be one of those overly keen teenagers who rattled on and on, hoping to sound like they knew what they were talking about. But by the looks of this one, she'd probably just trot out the standard 'How long has the company been in business?' and 'What opportunities are there for promotion here?'

But instead the girl shrugged, and asked, "Well, what are the men like?"

"Pardon?" Karen was so taken aback by the

unexpectedness of the question, that, for a second, she forgot all about her migraine.

"Well, me and my friend – Lisa Butler, she has an interview here tomorrow – we heard that there are supposed to be a load of fine things working in the call centre. Is it true?"

Karen had her out the door faster than an alcoholic's weekend. She smiled as she returned to her office. Fine things indeed! Courtney was probably right – there were lots of attractive young guys working in the call centre, but she was certain that the manager there wouldn't appreciate Karen employing a Britney Spears lookalike, whose sole intention was to chat up her co-workers. She checked her diary and found that little Miss Flirty was her last appointment this morning, and she had nothing pencilled in for the afternoon. It was just as well, she thought, because she didn't think she could bear it here much longer. She buzzed reception. "Pamela, I won't be coming back here after lunch. Can you hold any messages you have for me until tomorrow please?"

She hoped that it sounded to Pamela as though she would be away somewhere work-related, and not at home nursing her migraine.

She stepped out into the cool, crisp, afternoon. It was heading towards the middle of November, which meant that soon she and Catherine Mitchell would need to start organising the Acorn Fidelity Christmas party. Karen would also need to cut down on the amount of junk food she had been eating lately if she was going to fit into any of her remotely partyish clothes. Bias-cut backless dresses and love handles did *not* work well together. Shane was addicted to chocolate, and they were always pigging out in front of the television lately. Cable television was a terrible curse.

Karen sighed. She didn't see too much of Jenny these days. Her friend spent most of her time out with Roan, usually in the pub or at his flat. Karen frowned at the thought of it. She just wasn't at all sure about Roan Williams. The thing about him being engaged was a bit of a shock, but he and Jenny seemed happy enough.

He was strange though. Whenever he called for Jenny, Karen found it difficult to have a conversation with him. It was always small-talk and he seemed uncomfortable, and anxious to get away. She shrugged. Maybe some people were just like that.

As she crossed Portobello Bridge towards Rathmines, Karen worried about her friend and the changes that had come over her lately. She and Roan rarely joined the others on nights out any more. She had even missed the show that she had planned so eagerly with Tessa, before getting involved with *him*. Karen wished now that she hadn't said anything to Jenny about Roan that night in the pub. Shane had warned her not to get involved, but she wouldn't listen.

"I think he's a nice enough guy," he had told her afterwards. "There's no reason to believe that he's lying or messing Jenny around."

"You don't have the benefit of female intuition though, do you?" Karen had grunted. "And the fact that he is happy to sit for hours on end, arguing about football with you, is enough to make him a great man as far as you're concerned."

"Just give him a chance. If you start shooting your mouth off, you could end up losing Jenny as a friend. And, perish the thought, you might actually be wrong about him."

Karen shrugged. Maybe Shane was right. And of course, she sometimes tended to be a little over-protective of Jenny, as she always had been.

Feeling a bit peckish, she decided to pop into the Swan Centre to get something to eat before going home – maybe a salad roll, or at least something healthy. She tried her very best to ignore the mouth-watering smells coming from the chip-shop nearby.

As she approached the deli counter in Dunnes grocery store, Karen heard familiar male laughter coming from one of aisles behind her.

"Hey, whipped cream! You can have great fun with that!"

Karen looked around in surprise. What were Roan and Jenny doing here at this hour of the day? They should both be at work.

But catching sight of the couple behind her, Karen soon realised that Roan's companion wasn't Jenny. Tall and willowy, the girl was pretty and reminded Karen a little of the singer Alanis Morrisette, with her long, dark, glossy hair. Roan stood beside her as the girl picked up items from the dairy cabinet. Then he looked up. "Karen, how are you?" he smiled.

Karen didn't smile. What the hell was he playing at, she thought, frowning as they approached her.

Roan introduced his companion. "This is Alison – a friend from college. Alison, meet Karen – a friend from Rathmines," he laughed.

Karen watched the way this girl behaved with Roan, trying to establish how good a 'friend' she might be.

"I thought you'd be at work at this time of day, Roan," she said coolly.

"Nah, I have a few annual leave days left to take. I could say the same for yourself, though," he laughed, punching her playfully on the arm. "Dossing, are we?"

Karen looked at him in disgust. Why was he being so friendly all of a sudden? Normally, she couldn't get two words out of him! She picked up her basket and began to walk away. "I'm sure Jenny would like to meet you, Alison," she said, addressing the other girl, but looking Roan directly in the eye. "She's a good friend of Roan's too."

As she turned and walked down the aisle towards the checkout, Karen's face flushed with anger, unable to believe what she had just seen. The prat didn't even have the decency to look embarrassed at being caught! It was obvious what was going on – he was carrying on behind Jenny's back with that girl. Her suspicions from the beginning had been correct. Roan wasn't to be at all trusted.

How on earth was she going to tell Jenny?

Chapter 9

"So what do you think?" Barry Ferguson asked, "Jenny, do you think you could handle it?"

Jenny sat up. "Sorry, Barry, I wasn't concentrating – what?"

"I wondered if I could put you on the Foreign Exchange counter this week. I know you haven't been here long, but with Frankie leaving us next week, I'll need someone to take her place."

"OK, no problem," Jenny said, smiling at the Branch Manager. "I worked for a little while on foreign cash at a bank in Sydney. I might be slow for the first few days, but I'm sure I'll get better as I go along."

It was a lot busier at the Alliance Trust Dun Laoghaire branch than Jenny had expected. It seemed as though most, if not all, the local businesses had their accounts here. And most carried on as though they were the *only* ones with accounts there, each one more self-important than the next.

Jenny had been a little taken aback by the rudeness of

some of the customers. She wasn't sure why, but she had always assumed that everyone – customers and staff alike – at the Dublin offices of Alliance Trust, would be exceptionally mannerly and civilised. At home in Kilkenny, she knew most of the customers personally, so there was little need for formality. But her first day working at reception had quickly dispelled those notions. Jenny couldn't believe the way some of the customers barked down the phone at her, demanding to speak to this person or that person *immediately* and unwilling to be left on hold for longer than a few seconds.

Olivia, Barry Ferguson's personal assistant, had been highly amused when Jenny had told her this.

"Jenny, you'll soon find out that the shower of them can be like a pack of wolves –particularly on payday," she laughed. "Wait until you work downstairs. You'll think the ones you *don't* see face-to-face are absolute angels!"

Well, it looked as though she'd find out sooner than expected. She was enjoying working here so far. From the very first day in the staff canteen, everyone had gone out of their way to make her feel welcome, and to help her fit in.

She heard Barry talking to her. "You'll be fine, Jenny. I have every faith in you. You know we've all been very impressed with the way you've settled in here so far. I heard you on the telephone with Violet Madigan the other day, and she can be a tough cookie at the best of times. I don't know how many times I've been 'cut off' while talking to her myself!" He winked and Jenny hid a smile. "I think you'll be well able to manage downstairs. We'll put you beside Brendan Burke and, if you run into any trouble, he'll will sort you out."

Olivia popped her head around the door of Barry's office to announce his ten o'clock appointment, and Jenny took this as her cue to leave.

"Thanks, Barry, I hope I won't let you down," she said, as she left the room.

"Not at all. No better woman for it." The manager instantly turned his attentions towards his next appointment, the owner of a large Dun Laoghaire recruitment agency. "Kevin, how *are* you! Come in, come in!" Barry boomed, putting an arm around Kevin O'Leary and leading him into his office. "I haven't seen you since you made that birdie at the twelfth in Druid's Glen. You thrashed me that day – we'll have to organise a rematch."

As Barry's office door closed, Olivia saw Jenny's amused expression and rolled her eyes.

"I know," she said, closing a filing-cabinet drawer. "He can be so full of it sometimes, especially with the customers. He's a good manager though, one of best I've ever worked with."

"I just hope that I live up to his expectations then. He wants me to start on the Foreign Exchange counter next week."

"I wondered when they'd lay that one on you," Olivia said, sitting down in front of her computer, and putting on her headphones. "They'll be down an FX cashier when Frankie goes, and Christmas is on the way. You'll be fine though – it's not difficult at all once you get used to it."

"I think it's just the thought of all those queues. We were never that busy for foreign currency at home," Jenny frowned.

"At the beginning, let the rest of them worry about the

queues – you just concentrate on the customer in front of you, nothing else."

The telephone rang and Olivia answered it briskly. "ATB Dun Laoghaire, can I help you?"

Jenny returned to her desk. Olivia was so easy to work with; hopefully the others downstairs would be too. She'd miss the peace and quiet upstairs in the Accounts section; the main floor was manic at the best of times. Although her little stint here would stand to her. She now knew of most of the bank's biggest customers, and was aware that she would need to take extra care when dealing with some of them.

Additionally, she had got to know the Dun Laoghaire management team quite well. Barry Ferguson had told her that his door was always open, and that she should come to him if she had any problems. It was a nice change from Jenny's previous manager at Alliance Trust in Kilkenny who, in her opinion, had been an absolute ogre, and treated his staff little better than slaves.

She looked at her watch. It was nearly lunch-time. She wondered what Roan was doing now. Probably tweaking a line of Java code or something equally mind-boggling. Jenny barely knew how to use half of the features on her computer let alone program one of the things, but Roan seemed to love his work. She felt a small shiver of pleasure as she thought about him. It was hard to believe that she had only met him a few weeks ago, because it felt as though they had known one another forever.

If only Karen would stop acting so strangely, she thought, frowning. Jenny had explained the situation with Roan's ex-girlfriend to her a thousand times, but Karen was still suspicious of him.

"Why didn't he tell you about her from the start? Surely he knew it would come out eventually?" Karen had said, shortly afterwards.

"He told me that he wasn't sure how our relationship would progress, and if anything would come of it. He didn't want to lay anything heavy on me so quickly."

"You slept together after your first date, Jen – what do you mean he didn't know whether or not anything would come of it?"

"Karen I'm an adult. I like Roan and I'm pretty certain that he likes me. Why do you have such a problem with that?"

"I just don't want you to get hurt, that's all."

"Well, I appreciate your concern for me, but please try to remember that I'm no longer the fatso being bullied in the playground," Jenny said calmly. "These days I might still be a fatso, but we're not at school any more, and I'm more than able to stand on my own two feet."

"Funnily enough, Jen, I thought our friendship was based on a lot more than my standing up for you in the playground," Karen countered. "I thought we were good friends. And good friends give one another good advice."

"He makes me happy! Why can't you see that?"

And he *did* make Jenny happy. She could understand why he and his ex-girlfriend had broken up. If Roan thought that he and Siobhan were too young to be getting married, it was brave of him to have realised it before it was too late. He had told her that, after the engagement, Siobhan had talked about little else but wedding dresses, flowers, and church readings. It had all become too much for Roan, and he realised that he wasn't yet ready to settle down. He had wanted to put the wedding off for a couple of years, but Siobhan didn't agree and they had argued.

"We just didn't want the same things, Jen," he had said. "It hurt a lot, because we had been together for so long. She wanted me to give up my life in Dublin, and get a job in Kildare, and a house and a mortgage – she couldn't understand that I love my job. We were on two completely different wavelengths."

Jenny had decided there and then that she would never be like Siobhan. She would never ask Roan to give up anything for her. She wouldn't be that selfish.

Karen and the others just didn't understand. It was a pity, because it meant that she and Roan didn't spend as much time with Tessa, Aidan and Gerry and them all.

Still, as long as she and Roan had one another it didn't matter. Jenny picked up her typing file, switched on her Dictaphone and began to type.

* * *

Later that evening, Karen chopped peppers and onions in preparation for dinner. "I met Roan earlier today," she said airily.

"I know," Jenny replied, looking up from the magazine she was reading. "He told me on the phone that you were acting really weird towards him too. What's going on, Karen? It's obvious you don't like him, but could you not just be civil to him – for my sake?"

Karen was taken aback. The smart git had phoned Jenny afterwards! He was obviously covering his tracks.

"I was acting weird for a reason. He was with this girl and they –"

"For goodness sake, Karen, it was a friend of his from college! Is he not allowed to have friends now – is that it? I'm really getting sick of this!"

She threw down the magazine and stood up to face Karen at eye level. "Why the constant innuendo about him? It's not fair! I don't carry on like that with you about Shane!"

Karen felt the anger rise up from within. Why couldn't Jenny see what a chancer Roan was?

"You don't see Shane gallivanting around Rathmines with some slapper, do you?"

"Look, Karen, I've really had enough of this! Roan has done nothing wrong, yet you're carrying on as though he's some kind of criminal."

"You didn't see what I saw! They were joking and laughing and –"

"So, because he's joking and laughing with another girl, he's automatically cheating on me? That's what you're trying to say, isn't it?"

"Well . . . not exactly but – "

"But what?"

"I just don't want you to get hurt by him. He has a history and . . ." Karen trailed off and looked at Jenny, a pleading look in her eyes.

"A history? For goodness sake, we've been over this time and time again! OK, he was engaged and it didn't work out. Is he not allowed to move on now? I have a history too. I can't understand what the big deal is."

Karen was silent.

"Well, have you nothing else to say?" Jenny urged angrily.

Karen took a deep breath. "Jen, do you truly believe that it's all over between Roan and this Siobhan – his girlfriend of eight years?"

"Naturally, I believe him! If Shane told you something, you'd believe him too, wouldn't you?"

"But Shane is different and –"

"Oh, for goodness sake, Karen!" Jenny reached to where her coat was hanging on the door.

"Where are you going?"

"*Out!* Where I can get some peace, and I don't have to listen to you going on and on about Roan as if he's some kind of weasel!" She stood in the doorway, cheeks red and eyes flashing.

Karen chopped a pepper furiously. "Fine, suit yourself! But Jenny, you've changed a lot in the last couple of weeks. You have no interest in anything but Roan, Roan, Roan. You don't ask about anything that's happening in my life, and you tell me nothing about yours. You don't even go out with us any more and –"

"Go out! With you lot! Why would I want to – when all I hear is 'Be careful, Jenny. He has a history, Jenny.' Why the hell should I have to put up with that?"

She marched out the door, slamming it loudly behind her.

Karen stood transfixed in shock. The two of them hardly ever fought; it was a longstanding joke throughout their friendship that it was impossible to argue with Jenny. She went over to the window, and saw her friend walking purposefully down the street.

Shane had warned her not to get involved but how could she sit back and let her friend get hurt? Jenny hardly knew the guy but she had convinced herself that he was The One, just because of some stupid fortune-teller's 'prophecy'.

And he obviously had Jenny wrapped around his little finger.

"Well, if that's the way she wants it, let her make her own mistakes!" Karen said vehemently, turning away from the window and back towards the worktop.

She picked up a knife, and tried not to treat the unfortunate onion as if it was Roan Williams's head. She had tried her best to warn Jenny, so she needn't come crying to *her* if everything went pear-shaped between them. From now on Jenny and Roan could take a running jump as far as she was concerned!

Chapter 10

Karen snuggled in closer beside Shane. The colossal Screen 1 in the Savoy Cinema was without doubt her favourite place to watch a movie in the city and she and Shane were huge *007* fans.

"I'd better get some more Maltesers," Shane said, smirking at her through a mouthful of popcorn.

"Oh no!" Karen exclaimed, following his eyes and realising that she had practically eaten the whole packet by herself. "I'm such a pig!"

"You like your chocolate, that's for sure," he agreed, grinning, and moved out of the row of seats. "I'll be back in a minute."

Karen checked her watch as she relaxed in her comfy seat. Hopefully they would begin showing the trailers soon, and then they could watch James Bond getting stuck into all the inevitable baddies. While awaiting Shane's return from the sweetshop, she watched other cinemagoers being directed to their seats, and frowned when after a few moments she recognised someone sitting about three rows ahead of them. The girl stood up to let another couple pass her by and, as she did, Karen caught her profile. Jessie Kavanagh. She rarely went anywhere without her best friend which meant . . .

"Oh, Shane, stop it – I already have a stitch in my side from laughing," Karen heard Lydia Reilly gush from behind her. "We're sitting down here – oh! I didn't realise you were with anyone," she said, catching sight of Karen.

"Hello, Lydia," Karen greeted her calmly. *'I didn't realise you were with anyone!' And if he wasn't, what then, you silly wagon?*

"Right, well . . . I'll see you later, Shane, and thanks for the popcorn," Lydia grinned and deliberately ignoring Karen, pranced back down the rows to where her friend sat.

"Cow!" Karen grunted.

"Who – Lydia?" Shane was momentarily confused. "She's OK."

Karen was petulant. "What? Did you not see the carry-on of her with you just then – she was all over you, as usual. *"Thanks for the popcorn, Shane"'* she mimicked, wiggling her shoulders.

"What carry-on?" Shane looked amused. "Karen, just because you don't like Lydia doesn't mean that I shouldn't. She's Aidan's sister, and I've known her for longer than I've known you. I met her out in the lobby, and we walked back in together. What's the big deal?"

"The big deal is . . . oh, forget it – the trailers are about to start," Karen said bad-humouredly, as the lights went dim and the music blasted out of the surrounding Dolby speakers. She knew that she shouldn't let Lydia get to her but it really annoyed her that Shane couldn't see through the other girl's flirty act.

"I'll let you eat another whole packet of Maltesers if you forgive me," Shane said, making doe-eyes at Karen, and waving a piece of chocolate inches from her mouth.

Despite herself, she giggled. Shane put an arm around her shoulders and happily Karen snuggled into him. He was right, she thought. There was no point in letting the likes of Lydia Reilly ruin their night by putting her in bad form. She settled down to watch the delectable James Bond, all thoughts of Lydia forgotten.

Almost two hours later, when the movie had ended, she and Shane walked out of the cinema onto O'Connell Street.

"What did you think?" Shane asked.

"Brilliant!" Karen grinned, putting on her coat as they walked companionably down the street. "One of the best Bond movies in ages. We should really make the effort to go to the cinema more often, Shane. I really enjoyed tonight."

Shane said nothing and Karen stepped out onto the road, trying unsuccessfully to wave down a taxi.

They walked for a few moments more, before Shane stopped in the street, and kicked an empty burger carton out of his path. "I need to talk to you about something," he said, his tone serious.

"What, Shane, can't it wait? I'm trying to get us a lift home – hey, over here!" She waved furiously at a cab, which had already passed them by.

"Karen, forget it. We haven't a hope of getting one here

– there are too many others waiting. We might as well start walking home." He caught her hand and began to steer her towards O'Connell Bridge,

Karen walked along reluctantly beside him. "Shane, I don't fancy walking all the way back to Rathmines from here. If we wait long enough, we're bound to get a lift at some stage."

Shane stopped walking. "Look Karen, I wasn't going to say anything tonight but – I've got something to tell you."

She stopped alongside him on the bridge, suddenly aware of his discomfort. She frowned. What was wrong with him? "Go on, then, out with it."

"Well, you know that I'm not happy at Viking Engineering?" he began.

"And?" Karen looked over the bridge and down towards the murky waters of the River Liffey. Where was this going? She knew that Shane wasn't happy at work. He had taken a job there shortly after his degree, and over the last few years had come to the realisation that Viking Engineering was too small a company to secure the kind of contracts he really wanted to work on. Viking had only recently tendered for the construction of a new stand at Croke Park, and Shane was aware that such a small company hadn't a hope against the big-boys. He had been proved correct, when the contract had been awarded to another bigger, and ostensibly better, engineering company. It wasn't the first time it had happened – the bigger, better-known company nearly always secured the contract.

"The thing is," Shane continued, "my brother, Jack –

remember I told you he's the architect? Well, he knows someone, who knows someone from a large German engineering company, and apparently they're looking for Irish-trained staff."

"Terrific! Can this guy get you an interview?"

He wouldn't meet her eyes. "I've already had the interview. They sent a representative over last week and . . . they've offered me the job."

"That's terrific, Shane! What's the salary like?" Karen enthused, putting her arms around him. She knew that Shane had been a little distracted these last few weeks but typically he wouldn't tell her anything about the job until it was 'in the bag'.

She heard him answer her question about the salary. "It's out of this world, Karen. It's a huge multi-national company, and what they're offering is unreal for someone of my experience. But yet, they want me to work on the design team for this massive water-treatment plant they're planning to build. It'll be absolutely incredible – when I was in college, working on something like this was all I dreamed about."

"Great – where is all this happening?" she said. "I thought we had plenty of water-treatment plants around here."

The dreamy look disappeared from his eyes, and his expression again grew serious. "That's what I need to talk to you about, Karen. The project . . . the company is in Frankfurt."

Karen narrowed her eyes. "You mean . . . Shane, you're not telling me that you're thinking of working in Germany?"

He wouldn't meet her eyes. "I'm not just thinking of it,

Karen. I've already accepted the job – they want me to start next month."

Karen felt a myriad of emotions as she tried to make sense of what he had just told her – but anger was by far the strongest of them.

"How long have you known about this, Shane?" she asked finally.

"For a little while now, hon," he said softly, taking her hand in his. "I just couldn't bring myself to tell you before now. And I told you tonight because . . . well, I couldn't keep it to myself much longer."

Karen didn't know what to think. Shane, her Shane, was packing up and moving to Germany – just like that. How could he make a decision like that without telling her?

"Come on, let's go up to Bewley's and get a coffee or something – we can discuss it properly there," he said.

She looked at him through narrowed eyes. "Shane, I don't think there's anything to discuss. You're moving to Germany to start a new life and that's all there is to it. I don't know why you want to talk to *me* about it – you seem to have your mind already made up."

"Of course we need to talk about it!" Shane exclaimed. "Obviously, I've thought about how this might affect you and me and –"

"*Might* affect you and me? Are you mad, Shane? Naturally it will affect you and me! *Obviously*, you and me are finished!"

"Finished? What are you talking about? I thought maybe we could – "

"What – commute? Try a long-distance relationship?"

She pulled her coat tightly around her. "Forget it, Shane. It would never work – neither of us would be able to make it work."

"What? Do you mean to tell me that you're prepared to give up this relationship – this bloody *good* relationship we have together, just because I'm no longer living down the road from you?"

"Yes," she said shortly, "and you're the one who's made this decision – not me."

He gave her a strange look. "Karen, you're not prepared to even consider the possibility that we might be able to do this, are you? What does that say about you?"

Karen rounded on him, her eyes flashing with anger. "You have a bloody cheek, Shane Quinn! Tonight, you tell me out of the blue that you're swanning off to work in Germany – *next month*! You didn't even bother to let me know that something like this was in the pipeline. How the hell did you expect me to react?"

She turned on her heel and walked on. He followed silently.

She managed to flag down a taxi on Westmoreland Street, and she and Shane got into the car, both lost in their own thoughts.

Karen was so angry that she barely remembered telling the taxi driver where they were going. She hadn't expected this. She had thought that their relationship was going well, had thought that Shane might include, or at least consult, her with his plans. Here she was thinking they were happy together, and all the time he was planning on taking off to Germany, without giving her a second thought.

He obviously hadn't taken their relationship that seriously. They could pay lip-service to a long-distance relationship but that's all it ever would be. She knew that for her the fun that existed in her day-to-day relationship with him would be over, and it wouldn't be long before either of them began to play away. At least she could be realistic about it.

She stole a quick look at Shane, as he sat in silence staring out the window as the taxi sped towards Rathmines. He was probably feeling guilty for not having told her earlier. Still, it wouldn't have made any difference to his decision – he was going, and that was it as far as she was concerned. There was no point in either of them making promises she was sure they wouldn't be able to keep.

As the taxi crossed the bridge at Portobello, Karen asked the driver to stop at Leinster Square. Shane, who lived further up the road and closer to Rathgar, looked at her sadly, his face filled with hurt and disappointment.

"Can't we even discuss this, Karen?"

"Shane – there's no point in us talking any more about it," she said abruptly, "You've made your decision and that's it."

"For goodness sake, Karen – stop being so bloody stubborn," he said, his voice clipped, as the taxi turned into Leinster Square. "That's not 'it' and of course we need to talk about it."

Karen noticed the taxi-driver shift his position, so that he could get a better look in his rear-view mirror at the warring couple in the back of his car.

She sat up as the taxi approached the house. "Shane,

good luck in Germany. I hope you have a fantastic life. And *you*," she snapped at the unfortunate driver, "should mind your own bloody business!"

The poor man looked more than a little terrified when they came to a stop outside the gate. Karen thrust the fare at him and without another word to Shane, slammed the door behind her and stomped up the pathway towards the flat.

Watching the taxi move away, she battled with the double ache of disappointment and sadness. Stop, she warned herself. There was no point in getting sentimental about it. Shane had made his decision – she'd just have to get over it and move on.

Glancing towards the upstairs window, she noticed that the living-room light was on. She looked at her watch. It was nearly ten o'clock – unusual for Jenny to be here at this hour, as she usually stayed at Roan's on weeknights. She hoped he wasn't in there with her. Karen was *not* in the mood for making awkward small talk with the two of the – tonight of all nights.

On entering the flat, she took off her coat and went into her bedroom, before facing whoever might be in the living-room. But when Karen pushed open the living-room door, the sight that greeted her banished all thoughts of her situation with Shane completely from her mind.

* * *

Jenny had thought the day would never end. She hated late opening in the bank on Thursdays – there was always an endless procession of customers wanting to cash wages cheques, or make withdrawals in time for the weekend.

She just wasn't in the mood for a busy day and, sure enough, the majority of her customers were contrary. One woman had threatened to report her for having the audacity to ask for identification, before cashing a social welfare cheque.

"I'm entitled to it," the woman had said defensively. "Who do you think you are, telling me that I'm not?"

Jenny groaned inwardly, having had this argument with different people many times before. She tried to explain to the customer that it was actually the Social Welfare Department, and not the bank, that insisted on identification.

The woman wasn't having any of it. Snatching the cheque back across the counter, she turned, and marched upstairs towards Barry's office. Jenny knew that, if the woman made a complaint about her, the manager would explain that she had been correct in refusing payment without valid ID. Nevertheless she hated a scene.

It was to be the first of many that day, as customer after customer seemed to have some problem or another with her. It was as if they all knew that she was anxious to get away early that evening.

Another woman had chastised her for not smiling, while Jenny counted out her foreign cash to her. "I know it must be hard for you, exchanging money for those of us going off on holiday, while you're stuck here," she had said, "but the very least you could do is to be cheerful about it."

The customer was right – Jenny *was* being unnecessarily grumpy – but her mind was elsewhere, namely her appointment with the doctor after work.

Eventually, at four o'clock, the front doors closed, and the branch finally grew quiet. For the next half-hour or so, the only sound to be heard in the room was the whirr of adding machines as each cashier balanced the day's totals. Jenny had her Foreign Exchange cash balanced and totalled within fifteen minutes, and she watched the other cashiers anxiously, hoping that they too would finish soon, so that she would be in good time for her doctor's appointment.

Then she heard someone wail loudly from behind her.

"I don't believe it," exclaimed Joyce Ryan, the cashier working alongside her on the Irish cash counter, and a girl that Jenny didn't particularly like. She was a smug, unfriendly little madam who, according to Olivia, had got a job at Alliance Trust, not because of an impressive CV, but because her uncle was the Dublin South County Area Manager.

Joyce was frantically punching the keys on her machine. "I seem to be short about eight hundred euro!"

Jenny made a face. That meant they'd all have to stay late until Joyce managed to balance. Well, if she had her way, it would be sooner rather than later.

"Show me your dockets – I'll give you a hand," Jenny said, making her way over to the other girl who was anxiously double-checking her figures.

"The dockets are fine, thank you," Joyce glared defensively at her.

"Relax, Joyce," said Brendan. "She's only trying to help you so that we can all get out of here at some stage today – you might have made a mistake that you don't know about."

Jenny riffled through the pile of lodgement and withdrawal dockets, and compared them with the computer report. "Here it is," she said, spotting the mistake almost immediately. "You put four hundred euro through this account as a lodgement, instead of a withdrawal. You gave the customer four hundred, and yet you also lodged four hundred into his account. That's your eight hundred shortage. If you reverse the transaction, and afterwards make the withdrawal correctly, your totals should balance."

"Show me that," Joyce said, roughly grabbing the docket and scrutinising the relevant account on her computer.

"She's right," Brendan looked over her shoulder at the screen. "We can all go home now – good for you, Jenny!"

Minutes later, Jenny said a quick goodbye to the others before going upstairs to collect her coat. She looked at her watch as she walked nervously up the street. It was nearly five-fifteen, and her appointment had been for five o'clock.

As she sat in the waiting-room of the doctor's surgery, she tried to concentrate on the magazine she was supposed to be reading. She wished that she could just go on in to his office, and find out whatever she needed to find out.

"Jenny Hamilton?" the receptionist said pleasantly. "Dr Reilly will see you now. His office is down the hallway: the last room on your left."

Jenny's legs shook as she walked towards the office.

Dr Reilly looked up as she entered the room. "Hi, Jenny. Thanks for coming in today."

She clasped her hands tightly together as she stood in the doorway "What's wrong with me, doctor?"

He waved her inside. "Jenny, please come in and sit down. Don't worry, there's nothing seriously wrong with you," he reassured. "I just need to ask you a couple of questions, in order to find out what we're dealing with."

Jenny's mind raced as she did his bidding. Nothing seriously wrong? That meant that there was *something* wrong then, didn't it? But what?

Less than half an hour later, Jenny walked numbly out of the plush surgery. Dr Reilly had been lovely, though admittedly a little detached as he explained the situation to her. She felt the tears begin prick at her eyes as she walked along the street. She tried to bite them back, hoping not to cry – not here in front of everyone.

She walked quickly towards the seafront just in time to see a DART train pull out of the station. A sign proclaimed that there wouldn't be another train for at least twenty minutes. Trying to stay calm, Jenny walked across to the ferry terminal, and went inside to get something warm to drink. Though it was a mild evening, she felt icy inside. Clutching the warm paper cup, she went for a short walk along Dun Laoghaire pier.

As the evenings were now beginning to stay brighter for longer, the pier was packed with dog-walkers, joggers and, unfortunately for Jenny's sake, couples walking arm-in-arm. She watched one guy tenderly kiss his girlfriend's forehead, and wrap his arms around her as they looked out over the harbour at nothing in particular.

Jenny felt totally out of place amongst them all. Everyone seemed so happy and carefree, just going about his or her business on a fresh spring evening. Was she the only one that was aching inside? It wasn't fair.

She made her way back towards the Dart station, and this time managed to catch a train easily. As the train travelled along the coast towards town, Jenny thought she had never felt so alone. She wouldn't say anything to Roan, not yet. She wasn't sure how he might react to this. There wasn't anyone at work that she could trust with it either. She and Olivia had become very good friends over the last few months, and she had often confided in the other girl about her feelings towards Roan, and the fact that Karen didn't approve of him. What would Karen say if she knew Jenny's situation now? She couldn't tell her, that was for sure. She wouldn't know where to start. It was strange, because she and Karen rarely kept secrets from one another, but they had really drifted apart in the last few months. Jenny knew that it all stemmed from her relationship with Roan. While it hurt her to admit it, lately she had the feeling that maybe Karen had been right to warn her.

The train pulled in to Pearse Street station, and Jenny got off, walking quickly out of the station, and out onto the street. Her heart heavy, she signalled for a taxi and luckily one stopped at the kerb almost straightaway.

"Rathmines, please," she said to the driver, who grunted in response. Good, she thought, setting herself in the back seat. She wasn't in the mood for small talk.

As she stared at the streets outside, Jenny kept repeating in her mind everything that the doctor had told her. The longer she thought about it, the worse she felt.

Despite her best intentions to stay calm, Jenny felt a lump in her throat, and soon after she dissolved into silent tears. She turned her head towards the window, trying her best to ensure the taxi driver couldn't see her. He'd think she was some kind of madwoman.

After he had dropped her off at the flat, Jenny went inside and ran upstairs.

As she remembered the doctor's words as clearly as if he was sitting beside her, she was once more overtaken by a fresh bout of tears. Jenny sank down on the sofa and for what seemed like hours, cried as though her heart would break.

Chapter 11

Karen rushed in the door. "Jen! What's wrong?" She gathered her friend in her arms, but at this Jenny began to cry even harder. What the hell was going on? Karen wondered. Jenny looked as though she had been crying for days! "Jen, you're scaring me – please tell me! Has something happened between you and Roan – is that it?"

Seeing her nod, unable to speak for crying, Karen continued. "Did you have a fight, love? What has he done?"

Jenny sat up and wiped the tears from her eyes. Her hair was wet from crying and hung in strings around her face.

"I went to the doctor today . . . *hic* . . . and found out . . . I found out that I . . . *hic!*" She hiccuped furiously, unable to complete the sentence.

Karen's heart dropped like a stone as she engulfed her in a huge hug. "Oh, honey, I understand – I had a feeling in the last few weeks that something was wrong, and I suspected it might be this, but . . . "

110

Oh no, she thought to herself. Not this. Not Jenny.

"The doctor must have thought I was a right tramp. Oh, it's my own fault, Karen! I thought it would be OK not to use condoms, because I'm on the Pill."

"Yes, love, but the Pill isn't a hundred per cent effective – I thought you knew that," Karen interrupted with a consoling smile.

Jenny looked confused. "It's not effective *at all*, Karen, in this case – what are you talking about?" Then she realised and her hand flew to her mouth.

"Look, Jen, it's OK – I'll be there for you," she soothed, "and I'll help you tell your parents if you like."

Jenny gave her a lopsided smile. "'Somehow, I don't think I'll be telling Mum and Dad about this. I'm not pregnant, Karen – that's what you think, isn't it? It's nothing like that, thank goodness. But," her voice dropped to a low whisper, as she struggled to say the words, "I've picked up, some kind of . . . infection, and I must have picked it up from Roan. A sexual infection." She looked away, mortified.

Karen stared at her friend, open-mouthed. She tried to say something but, for a long moment, words escaped her. "What?" she whispered eventually. "Well, what type of infection? I can understand if you don't want to tell me but . . . how serious is it, Jenny? It's not –"

"It's gonorrhoea, Karen. I've been having a few problems, so I went to get it checked out, and the doctor called me in today to give me the results. I didn't think . . . I mean, I had no idea it could be something like this – I just feel so disgusting!"

"Oh, Jen, you poor thing," was all that Karen could

manage, and as she hugged her friend again, her thoughts descended into fury.

The bastard! The good-for-nothing bastard! How dare he? She'd kill Roan Williams when she got her hands on him. She knew it. He had finally tripped himself up – but how! Poor Jenny didn't deserve this. No one did. She'd love to see him strung up by his –

"I haven't said anything to him about it, yet. I suppose I'll have to, but I just don't know what he'll say. God, I feel so dirty, Karen!"

"Don't you dare blame yourself for this – you're not the one that's dirty! The sod – I knew it!" Her voice softened when she saw Jenny's hurt expression. "Honey, please don't think that I'm pleased about this – I'm not and I'm *definitely* not going to say I told you so. But even you have to admit now that he's not to be trusted. I mean, he's obviously been two-timing you and with God knows who, or *what*? You have to find out, for your own sake."

"I've suspected for a while that things haven't been going well. This confirms it all though." Jenny smiled ruefully. "What a way to find out that your boyfriend's been cheating on you!"

Karen hugged her again. "Don't worry, Jen, you'll be much better off without the two-timing prat. I swear to God, if I get near him, I'll murder him!"

Despite herself, Jenny had to laugh at her friend's vehemence. "You know, I've kind of missed having you stick up for me, Cassidy." She pushed her hair out of her eyes.

"I know it's been hard for you to hold your tongue

about him, but I was too pig-headed to listen in the first place. I should have known that you were only saying those things out of concern. I'm really sorry, Karen."

She sniffed, and the two of them looked at one other momentarily, before they burst out laughing.

"What a pair we are," Karen said, shaking her head, "the two of us discovering on the same night that our men are complete and utter bastards."

Jenny sat up quickly in surprise. "What do you mean – what's Shane done?"

Karen told her about Shane's decision to move to Germany and it was Jenny's turn to be sympathetic.

"So what are you going to do now?" Karen asked eventually.

Jenny had brightened considerably since telling Karen about her predicament.

"Well, I'm not looking forward to it, but I suppose I'll have to confront him."

"And?" Karen probed, hoping that Jenny was going to dump the rat. She'd have to dump him!

"And – I'll tell Roan exactly where to go. I don't need someone like him, Karen. I can't believe that I fell for all the lies he must have been telling me. Remember at Christmas, when he was supposed to come home with me to meet Mum and Dad? And he cried off with the flu? I believed him, but that was probably a lie too."

Karen nodded sagely.

"But why didn't I see it before now?" Jenny asked, and then answered her own question. "There were signs from the very beginning, but I just ignored them all, because I wanted to believe that Roan was The One."

Karen said nothing. She didn't want to go down this road again.

"Right," she said brightly, jumping up from the sofa, and taking two wineglasses out of the cupboard. "After all that, I think we could both do with a drink."

Jenny gave her the thumbs up. "Karen – are you absolutely sure that you and Shane are finished?" she asked, while Karen rummaged in the drawer for a corkscrew, "After all, he'll only be an hour or two away on a plane. A long-term relationship might not be as difficult as you think."

Karen shook her head firmly. "No, he made his decision without consulting me, so why should I be the one doing the running? As if it wouldn't make any difference to our relationship," she drawled, rolling her eyes. "Seriously, did you ever hear such rubbish in all your life?"

Jenny shrugged. "But do you think it's wise to make such a snap decision? You and Shane have been together for a while now."

"That's exactly my point. If the relationship meant anything to him, he wouldn't be swanning off without a second thought, would he? Anyway, I don't want to talk, or even *think* about it any more." She filled each wineglass to the brim, and slowly handed one to Jenny, careful not to spill any. "So what about this infection thing then? It's curable, isn't it? I mean . . . it won't affect you permanently or anything?"

Jenny shook her head. "Apparently I caught it in time and, according to Dr Reilly, it's supposedly easy enough to get rid of. He gave me some antibiotics and told me to abstain from sex for a while, which *won't* be a problem – so, hopefully, I'll be fine."

That was a relief, thought Karen to herself. She had read enough about sexually transmitted infections in women's magazines to know some of them, if left undetected, could be very dangerous. She was glad that Jenny hadn't been too embarrassed to go to see a doctor about it. At least she was prepared to admit now, even to herself, that everything hadn't been right with Roan.

With the way things were going, and now that there were no longer any barriers between them, she and Jenny would be back to normal in no time. She was looking forward to it. Now they could have a bit of a laugh together, just like old times. She'd arrange it with Tessa for the three of them to go on a rip-roaring girls' night out in town soon.

And Roan Williams and Shane Quinn could go take a hike.

* * *

"Roan, we have a bit of problem." Jenny tried to stop her hands from shaking.

"What's wrong, Jen? Kevin told me that you called earlier. I had to work late tonight, sorry."

Roan moved to kiss her on the lips and Jenny quickly stepped away from him. He stood back, surprised.

"As I said, we have a bit of problem. I went to the doctor a few days ago and – "

"Whoa! Don't tell me it's that kind of problem," he interrupted. "I thought you were on the Pill." Jenny flinched at this reaction and seeing her face, he softened his tone. "It's not that, is it, babe? You're not pregnant, are you, cos you know we're both young and –"

115

"I'm not pregnant."

His expression visibly relaxed.

"But I appear to have caught an STI from you." Jenny was amazed at how calm she sounded, when her insides were churning.

"Caught? What? From me? What are you talking about?" Roan said, obviously thrown completely off balance.

"It appears that I have caught gonorrhoea from you, Roan."

There, it was out. She waited for his reaction.

He turned away from her, and ran his hands through his thick dark hair. When he turned back to her, she saw a look of utter horror on his face.

"My God! You don't think . . . my God! You think that I gave you that? Jenny, how could you think something like that?"

"Well, who else could I have got it from, Roan? I hope you're not suggesting – how dare you? I haven't been sleeping around, you know!"

Jenny eyes were bright. Karen had thought that he might go down this particular road but, up until now, Jenny didn't believe that he could be so low.

"No, no, that's not what I'm saying at all," he said, cupping her face in his hands. "I know you wouldn't sleep around. I trust you, Jenny. You wouldn't be unfaithful to me," he gazed at her steadily, "in the same way that I wouldn't cheat on you. Surely there are other ways you could have picked up this thing?"

Jenny was confused. "What are you talking about? Naturally, I caught it from you. What are you saying? I don't understand."

"Well, what about your boyfriend in Australia? I'm not trying to be mean but . . . didn't you tell me that he had been cheating on you?"

"Well, yes, but . . ." Jenny slumped down on the couch, no longer so sure of herself.

Roan seemed so hurt by the suggestion and was so adamant that he hadn't been unfaithful. She supposed that it was a possibility that she could have got the infection from Paul. The doctor had told her that these things could lie undetected for some time, and there was no way of knowing how long she had had it. In fact, now that she thought about it, she'd ignored the symptoms for a long time before having it seen to. The problem was, she couldn't remember exactly when the symptoms started.

"I hadn't thought of that," she admitted in small voice.

Roan knelt down in front of her, and held both her hands in his.

"Think about it, Jen. How else could you have picked it up? You and I are in a serious relationship together. There's no one else involved here." He put his arms around her and gathered her towards him.

"Oh, I didn't know what to think," she cried, tentatively returning his embrace. "I thought that maybe you had been, you know . . . I just wasn't sure."

"Sssh, it's OK. I understand," Roan soothed, "but we've been together for months now, and you're the only person I've been with since Siobhan. Please believe me," he stroked her cheeks with his thumb, wiping away the tears, "I wouldn't do anything to hurt you like that. You have to trust me."

Relief flooded through her and, as she saw the hurt

and pain in his eyes, she knew that she had made a mistake. How could she have doubted him like that? And how stupid of her to automatically assume *he* was being unfaithful, when there was concrete proof that Paul had been! She was an untrusting cow!

"I'm so sorry. You must think I'm awful, accusing you like that." She looked up at him, her face full of remorse.

"No, it's OK. I know it must have been a bit of shock to you. I wondered why I hadn't heard anything from you in the last few days. You poor thing – how are things now? Did the doctor get it sorted?"

The look of utter concern on his face made Jenny feel like an absolute heel. Here he was, all concerned about her, after she had thrown something like that in his face.

"No, I'll be fine but . . . " Jenny grimaced, embarrassed, "you'll have to be treated too. Roan, I don't know what you must think of me. I should have trusted you, and I should come to you, before automatically accusing you and –"

He took her in his arms again. "It's fine, as long as you know now that I wouldn't do anything like that." He looked directly into her eyes. "You do know that, don't you?"

She smiled tearfully at him. "I wouldn't blame you if you never wanted to see me again."

"Don't be silly. It was just a little misunderstanding. But I take it that we have to behave ourselves for a while?"

Jenny nodded and he kissed her on the nose. "Look, why don't you go into the bathroom and fix yourself up, and we'll go for a nice quiet pint somewhere."

He patted the pockets in his jeans. "The thing is, I

118

haven't been able to find my wallet anywhere today so I might have to –"

"Oh, I can sort us out!" Jenny piped up quickly, eager to please.

"Are you sure? It should be around here somewhere but –"

"It's no problem, Roan. The least I can do is buy you a few drinks after my performance just then."

"Well, if you're sure." Roan flashed her a winning smile.

Jenny went into the bathroom and splashed cold water on her face to get rid of the tearstains on her cheeks, pleased that things were back to normal between them. As they left the flat and walked down the street, Roan put his arm around her and smiled. Jenny shivered with a mixture of relief and delight. She was really very lucky that Roan had been so understanding about it. After all, if she had been in his position, she would have been appalled.

She remembered what the fortune-teller had told her about 'the upheavals' she and Roan would experience throughout their relationship. But didn't she say too that they would work their way through all of those problems? She hoped that there wouldn't be other problems because, if there were, she wasn't sure if she would be able to handle them.

Not to worry, she thought, as they reached the pub. The main thing was that they *had* been able to work through their problems. And she'd make it up to him. She'd make sure they had a great night out tonight and then, at the weekend, she'd take him out to dinner and wouldn't let him put a hand in his pocket. She owed it to him after everything she had put him through.

Chapter 12

"How could she be so bloody stupid, Tessa?" Karen groaned. "She seemed so determined to finish with him. I can't believe she fell for it!"

She stared out of the window of the coffee shop at a crowded O'Connell St. It was the following Saturday afternoon, and the city centre was packed with shoppers and tourists. She had felt bad telling Tessa about Jenny's situation, but was so annoyed with her friend that she had to tell someone. A nurse by profession, maybe Tessa might be able to shed some light as to how Roan could get away with such lies.

When Jenny had returned from her supposed confrontation with Roan, Karen had known by her face that she hadn't dumped him as she had intended.

"Maybe I've been a bit hasty in judging him," she had said, when Karen asked her how it went.

Karen had jumped up from the sofa in disbelief. "Hasty?

What are you on about? Look what he did, for goodness sake!"

"He said it wasn't him," Jenny had said quietly, refusing to look at her friend.

Karen could hardly believe it.

"Jenny, that's why these things are called STI's. They are *sexually transmitted*! How *did* he think you caught it?" She gave her friend a warning look, as the thought struck her. "Don't you dare tell me he says you got it from someone else!"

Jenny looked at Karen imploringly. "He thinks that I could have picked it up from Paul. He says there's no way that he'd be unfaithful."

"What!" Karen was incredulous. How did he come up with this crap? "You and Paul broke up months ago! How would this take so long to manifest itself?"

Jenny winced. "I've had the symptoms for a while – I just kept putting off going to the doctor, hoping things would get better. Roan has a point – it could just as easily have been Paul."

Karen shook her head. "I really don't think so, Jen. It sounds a bit far-fetched to me. And you said yourself that you had some doubts about Roan before you even found out about this."

"Yes, but maybe I misjudged him, and this just magnified everything unrealistically. You should have seen his face when I told him – he was really upset about it. I felt so guilty for jumping the gun, when there could have been a reasonable explanation. My heart went out to him."

Karen didn't know what to say. She felt like catching Jenny and shaking her until she saw reason. Obviously, all her great intentions the other night for dumping Roan had gone out the window now. And the sly bastard knew exactly how to cover his tracks too. What was wrong with Jenny? Why was she so blind as to what was really going on?

"I just can't understand it," she said to Tessa.

The other girl sat back in her chair. "What can you do? If she's prepared to go along with what he's told her, then there's absolutely no point in *you* worrying yourself over it. She's a big girl now, after all." She took a sip from her cappuccino. "But I have to admit, I'm surprised at Jenny. Now I know exactly what they mean when they say love is blind."

Karen rolled her eyes. "Blind being the bloody operative word. Seriously, Tessa, what's wrong with her? Is he that good a liar?"

Tessa paused. "Well, it might have something to do with this fortune-teller – "

"I know – it's absolutely crazy stuff! Why would anyone over the age of ten believe all that crap?"

"Now, hold on just a moment," Tessa said levelly. "You're a sceptical person by nature, Karen, and that's your business. But Jenny isn't. She put her faith in this woman, at a time in her life when she was unsure and afraid. She had just broken up with this Paul, had come back from Australia and to what? She wasn't sure of herself, and was obviously frightened. I suppose she needed to know what the future held for her – a little bit of hope if you like."

Karen was still shaking her head. "Tessa, come on – nobody knows what the future holds for them, least of all these blasted fortune-tellers. If that's the case, why aren't they all out betting on horses, or doing the Lotto, instead of warping people's minds?"

"That's not the point though, is it?" Tessa argued. "Sometimes it gives people a little confidence – even gives them something to look forward to. It's not a bad thing, Karen – no worse than reading your horoscope, which I've seen you do on a regular basis!"

"But that's different, surely? I don't follow blindly what my horoscope tells me and another million Aries! What happens, happens, and we all have to make our own decisions regardless." Karen ran her hands through her hair, exasperated. "Jenny's staying with Roan because she's convinced herself that he's The One, and I think that is total bullshit."

Tessa bit into her croissant. "Did you ever think that she might be staying with him because she loves him, and wants to believe that he's telling the truth?"

Karen shrugged. "I suppose it's a possibility. But for what it's worth, *I* don't think he's telling the truth. I know for a fact that's he's a lying, cheating, scumbag."

"How?"

"How what?"

"You said that you know for a fact. How do you know that?" Tessa repeated, folding her arms across her chest.

"Well, I told you about that girl he was with, that time in the shopping centre."

"Oh? And were they at it on the floor of the fruit and veg aisle, or something?" Tessa asked, with an amused glint in her eye.

"No, but – "

"So, how do you know that she wasn't just a friend?

And, isn't it possible that Jenny *may* have picked up this thing from her ex-boyfriend? Some STI's can often be asymptomatic."

Karen raised an eyebrow. "Can you explain that in English, please, nurse?"

"Well, I'm not saying that this is exactly how it happened, but there is a possibility that Jenny could have picked it up from Paul sometime last year, and didn't even know she had it. Eventually, she goes to her doctor complaining of mild symptoms and it shows up on her cervical smear."

"You think that's a real possibility?"

"Why not?" Tessa shrugged. "Women have a tendency to stick their heads in the sand over these things – I see it myself all the time. Karen, give the poor guy a break, and try and accept the possibility that you might actually be *wrong* about him."

Karen remembered Shane telling her the exact same thing. Could she be mistaken about Roan? She didn't know. All she knew was that her head was going to explode if she thought about Jenny's situation any longer. Goodness knows she had her own problems. Shane was leaving in a few weeks' time.

Karen hadn't seen him since that night at the cinema, and he hadn't been in contact with her. She was surprised. It wasn't like Shane to hold a grudge or to sulk.

She had to admit to herself that she missed him already. But what was the point? He was going to Germany and she wasn't – end of story. It would be a lot easier this way. Still, Karen couldn't ignore the ache she felt in the pit of her stomach whenever she thought about him.

"Have you seen Shane around lately?" she asked Tessa, trying to keep her voice light.

Tessa brought her cup halfway to her mouth and then stopped. "Ah, I wondered when we might get to that."

"What do you mean? It's over between us."

"You could at least talk to him about it. He's really upset, you know."

Karen felt her heart thump loudly in her chest. "Has he said something to you?"

Tessa shook her head. "Not to me – to Gerry. He reckons he's really cut up over it. Now he doesn't know whether or not he's made the right decision. You should talk to him, Karen. You're not being fair."

"Hold on a minute! I wasn't the one that decided to up and leave for Germany, just like that, was I?"

"No, but I think that you both should at least talk about it before he goes. You said yourself that you didn't give him a chance to explain."

Karen bit her lip. She desperately wanted to talk to Shane before he left, but she wasn't going to make the first move.

Tessa read her thoughts. "He's afraid to ring you. He thinks you'll tell him where to go. You know what he's like, Karen – he doesn't know how to handle this at all."

Karen felt a surge of annoyance as she remembered their last conversation. "Oh, I see. He thought I'd say, 'Terrific, Shane! Whatever you want, Shane! I'll come and see you every weekend, Shane!'"

"It's not that," Tessa had to hide a smile at Karen's stubbornness. "He didn't think that his moving away would mean the end of your relationship. He thinks a lot of you, you know. Gerry reckons he's never seen him so upset. You must be a right cracker in bed!"

Karen laughed at this. "I was so angry with him that night, Tessa. He'd made the decision without saying anything to me, and then expected me to go along with it. It was unfair of him to expect that I wouldn't be shocked and upset. After all, he'd known about it for ages but for me it had all come completely out of the blue."

Tessa was soothing. "There's no point in being pig-headed about it now. He's leaving in a just few weeks' time. Talk to him about it with a clear head. Then you'll both be in a better position than before to make any decisions about whether or not you'll stay together."

Karen shook her head, laughing as she did. "You know, you talk an awful lot of sense for a Corkwoman."

Tessa made a face at her.

"Still, I know what you mean," Karen continued. "I think I would like to talk to Shane, but with everything that's been happening with Jenny, I've been a bit distracted."

"Why don't you call over when we're finished here?" Tessa suggested. "He'd be delighted to see you, Karen – I know he would."

"OK then, I'm convinced! Anything to get you off my back." She finished eating, satisfied that the decision had been made for her. She might as well go and see him. There was no point in carrying on like this.

Tessa pushed her plate away and stood up. "C'mon, I've bought nothing yet, and I'm really in the mood for a bit of a splurge!"

Karen picked up her bag, and followed her friend out

onto the busy street, wondering why they repeatedly subjected themselves to shopping in the city centre on a Saturday, when everyone else in the city had the same idea. They struggled through the oncoming crowds towards Grafton St, Karen feeling in much better form after the chat and the food.

"Oh wow! Look at that dress – it's absolutely fabulous, Karen!" Tessa stood in front of Top Shop, pointing at the window display. "Come on – I have to try it on!"

She stood outside the changing room as Tessa pranced around in a wispy dress that looked amazing on her. Being as she was, a supposedly healthy size twelve, a dress like that still wouldn't go near Karen in a million years. She'd love to have Tessa's gamine looks; it seemed all the rage lately. That Ally McBeal had a lot to answer for.

Nothing in Top Shop would fit her, she thought, examining a boob tube that would just about cover *one* of her breasts. She'd get Tessa to go down to Jigsaw or Principles with her afterwards. At least they did normal sizes!

* * *

Later that afternoon, Karen left a happily fulfilled Tessa, after a successful bout of retail therapy.

She decided to pop back to the flat, and get changed before calling over to Shane's. Now that her mind was made up, there was no point in delaying things. She'd have a good long chat with him, and maybe later they could go out for a quiet pint to discuss everything properly, and to ensure that they didn't start arguing again.

Who knows, maybe the move mightn't be such a bad thing after all, she thought. A break might actually be good for them – absence makes the heart grow fonder, and all that.

As Tessa had said earlier, she should stop behaving like a spoilt child, and start to show Shane some support. After all, Karen reasoned, it couldn't have been an easy decision for him, leaving all his friends and family to start life in a completely different country. She'd sort it all out with him, and make sure that before Shane left for Germany they would both know exactly how they stood with one another.

She decided against taking the No 15 bus to Rathgar, where Shane lived, preferring instead to walk the short distance and make the most of the fine evening.

Taking in the hustle and bustle around her, she marvelled at how easily she had warmed to Dublin and city life. She loved the fact that she could hop on a bus and be in the city centre within twenty minutes. She couldn't imagine living anywhere else, and hoped that someday she'd end up settling down somewhere nearby. Rathmines had everything – pubs, shops, restaurants and most importantly, good friends and great memories. Shane would definitely miss all this.

She was looking forward to seeing him. She and Shane had rarely spent a night apart since they'd started going out, and it had now been nearly two weeks since the argument.

Ignoring one another was pointless; they needed to sort it out sooner, rather than later.

Just before Karen turned onto the road leading to Shane's flat in Cowper Downs, she stopped off at the corner shop for a packet of Cadbury's Fingers as a peace offering. Or as blackmail, she thought, smiling to herself as she paid the shopkeeper.

She walked down the steps to Shane's basement flat, and rapped loudly on the door. There was no doorknocker, and the intercom hadn't worked in years.

No answer.

She knocked loudly again and, when there was still nothing, she peered in the living-room, looking for signs of life. Then she heard some shuffling in the hallway.

Shane opened the door in his boxer shorts, eyes half-closed as he struggled to see against the bright daylight.

"Hello," Karen said shyly, a little taken aback. Now that she was here, she didn't know what to say to him. He must have been asleep, because he looked awful. And his breath stank of drink.

Shane finally recognised her. "Uh, Karen – what are *you* doing here?" His speech was fuzzy and his expression wide-eyed.

Karen was a bit put out. For someone who was supposedly pining over her, he didn't look that happy to see her.

"Can I come in, Shane? I thought we should talk. I haven't seen you in a while."

Shane scratched his head and looked around him. He stood in the doorway, shuffling from side to side, and seemingly not knowing what to do.

"I don't think it's a good idea, Karen. Can I meet up with you later or something?" Karen saw the glazed look in his eyes, and immediately realised why he was acting so strangely.

"Shane, you're drunk! It's seven-thirty in the evening, for goodness sake! Have you been in the pub all day?"

"Karen, you can't tell me what to do any more – it's over between us. You said so yourself and – "

"Love, it was just a silly argument. I was shocked when you told me you had made up your mind about Germany so quickly, that's all. I hadn't time to take it all in. It's not a big deal – now stop being so stupid, and let me come in, so that we can sort it all out."

"Karen – it's really not a good idea," Shane said, uncomfortably.

Then suddenly she realised why he was being so cagey

"Get out of my way," she said, brushing roughly past him, through the doorway, and into the living-room.

"Karen, what are you doing here?" Lydia Reilly purred like a cat that had just been awarded a lifetime's supply of cream. She lay barelegged on the couch, and was just about dressed in a U2 T-shirt that belonged to Shane. Karen knew it belonged to Shane, because the T-shirt had been a present from her last Christmas.

Lydia smiled broadly, obviously thrilled with the look of utter disbelief on Karen's face.

Karen was so shocked she was unable to utter a single word.

For the moment.

Shane visibly paled. "Karen, I know it looks bad, but there's nothing . . . I was drunk . . . I didn't know that you . . ." He held his hands out in despair.

Karen turned on him, her eyes flashing and her cheeks red with fury.

"It didn't take you long, did it? Here I was feeling

130

sorry for you, thinking that I had let you down somehow, when all the time you've probably been screwing Miss Piggy here." She eyed Lydia's chunky thighs pointedly.

Lydia stood up, her hands on her hips. "How dare you talk to him like that!" she began. "And don't think you can come in here and insult me, you stuck-up culchie cow!"

Karen rounded on her with such venom in her eyes that Lydia actually jumped backwards. "Listen here, you silly little bitch – you can just shut your ugly, over-made-up, little trap! You're a desperate slapper who can't get a man to go near you sober, so you have to rely on drunken rejects like *him*. And you!" She stabbed Shane's chest with her forefinger. "I'm only sorry I wasted so much of my time on a brainless cejit. God knows, it wasn't worth it! As far as I'm concerned, you're welcome to one other, and you can both take a running jump into the Grand Canal!"

With this, Karen raced out the door, up the steps and down the driveway, her entire body shaking, with both shock and fury. She barely heard Shane calling after her.

The bastard! How could he? Just like that – after all the time they'd been together.

Karen tried to keep her feet moving forward, her entire body convulsed with fury as she walked. She turned onto a side road, not wanting to face the busy Rathgar Road in the state she was in.

Noticing that she still had the chocolate biscuits she had bought Shane earlier, Karen cursed loudly, and threw them across the road with such force that they landed in somebody's front garden. For some reason, she found this hysterical, and she laughed out loud, before seconds later bursting into tears.

She used the sleeves of her sweater to dry her drenched cheeks and, as she did, she noticed Shane come up behind her, dressed in just a shirt, a pair of boxers and boots with no socks.

"Karen, please talk to me – I'm so sorry – I didn't mean – I was out of control – nothing happened – please!" There were tears in his eyes as he approached her.

"Don't you come near me. Don't you even *think* about coming near me, you stupid bastard!" Karen hunched her shoulders and turned away, walking quickly down the road away from him.

Shane followed, shouting after her, "Karen, please! If you would just let me explain!"

"Explain?" She stopped and faced him, her eyes steely, "Explain what? Oh let me guess. You and that little tramp were just swapping clothes – was that it? Shane, you're pathetic, unbelievably pathetic!" She walked ahead of him again.

"I know, Karen. I know I've been an absolute fool. Look, Lydia was just hanging around in the pub earlier. I'd had a lot to drink and – "

"Oh, don't you dare!" Karen waved a finger at him. "Don't you think that I have any interest in hearing how this little shag-fest came about. What are you trying to do, Shane? Make it worse – is that it? Because that's exactly what you're doing!"

"Karen, I swear to you that nothing happened!"

"Look, *just leave me alone!*" she roared, not caring who heard her. "I don't want to hear it, Shane, and to be honest, I couldn't give a flying fuck. What you do now is your own business, and has nothing whatsoever to do with me. So you can just go to Germany, or go to hell. Either would suit me just fine."

She stormed off again.

Shane went to catch up with her but decided against it. Standing as he was in the road barely dressed, he noticed some passers-by stare at him with unconcealed amusement. Karen was right, he thought. He was fucking pathetic.

He made his way back to the flat, and found Lydia still there; lazing on the sofa and drinking another can of Budweiser from the crate she had bought earlier. She looked up, and smiled smugly when she saw him come in.

"Hi, I hope I didn't cause too much trouble earlier."

Shane ran both hands through his hair in despair. "Lydia, look . . . can you leave please? I need to be by myself for a while."

"Oh, what's wrong?" She stood up and put her arms around his neck. "Whatever it is, I'm sure I can make you forget about it. I did earlier, didn't I?' She giggled, nuzzling his earlobe.

He pushed her away from him. "Look, Lydia, forget it. OK? I'm sorry, but this was a mistake. I should never have kissed you – "

"Oh, come on, Shane, don't give me that!" Lydia was petulant. "You were up for it as much as I was – more so, as I recall." She reached for him again. "Look, forget about her – let's continue where we left off."

"Lydia, please! Just go, will you?" Shane shouted.

Lydia flinched slightly but said nothing. As she left the room, Shane called after her. "I'm sorry, Lydia. It's not your fault. You didn't ask to get caught up in all of this."

His voice softened as she appeared again in the doorway. "I think it's better if we forget all about this for now, OK?"

She nodded, her lower lip wobbling.

"Look, Lydia, we're mates, aren't we? I know I'm being a bastard to you too, and I'm sorry. What happened here was a big mistake. I love Karen, and I've been an absolute idiot. I'm very, very sorry."

Lydia said nothing. She went back into the bedroom and quickly got dressed, before walking out, slamming the front door behind her.

Shane flopped down on the sofa, and put his head in his hands.

He'd made such a mess of everything. Karen would never forgive him – now he'd probably lost her forever. How could he have been so stupid? What in God's name was he supposed to do now?

Chapter 13

Karen arrived back at the flat, her entire body shaking with fury. There was no sound from inside, so maybe Jenny wasn't home. Karen half-hoped that she wouldn't be there. She didn't know if she had the strength to tell anyone what had happened. How could she have been so stupid? Here she was, dishing out advice to Jenny about her love life, and accusing Roan of playing around. Little did she know it was her own boyfriend she should have been watching.

She replayed the scene at Shane's flat over and over again in her head, seeing clearly that stupid bitch Lydia gloating over her. God, the cow must have thought all her birthdays had come at once, when she saw Karen standing at the door.

How Karen didn't catch her and choke her there and then, she'd never know.

And as for Shane, that was a different story. Karen didn't realise that she could feel such anger and resentment towards someone, while feeling so hurt and betrayed by them at the same time. If she was being perfectly honest with herself, she hadn't realised her feelings for Shane had been so strong until now. She felt as though her heart had fallen into the pit of her stomach when she saw the two of them together. Karen shook her head as she felt tears form in her eyes again. She wasn't going to cry this time, not again.

The door finally opened, and Karen walked in to see Jenny and Roan sitting in silence at opposite ends of the room. Neither of them looked at her as she entered. Karen, head bent, said a quiet hello, and went quickly to her bedroom.

She lay on the bed for a little while, and then, after a few minutes, sat up and wiped her eyes on the edge of the duvet. She thought for a minute, before getting up and examining her reflection in the mirror. She wiped her face, and put on some make-up to try and conceal her blotchy cheeks, and red-rimmed eyes. It was a difficult job, but she managed to look some way normal when she re-entered the living-room, a few minutes later.

"Jenny, I'm going out again for a little while – I'll see you later."

Jenny nodded, distractedly.

"Bye, Roan." Karen was sorry she'd said anything, when she barely got a grunt in reply.

Karen strode down the Rathmines Road, feeling a lot better now that she knew what she was going to do. Some of the girls from the office usually met up for drinks in the Turk's Head on a Saturday night. Tonight, Karen was going to join them, and she was going to get well and truly smashed!

* * *

"Roan, this is stupid. I don't know why you're getting so upset about it." Jenny moved over to sit beside him on the couch. "I wasn't implying anything. I was only asking."

"You were implying that I don't pay my way, Jenny," Roan said huffily, his arms folded across his chest, refusing to look at her.

"That's not at all what I was saying. It's just that I'm a bit short this month, and I wondered if you could pay back some of the money I lent you before, that's all," she said nervously. He was upset now – she shouldn't have said anything. She didn't like it when he sulked like this. He had already been sitting there for nearly an hour, without saying a single word to her.

"Come on, Roan. Just forget I mentioned it, OK? It doesn't matter. I'll sort something out with Karen for the rent."

Silence.

"OK, OK I'm sorry! I don't know what else you want me to say!" She moved away from him again. He was being really childish behaving like this!

"Well, it's nice to know that you appreciate my bringing you off on holiday for a week," Roan said sulkily.

Jenny's heart dropped to her stomach. That was a bit low.

Roan had announced only a few days earlier that he was taking her on holiday to Venice, for a week in early June. While she had been thrilled at the prospect of going away somewhere romantic with him, and equally delighted that their relationship hadn't been affected by her 'accusations', Jenny knew that if she had to be perfectly honest, she would have preferred that he paid back the money he owed her.

"Fine!" she said shortly and, to her surprise, Jenny felt herself getting annoyed at him. "Thank you so much Roan for booking this holiday for me. The thing is," she continued, "I didn't expect that you'd pay me back like this, and I myself owe Karen for covering my rent for the last three weeks."

Roan looked at her, incredulously. "Come on, Jenny – you're the one with the big job in the Bank, of all places! Surely you'd be the last one stuck for a few bob!"

"Well, you obviously haven't seen my wages slip, Roan. Otherwise you'd know that my wages are nothing to shout about."

"Fine!" he shot back. "I'll get you your bloody money. But I'm surprised at you, Jenny," he said, his voice lowering, "I didn't think you were that kind of person."

"What kind of person? What are you talking about, Roan? I've lent you over five hundred euro in the last few months, and I haven't seen a penny of it! I'm not made of money, you know."

Bzz! Bzz! Buzzzzzzzzzzzz! The intercom buzzer startled them both. Jenny jumped up quickly to answer it.

"Jenny, is she all right? Buzz me in – I need to talk to her!"

"Tessa? Is who all right? What are you talking about?"

"Look, just let me in, will you?"

"OK, OK!" Jenny pushed the door release and replaced the handset. Everyone seemed narky today! Karen had come in earlier with a face on her that would stop Big Ben! What was Tessa's problem?

Tessa appeared in the living-room, breathless after racing upstairs.

"Is she all right, Jenny? Gerry just told me . . . oh, the stupid gobshite! I'll kill him! Is she all right?"

"Tessa, look, will you calm down for a minute – what's going on?"

Tessa paused as she caught her breath. "It's Shane. Karen called up to his flat earlier to make up with him, and she caught him with Lydia. Hasn't she come home yet? I wonder where she is? God – I hope she's OK."

Jenny looked at her, wordlessly. Why hadn't Karen said anything?

"She's gone out, Tessa," she managed to say. "She left about fifteen minutes ago."

"What? You let her go off on her own, in that state?"

Jenny looked at Roan. "I didn't know – she never said a word. She seemed upset about something, but we were in the middle of a discussion, and I didn't get a chance to talk – "

Tessa rolled her eyes to heaven. "Jenny, get a grip! Karen is your best friend, and you're too wrapped up in lover-boy here to even notice she's upset!" She gave Roan a contemptuous look. "Get up off your lazy backside, and give me a hand to look for her, will you?"

Roan said nothing, stood up, picked up his jacket and walked towards the door. "Look, I'm outta here. I've put up with enough crap today already. See you later."

Jenny watched open-mouthed as he disappeared down the stairs, then she turned back to Tessa, who was glaring furiously at her.

"Well? Where did she say she was going?" Tessa spat. "Will she be gone for long?"

"Look, I knew nothing about this, Tessa! Karen said

nothing to me. She just walked in here, stayed a while in her room, and then told me she was going out again. How was I supposed to know what had happened? I'm not a mindreader, you know."

"You're right. You're right. I'm sorry, Jen. It's not your fault." Tessa began to pace the room. "It's just – she must have got such a shock. And Shane is in an awful state . . . he tried to go after her, but she blanked him and . . . "

Jenny tried to take it all in. Apparently Karen had caught Shane with Aidan's dreadful sister! *What* was he doing with her? She knew that he and Karen were on frosty terms but this was awful!

"Tessa," she began, "it might be the best thing for Karen to get away from here for a while. It'll give her a chance to calm down a bit, and maybe see things more clearly. There's no point in us running around trying to bring her back. She's better off."

"Are you sure? What if she does something stupid?" Tessa wasn't totally convinced.

"Look, Tessa, I *know* Karen. This is her way of coping. She's never been the type to sit around, thrashing things out with everyone else. She'll deal with it when she's good and ready."

Tessa nodded, contrite. "I suppose you're right, and at least you know what you're talking about. I'm sorry I snapped at you and Roan earlier – I was acting like a right old wagon."

"I know you're just worried about Karen, but she'll talk when she's ready to talk – we'll just have to wait until then." Jenny filled the kettle. "Now, will you sit down and take your coat off?" she urged. "I'll make us a cuppa, and you can tell me exactly what happened. You say you've spoken to Shane?"

Tessa sat on one of the high stools, and propped her head up on the counter with her elbows. "Yes, he arrived at our place in an awful state looking for Gerry. Luckily Aidan wasn't around – he normally has dinner with us on a Saturday after he and Gerry finish football training, and I don't know who he'd murder first, Shane or Lydia. Aidan is very protective of Lydia, God knows why, because I think it's everyone else that needs protecting from her!" She searched in her handbag for her cigarettes. "Do you mind?" she asked as she lit up a Marlboro Light.

Jenny shook her head. "But why was Shane so upset? I mean, obviously he knew what he was doing – was it just because he got caught?"

Tessa exhaled a cloud of smoke. "Well, ever since he and Karen had that first argument, Shane has been hitting the bottle big-time." She took another long drag from her cigarette. "He didn't expect Karen to finish with him just like that, and he took it very badly when she refused to talk to him afterwards."

"That's just Karen, though. She can be very stubborn."

"I know," Tessa agreed, "and we tried to tell Shane that, but he wouldn't have any of it. I've never seen him in such bad shape – he's been out on the beer nearly every night since."

"I didn't realise," Jenny said. "I don't think Karen did either. Why didn't he let her know he was upset?"

Tessa shrugged. "Search me – maybe he didn't think there was any point. You know what Karen is like – once she makes her mind up, even the likes of Uri Geller couldn't change it. Maybe he hoped that she'd come to her senses before he left – and unfortunately she did."

"But where does Lydia come into it?"

Tessa's eyes narrowed at the mention of the other girl. "You know what that one is like. She was probably hanging around like a bad smell. When she saw that Shane was suitably pissed, she more than likely leapt on him."

"Well, it takes two to tango, as they say. Shane couldn't have been that innocent either."

"Yeah, but as far as he was concerned, he and Karen were finished. He needed a little comforting, and sure enough, Lydia was only too happy to oblige. The problem is that I convinced Karen, only this morning, to make up with him. She just happened to call at the wrong time – thanks." She took one of the biscuits Jenny had laid out for them and bit into it. "I feel like it's all my fault now. I should never have convinced Karen to call up to him unannounced. But, I didn't think Shane would be drinking at that hour of the day, and I *certainly* didn't think he'd be with that tramp." She shook her head and looked forlornly around the room.

"Don't blame yourself. It was just a pity that the two of them couldn't have sorted things out sooner."

"Amen to that. And seeing that Karen is gone AWOL, and Shane is leaving soon, it seems unlikely they'll sort out anything at all at this stage."

"It's such a pity," Jenny said. "I know that she always pretended she wasn't that serious about him, but they were getting on so well. I thought they were a great match."

"Don't I know? But Shane's messed up big-time now."
Jenny thought for a second.

"I'm not saying for one minute that I agree with what
he did but, to be honest, Tessa, I feel a little bit sorry for
Shane. I mean, Karen finished with *him*. It was just an
awful pity that, when she changed her mind, it was too
late."

"I know what you mean," said Tessa nodding. "That
won't mean much to Karen though."

"It's a bit of mess all the same though, isn't it?" Jenny
said, her face clouded in anger. "I bet Lydia is thrilled to
be stuck in the middle of it all."

"I'm sure she was bloody delighted when the two of
them got caught like that. God, I'd like to slap her hard!"
Tessa said, vehemently slamming her fist on the counter
top.

"You and me both," Jenny said quietly. "You and me
both."

* * *

Roan furiously kicked a Coke can out of his path as he
marched down the road. Women! Why did they always
have to be so difficult?

Of course he'd pay Jenny back her money – he wasn't
some kind of leech. He'd only asked her in the first place
because he was a little bit behind on his rent, and there
wasn't much overtime going at work these days. But he
would never have asked her for a few bob if he thought
he'd get this much grief over it.

Talk about ingratitude! Here Jenny was, mouthing off
about money, and he was taking her off to Venice on the

romantic trip of a lifetime! Any girl would kill for a chance like that.

Then again, he hadn't actually *paid* for the trip, but Jenny didn't have to know that.

His winning that competition on Today FM that time had been a blessing in disguise, even though he entered the bloody competition on the wrong week, and thought he was competing for a trip to Barcelona, which had been won the week before. Roan would have loved to have gone there, and maybe he and Jenny could've caught a football game at the Nou Camp Stadium.

Anyway, maybe it wasn't such a bad thing that he had ending up winning a romantic trip to Venice instead. Jenny had been delighted, and it seemed that she had always wanted to visit Italy.

He was pleased for her, really. She deserved a bit of a treat, after what she had been through recently. That thing with the STI had rattled him a bit, and it wasn't fair on poor old Jenny to end up getting something like that.

When he found out, Roan knew there-and-then that he'd have to cop on to himself. If he was tempted to do the dirt again (although he was sure he wouldn't) he would have to start making sure that he always wore a condom.

He had been lucky to get away with it, though. Luckily, Jenny believed that she might have picked it up from someone else. Anyway, your man in Australia wouldn't know the difference. Naturally, he had felt bad lying to Jenny, but he didn't want to lose her, and he had come very close. She had been so upset about it all that it had nearly broken his heart.

Luckily, she had also believed him about Siobhan. He nearly had a heart attack when that Lydia one started going on about it that time. Needless to say, he couldn't tell Jenny that Siobhan had been the one to end their engagement because she had copped on to his roving eye. Now, he and Siobhan hadn't *actually* broken up – they still saw one other now and again when they were both at home, but it was more out of habit than anything else. Anyway, Siobhan had turned into a bit of moan lately.

Roan wished that he had more willpower when it came to the women. But there were so many babes out there – it was impossible to stay with just one!

This time though, he was determined to try. Jenny was a great girl, they had a laugh together, and she was a right goer in the sack. And she really seemed to care about him. Better still, she didn't nag him to death over this, that and the other, like Siobhan did.

Yes, he was definitely going to change his ways. No more messing around behind Jenny's back, or flirting with the girls at work.

In the meantime, he'd better give the boys a few bob before they kicked him out of the flat altogether. Even Kevin, his so-called mate, had been very short with him these last few weeks, suggesting that he might be able to pay the rent if he cut down on the drinking! The cheek of him! Just because Kevin's ma and da were loaded – with their horses, and their fancy pad up in Monaghan. *He'd* never have to worry about money, that was for sure. Anyway, he'd pay Jenny back, catch up on his rent and then things would be grand again.

In the meantime, he might go for a quick pint while he

had nothing else to do. He might call up to Quinn and see if he wanted to come out for one, seeing as he was in the doghouse too. Your one Karen would be a lot harder to get around though. She was such a narky oul bitch. Pity, 'cos she had a fine body on her.

Roan scowled. He hated fighting with Jenny, but hopefully she would calm down soon enough. He might even take her out for a meal to try and make it up to her. Jenny was normally such a happy-go-lucky kind of girl and he hated it when she got moody. A good night out would cheer her up, and they'd be back to normal in no time.

His mind at ease, Roan began to whistle happily to himself as he continued on his way.

Chapter 14

"Mmm, this is out of this world!" Tessa declared, eating a forkful of banoffee pie. "This dinner was a brainwave. I can't remember the last time I was on a night out without Gerry."

It was a Saturday night, and Jenny had booked a table at Luigi Malone's, one of Temple Bar's most popular eateries. The three girls had just opened a third bottle of Chianti and were thoroughly enjoying themselves.

Karen smiled. "Yeah, thanks, Jen. I know you're trying to cheer me up and, believe me,"' she said, clinking wine-glasses with her, "it's working beautifully."

"It's a pity that we couldn't get tickets for that show though, Jenny," Tessa said, biting her lip.

Karen tried to hide a grin. She knew that when Jenny had spoken about a girls' night out to Tessa, the other girl had eagerly suggested that they go see her idol, Joe Dolan and his band, who just happened to be playing at a venue in town. Jenny had immediately headed her off at the pass, proclaiming vehemently that she had heard over the radio that it had been an instant sell-out. She had heard no such thing, but was loath to subject either herself, or Karen, to the show. Poor Tessa had been terribly disappointed. Karen and Jenny had been terribly relieved.

"It's such a shame that it was all sold out." Tessa looked mournfully at her plate.

Thank God, Karen mouthed to Jenny, who was trying her very best to smother a giggle. She was really enjoying herself tonight. Going out with Tessa and Jenny had really cheered her up, and after everything that had happened recently, she needed cheering up. She had drunk herself silly that night in town with the girls from work. She still felt embarrassed every time she thought about it. She didn't tell them about what had happened with Shane – she didn't want anyone to know how much the bastard had hurt her. He was leaving next week but so what? She had had enough of Shane Quinn. He and Lydia were welcome to one another, and now there was nothing to stop her having some fun of her own.

"Will we go for a drink somewhere else afterwards?" she said to Jenny, who was already well on the way to total drunkenness.

"Of course," Jenny said, signalling for the bill. "The pubs won't know what's hit them once we're finished here. Right, Tessa?"

Tessa shook her head eagerly and a short time later the three girls moved on to a trendy disco bar nearby. Karen watched Jenny flirt unashamedly with the barman as she ordered another round of drinks. She also seemed to be enjoying the night, and it was a nice change to see her out without Roan for once.

Although lately, Karen thought, he had been behaving like the perfect gentleman and the two of them had actually held what amounted to a decent conversation the other day. While waiting for Jenny to get ready for a night out, Roan had sat down and chatted away to Karen about the film she was watching. She would never have pegged Roan as the romantic type, and she had nearly fallen off the sofa when he told her that *Pretty Woman* was one of his favourite movies of all time. She wondered if maybe he fancied himself as a bit of a Richard Gere, although it was a lot more likely that he just fancied Julia Roberts. Since discovering that her own relationship may have been one giant fiasco, Karen was willing to forget about her earlier distrust of Roan, and decided to try to be a bit nicer towards him.

Speaking of nice, you ain't half bad, mister, she said to herself, spying a tall fair-haired guy smiling at her from across the room. She smiled back at him, and within seconds he had made his way through the crowds and over to them.

"Hi," he said, eyeing Karen appreciatively.

"Hi, yourself!" Karen smiled back, and Jenny and Tessa looked on with interest.

"I was going to say something about fathers, and thieves, and stars," he said, "but something tells me that you're not the kind of girl that falls for corny chat-up lines."

"You'd be right. But isn't *that* a roundabout kind of line, all the same?"

He held his hands up. "OK, you've got me there. Should I quit while I'm ahead . . . ?"

He smiled lazily, and Karen noted that he had the unusual combination of brown eyes and fair hair. His colouring was so dark it made him looked foreign – maybe Danish, or Swiss. No, she didn't want this guy to back off, not at all.

"So, are you here with some friends?" she asked, eyeing him flirtatiously through her dark eyelashes.

"Yeah, we're got seats over there – would you girls like to join us?" He indicated a small group behind him who had somehow managed to secure a precious table.

She looked at Tessa and Jenny, and they both shrugged.

"Lead the way!" Karen enthused, winking at Jenny, as she followed him across the room. They were introduced to the others, and Karen soon discovered that her 'friend' was called Charlie, and was neither Danish nor Swiss. He was from Wicklow and he and his friends had come to Dublin for a birthday night out, and were staying in the Conrad Hotel for the night.

"Mmm, the Conrad, very swanky," Karen said, before downing her bottle of Budweiser in one.

"We could go back to the residents' bar for a drink if you like," Charlie suggested, unable to take his eyes off Karen. "It's nearly closing time here, and we should get a few late ones there."

"Lead the way then!" Tessa said, nicely drunk, and anxious for a few more drinks to keep her going.

After waiting forty minutes at a taxi rank on Dame St, the little group eventually decided to walk to the hotel. Jenny tottered along drunkenly on her high heels, holding on to an equally wobbly Tessa for support. "I'll never be able to make it in these shoes!" she moaned.

One of Charlie's mates, Brian, knelt down in front of her. "Here, I'll give you a piggy back," he said.

"Are you sure you can handle it? I'm no Kate Moss, you know," Jenny laughed, wrapping her arms around his neck.

"I'm a big strong Wicklow farmer – the likes of me could carry twenty Kate Mosses," he said, feigning a thick country accent, as he lifted Jenny off the ground.

"Well, good, because you might have to," she giggled, as Brian began to carry her up Grafton St. He kept going until they reached St Stephen's Green, and then he had to let her go.

"Your mate's a good sport, isn't she?" Charlie said. "Girls her size are usually very self-conscious about their weight."

"I know," Karen said fondly. "She could teach us all a thing or two. I think that *I'm* more self-conscious about my weight than Jenny is."

"You shouldn't be – you look fantastic." With this, Charlie leaned forward and kissed her firmly on the lips.

Karen instantly pulled away.

"I'm sorry," he said, genuinely. "I'm sorry if I was a bit forward. But I thought that you. . . "

Karen exhaled loudly. He was nice, he was gorgeous and he was funny. But he wasn't Shane.

"*I'm* sorry, Charlie. I thought I did too. But I've just come out of a relationship and . . ." she shrugged.

Charlie smiled. "It doesn't matter. I knew it was too good to be true that a fine thing like yourself would be interested in someone like me. Never mind," he said, catching her hand, and quickening his step to catch up

151

with the others. "Let's go and have a drink and a bit of a laugh anyway – no funny business, OK?"

"OK," Karen said, letting Charlie pull her along beside him, relieved that he hadn't made a big deal out of it.

She must be crazy. Any girl would be crazy to knock back someone like him. But it was too soon. No matter what he had done, and no matter how much he had hurt her, Karen was realistic enough to know that it would a very long time before she got over Shane Quinn.

But in the meantime, and to help her along the way, a bit of a laugh would be the next best thing.

* * *

"What's this?" said Karen to Jenny in surprise, a few days later.

"I'm not sure. It was on the floor when I got back from work earlier. Someone must have put it under the door."

Jenny didn't like lying to her friend, but she couldn't tell Karen that Shane had dropped in the note on his way to the airport. Karen would go ballistic. She was still raging with him and had insisted that she never wanted to see him again. She had so far refused to take any of his phone calls, and wouldn't talk about him under any circumstances. Jenny knew better than to risk Karen's wrath by telling her that she had spoken to Shane the day before, when Karen had been at Tessa's. He was flying out to Germany that very morning.

"If I could just tell her that nothing happened, Jen," he had said, still clearly upset, "but she won't listen to me. She won't let me explain –"

"Shane, she's still hurting very badly. It was a terrible thing for her to find you two together. Maybe nothing had happened, but still –"

"I know, I know . . . I've been such a fool. I just wish she'd talk to me! Will I take a chance and call down to Tessa's before I go, do you think?"

"It wouldn't be a good idea, Shane," Jenny said softly. That was putting it mildly. Jenny couldn't be sure what Karen might do or say, if he went near her.

"Well then . . . " He stood up and took something out of his back pocket. "I suppose I have no choice but to leave this here." He handed Jenny a small white envelope addressed to Karen. "Maybe if she won't listen to me, I can explain things another way."

Jenny took the envelope from him, and promised to pass it on to Karen.

Karen held the envelope in her hand for a few seconds before opening it. "I hope it's not from that lying bastard," she said vehemently, although Jenny saw that it had piqued her interest.

"Why don't you go into the bedroom and read it in private?" she suggested, busying herself with the washing-up.

Karen sat on her bed and carefully tore open the envelope. Her heart was pounding as she did so. Was it from Shane? If so, what could she expect from this? Would it be good or bad? Karen didn't know. She had spent night after night, lying awake, tossing and turning, trying to get the image of Lydia and Shane out of her head. She had thought about nothing else over the following days. She couldn't face talking about it with anyone, not wanting to let anyone know how much the bastard had hurt her. She opened the note and began to read.

Karen read, and reread the note a few times, before going back out to the living-room.

Jenny looked at her curiously. "Well?"

Karen rolled her eyes. "He's just feeling sorry for himself," she said airily, but her eyes were bright.

Jenny read the note and her eyes were glistening when she looked up. "Oh, Karen, he's really suffering over this. You have to try and contact him."

"Just because he comes up with this soppy rubbish doesn't mean that I'm going to run back into his arms," Karen said vehemently. "That's it, as far as I'm concerned. He said in the letter that I deserve better, and he's right. I *do* deserve better."

Jenny shook her head as she handed the letter back. "Sometimes, I just don't understand you at all. I mean, the guy has told you everything any girl would want to hear and, after all," she said, her voice lowering, "you dumped him before he went near Lydia."

Karen sank down on the sofa, and folded her arms defiantly. "That's not the point, Jen, and you know it! How you would you feel if Roan went off and shagged someone else and you caught the two of them at it? It's no fun, I can tell you!"

"They didn't actually sleep together though, did they?" Jenny retorted, unable to understand her attitude. She knew how hard it had been for Shane to write that letter. Her friend really was too stubborn for her own good. The poor guy had explained himself, and it still wasn't enough for Karen. In fact, Jenny thought, Karen was partly to blame.

They had both made mistakes but obviously still had feelings for one another, so what else mattered?

Both girls were silent for a while, before Karen stood up and stretched her arms out above her head. "Ah forget it!" she said, "I don't want to talk about it any more. He's leaving anyway, so that's the end of it. What's the story with you and Roan anyway?" She deftly changed the subject. "Are you two OK after that argument about the money?"

Jenny smiled. "We're fine. I haven't seen much of him lately though – he took on a lot of extra hours at work so he could pay for this trip. Of course, I'll have him to myself for a whole week then!"

Karen grinned at her, feeling more gracious about Roan these days, particularly since she had found out about Shane. "Yeah, Venice is coming soon, isn't it? The break will do you good – you must be really looking forward to it"

Jenny was. Only last weekend, Roan had been talking nineteen to the dozen about the trip, and making plans as to where they should go, and what they should do when they got there. He had taken her out to dinner, and had promised to pay back the money he owed once he got paid at the end of the month, which Jenny reasoned should have been the previous weekend. But of course, she hadn't seen him then, what with her being out with the girls on the Friday night, and he out with Kevin on the Saturday night. She was looking forward to spending time with him on the trip, and knew that Roan too would need the break, what with all the overtime he was doing.

"I am looking forward to it," she answered Karen.

"It'll be nice to be able to spend a bit of time together on our own. Anyway," she said, winking at her, "this manless spell you and I are having at the moment could well work to our advantage. We should give Tessa a ring and arrange another night out in town, just the three of us.

"No men involved? Suits me down the ground," Karen said, rubbing her hands together with glee. "I've had enough hassle with the opposite sex lately to put me off them altogether!"

With this, she tore up Shane's note, and cheerfully tossed it into the dustbin.

Chapter 15

Jenny examined the contents of her wardrobe, and wondered what she should pack in her suitcase. She wasn't sure what kind of weather to expect in Venice at this time of the year. It was bound to be warm though – Italy was a warm country, wasn't it?

She and Roan were due to fly out tomorrow morning.

This holiday would be a celebration for Roan, because the company he worked for had this week been taken over by an American firm. It seemed that not only would Roan be earning more money, but he would be moving to another department, where he would get a chance to work on, what he called, 'some serious stuff'.

Maybe she should pop down to the Swan Centre and pick out a few new bits and pieces to take on holiday with her, she thought. Still, money was tight and she'd need some spending money during the trip too. She certainly couldn't expect Roan to pay for everything! She might leave the clothes shopping for the time being, and make do with what she had. Luckily she remembered to bring a lot of her summer clothes back with her, the last time she had been home.

But she still wasn't sure what she should bring. This capsule wardrobe that they were always going on about in the magazines looked easy, but just didn't seem practical. For one thing, she wasn't sure whether or not they would be going out to formal restaurants, or casual pizzeria-type places for dinner, and what if they went sightseeing? She would need to bring comfortable clothes for that, and dressy clothes for going out in the evening.

Maybe the likes of Tessa, who was so tiny that she could fit most of her clothes in her back pocket, could get away with a capsule wardrobe, but for Jenny, putting the whole lot on a freight container would be more like it.

She should give Roan a ring and ask him about it. Then she could decide once and for all. She went downstairs to the public phone and dialled the number of Roan's flat expectantly. Kevin answered on the first ring.

"Hi, Kevin, it's Jenny. Is Roan there?"

"Jenny, how's it going? No, he's not here – he went home to Kildare for a few days to . . . um, get some stuff. How are you?"

"I'm fine, Kev – I'm really looking forward to this trip. I'm getting the suitcase organised as we speak."

"Uh – right, right," Kevin sounded uncomfortable. "Do you want his home number, Jenny? You'd probably get him there now."

"That would be brilliant, thanks."

"Right – hold on."

Jenny heard shuffling as Kevin searched for the

number. A few seconds later, he came back to the phone and read it out to her. Jenny scribbled the number on the front of her hand.

"OK, thanks again. See you soon. Byee!" she said gleefully.

Of course! Roan had probably booked the trip while he was at home in Kildare, and needed to collect the tickets from the travel agents down there. Jenny decided that she'd better ring the house and find out when he would be back – or to make it handy, she could just meet him at the airport. She dialled the number that Kevin had given her, and waited as it rang a few times. Then she heard a friendly female voice answer.

"Hello, Joan Williams speaking."

"Hello, Mrs Williams. I wonder if I could speak to Roan please?" Jenny said pleasantly.

"Roan? Oh, he's not here, I'm afraid. He left not long ago. Would you like to leave a message?"

Pity, Jenny thought. She'd missed him again. "Yes, if you wouldn't mind. Could you tell him that Jenny called, please?" She waited for any sign of recognition at the mention of her name. "Jenny Hamilton? I'm calling from Dublin."

"Jenny? Yes, I'll tell him that. You must be a friend from work. Is that right?"

Jenny's heart sank. Mrs Williams didn't know who she was. The name Jenny didn't seem to mean anything to her. Maybe Roan hadn't told his mother that he had a girlfriend in Dublin. But, surely he must have told her about the holiday? She was starting to say something when Mrs Williams continued.

"He's in great form altogether these days," she said,

not noticing Jenny's silence. "I suppose he's delighted with the takeover. Same as yourself, I'd imagine."

"Well, I don't work with him, actually. I –"

"Oh, sorry love," she laughed pleasantly, "I can't keep up with all his friends these days. Between the ones here, and the ones in Dublin, you couldn't keep track of him. Anyway," she continued, "they left for Dublin not long ago. They're staying in some hotel near the airport tonight, because of the early flight tomorrow morning. Venice, imagine? I don't know where Roan gets it. His father hasn't a romantic bone in his body."

Jenny's heart lifted. Roan was on his way back to Dublin and he had arranged for them to stay in a hotel tonight. What a lovely surprise!

"Well, that's why I'm ringing actually," Jenny said. "I was wondering about the time of the flight."

"Oh, are you collecting them from the airport when they come back, love? I wondered about that, because Siobhan's car is in the garage."

Siobhan? Roan hadn't mentioned that they were still on speaking terms. But then again, they were bound to be still friendly, thought Jenny. Hadn't they grown up together in the same town, and known each other for years? It was only natural that Roan might expect Siobhan to drop him back to Dublin, if it was on her way. Pity her car was out of action though, Jenny thought. She wouldn't have minded a look at the other girl to see what her predecessor had been like.

Mrs Williams' voice interrupted her thoughts. "You should have seen Siobhan last night – she's a gas woman altogether. I don't think I've ever seen her so excited. And the same one flies here, there, and everywhere, all the time! Still, I suppose it's different when you're working. Anyway they deserve this trip, the two of them. She works away so much they hardly see one other, and then what with Roan working so hard all the time . . ."

The two of them? Jenny felt her knees weaken, and her heart quickened in panic. For a split second, she wondered if maybe she had rung the wrong number.

Roan was taking Siobhan to Venice with him?

She thought she heard Mrs Williams' voice but she hadn't a clue what the woman was saying. Maybe she had taken it up all wrong. Or, maybe *Mrs Williams* had taken it up wrong. That was it, Jenny thought quickly. Maybe Roan hadn't said anything to his mother about the break-up with Siobhan. The woman sounded as though she was quite fond of the other girl. Maybe Roan thought she would take it badly.

"Hello? Are you still there, love?"

Jenny clasped the receiver tightly. "Mrs Williams – hi, I'm here. I'm sorry – someone just interrupted me there. You were saying? About the holiday?"

"Oh, I was just saying that with the amount the two of them were packing here last night, I doubt that they'll fit their suitcases on the plane, let alone in your car!" She laughed loudly. "Roan was nagging Siobhan like there was no tomorrow about all the clothes she was bringing. You'd swear they were already married, with the way they were carrying on."

Jenny felt as though she had been hit with a sledgehammer as Mrs Williams continued.

"It's very funny altogether! They've been together so long now, that the two of them are just like an old married couple!"

Chapter 16

"What the hell?" Karen looked in disbelief at the person standing before her in the doorway. "What are *you* doing here?"

"Can I come in for a few minutes, Karen?" Shane asked, nervously twisting a piece of tissue paper in one hand.

"I'm not sure . . . "

"Please, I really need to talk to you." He looked up at her with such a mournful expression that Karen faltered. She stood back and waved him in and as he passed her she caught the familiar scent of his *Obsession* aftershave – her favourite.

She tried to collect herself as she walked upstairs behind him. Her heart was pounding so much, she could hardly breathe.

She was alone in the flat, poor Jenny having gone home for a few days, upon discovering that Roan had upped and off to Venice with his supposed ex-fiancée.

"What do you want, Shane?" Karen asked, when they were both inside the flat. "Why aren't you in Germany?"

She made no motion for him to sit down, so he didn't dare.

"Did Jenny give you my note?" he asked hesitantly.

Karen shrugged her shoulders, her expression defiant. "I don't know what you expected, Shane. I haven't changed my mind about anything, if that's what you want to know."

"But you believe what I told you – about Lydia that day?"

"I'll never know one way or the other, will I? But, I hope you haven't come here expecting forgiveness and happy ever after, because you won't get it. You made an absolute show of me that day, Shane. Lydia must have been thrilled –"

"Lydia wasn't thrilled," Shane interjected flatly. "She didn't set the whole thing up just for you to find us, you know."

Karen sniffed. "I wouldn't be surprised if she had."

"Believe what you like. But did you ever consider the possibility that Lydia might be hurt by all of this too?"

That was enough for Karen. How dare he come in here and start defending *her*?

"And do you think I care?" she said, rounding on him. "Do you think I give a shit about your little girlfriend's feelings in any of this?"

"I know you don't care. But *I* do. Lydia's all right, and it wasn't fair of me to do what I did to her. She has a bit of a thing for me, and I took advantage of that."

"Spare me the details, Shane. I have no interest in 'what you did to her' that day."

163

Shane shook his head from side to side.

"Oh, you know damn well that nothing happened between us – you're just too stubborn to admit it. You won't give an inch, will you, Karen?"

Karen put her hands on her hips. "Tell me, why the hell should I? Did you call in here expecting me to run to you with open arms? If you thought that, then you can think again. It's just not that simple." Karen felt her hands shake as she spoke. It was so difficult having Shane so near to her, and yet she couldn't bring herself to forgive him. It was too hard. Although she knew from his face that he was telling the truth. She also knew that if he *had* slept with Lydia that day, he would have admitted it. It wasn't in him to lie.

But what should she do now? She wasn't going to run back to him just like that. And what about Germany – why wasn't he . . . ?

"Will you marry me, Karen?" Shane asked suddenly.

She looked at him, stunned. "What did you say?"

He moved closer and, taking both of her hands in his, he looked deep into her eyes "You heard me, and I mean it. I love you, and I want to marry you. You're the most important person in the world to me, and I realised just how important you were when I lost you." When she said nothing, Shane continued, "I went to Germany and started the new job, got a new place to live, met some new friends, you know – the whole shebang."

Karen smiled despite herself, at the catchphrase.

Buoyed by the softening of her expression, he went on. "Everything was going brilliantly. The job is terrific and the social life is just like being here at home, there are so many other Irish lads over there. I had no problems fitting in but –"

"But what?" Karen interrupted, dropping her hands, and placing them on her hips. "Let me guess," she said nastily, before she could stop herself. "You missed Lydia so much you had to come back here, is that it?"

She saw something in his eyes then, and instantly regretted her outburst. Shane looked at her as though she had just slapped him across the face. He stood back.

"What's the real problem here, Karen?" he said, and she heard his voice begin to rise as something snapped within him. "Why are you acting like this? I've been nothing but honest with you about everything from the very beginning. OK, we've had our ups and downs. . . no," he shook his head, wagging a finger at her angrily, "I take that back – we've had *one* down, and *plenty* of ups throughout this relationship and you're carrying on as though I'm some kind of bastard! I've told you time and time again that nothing happened between Lydia and me. I've *never* been unfaithful to you. I made one stupid mistake in not discussing my plans for Germany, and now I'm back. I've even given up the stupid job for you! And it's *still* not enough! What more do you want from me – Jesus!" Shane walked back and forth, running his hands through his hair. "I just can't win here, can I? No matter what I say or do, I just can't win."

Karen wasn't sure what to think. She'd never seen Shane so angry. *She* was usually the one that needed calming down in any arguments they had – it had always been Shane doing the calming. It wasn't a pleasant experience. His face was bright red and his fists so clenched she was afraid he might try to put one through the wall.

"Look, I'm sorry," she conceded. "It's just a shock, seeing you here – I suppose it's just my way of hitting back at you." She shrugged her shoulders again. "Please, go on with what you were saying . . . about Germany, and everything."

But Shane seemed to have lost all patience with her. "It doesn't matter," he said, waving her away, as he stomped towards the door. "Forget I said anything. Forget about the whole bloody lot of it." He opened the door, went to walk through it, then paused and looked back at Karen, his eyes tired and sad. "I think I have your answer now anyway."

He walked out the door and began descending the stairs.

Karen stood alone in the flat, her mind racing, as she tried to get to grips with her feelings. Shane had just proposed to her! And all she could do was stand there and insult him! She ran out the door and caught up with him on the second floor landing. "Shane, wait!"

He stopped and looked up at her from the steps below, the expression on his face unreadable. "Yes, Karen?" he sighed.

"What do you mean? I haven't given you an answer yet," she said indignantly. "You can't propose to someone, and then tell them to forget all about it! You have to wait for an answer at least."

They looked at one other for what seemed like an age. Then, to Karen's surprise, she saw Shane's mouth break into a wide grin. "You're just so bloody stubborn, aren't you?" he said, shaking his head and smiling as he started up the stairs again. "You have to have the last word all the time, whether you're wrong or right."

"I don't always have to have the last word," she said contritely.

"Well, are you going to apologise?"

"For what?"

"For *once*!"

A flicker of a smile crossed Karen's lips, but she didn't apologise.

Shane shook his head and smiled. "I just don't know what to do with you, Karen Cassidy."

"Well, what *are* you going to do with me?" she grinned, as he took her in his arms and kissed her.

"I'll show you."

He scooped her up in his arms, and went back upstairs to her bedroom, kicking a pile of Karen's discarded clothes and shoes out of his path as he went.

Laying her carefully on the bed, he kissed her deeply with a raw, passionate kiss. Then he made love to her with such intensity, that Karen thought it had nearly been worth all the time they had spent apart.

Much later, they lay underneath the covers, bodies entangled.

Shane looked at across at Karen and smiled. Then his eyes lit up, as if remembering something. Suddenly he threw back the covers, and jumped out of the bed and onto his knees. Karen watched him with undisguised amusement, and a little surprise.

Shane grinned, as he took her hand in his. "Karen, for the *second* time, will you marry me?"

Tears of happiness pricked the corners of her eyes.

"Well, what's your answer, Cassidy?" Shane asked impatiently.

This time there was no hesitation in her reply.

"The answer's definitely yes, Shane," she said giggling. "How could I say no to a proposal like that?"

* * *

"Oh – that's fantastic news!" Jenny said, with genuine enthusiasm. An excited Karen had just phoned her. "I can't believe Shane came back from Germany and proposed. How romantic!"

"Well, it wasn't exactly romantic, Jen," Karen said, laughing. "We had a bit of an argument beforehand, and I made it very hard for him before I eventually said yes."

"Typical," Jenny said, with a grin. "You're a hard woman, Karen. Poor old Shane has got his work cut out for him."

"Poor old Shane? You traitor – don't you mean poor old me? Anyway, Jen, I didn't know whether to ring you or not. I know what you're going through now, and I wasn't sure –"

"Karen, are you mad? I'd murder you if you didn't tell me. This is terrific news. It's just what I need, to be honest."

"How are you feeling?"

"A lot better now, I think."

"Good. Well, come back whenever you feel like it. We're going to Shane's house on Saturday, but otherwise I'll be here at the flat. Give me a ring when you're coming back, will you?"

Jenny nodded, forgetting that Karen couldn't see her.

"Thanks for ringing. And tell Shane I said congratulations too. We'll have to organise a big celebration soon."

Jenny tried to sound brighter than she felt. Although she was genuinely delighted for her friend, she couldn't help feeling a tiny bit envious. It was the same old story, really. Her love life was in tatters, while Karen's couldn't be better. Her friend was on top of the world, while Jenny was so low she thought her feet might pop out down in Australia somewhere.

She was so pleased for Karen, though. She had handled the break-up with Shane brilliantly. Having had a quick cry about it, she had taken some time out to be on her own, and then got on with her life. She hadn't collapsed in a heap and wanted to crawl into a hole, shutting herself away from everything.

Not for the first time, Jenny wished she could possess just a tiny piece of her friend's strength. These last few days had been an absolute nightmare, and she hadn't slept more than a few hours all week. Her father had been very curious as to why Jenny wasn't at work, but her mum had been a little more sympathetic because she had known about the trip, and had obviously figured things out for herself.

Jenny had lied when she told Karen she was feeling better. The numbness was there constantly, underlying all the confusion and disappointment she had felt since discovering that Roan had gone to Venice without her.

In fact, Jenny thought, as she hung up the phone, she had hardly stopped crying since that night. As she had nothing else to do but think about the entire situation and feel sorry for herself, it was impossible to stop the tears from flowing. With the amount of water that had fallen from her eyes, Jenny thought, she could do away with at least half of Africa's drought problems.

Wearily, she went upstairs to her bedroom hoping to sleep for maybe an hour or two.

Hours later, she was still lying on the bed – her eyes wide open.

So many thoughts just kept going round and round in her head. Why did she have to mess everything up like that? Roan loved her, didn't he? Despite all the accusations she had made, and despite the fact that he must think she didn't trust him. Why wasn't that enough for her? Jenny wondered. What more did she want?

She thought about Roan and Siobhan together in Venice. Were they in bed together now, at this very moment? Was he making love to Siobhan, like he made love to her so many times before? Was the sex better with Siobhan? Of course it would be better, she thought, the tears smarting at her eyes again. Venice was one of the most romantic places in the world. They were probably at it like rabbits, just like the way she and Roan had been at the beginning, before she had lost the plot and started behaving like some kind of crazed psycho-girlfriend. That time watching *Fatal Attraction* with Karen must have had affected her subconscious – *something* definitely had.

Why had she been so stupid? If she hadn't been so insistent about his paying back the money, and being an ungrateful cow, then she wouldn't be in this situation now.

Naturally, he would bring someone else – someone that would at least appreciate the thought and effort that had gone into it all. She had been so unfair to him all along – firstly accusing him of giving her that STI and then practically throwing the holiday back in his face! Why did she have to be such a fool sometimes?

Jenny turned over onto her stomach to try and get comfortable. She was sick of torturing herself. She so longed for Roan to take her in his arms, and tell her that everything was going to be fine, that it was all a big mistake and Siobhan meant nothing to him.

Jenny shook her head violently from side to side. Why couldn't it all just go away? She was so sick of trying to figure it out, so sick of all the questions. It was her own fault for messing things up, with her accusations and moaning about money.

Jenny sat up and studied her reflection in the mirror for a long, long time. Her hair was stringy and full of split ends, her skin raw and red from crying. She couldn't look any worse if she tried.

Lydia had told her that Siobhan was tall and stunning, with a perfect figure. The girl was a model, for goodness sake – she was probably *better* than perfect! Jenny sighed. Siobhan and Roan must look so right together, the perfect couple.

People on the streets – or, more likely, the canals – were probably stopping the two of them, wondering if they were famous Hollywood stars, or something.

Jenny critically looked at her reflection once more. Why would Roan want an ugly, overweight whinge for a girlfriend, when he could have somebody like Siobhan?

Chapter 17

"Which one do you think I should wear – the cardigan, or the jacket?" Karen asked Jenny. She and Shane were going to Kilrigh for the day to meet Shane's mother, and even though she kept telling Jenny that she wasn't nervous, Karen had to admit to herself that she was.

"The cardigan," Jenny said firmly. "The jacket is too . . . officey, or something?"

"Officey? What kind of a word is that?" Karen asked, whilst studying her reflection. The black fitted cardigan did look better with the dress she was wearing and she knew what Jenny meant. She wanted to look smart, but not too formal. The dress was elegant, but the cardigan made the outfit look casual and easygoing, the image that she wanted to project to Mrs Quinn.

"I don't know what I'm so worried about, anyway," she said, trying to find a stray shoe from the pile at the bottom of her wardrobe. "We're already engaged – it's not as though I have to pass a test." She found the black sling-back she was after, and dusted it off with a tissue.

"It's a test of sorts though, isn't it? She's going to be your mother-in-law, after all," Jenny said seriously, fully aware of Karen's nervousness, and trying her best to stop herself from laughing. "If she doesn't like you, she could make your life hell. You read about these things in the problem pages all the time."

"Well, if she doesn't like me, it's her tough," Karen said airily, studying her make-up closely in the mirror. Was she wearing too much mascara?

Jenny collapsed on the bed laughing. "I'm only joking, you fool! Sure she'll like you, why wouldn't she?"

"Oh, stop trying to make me nervous."

"All right, I'm sorry – I admit it. I *am* trying to make you nervous," Jenny said, lying back on the bed, her hands behind her head. "I'm sure you'll get on fine. Shane is normal enough. I'm sure his mother will be too."

"We'll have to see."

They went back into the sitting-room to wait for Shane.

"What are you going to do this weekend?" asked Karen. "Will you be all right on your own?"

"Yep," Jenny said, brightly. "I'm going to take a leaf out of your book, by not spending another second crying over men. I've got the new Patricia Scanlan novel, and a tub of Ben & Jerry's to keep me going for the night, and then tomorrow I'm meeting Tessa in town for a bit of shopping."

"Good stuff, Jen, that's what I like to hear," Karen said, although secretly she worried about her friend. Jenny had been a little too sprightly since coming back from Kilkenny the day before. Karen knew that Roan should have been back from Venice this morning, but Jenny hadn't mentioned him at all. She suspected that she was just trying to put a brave face on it. She couldn't have put it all out of her head in the space of a few days.

A car horn beeped twice from the street outside.

"Right, that's Shane," Karen said, standing up and looking out the window at the street below; where Shane waited in his newly-bought two-year-old Opel Astra. "I'll see you later, Jen – wish me luck, OK?" She checked her appearance once more in the mirror, before rushing out the door.

"Don't worry. You'll have a great time," Jenny shouted down the stairs after her.

She slumped back down on the couch, and checked her watch. Roan would be here in less than an hour.

* * *

Roan paid for the flowers, and put the change in his pocket. He'd have to think quickly. Jenny would probably give him hell and, in fairness, he wouldn't blame her.

But what could he do? Siobhan had come home early from a cancelled assignment and had phoned him, all excited about the trip. His mother had told Siobhan's mother about his winning the competition and all of a sudden Roan was backed into a corner that he couldn't get out of. He *had* to take Siobhan. It wasn't easy – nor was it bloody cheap, Roan thought grudgingly – getting the airline to change the passenger names at such short notice.

And after all that, now he was sorry that he *hadn't* brought Jenny. She was great fun, and rarely whinged at him like Siobhan did. He frowned. Siobhan had been very difficult company on the holiday. She hadn't appreciated the trip as much as he'd thought she would. In fact, she carried on as though it was her due. OK, they hadn't spent much time together lately, but that was more her fault than his. He couldn't help it if his girlfriend was in such demand that she was never in the country, could he? He was seriously thinking of finishing with Siobhan at this stage. Kevin had given him a right ear-bashing about doing the dirt on Jenny when he came back from Venice. Apparently, Jenny had phoned the flat, and Kevin had stupidly given her his home number.

"I didn't know what to say to the poor girl when she rang, all excited about going away with you," he had said, "and you off gallivanting with no intention whatsoever of letting her know she wasn't going. I've had enough, Roan. I'm not covering your ass any more."

He hadn't wanted to hear Roan's side of the story at all, and had barely spoken to him since. That bird Andrea he was seeing was causing most of the problems between them, he reckoned. She reminded him a lot of your one Karen, with the way she carried on – always so touchy about everything. She had Kev wrapped around her little finger, with all her moods and tantrums.

Kevin had changed all right, he thought, shaking his head. Just because he was settling down with one woman didn't mean that everyone else had to do the same. There'd be plenty of time for that later. *And* he had covered his friend's ass to birds, many times over the years.

Luckily, he had a good story and, if Jenny forgave him as Roan was sure she would, things could get difficult if Kevin refused to cover for him.

He frowned. It might be time to say goodbye to Siobhan – for a while, anyway. He'd get Jenny back on side for now, and afterwards, he could start paying Siobhan a little attention again. As usual, she'd come running back. No problem.

Roan pressed the doorbell outside Jenny's flat. She buzzed him inside without answering the intercom, and when he saw her standing at the top of the stairs with her arms crossed, he knew that this mightn't be as easy as he'd thought. He'd have to play a blinder.

"Hi," he said, handing her the flowers, and giving her a kiss on the cheek.

"What do you mean 'hi'? And if you think that a cheap bunch of supermarket flowers will soften me up, you have another think coming." That was good, she thought, that was exactly like something Karen would say. Act tough, and don't let him away without a proper explanation.

"Did you have a nice time in Venice?" she asked, turning her back to him, her arms folded.

"It was OK," he said. "I missed you though."

Jenny spun around in surprise. "You missed *me*! Where did you get the time to miss me, Roan? I thought you would have had enough on your hands with Siobhan." She felt her hands shake as she spoke. This was no good – she was going to crack soon. She had had great intentions of acting cold and unforgiving towards him, but it was so hard now that he was here.

"Siobhan? What are you talking about?" Roan asked, with what sounded like genuine surprise.

"Siobhan, your supposed ex-girlfriend – the one you brought to Venice instead of me?"

176

"What? I didn't go with Siobhan – who told you that?" Roan said, incredulously. "She gave me a lift to the airport, that's all."

Jenny stopped short. That's exactly what she had thought at the time. Was there a possibility that she might have been right – that Siobhan had just given him a lift, rather than gone on the trip with him? "What? Then, who *did* you go with?"

"I went on my own, obviously. Jenny, you don't seriously believe that I would do something like that, do you?"

"Your mother said . . ."

"Oh, for goodness sake, Jen, my mother doesn't know her arse from her elbow. She gave you her version of events, that's all. I've told her a million and one times that Siobhan and I are finished, but she won't accept it. She and Mrs Hennessey – Siobhan's mother – are always trying to get us back together."

"But why did she say that you were like an old married couple, then?"

"She does that all the time. When you phoned the house, she assumed, correctly, that you were someone I was seeing. She wanted to throw you off, afraid that it might get serious between us. Obviously it worked." He paced angrily up and down the room.

Jenny felt unsure of herself. Now she'd lost her nerve a little. He had behaved as though nothing at all was wrong and sounded thrilled on the phone earlier. Then he turned up here with a bunch of flowers and a big smile. What was going on?

Was it possible that Mrs Williams had lied to her? But

she would have to be an awful cow to do something like that, just to try and get him back with Siobhan. No mother would do that to her son, would she? Yet Roan seemed adamant that he had gone to Venice on his own.

"But why on earth did you go on your own? Wasn't I supposed to be going too?" Jenny said, her thoughts spinning.

Roan slumped down on the sofa. "I was angry with you. When I saw you with that other guy . . ."

"What other guy?" she asked. What was he talking about?

"The guy on Grafton St. I was in town for a few pints with the boys, and we were on our way out of Bruxelles, when we saw you pass by on the street, laughing your head off in the arms of some other guy. I was absolutely mortified, I can tell you."

"What?" For a moment Jenny didn't understand what he was talking about. Then she remembered. The night out with the girls. Charlie's friend Brian giving her a piggy-back up the street. Roan had seen them!

"But that was nothing! We were out that night, just having a laugh. This guy started chatting up Karen and his friend – "

"Started hitting on you?" Roan finished shortly. "I know how it works, Jen, and I know what I saw. You looked as though you were having a great time. Do you have any idea how embarrassed I was? All the guys saw it too, you know."

Jenny tried to gather her thoughts. Her mind was racing a mile a minute.

"So you went off to Venice without me because you

wanted to get back at me? Why the hell didn't you ask me about it, or at least have it out with me?"

He wouldn't look her in the eye. "I was annoyed with you, Jen. I organised this trip for us, and you didn't seem at all pleased – you just kept going on at me to pay back the money I owed you. Which I would have done – actually," Roan stood up and put a hand in his pocket, "here's some of it." He threw a roll of notes on the breakfast bar. "When we had that argument, I felt bad about the money and decided I'd try and make it up to you by bringing you out for a slap-up meal. I told you I'd pay you back at the end of last month, but you didn't seem happy with that. I knew you were annoyed but – "

"So when you saw me that night on Grafton St, it was the last straw . . . " Jenny sat back on a stool, guilt flooding through her. Why had she carried on like that with Charlie's friend? She should have been more careful. Naturally, Roan had got the wrong idea. She wouldn't have too impressed to see *him* crawling all over some strange girl like that, would she?

"Exactly," he answered. "I'll admit I was stupid not to ring you – I have a tendency to sulk a little, and for that, I'm sorry. But the trip was coming up, I had the tickets and I had to use at least one of them. So, I decided to go off on my own, and have a think about things, about us, and what would happen when I got back."

Think about things? Oh no, Jenny thought – now she had really ruined everything. She hadn't meant to go overboard about the money. She was just trying to stand her ground, and look what had happened? When she thought about everything she had accused him of, and everything that had happened, she couldn't blame Roan for being angry with her.

"Look, I'm really sorry about everything," she said to him. "I know I shouldn't have gone on at you like that, and I can understand why you thought I was being ungrateful about the trip. But when I rang your mother, and she told me about Siobhan, well . . . I just didn't know what to think. Put yourself in my position – what would you have thought?"

"*You* put yourself in *mine*, Jenny! What would *you* have thought? One week, you accuse me of sleeping around and giving you some sexually transmitted disease. To try and cheer you up I organise a romantic – not to mention *expensive* – holiday away for the two of us. The next week, you're shouting and roaring about this money that you lent me, and soon after, I see you all over some stranger in the street. I snapped, Jenny! I've done everything I can do to try and make you trust me, but you still don't. And I've done nothing wrong." He sat down and put his head in his hands. "I missed you so much when I was away, and then I come back to this! What do you want from me?"

Jenny sat down beside him and tentatively put her head on his shoulder.

"I'm so sorry, Roan, really I am. I just didn't know what to think or who to believe. I was out of order about the money, and about the trip. I know that now. I do trust you. It's just sometime things happen and – "

He pulled away from her and stood up. "Look, let's just forget it. Let's forget about the whole thing. I've always tried to be as honest with you as I could possibly be, but I'm sick of it now. If you can't trust me, then I'm wasting my time." He walked towards the door, and then turned back to her. "It's a pity, because I really care about you, Jenny." He looked away for a moment, before opening the door. "I'll make sure you have the rest of your money by the end of the week."

"Wait, Roan, please!" Jenny said tearfully. This was awful. What had she done? "I don't want to lose you. Please don't leave . . . "

She ran into his arms and, just before she kissed him, Jenny was sure that she saw a flicker of something in his eyes – relief, maybe? It didn't matter. She and Roan were together again. *That* was all that mattered. There were a few things that they needed to sort out, but those things could wait.

She felt his arms wrap tightly around her as the kiss became hungrier, and more passionate. They walked backwards together towards the bedroom and lay down on the bed. As he kissed her, Jenny felt all the doubts and despair melt away. She was going to make it up to Roan and make sure that this relationship would work. She was lucky that he hadn't dumped her long before now, what with all her accusations and recriminations. Poor Roan, he must have been through hell these last few weeks. Well, no more, Jenny decided. From now on, she would make sure that everything was perfect. After all, hadn't he proved himself to her, over and over again?

Chapter 18

Shane looked up in surprise when Karen came in and slammed the living-room door behind her. They were at his flat, having decided to stay the night there, after coming back from Rathrigh, earlier the same evening.

"What's up with *you*?" he asked, seeing her dark expression.

"You'd better keep me away from Roan Williams for a while," she said angrily, "or may God forgive me but I'll end up doing damage to him. That was Jenny on the phone. You won't believe it, but she's gone and fallen for his lies again."

Shane was confused. "Who has? What lies?"

"Oh, bloody Roan has concocted some cock-and-bull story about why he went off to Venice without her, and Jenny believed every word that came out of his mouth. What is wrong with her?"

"Ah, Roan's not that bad," Shane said. "Me and Aidan met him down the pub the other night, and he bought me a congratulatory pint. We had a right laugh – he cheered Aidan up no end."

Earlier that week, Aidan had come off duty, tired and depressed, having attended a particularly horrific fire the night before. Their unit had saved three children from a burning two-storey house, but unfortunately they hadn't been able to save the parents. Afterwards, Aidan had found both charred and blistered bodies, lying, arms entwined, under a bed. As was often the case in his line of work, the incident had affected him deeply, and Shane had insisted on bringing his friend out for a quiet drink, to try and prevent him dwelling on the episode.

"He's not that bad? Just because he bought you a pint?" Karen said. "Come on, Shane – be honest, the guy's a snake."

"I don't agree, as it happens," Shane said calmly. "I think he's all right, and I don't know what you have against him. OK, he can be a bit of a lad but that's no crime, is it?"

"You don't know what I have against him . . . " Karen was stunned. "Am I the only one around here that can see through it?"

"See through what?"

"This big act that he has going! For goodness sake, it's sticking out a mile that he's bogus. Jenny's being taken for a ride."

Shane shook his head. "Karen, I told you before that you shouldn't get involved. Jenny's relationship is her own business. How would you feel if she started questioning your relationship with me? Wouldn't you resent it a little?"

"Maybe, but I might at least listen to what she had to say! But no, Jenny sticks her head in the sand, and believes every word that comes out of his lying little trap. It'll end in tears, Shane. I guarantee you that."

"Well, if it does, just make sure that *you're* not the one doing the crying. Anyway, Jenny's a big girl – she doesn't need you to look out for her. I'm sure she knows exactly what she's doing."

"Maybe, but I'm glad I'm not staying at the flat tonight. I couldn't be responsible for what I might do – to either of them."

Shane put down the newspaper he was reading. "Speaking of which, what did you think about what Mam said earlier about the house?"

Karen shrugged. "I suppose there's no harm in looking."

Shane's mother, Nellie, had suggested that she and Shane start looking immediately for a house of their own.

"There's no time like the present, and if you wait much longer, house prices will just keep getting dearer," she had said, in the bossy tone that Karen had noticed she used, whenever she spoke to any of her children.

Nellie Quinn seemed a nice enough woman, and had been very gracious and friendly towards Karen throughout the visit, but she had quickly got the impression that the older woman wanted to retain a certain level of influence over Shane's future. For this, she supposed she couldn't blame her. Just because Karen's parents were happy to let her live her life without any interference, didn't mean that Shane's family dynamic would be the same. She had sensed this instantly upon her arrival, when Nellie had hugged Karen and said, "So you're the reason he gave up that great job in Germany!"

She had taken this as a joke at the time but as the evening

went on, she wondered if there was a little resentment towards the fact that Shane hadn't taken advantage of the opportunity proffered by his brother Jack.

Jack, back from London for the weekend to visit his mother, was also present at the Quinn house, but came across to Karen as a very serious type and not at all friendly. He had barely uttered a word to her throughout the visit, but then again, she thought wryly, he would have hardly had a chance.

Shane's house had been absolute bedlam. He had warned her about Paddy the family dog, who tried continuously to hump visitors' legs, and that was fine – Paddy behaved as exactly as predicted. But he *hadn't* warned her about the kids. Shane's sister Marie had brought her toddlers to the farmhouse for the visit, and although there were only three of them – a five-year old boy and two younger girls – to Karen it seemed like she was caught in the middle of a chimpanzees' day out at Disneyland. They seemed to be everywhere all at once – the baby screaming constantly, the other girl demanding that Karen brush her Barbie doll's hair, and afterwards brush her own with a sticky, sweaty comb – then more screaming when the boy decided *he* wanted attention, and frazzled said Barbie in the microwave.

By the time she left the Quinn household, Karen was doubly determined that she would never put herself through the misery of having kids. Never a child-lover by any means, her experience with Shane's nieces and nephews not only put the final nail in the coffin that was Karen's maternal instinct, but encased it in reinforced steel. She had had to sit through the usual, wait-until-you-have-your-own apologies and eye-rolling from the unfortunate mother of the three gremlins.

"Karen, you have it all ahead of you," Marie had said, while trying desperately to prevent her eldest from choking his sister under the coffee table. "They're just at that stage where nothing will keep them quiet."

A good kick up the backside might keep them quiet, Karen thought, but kept her counsel to herself. She smiled sympathetically at Marie. It was obvious that the poor girl hadn't an ounce of control over any of her boisterous kids. Nope, she told herself – as the baby screeched loud enough to almost shatter Karen's eardrums – she was *never* having children.

But she couldn't be too sure that Shane felt the same way. He seemed delighted with his nieces and nephews, picking up each of them in turn, and floating them above his head, pretending that they were aeroplanes.

The noise levels didn't seem to affect anyone else in the Quinn household either.

During dinner, while ducking a spoonful of baby food that came hurtling through the air past her nose, Shane's mother Nellie had suggested that Shane and Karen begin searching for a house.

"There's a site going over by John Corbally's," she had said to Shane, and Karen realised to her horror that Nellie was talking about somewhere local. "You should ask him about it."

"Oh, we were hoping to settle in Dublin," she had said quickly, before Shane answered. They hadn't really spoken about where they were going to live – in fact they hadn't made any plans other than getting engaged – but there was no way that Karen would even consider living up in the wilds of Meath.

To her relief, he had agreed. "No, Mam, we'll more than likely be getting a place in Dublin. The two of us have good jobs up there."

"I could get Karen a job at the council offices," Marie had interjected. "My husband works for the County Council," she explained to Karen proudly.

Karen had been so shocked that she was unable to answer. As if she was going to up and leave her job in Acorn Fidelity, a position she had worked so hard for, and take up some crummy job in the council! The cheek of them, trying to organise her life for her!

"Thanks, Marie, but Karen is happy where she is, aren't you, hon?" Shane said quickly, noticing the look of horror on his fiancée's face. "Anyway we've already begun looking for a place in Dublin." He took a bite from his thickly-buttered scone, and washed it down with a mouthful of tea.

Upon hearing this, Karen felt momentarily relieved. It was obvious from Shane's behaviour, that his family must often interfere like that, and he had lied simply to put them off. But the visit had shaken her a little. The Quinn family all seemed so involved in one another's lives, whereas her parents had always left it up to Karen to decide how she wanted to live her life. When she and Jenny were under age, they used to escape out of their respective bedroom windows, to sneak off to the local disco. One night, they were seen by the local busybody who took great pleasure in afterwards outlining events to the Hamiltons and the Cassidys.

While Jenny had been given a right rollicking by her parents, and had been grounded for a month, Jonathan and Clara Cassidy had simply shrugged and said, "Why didn't you just tell us you wanted to go out? We wouldn't have minded."

At the time, Jenny had thought that Karen's parents were 'the coolest in the town', as did Karen, until she realised that her parents' were just so busy with their own lives that they were happy to let their only daughter live hers as she pleased. As a result, Karen had grown used to her independence, and had come to value it. She wouldn't tolerate her parents' intrusion in her life now, in the same way that they wouldn't appreciate her interference in theirs. They had, naturally, been thrilled with the news of Karen's engagement, but still had no intention of rushing away from their business in Tenerife, 'even to see the ring', as Jenny had said one day, wondering why Karen's parents didn't seem that excited about the news. But Karen didn't expect them to rush home. She and Shane would go out and visit them sometime this year, and it would be way too much to ask for them to come back to Ireland, just to pass on their congratulations.

But she sensed that things were different in the Quinn family.

"Was Jack upset with you for not taking the job in Germany?" Karen asked.

Shane shrugged. "I suppose he was a bit miffed about it. After all, he had pulled a few strings to get me the job in the first place. You have to understand that Jack is more like a father than an older brother in our family. I suppose he took Dad's place, in a way." Shane's father had died from a heart attack when Shane was ten years old. Karen had suspected from his demeanour and his siblings' reverential manner towards him, that Jack was considered something of a father figure in the Quinn household. Shane had just confirmed that.

"Anyway, about the house," he said, "I'll have a chat with a guy I know from college – he works for an estate agent in town. I'll ask him to put a few feelers out and see if he can come up with anything around here – what do you think?"

Karen grimaced. "Around here? Shane, do you think we could afford to buy in this area? The house prices are manic."

"Well, I know you don't want to have to commute. I don't mind because with this job, I'll have to travel from place to place anyway."

Since his return from Germany, Shane had managed to secure a job with McCann Engineering, an older, more established civil engineering firm. He was currently working on the design team for the construction of a second toll bridge on the M50 motorway. The company's offices were based in town, but Shane often had to liaise with various project managers on-site.

"Anyway," he continued, "I'd like to live in Dublin. We're happy here, our friends are here – why not?"

"Well, there's no harm in having a look, is there?' Karen said, thrilled that Shane felt the same way she did, "and we're in no rush – we can wait until something decent comes on the market, and with your friend on side, I'm sure we'll find something we like."

"Great." Shane put his arms around her. "I'll ring

Steve tomorrow. I know he'll be only too delighted to help."

* * *

"Are you coming into town with me today, or what?" Karen asked impatiently, "I need to get Shane a birthday present, so, if you're coming, get your ass in gear."

Jenny had been going on about Roan and his pathetic excuses for the last ten minutes, and Karen didn't think she could put up with it much longer. She couldn't understand why Jenny had let him get away with the Venice thing. But, she had to admit that her friend had been in great form these last few days, so she wasn't going to say anything.

Jenny put her hands up. "OK, OK, I get the message!" she giggled. "Sorry, Karen, I should get myself a dog, or a cat or something, then I could natter away to my heart's content."

"Out – now!" Karen said, feigning sternness, as she locked the door behind them. "Just be careful, Jenny, that's all. I know I've said this before, but just make sure that you know what you're doing, OK?"

"Yes sir," Jenny mock-saluted her, and they went to collect Tessa from her flat, before catching the bus into town.

Two hours later, and after a fruitless search for a suitable present for Shane, the girls decided to take a break from the madness of Grafton Street on a Saturday.

"What about a PlayStation game, or something?" Jenny suggested, as they sat at a table in the Kylemore in St Stephen's Green shopping centre. "Isn't he into all that *Tomb Raider* stuff?"

Karen rolled her eyes. "Don't remind me. That Lara Croft one is enough to give any woman a complex. Have you seen the figure on her?"

Jenny laughed. "Have I what? They have a big poster of her up on the wall in Roan's flat." She took a large bite of her cream slice.

"What figure?" Tessa exclaimed. "She's a computer-generated image, for goodness sake. Imagine getting all excited over a few million gigglebites. Gerry's just as bad – I've never come across anything as stupid in my entire life."

"Well, there won't be any posters of her in our new house – I can tell you that straight and fair," Karen said, spooning sugar into her mug.

"What new place?" Jenny asked easily.

It took Karen a second to realise what she had said. "Oh, Jen, I'm sorry. That just slipped out. I wasn't going to tell you until I had something concrete, but . . . Shane and I are thinking of buying a place together."

"Oh!" Jenny was taken aback.

"It won't be for a while yet, though," Karen added quickly. "I mean, I'm not going to leave you in the lurch, or anything. It's just we've decided to find somewhere before we get married. I'm sorry."

Jenny waved the thought away. "Not at all. Don't be silly. Of course you'll be moving in together. I wondered about that when you got engaged. There's no point in the two of you renting separately for the next few years, is there? It'd be dead money." She smiled at Karen, who was sitting there with a rueful expression. "Don't look like that – it's fine, really."

"Are you sure you don't mind?" Karen felt like an absolute heel. She was planning to tell Jenny, but the time was never right. "As I said, it won't be for a while yet."

"Where are you planning to buy?" Tessa asked

"We were thinking of somewhere around Rathgar or Terenure."

Tessa looked at her. "You do realise that it'll cost you a small fortune for a house around either of those areas," she said.

"Well, we're not necessarily looking for a house, maybe just an apartment or a duplex. Whatever comes up, really." Karen took another mouthful of tea. She didn't yet want to tell them that something had already come up. A block of newly-renovated apartments in Terenure village had come on the market, and she and Shane were going to take a look at one of them the following week. It would probably come to nothing anyway, she told herself. She just didn't want Jenny to think that she had it all planned without saying anything to her first. After all, when Karen moved out, Jenny would have to find someone else to share the flat in Leinster Square.

"Well, I think it's brilliant," Jenny enthused. "Imagine owning your own place in Dublin, Karen!"

"Imagine having a man that wants to marry you," Tessa said glumly. "Don't get me wrong – you know I'm thrilled for you, but I just wish Gerry would hurry up and produce the ring. I've dropped so many hints since you two got engaged that I'm surprised he hasn't fallen over them by now."

Karen winked at her. "You might beat me to it yet. We decided not to set a date for the wedding until after we get a house sorted – and that could take ages." She wolfed down the last of her doughnut, and licked her lips with relish. "Anyway, getting engaged means meeting the rest of the family, which isn't much fun, I can tell you."

Jenny giggled, having heard the tale of the terrible toddlers. "Tell her about the children's names," she urged Karen.

Karen rolled her eyes. "I know you worked as a maternity nurse, Tessa, so you've probably heard worse, but Shane's nieces and nephews have the strangest names I've ever come across."

"Go on," Tessa leaned forward.

"The oldest fella is called – wait until you hear this – Keanu! I nearly fell out of my chair when Shane's sister started shouting." Karen adopted what she thought was her best country accent. "'Keanu, Keanu – I'm warning you, leave Honty alone – stop choking her!'"

"Tell her what Honty stands for," Jenny said, with tears of laughter in her eyes. Although she had heard the story before, and had never met the other woman, Karen's impression of her future sister-in-law had her in fits of laughter.

"It stands for Pocahontas," Karen said flatly, while trying to keep a straight face. "Honty stands for Pocahontas. The woman called the poor child after a Disney cartoon character."

"That's not unusual, by any means," Tessa grinned, "I've come across a few Pocahontases in my time. When that film was out a few years ago and I was in Holles St Maternity hospital, we had lots of them."

"Are you serious?" asked Jenny.

Tessa nodded. "Yep – but the best I ever heard was the one about the mother who called her child Femaalay."

"Fema . . . what?"

"Well, it's a bit of an urban legend around the hospitals, but I'm sure there's a grain of truth in it somewhere," Tessa explained. "Apparently, this woman gave birth to a girl but didn't name her straight away. When the nurse brought the baby to her mother's bed the next morning, the woman took one look at the pink tag on her daughter's wrist and said, 'Femaalay Kelly – that's a grand name for a young one.'"

"Femaalay? I don't get it," said Jenny, confused.

"I do!" Karen said, in fits of laughter. "The woman read the tag as Femaalay Kelly, when it actually said *Female* Kelly – isn't that it, Tessa?"

The other girl nodded with a smile. "I don't know if it's true, but believe me – anything's possible."

"And I thought Keanu and Pocahontas Byrne were bad," spluttered Karen, through a mouthful of tea.

Thank goodness that Jenny didn't seem to mind her moving out, Karen thought, as she watched her friend laughing with Tessa. Maybe she was thinking of keeping on the flat herself. Still, the rent was expensive for one person, and it would be crazy to let the extra bedroom go to waste. Enough, she scolded herself. There was no point in her wondering about what Jenny might do. At least she knew now that a move was in the offing. Anyway, she and Shane were only starting to view properties next week. They mightn't end up moving for ages yet and there she was running away with herself already.

Chapter 19

Karen and Shane looked around in dismay at the apartment they were being shown.

"It's a little bit small," Shane said to the estate agent.

That was an understatement, Karen thought. The place was a like a shoebox. How could anyone be expected to live here?

"It may look a little small, but the designer has made amazing use of the space available," said the estate agent, a man to whom she had taken an instant dislike. Although hardly even a man, Karen thought, with a smile. He looked as though he was barely out of secondary school. He had been quite rude with Shane earlier, when he had enquired about the asking price.

"Asking price?" he had said, in an annoying, affected, South Dublin accent that had got right up Karen's nose. "These apartments will be snapped up at *auction*. They're in a prime location, as I'm sure you already know. The *guideline* price means nothing when it comes to property like this."

"Amazing use of space, huh?" Shane repeated, catching Karen's eye, and nodding towards the doorway. She followed his gaze, and noticed that the living-room and bedroom doors were not yet hung, which instantly gave the impression of additional space. There was no way that even a two-seater sofa would fit there, once the doors went in. The flat in Leinster Square was bigger than this *'exceptionally spacious and tastefully decorated de luxe apartment'*, as the estate agent's brochure had proclaimed.

"If that's what we're up against, this is going to be an absolute nightmare," Karen said afterwards, when they had made their excuses, and went to the nearest pub for lunch. That afternoon, they were going to see a townhouse in the same area.

"I think it's probably the location, love," Shane said, tucking into his roast beef dinner. "Property around here is never going to be cheap."

"I don't fancy living outside Dublin, though, do you?" Karen said. "I'd hate to have to spend hours every day commuting. Neither do I want to settle for something resembling a dog box."

"Don't panic, Karen. That's not an option yet. Anyway," he said, with a glint in his eye, "I have a bit of an ace up my sleeve."

"What do you mean?"

"Well, you know how we only qualify for a small mortgage at the moment? Well, Jack knows a guy that can grant us more money."

"Your brother Jack? How?"

"He knows a guy who works as a mortgage adviser with one of the building societies over here. Jack owns a house at home in Meath that he's renting out, and he's going to put that house up as collateral for whatever extra money we need. What this means is that we can get a much bigger mortgage than what they offered us at the bank. The salary restrictions will still apply, but because there's a guarantee, this guy can organise for his building society to give us a bigger mortgage."

Karen was stunned. "He'd do that for us? Why?"

Shane shrugged. "Jack knows the property score over here, and how hard it is to get anything decent. As well as that, he already owns his apartment in London, *and* another house of his own back home. It's nothing to him. The only risk he's taking is that we might default on the mortgage repayments, and he knows that that won't happen. McCann's pay very well, and I'll be due a salary increase every year, as well as bonuses. And of course, you have a secure job with Acorn Fidelity."

Karen was contemplative. This was very generous of Jack.

"And how did he come up with this idea?" she asked.

"He reckons this kind of thing happens a lot in England, except it's usually the parents putting forward the family home as a guarantee for their children. It'll have to start happening here soon too. Our generation can't get adequate mortgages any other way."

"So you have it more or less worked out already?"

Shane speared green beans onto his fork. "More or less. We just have to find a place first. It gives us a bit of headstart on everyone else, though, doesn't it?" he grinned.

"I'll say! Shane, this is brilliant. Why didn't you say anything about it before?"

He shrugged. "I wasn't really sure what we were up against price-wise. But, after seeing that cubby-hole of a place this morning, I knew we'd have to pay more than what the bank have offered us for anything even half-decent."

This was great news, Karen thought, finishing the remainder of her club sandwich. With Jack's offer, they now had some leeway with regard to the price. They'd have to arrange to go over to London, and thank him properly. After all, he barely knew Karen, and here he was offering the deeds of his own house, lock, stock and barrel to them. Imagine Jack owning his own house in Meath *and* a London apartment – and he a single man, and only in his thirties! He must be loaded!

"It's almost two o'clock," Shane said eventually, pushing his plate away from him.

"We'd better head on up to that mews and see what it's like. Who knows,' he said, winking at Karen, as he went to pay their bill, "it might just be the house of our dreams!"

* * *

"Far from it," Karen said grumpily to Jenny, back at the flat afterwards. "The place was an absolute dive! We'd have to put the asking price and more back into it, to try and make it anyway livable. It's so depressing!"

"It sounds tough," Jenny said, regarding her friend thoughtfully. "Why don't you start looking outside Terenure? It's always been an expensive area. Maybe somewhere further from town might be better."

"Well, it's not really the money that's the problem, Jen –" Karen then told her about Jack's offer. "We just want somewhere that's a decent size, and needs nothing much doing to it. Honestly, Jen, I never imagined that finding a house would be so much hassle."

The intercom buzzer went and Jenny ran to answer it. "Hi," she said breathlessly, and buzzed their visitor in.

Karen rolled her eyes. "Lover boy, I take it?"

She nodded. "I hope you don't mind, Karen, but we're getting a video. Do you want to watch it with us?"

"Ah, Jen, I wish you'd have told me! I was planning to watch the *X files* later. It's the second of a two-part episode that I'm following."

Seconds later, Roan appeared at the top of the stairs with a video and a six-pack of Carlsberg, and behaved as if Karen wasn't even in the room. Since the Venice trip, their truce had been broken, and swords were drawn once more.

"I got the new Vin Diesel flick, Jen – it's just out today and it's supposed to be brilliant," he said.

"What? I thought you said you'd get *Titantic*! You know I've never seen it!"

"I know, but I couldn't sit watching that soppy crap for over three hours. Come on, that's more of a chick flick, and you know what I'm like." He gave a lopsided grin, and immediately Jenny relented.

Yeah, we all know exactly what you're like, Karen said sourly to herself. The cheek of him! She had decided to go over to Shane's but there was no way she was going anywhere now. It would annoy Roan if she stayed around and played gooseberry and she could get Shane to record the *X-files* for her. Stuff him! She paid the rent, why should she make things all nice and easy for Mr Smooth?

"Great! I love Vin Diesel," Karen smiled sweetly at Roan, and eyed the off-licence bag. "Did you bring any beer for us?" *As if!*

"I didn't think there'd be anyone else here," he said rudely.

Karen raised an eyebrow. "Oh? And where did you think *I'd* be?"

"It doesn't matter," Jenny said, hastily taking the beer from him, and putting it in the fridge. "We'll watch the video after the *X-files*."

"It's all right," Karen said, with a sigh. "You can put it on now if you want."

"Are you sure?" Jenny asked gratefully. "We can wait if you like."

"I don't know how anyone can watch that heap of shite," Roan said sourly. "All that crap about aliens running around – it's a load of rubbish if you ask me. That red-haired one isn't bad looking though," he added.

Jenny looked as though she wished the ground would open up and swallow her.

She smiled, obviously struggling to keep things lighthearted. "What would you know, Roan? I mean, look at your choice of video!"

Roan grunted and said nothing, then flopped down on the sofa. He unlaced his boots and to Karen's disgust, took them off and left them in the middle of the carpet.

Jenny changed the television channel, and put the cassette into the VCR before sitting down beside him. She pressed 'play' and as they watched the trailers the room was silent.

"Any chance of a beer before it starts, Jen?" Roan

asked, leaning over and chuckling as he whispered something into her ear. Karen thought she had never met anyone who could be so unashamedly rude.

Jenny jumped up from her seat. "Sure – Karen do you want anything?"

Karen shook her head. "No thanks, Jen. But if I did want something, I'd get it myself." She glared at Roan, and if he realised that she was making inferences about his behaviour, he said nothing.

About half an hour into the film, Karen stood up to visit the bathroom. She was about to return to the living-room, when she caught the tail-end of a conversation Roan and Jenny were obviously having about her.

"I just wish she'd go – then I could have you all to myself," Roan was saying, none-too-quietly. "Why doesn't she just move in with Quinn now? It would be better for all concerned."

"Roan, stop," Jenny said, her voice low. "This is still her flat. She's entitled to stay here for as long as she wants. We'll just have to wait until she's ready."

"You certainly will!" Karen exclaimed, bursting open the door, unable to contain her anger. The little prat! How dare he talk about her like that behind her back?

She glared at Jenny, who looked from her to Roan and back again, not knowing what to say.

"What's going on, Jenny? Why are you two plotting behind my back?"

"Karen, calm down. We haven't been plotting anything. It's just . . ." she faltered, not sure what to say to her angry friend.

Roan brusquely finished the sentence for her. "Jen and

I were planning on moving in together, and seeing as you're getting a place of your own, we thought you might as well move out with Quinn, and let me move in here." Clearly bored by it all, he turned back to the television, leaving Jenny to deal with the aftermath.

Karen looked at the two of them in disbelief. "I can't believe this. Jenny, why didn't you say something?"

"I'm sorry, Karen," she said uneasily, "but it's not how it all sounds. I mean, the obvious solution is to have Roan move in here after you're gone. I wouldn't be able to manage the rent here on my own."

"Why didn't you just say something then? Why all the secrecy?" Karen couldn't help but be angry with her. Now Jenny was getting as bad as he was for sneaking around. If she and Roan were thinking along those lines why didn't Jenny just say so?

"I didn't want you to feel under any pressure to move out. And there isn't any pressure," Jenny said. She looked at Roan again for back-up. "Look, don't mind him. We're fine the way we are at the moment. We have every intention of waiting until you and Shane find a place to live. There's no rush or anything, is there, Roan?" She nudged him hard.

"No, there's no rush, Karen," Roan drawled sarcastically, without once taking his eyes off the television screen. "You just take as much time as you need." Then he added under his breath, "You will anyway."

Jenny looked at him, horrified at his behaviour but unable to say anything.

Karen was fit to be tied. "Now look here, you," she began, fully prepared to put Ignoramus in his place, once and for all, "it's time you were told a few home truths, Williams. I . . ." Karen stopped herself from saying any more, when she saw the horrified look on Jenny's face. It wasn't fair to Jenny, nor was it her friend's fault that Roan Williams was the scum of the earth. She took a few deep breaths to try and calm herself. "I'm going to bed," she said instead and, picking up her slippers from the floor, Karen promptly marched out the door.

"Hold on a second." Jenny got up from the couch and followed her.

The two girls faced one another in the hallway.

"I don't know what to say about that, Karen. I'm very sorry. I know he's been under a lot of pressure lately with work and . . . and one of the lads in the flat he's in now isn't paying his way. They all have to make up the shortfall in the rent. It's nothing personal."

Karen shook her head. Under pressure, my ass!

"Jen, that was rude of Roan – plain and simple," she said, unafraid to let him overhear. "I don't know how you put up with it."

"He has a few drinks in him, that's all. He'll be mortified in the morning, when he remembers what he said. Don't think that I'm trying to get rid of you. Roan will move in only when you're ready to move out, and not before, OK?" She reached out and touched Karen's arm. "Please don't be angry with me."

Karen looked at Jenny's forlorn expression, and immediately felt guilty. "Come here, silly," she said, engulfing her in a hug. "I can never be angry with the likes of you for very long anyway."

Chapter 20

A few weeks later, Jenny visited Karen and Shane at their new house. They had finalised the sale just days earlier, and were moving in immediately, the previous owners having moved abroad before everything was signed and sealed. They had left instructions with the estate agents for a quick sale, and Karen and Shane had been the very first people to view it. Shane's estate agent friend had come good for them. They had snapped it up immediately, albeit paying a little over their budget, but agreeing that it was worth it.

The house was situated in Harold's Cross, which suited both Karen and Shane with regard to commuting for work. It was a two-bedroom townhouse, but much 'roomier' than anything else they had seen, as Karen explained to Jenny shortly after viewing it.

"It's gorgeous, Karen," Jenny said, looking around the living-room with genuine enthusiasm. A large bay window looked out onto a good-sized front garden, which wasn't unusual for most Georgian houses in Dublin but very unusual for a smaller, modern property such as this one. The window gave the living-room definite character, despite the dreadful swirling wallpaper and heavily patterned carpet. She followed Karen upstairs to see the bedrooms. The master bedroom contained mirrored 'sliderobes', and Karen slid back one of the doors for Jenny's perusal.

"These things could have been designed just for me," she said elatedly, pointing at the collection of shoes, and the piles of clothes bundled in the wardrobe. "I don't have to keep everything all tidy and folded because they'll never fall out and," she promptly slid the door shut again, "the mess just disappears in an instant!"

Jenny laughed, watching her friend's expression in the mirrored door. Karen was deliriously happy with her new home, and rightly so.

"You're so right, you know – these things must have been designed for, or *by*, people exactly like you."

She had a quick look around the other bedroom, which judging by the *Barney* wallpaper, had been used by the previous owners as a children's bedroom.

"You'll have to do some work on that one," Jenny said, nodding at the dinosaur décor, "I know you have a bit of a thing for purple, but that's a bit much!"

Karen laughed. "I know. There's no rush with it yet, though. We'll probably just use it as a storage room at first, and then do it up as a guest room."

"Imagine you with a *guest room*?" Jenny mimicked her in a posh accent. "Hello, would you like to stay in my *guest room*? I can't promise that you won't have to climb over a mound of clothes and shoes, but you'll get a bed at least!"

She laughed, as Karen pretended to push her down the stairs.

"What were you two skitting about?" Shane asked, as they joined him downstairs in the kitchen, where he was busy washing the insides of the cupboards.

"I was just teasing your wife-to-be about her house-proudness, if there is such a word," Jenny said, giggling as she sat down at the small kitchen table. The kitchen was small, but manageable, she thought, looking around. There were plenty of cupboards, and the floor had been tiled with unusual but attractive slate-coloured tiles. The kitchen units were old, but Shane had already undertaken to replace those as soon as he had the time. Jasmine-coloured tiles surrounded the worktop and the hob-plate cooker. Jenny loved it.

"Tell that Williams fella to get his ass down here some Saturday. He promised me in the pub the other night that he'd give me a hand with laying the wooden floor."

Roan – laying a wooden floor? Jenny was astonished. He must have been full of drink if he promised Shane something like that. But she was pleased that the two of them seemed to get on so well together, and it often helped diffuse the frosty atmosphere between Roan and Karen, especially when the group went out together.

"We don't yet have a washing machine, or tumble dryer so we're going to Curry's on Saturday, aren't we, hon?" Karen said, winking at Jenny.

Shane groaned, washing out the J-cloth he was using in the sink. "This is the bit I hate, Jenny. It's all very well getting a new house, but I didn't realise I'd be dragged around the place looking for stuff to fill it."

"That's domestic life for you – you're stuck with it now," Jenny said, laughing as Karen handed her a freshly-made cup of coffee.

"Am I what! Do you think there's any way I might get out of it at this stage, I wonder?" He grinned mischievously at Karen, "Maybe the ink hasn't dried on the mortgage contract yet."

Karen slapped him away with a J-cloth. "Less of the whingeing please – you should be happy we have the place at all!"

Jenny watched them both enviously. They were so happy, and so lucky. Imagine owning a house like this, and having everything to look forward to? She'd love it if she and Roan could go down that road eventually. They had only been living together for a few weeks, Karen having moved in with Shane, while they were waiting for the sale on the house to go through.

So far it had been working really well. Jenny enjoyed coming home from work and having him there most of the time. Sometimes he even made dinner. The only snag so far, she reflected, was his unwillingness to share in the housework. Roan wouldn't dream of picking up a sweeping brush or a cloth, not to mention cleaning the bathroom. Jenny had thought that Karen was untidy, but at least she did her share of the housework. With the long winter nights drawing in, the last thing Jenny wanted to do when she got home from Dun Laoghaire was housework. She would have much preferred to flop on the sofa, in front of the telly. But if she didn't make the effort, their flat would end up like his old flat – an absolute disgrace.

Then of course, Roan did work a lot harder than she did, and often for longer hours.

Since the takeover of Euramax, by the American company, he had confessed to Jenny that he had never worked so hard in his life. The CEO of Evanston Technologies, an American company based in New York, had purchased Euramax to take advantage of the skilled staff and tax breaks offered by the IDA to foreign technology companies. The MD expected nothing but complete dedication from his staff, and if this meant coming in earlier in the morning, and staying on later in the evening to complete a project, so be it.

She shouldn't really expect him to do too much around the flat, Jenny mused. After all, he had enough on his plate. He couldn't even come here with her tonight because he was working late.

And then there was the problem with the boys. Apparently there was some dispute over the rent he owed at his last flat. Jenny wasn't sure what it was all about, but until everything was sorted out, Roan wasn't able to contribute to the rent. He would eventually of course, but for the moment, things were a little bit up in the air.

"Have a biscuit, Jenny – there's loads." Shane pushed a plate of chocolate digestives towards her.

"Thanks – tell me, now that you have the house sorted, have you had any more thoughts about the wedding?"

"Nah! Plenty of time for that," Karen said dismissing the thought with a wave of her hand. "We have so much to buy for the house this year, we can't even think about getting married, unless we run off and do it in secret on the cheap. Give it another year or two, and we'll see what happens."

Shane rolled his eyes and groaned. "The thoughts of it. All that money on one day! I don't know how people do it."

"We know a girl who spent nearly twelve grand on her wedding," Jenny said. "Remember Frances Kiely?"

"That's right!" Karen exclaimed. "She got married a few years ago, and invited practically the whole village to the wedding. The dress was like something out of High Society Brides – I believe that it cost nearly five grand alone! Lovely dress, shame about the bride," she giggled.

"Well, spending that much on the wedding didn't do them any good. The marriage broke up a few months ago. I believe she's back living at home with Mummy and Daddy Kiely."

"You're kidding!" Karen's eyes widened. "I never heard that! What happened?"

Jenny shrugged. "Apparently the husband, who according to Mrs Kiely had been 'a terribly successful financier', was actually a dodgy dealer. He was caught by the Revenue for tax-dodging, and now he hasn't a penny. Frances couldn't take the scandal of it all, and scuttled back home to Mummy."

"Nice wife," Shane said wryly. "What about 'for richer or poorer'?"

Jenny giggled. "Actually, Frances went around reminding anyone that was interested that they had written their own vows for the service, and that that particular vow had been left out. She hadn't promised anything!"

"Talk about covering your ass, and keeping your options open," Karen grinned.

"Stop it, the two of you!" Shane put his hands over his ears. "Don't be putting ideas in her head. She's bad enough as it is, about the wedding. 'Now don't think I'll be into all this honour and obey stuff'," he said, mimicking Karen. "Would you believe she actually said that to me, on the night I proposed!"

Karen laughed. "Come on, we're not living in the Middle Ages! All that stuff freaks me out. It's you, and not me that should be doing the obeying." She ruffled his hair. "Now, get cracking on those cupboards, so we can at least make this kitchen livable."

Shane raised his hand to his forehead in mock salute. "Yes, sir – right away, sir! See what I have to put up with, Jenny? And we're only here a few days. What'll she be like in a few years' time?"

"You're so lucky." Jenny said later, as she got her coat. "Shane is such a pet."

Karen smiled. "I suppose I am. But, I could have murdered you when you brought up the wedding. It's been a bit of a bone of contention between us lately."

"What do you mean?"

"Well, Shane is like yourself. He thinks that now we've got the house, we should be making plans for the wedding, but I want to put it off for a few more years."

"But why? Why get engaged if you don't want to get married?"

"I do want to get married, but not just yet. The mortgage repayments are very high and I want to try for a promotion at Acorn. I want us to be financially comfortable, and not have to give up our social lives, in order to save for a wedding. There are a few things to do with the house, and I just don't think we're ready yet."

"I suppose you got the house sooner than you expected," Jenny mused, "but does Shane know how you feel?"

"We've talked about it, and he sees no reason to wait. He reckons that things are tight for everyone starting out. But I don't see why it has to be that way. If we start saving for the wedding – now on top of everything else – Jen, you'll probably never see us out again. We're much too young for a life of cosy domesticity. Anyway we're as good as married now – what's the difference?"

Jenny shook her head. "Maybe, but you have to tell him how you really feel. If you keep putting off the wedding, Shane's going to think you're having second thoughts about it."

"I know, I know. I just don't know how to broach the subject just yet. I'll wait until we're settled here, and then I'll say something."

"You should. It's not fair to Shane otherwise."

"I promise I will. Just don't say any more about the wedding in front of him, OK?"

Jenny smiled and nodded. "Look, I'd better go. I'll talk to you during the week."

As she walked down Kenilworth Road towards Rathmines, Jenny couldn't help thinking about what Karen had just told her. She would love to be in Karen's position now – a gorgeous new house, an obviously devoted fiancé and a romantic wedding to plan.

Still, she supposed she wasn't doing too badly. She

had a gorgeous boyfriend, who was madly in love with her, and now they were living together. Who knows what might happen next?

Jenny quickened her pace and hummed to herself as she walked towards home.

* * *

Barry Ferguson, Manager of Alliance Trust Dun Laoghaire, studied the sheet in front of him for a few moments, and then slid it back across the desk to Marion.

"Whom do you think we should put forward?" he asked her.

"Well, Brendan and Robyn are here longer than the rest of our bank assistants, so in terms of seniority they should be next in line for promotion to Senior Bank Official," the Branch Administrator said.

"But you're not so sure?" Barry said, studying her expression.

Marion shook her head. "Brendan is fine, he's a good worker but, as you know yourself, Robyn is more than a little unreliable. She's missed a lot of days over the last few years, and has put us on the spot a few times in trying to get cover for her absences. I really don't think that promoting her will benefit anyone. This is just a job for her, and I'm certain that she doesn't have aspirations for a real career with this bank."

"Then who else? All the other bank officials came in after the last recruitment drive. We have the chance to put two people forward for promotion, Marion, and we have to take it. This branch has too many bank officials, and not enough seniors."

212

"I know. And with Olivia leaving at the beginning of next year, we'll only have three SBO's left on the staff."

"So what do you recommend?"

Marion sat back in her chair and crossed her legs. She didn't know what Barry was going to make of this, but she might as well just say it.

"I've spoken to Brendan, and he doesn't have a problem with it. He's happy enough on the cashier's desk, and he doesn't want the responsibility. I suggest that we put Jenny Hamilton forward for the second SBO position here."

"Jenny? But she's only in the door!"

"I know that, Barry, but her work rate is excellent. She has plenty of experience, what with working in Kilkenny, and then at the bank in Australia. We put her on the Foreign Exchange desk not long after she started, and I can honestly say that she's one of the most efficient cashiers I've ever come across. Her paperwork is always perfect. I don't think she's ever had a single cash difference, and she's excellent at clearing the queues – not to mention all the help she gives the others."

"I'd noticed that from the reports, all right. And her pension and insurance referrals have put us top of the District in Sales. But she's hardly ready for promotion, Marion."

Marion shrugged her shoulders. "She knows most of the business customers by name and face, from being up here working with Olivia. The customers know and like her. She's extremely diligent, Barry. I can't think of anyone else I'd prefer to put forward, to be honest."

Barry stroked his chin and pondered the thought. "And you're sure Brendan doesn't mind?"

"Not at all. He thinks it's a great idea."

213

"Good. I like Brendan and I wouldn't like him to think he was being passed over."

"He's happy enough to go along the present salary scale. He's just a young fellow, Barry – he works all week to go out at the weekends. He's still living at home and doesn't want or need the hassle, as he put it himself."

He nodded in agreement. "Jenny it is then. Have you mentioned anything to her?"

"I wanted to see what you thought first."

"It's fine by me. It's a little unusual, though. She hasn't even been here a year."

"But she's been with the bank for longer than that, Barry. Look, the District office is giving us the option to promote. If they're offering us the chance, then why not take it?" She picked up her pen and made some notes. "I'll be sorry to lose Olivia though. I was hoping to train her in on the Lending soon. The bank's salary just can't compete with these IT companies any more."

"Not to worry. We'll sort something out," Barry said, in a tone that Marion knew meant that *she'd* have to sort something out.

Being the branch administrator, she was responsible for the staff and the day-to-day operation of the bank. In fact, she did most of the managing. Barry never had to worry about who might cover the Foreign Exchange desk in the middle of July, when the usual cashier was out sick, or the Customer Services desk when the new student year began, and every second customer wanted a new student account. It wasn't easy.

The prospect of promotion for two of her bank assistants would ease a number of headaches for Marion. Promotion brought responsibility, and generally bank assistants could not fill Lending or Accounting roles in the bank. The more SBO's on the branch staff, the fewer problems for Marion.

Barry looked at his watch, a sure signal to Marion that the meeting was over. "Right, I'll leave it in your very capable hands. Have a chat to Jenny about it and see what she says. Stress how important it is that she grab this chance with both hands." He stood up. "I won't be back in the office this afternoon – I've a meeting with Jimmy Fitz from FitzGerald Press. If anything important comes up, refer it to Mick, will you?"

"Of course," Marion picked up her folder. "Enjoy your game," she said with a smile, before closing the door behind her.

Barry grinned to himself, as he put on his overcoat. You couldn't put much past that Marion. She knew damn well that he was meeting Jimmy FitzGerald on the golf course. Still, she was a good sort, and he'd never forget that time she covered for him. He had gone AWOL on the session the weekend after Wexford won the All-Ireland Final, and the District Manager had paid a surprise visit to the branch the following Monday morning.

It wasn't all fun and games on the golf course like Marion thought, though. Some fellas would only open up over a round or two. You couldn't hammer out anything with the likes of Jimmy Fitz in the office. Anyway, the bit of fresh air would do him good, away from all the hassle of being Manager in a busy spot like Dun Laoghaire. Barry wished sometimes that he had ended up in one of those quiet branches down the country. Now that would have been an easy life.

Chapter 21

"Jenny, guess what? Gerry proposed! We're getting married before the end of this year!" Tessa squealed elatedly down the telephone line.

"Tessa, that's brilliant. I'm really pleased for you! When did this all come about?"

"He just popped the question out of the blue, although I thought it might be on the cards – remember I was telling you that I thought we might get engaged for my birthday last month? Well, we went out to dinner at the weekend for no reason at all and he completely surprised me!"

"That's great news. What's your engagement ring like? Did Gerry pick it out himself?"

"He wouldn't dare! No, we're going into town to pick it out together on Thursday evening, so I suppose it's not entirely official yet!" she giggled. "Anyway, we're all getting together on Friday night to celebrate. I've booked a place in Temple Bar for food, and then we'll go on a bit of a pub-crawl in town. What do you think?"

"I wouldn't miss it for the world," Jenny said warmly. "What time are you going out?"

"Well, we've agreed to meet up at about eight o'clock outside the Central Bank. Is that all right with you and Roan? If not, I'll have my mobile on, and you can give me a buzz on that?"

"No, that's fine by us. We should be there by then. Tell Gerry I said congratulations, won't you? I can't wait to see the ring."

"Me neither! See you Friday then. I've a few more people to phone."

Tessa rang off, and Jenny slowly went back up the stairs. Not another one! Everyone she knew seemed to be getting engaged these days. Olivia had announced her engagement months back, her boyfriend having proposed on holiday. *And* one of her sister's friends from home had got engaged only last week. Was there something in the air lately? First Karen, then Olivia, and now Tessa. Why was it that all her friends were planning their future with eager partners, and she was in a relationship that at the moment, seemed to be in a bit of a rut?

Things had started to get a little strange soon after her promotion, Jenny reflected. She couldn't believe that she had been put forward by the bank so quickly, and then to have got the Senior Bank Official position soon after! It had all happened so fast – she hadn't really had the time to consider what it would all mean. If she had known how hard it was going to be, she might never have agreed to put her name forward so readily. The way things were, she didn't know whether she was coming or going at work. When she got the SBO position, Marion had taken her off the Foreign Exchange desk, and practically dumped her into the Customer Services, with little or no experience. It had been an absolute nightmare. They had been so busy that Amy, the regular Customer Services official, didn't have a chance to answer Jenny's questions or give her a hand with any difficulties. Jenny discovered very quickly that the Customer Services desk was a completely different ball-game to working on the cash desk. She remembered walking out of the branch one day in tears. Something like that had never happened before – Jenny rarely let work get on top of her. Then there was the short stint she had in the Accounts section on her own after just a few hours' training, and she was expected to deal with the accounts of some the branch's biggest customers.

Jenny hadn't realised how tiring it could all be. What with trying to take in everything she needed to do as part of the day-to-day tasks, as well as coping with the dozens of phone calls from customers – that seemed to be coming through by the second – Jenny could barely keep her eyes open on the Dart going home in the evenings.

It was getting a bit too much for her even then, but today, Marion had announced that she was about to be trained as a replacement for Olivia, who had been earmarked for a Lending role before her departure. Jenny had been shocked upon hearing this. How could she go from being a simple cashier to a Lending Officer in just under twelve months? But she couldn't say anything to Marion about it. After all, Marion had been the one who had been behind her promotion in the first place. She couldn't start whingeing and whining about it now. She had soon realised that her promotion came about more from a staffing shortage than anything else, but didn't they realise that they were bombarding her with too much?

Jenny moaned to herself as she caught sight of Roan asleep on the sofa, the dirty dishes from the dinner piled high on the counter. Could he not make the effort to help out – just once in a while?

Things hadn't been that great between them lately, she reflected, rinsing the dishes under the tap. He didn't seem to understand the pressure she was under, couldn't see why she went on at him to give her a hand with the housework. He still insisted that he worked too hard without having to come home and do all that 'woman's stuff' as he called it. Jenny had learned from a few weeks of living with him, that Roan had never done a tap of housework. His mother had obviously let him get away with murder. He was lucky he hadn't been born in the Hamilton household! Her brothers Eric and Thomas had been well trained by their mother in everything from making beds to cooking stew.

Roan moaned loudly, obviously annoyed that she was making so much noise with the washing-up. Tough, Jenny thought, scraping the leftovers into the bin with a little more enthusiasm that was strictly necessary.

"Do you have to be so noisy doing that?" Roan growled.

"No, I don't *have* to be so noisy – maybe you'd like do it instead for a change?" she said, waving the washing-up-liquid bottle at him.

"Ah, don't start. Jenny. I've had a balls of a day," he

said, rolling his eyes to heaven. "The insurance company is putting the pressure on, and we need to get everything finished before the end of this month. I get enough hassle at work, without having to put up with it when I come home."

Something snapped inside Jenny. She'd just about had enough of Roan and all the hassle he was supposed to be under. She whirled around to face him, her face scornful. "Well sorr-y! But you're not the only one under pressure at work, you know. Not only that, but I have to come back to this pigsty, and clean up after you and – "

"Jesus, if it's that much hassle to do the feckin washing-up, give it here!" He jumped up and nudged in beside her at the sink. "Talk about a bloody nag," he whispered under his breath.

"Roan Williams, I am not a nag," Jenny retorted, "but even if I was, I don't have any choice. You make as much of a mess around here as I do, and yet you expect me to clean up after you – why is that? I'm not your personal slave, you know!"

"What? What are you on about? Wasn't I the one that did all the shopping last week?" Water splashed out of the sink and onto the floor as he scrubbed the saucepan vehemently. "Anyway, the place is never that bad – you just have some kind of a cleanliness obsession or something."

"It's not that bad, Roan, because I make sure it doesn't get that bad!" Jenny was getting angrier by the minute.

Roan threw a handful of cutlery into the water, then turned and glared at her. "I don't know what's wrong with you lately. Since you got that bloody promotion you've become really up in yourself."

"What? What are you on about?"

"It's true! You act like you're the bee's knees, thinking you can boss me around like you do everyone else in that job. Well, I'll tell you one thing for nothing – you won't treat me like some nerdy office boy!"

Jenny opened her mouth but no words came out. She couldn't believe what she was hearing. How dare he accuse of her of bossing him around, when all she wanted was a bit of help with the tidying-up!

"Roan, you're being very unfair here. I hardly ever ask you for help, unless I'm very tired. And I'm very tired tonight. Coming in here and seeing you all tucked up and snoring on the couch doesn't exactly improve my mood, you know."

"Well, Jenny, I've had enough of your moods lately. I don't know what's got into you. You're no crack any more. It's like you've aged about twenty years since you got promoted." He looked at her disdainfully. "You've let yourself go too."

Jenny looked back at him through narrowed eyes. "What the hell does that mean?"

"Oh, come on, Jenny – you dress like a dowdy schoolteacher these days, you hardly ever wear make-up, and you haven't bothered getting your roots redone in a very long time. It's like living with my mother! You haven't made much of an effort to shift the extra pounds either."

Jenny's heart sank. How could he say those things to her?

When he saw her expression, Roan's voice softened. "Look, I'm sorry, Jen. I didn't mean to hurt you. I just lashed out at you because I'm tired, and you were ranting on at me for being lazy." He came across the room and pulled her towards him. "I'm not trying to be hurtful, hon – I'm only telling you these things for your own good."

Jenny looked behind Roan to her reflection in the mirror over the fireplace, as he held her. Maybe he was right. She had been so keen to do well at work, and so tired lately that she hadn't really bothered with the things she used to love doing. She had been putting off a visit to the hairdresser for ages. And he was definitely right about the weight gain. She had got into the very bad habit of getting takeaways in the evenings, instead of making a proper dinner. She was just too bloody tired all the time.

Roan had told her some home truths, however hard they might have been to hear. No wonder he had lost interest in sex lately. At the beginning, they had been tearing each other's clothes off at every available minute – these days, they were lucky if they managed it once a week. Maybe it was all her fault, Jenny reflected. After all, Roan worked hard too but he still managed to keep himself in order.

Roan hugged her tightly once more, before releasing her and kissing her softly on the forehead. "I'm sorry again, Jen. Look, I know you're under pressure too, getting used to having to work hard and all that. I tell you what, why don't you sit down and put your feet up while I finish this, and then I'll make you a cuppa, all right?"

She hesitated for a minute. "I'm sorry too. I probably have been difficult to live with lately."

"It's OK, babe." He patted the sofa cushions. "Go on, sit down and take it easy."

Jenny looked at him gratefully. "Are you sure? I'm really wrecked, Roan – I wouldn't mind a chance to sit down for a minute."

Then, I'm putting on my tracksuit bottoms, and going for a good long jog, she thought, wondering if any of the salons in Dun Laoghaire might fit her in after work the next evening. She'd make sure she was looking her best for Tessa's engagement party on Friday night. After all, Tessa rarely looked anything other than stunning. Which was probably why Tessa was the one shopping for engagement rings, Jenny thought glumly.

* * *

Roan flicked through the TV channels, trying to decide what to watch. He had finally settled on Eurosport when Jenny appeared out of the bedroom dressed in sweats, and announced that she was going jogging.

Well, he thought, his earlier comments seemed to have had some effect on her at least. Jenny had gained a little weight all right, but not that much that you'd notice. It was only because she had nagged him so much that he had said that to her. Still, she hadn't been making much of an effort with her appearance lately, and it was his duty to tell her these things. After all, he'd expect her to tell *him* if he was losing his looks. He stroked the underside of his chin. Not likely. If he thought for a minute that he was putting on weight, he'd be on the treadmill fast as lightning! There was no way he was going to end up with a big beer belly, and a double chin like his oul' fella.

He had to laugh at Jenny, going on about the pressure

she was under at the bank. She didn't have a notion of what real pressure was like. Since his transfer to a different department, work had been much harder than he'd expected. Sure, the money was great, and the benefits were second-to-none, but you paid for it through blood, sweat, and tears. His boss, McNamara, was a slave-driver altogether – he'd have them working every hour God sent, if he could! Still, at least they were a decent crowd to work with. The lads on his project team were all about the same age as himself, and were always up for a laugh in the pub on a Friday evening. Not to mention the babes. Jeez! He had had to pinch himself when he walked into the office that first day. There was one girl there, Cara, the foreign-looking one with long curly hair, sultry dark eyes, and sexy legs up to her armpits. All the lads in the office were convinced that she wore those tiny skirts, and high heels, just to torment them. She was one sexy bitch! So far, Roan had resisted her charms. So far.

He had been trying to behave himself since he and Jenny had moved in together, in order to give the relationship a chance. The truth of it was that he had felt really guilty after the Venice thing. She had been very hurt by that, and he didn't want to upset her again.

But lately, Roan thought, flicking through the channels again, lately things weren't going so well with him and Jenny. She had imposed some kind of nookie ban on him these days. He had tried it only last night, but she had told him that she was in work early for some meeting or other. He couldn't remember the last time they had a decent shag. Jenny had better cop onto herself, or he'd have no choice but to go looking elsewhere. They weren't some middle-aged married couple after all – at their age, they should be gagging for it every night!

Roan sank back down on the sofa, closed his eyes, and began to imagine what it would be like to do the business with someone like Cara. He could almost feel that silky hair sweeping across his bare chest, and those long, dark legs wrapped tightly around his own. Roan smiled. If he ever got the chance he'd give her the shag of her life.

Chapter 22

Tessa hugged Karen and Shane enthusiastically when they entered the restaurant in Temple Bar. "What do you think – isn't it gorgeous?" she said, proudly displaying the large, almond-shaped solitaire on her engagement finger. "Gerry wanted to get something smaller, but once I had seen it, I knew it was the one for me."

"It's fabulous," Karen said, trying it on her own finger, and wondering how on earth Gerry could afford such an expensive ring on his salary. The setting on her own engagement ring looked tiny in comparison.

Not that it mattered, she thought, looking lovingly at the back of Shane's head. He could have done a Homer Simpson on it, and bought her an onion ring for all she cared!

She waved at the others, who were sitting at the bar with some girls that Karen didn't recognise – probably work friends of Tessa's, she decided.

"Where are Jenny and Roan?" Tessa asked, looking

anxiously towards the door. "Everyone else is here, and I thought they'd be coming with you two."

"Don't ask," Karen said dryly.

Tessa raised an eyebrow. "Trouble in paradise – again?"

"Paradise it ain't, not these days, anyway. We arranged to call for them tonight in the taxi, and when we got there, Jenny came to the front door and told us to go on ahead – that Roan wasn't yet back from work, and that they'd meet us here later." She shook her head. "It was obvious that she was lying, Tessa. I'd say your man was upstairs and they were having an argument."

"It's happening a lot lately isn't it?" Tessa said. "Since they moved in together, I mean."

Karen lit a cigarette, hoping there were no non-smoking signs anywhere.

"Jenny's not the same girl at all these days." She shook her match and took a large drag from the cigarette. "She's been under a lot of pressure at work, and he's not giving her a lot of support, from what I can see."

"I haven't seen them out together in ages. I really hope she comes out tonight though, for her own sake as well as anything else."

"We'll see," Karen said, "but I'd be very surprised if he's with her. After all, he doesn't exactly make much of an effort where Jenny's friends are concerned, does he?"

"Tell me about it. He hasn't said more than two words to me since the day I bawled him out. Remember? The day you went home after . . ." Tessa inclined her head towards Shane.

"Don't remind me!" Karen said. She winked at Shane who was making his way over to her.

"What are you two nattering about?" he asked, putting his arm around her waist. "Discussing wedding dresses, I suppose?"

"Nothing of the sort," she said shortly, taking a mouthful of wine. Tessa looked at her questioningly.

"No, we were wondering if Jenny and Roan were coming," Tessa said, checking her watch. "Our table should be ready soon."

"Well, wonder no more," Shane said, pointing to the door behind her, where a harassed-looking Jenny had just come in.

"Told you he wouldn't come," Karen murmured under her breath, as Jenny approached them.

"Hi, everyone!" Jenny waved.

She didn't look at all well, Karen thought, studying her friend, as Jenny examined Tessa's engagement ring. For an occasion like this, the old Jenny would have dressed up to the nines. Instead, she wore a long black shirt, black trousers and very little make-up. Her hair seemed lighter than usual, too. As they were led towards their table, Karen wondered if Jenny had changed her hairdresser.

Jenny smiled at Karen from across the table as they took their seats. "Before you ask – I don't know where he is, he hasn't come back from work yet, and I haven't been able to contact him. He hates mobile phones."

"Jen, it's none of my business." Karen looked down at the menu, and tried to bite her tongue. Typical Roan! He had obviously ducked out of going to the party at the last minute, letting Jenny down again. She could kill him!

"Jenny, your hair looks different. Did you get it cut?

Ow!" Shane felt the full force of Karen's kick, and a low blush appeared on Jenny's face.

"I know – it looks awful," she said, touching her hair self-consciously. "I got one of those home hair-colouring kits and coloured it myself yesterday. I usually get it done at the hairdresser's. That's why it looks a bit off." She smiled shyly around the table.

"No, no, I meant it looked nice." Shane was relieved when the waitress appeared beside him to take his order.

"It's unusual for *you* to do things by half, Jen," Tessa said, trying to make light of the situation, "but I tell you, for a home kit, it's not bad at all."

Karen's heart went out to Jenny – she looked so embarrassed. Jenny had to resort to a home kit because she obviously couldn't afford to have it done at the hairdresser's. And probably for the same reason, she hadn't bought anything new to wear out tonight. Come to think of it, she hadn't seen Jenny in anything new for a long, long, time! Damn it – the bastard still wasn't paying his share of the rent, and Jenny was making up the difference! He must owe her a fortune!

Her friend wasn't particularly talkative throughout the meal, and it seemed to Karen as though her mind was totally elsewhere. Probably wondering where that shit Roan is, she thought sourly.

When the last plate had been cleared away, and they were tucking into dessert, Tessa announced that she wanted to do a pub-crawl in Temple Bar starting with Buskers.

Shane groaned. "The last time I was in that place, I ended up getting thrown out."

Karen looked at him curiously. "Why – what did you do?"

"I remember that," Aidan laughed from the other end of the table. "He fell fast asleep while sitting on the bog. They threw him out because it was nearly three o'clock in the morning, and they were trying to clean up. Some poor bugger had to climb over the door to wake him up. Imagine the sight – Quinner snoring away with his kaks around his ankles!'

Shane looked mortified and everyone else roared laughing.

"Hmm. I hadn't heard that one before," Karen said, feigning sternness. "What else don't I know about you and your drunken antics?"

"None of that tonight, Shane, please," Tessa scolded, catching sight of Shane's mischievous grin. "I don't want you getting my fiancé in any trouble."

"See – you're a bad influence, Shane Quinn," Karen said, laughing. "I'd better keep an eye on you tonight – you'd never know what you might do."

Chapter 23

Jenny looked wistfully at both couples walking hand in hand in front of her. They were so lucky she thought, watching Shane put his arm around Karen, and plant a kiss on the top of her head. And from the looks of it, Tessa and Gerry were just as happy, and had everything to look forward to.

Watching them all together just made her feel worse about Roan. She had told him about tonight earlier on in the week, and he had said he would come, so where was he? He had told her that they were a little behind on their current project, but surely they weren't expected to stay there until all hours on a Friday night? Then again, his boss was supposed to be a bit of a slave-driver – maybe he had no option but to stay late tonight. He could have let her know though.

Tessa looked really gorgeous tonight, she thought, admiring her friend who was wearing a backless, silver-grey, chiffon dress under a fake-fur jacket. There wasn't a bulge to be seen on her anywhere, and for a figure-hugging dress like that, it was no mean feat, Jenny thought enviously.

If she wore a dress like that, people would think she was pregnant, she had got so fat. The black shirt came in handy that way; at least it hid her bulging stomach.

Roan was spot on. She'd have to try and lose all this weight. Funny, she'd never really bothered about it before – it must just be age catching up with her. She had read in a magazine once that as you grow older, you gain so many pounds per year as your body muscles start to sag. That must be what was happening to her. She'd have to watch herself. She was only twenty-eight after all – if she didn't do something soon, she'd be massive by the time she was thirty!

"Come on, guys, we're going in here for one!" Tessa signalled for everyone behind to follow her into the pub, which was packed to the gills with revellers. Temple Bar was a busy spot, especially on Friday nights.

She went to get a drink and, as she caught sight of herself in the mirror behind the bar, Jenny grimaced. Her hair looked dreadful! Never again would she use one of those home-colouring kits. The bleach had covered her roots as she'd hoped, but had also dried up her hair so that her curls were now a mass of frizz. She couldn't get an appointment for love nor money with a hairdresser in Dun Laoghaire.

"Jen, over here!" Karen smiled and patted the seat beside her.

"Busy in here tonight, isn't it?" Jenny said, putting her drink on the table, "We're lucky to get a seat."

"Definitely," Karen lit up another cigarette. "Tessa leapt

in as soon as she spotted a crowd of girls getting ready to leave. Did you see the get-up of them? They looked like they were on a hen night or something."

"Tessa's will be next," Jenny said. "I'm amazed that they're getting married so quickly. November doesn't seem that far away at all."

"I know, but she has practically everything organised already. She was a woman on a mission once he popped the question."

Jenny looked at Karen thoughtfully. "Well, have you said anything to Shane yet?"

She shook her head. "No, I'll have to soon, though. He keeps dropping hints and it's starting to annoy me."

Jenny laughed. "I don't understand you at all, sometimes. Usually the women are mad to get cracking on the wedding plans, not the other way round!"

Karen rolled her eyes. "To be honest, the thoughts of organising hotels, and guest lists and all that, fills me with absolute dread. Not to mention trying to find the so-called perfect dress. It's enough to put anyone off getting married altogether."

"Not me," Jenny said. "I'd give anything to be in your position now."

Karen said nothing.

Tessa walked over to the table, one arm in one sleeve of her coat. "Right, come on you two. Drink up – we're moving."

"Already?" they said in unison. "But we've just got a seat!"

"Hey, we're on a pub crawl here, and we've got at least another ten pubs to do. Get going!"

"If this is her engagement party, what'll her hen night be like?" Jenny laughed, as she walked out the door in front of Karen.

They didn't manage ten pubs Tessa had hoped for, because after a short while Gerry had begun to get a little worse for wear. The other lads had each bought a shot of Southern Comfort every time they moved, so by pub five, her fiancé was more than a little inebriated.

"I don't believe this," Tessa exclaimed, only starting to feel tiddly herself. Gerry was face down on one of the tables. "I'll have to take him home soon – he won't last much longer at this pace. And I wanted to go dancing tonight!"

"It's all right. I'll look after him," Shane said. "I've to go in to work for a half day tomorrow, so I promised myself I wouldn't stay out too long tonight."

"Oh no!" Tessa wailed. "Karen, you'll stay out, won't you?"

"Of course I'm staying out. I don't have to get up early tomorrow," she said, putting her arms around Shane. "You don't mind, do you?"

"No, by the looks of it I'm better off getting out of here while I can. There's no way I'm ending up in Copper Face Jack's tonight!"

Jenny came back to the table, looking slightly the worse for wear. "Aidan made me knock back a treble tequila with him at the bar – yeuch!" She stuck out her tongue. "Who's going to Copper Face Jack's?"

"Not me! I'm off," Shane said, getting to his feet. He gave Karen a quick kiss goodbye, and after some difficulty, eventually succeeded in getting Gerry out of his seat.

Tessa watched them leave, and then rubbed her hands with glee. "Right, now I can really let loose. Who's for a flaming sambuca?" she said running off to the bar like a child let loose in a sweet-shop

Hours later, Jenny, Karen, Tessa and a much-depleted crowd made it to the nightclub.

"Ouch! My feet are bloody killing me!" Tessa said, after leaving her coat in the cloakroom. "I don't know why we had to walk all the way up Grafton St. We should have got a taxi!"

"Oh yeah? And who's the one that wanted to go window-shopping?" Karen teased. After a few sambucas, Tessa had got the drunken idea that she should start looking for her wedding dress, and had dragged Jenny, Karen and her other friends Katie and Caroline to a window display at a bridal boutique on Grafton St. The girls had walked to the nightclub from there, and were to meet Aidan and the others in Copper Face Jack's.

"Can you see any sign of the others?" Karen shouted, craning her head to see around the dance-floor, as she made her way through to the crowded bar.

"If they're here, the dance-floor is the last place they'll be," Tessa said, wiggling her hips to a dance remix of U2's *Lemon*. "They're men, remember?"

"They might be at the upstairs bar." Jenny struggled to be heard over the music. "Let's get the drinks in anyway – oh, thank you!" Tessa said, beaming at a guy who stood back to let her in front of him at the bar.

Karen rolled her eyes at Jenny as they watched Tessa making big eyes at a barman, trying to get him to notice her. It was an old trick of hers, trying to get him to feel sorry for her by looking as though she had never bought a drink at the bar in her life. It worked – the young barman was over to her in a shot, ignoring everyone else.

Drinks in hand, the girls moved over to where Katie and Caroline stood near the dance floor.

"Looks like it's becoming a girls' night out," Tessa said, after searching for the others to no avail. "Oooh, listen – I love that song! Come on!" She caught Karen and Jenny by the hand, and practically dragged them towards the dance floor.

"No, I'll stay here with the drinks," Jenny said, and the others looked at her in amazement.

"But you love this one!" Karen exclaimed.

"No, you go on ahead – seriously."

Jenny watched the girls try to strut their stuff on the overcrowded dance floor.

She didn't quite know why, but her exuberance had suddenly left her. She didn't really want to be here at all. The crowds and the noise were getting to her. Even the drink didn't seem to be having much of an effect, at this stage. It must have been the walk from town to here, she thought. The fresh air must have sobered her up. She looked up sharply as a tall girl in high heels swayed towards her, and nearly knocked her over.

"Hey, watch where you're going!" she said, starting to feel more and more annoyed and uncomfortable by the minute.

A few songs later, the girls came back from the dance floor, giggling and damp with sweat from their exertions. Jenny wondered why they all seemed to be giggling and whispering amongst themselves. She felt annoyed again, and was just about to tell them she was leaving, when she heard another song start. Then she knew why the girls were whispering.

"It's your favourite!" Karen exclaimed. "We got the DJ to play it. He was supposed to play a request for you but he must have forgotten. Come on – you have to come out dancing now!" She took the drink out of her hand. Jenny had no choice but the follow the girls onto the dance floor, leaving her drink with Katie, who was a grunge fan, and refused to dance to anything resembling pop music.

Jenny, Karen and Tessa linked arms in an attempt to make some more room for themselves on the floor as they danced, Jenny belting out the words of the song as she did. This was much better, she thought.

She was beginning to really enjoy herself until she saw something at the edge of the dance floor – something that shattered her world into a million different pieces.

* * *

Roan couldn't believe his luck. The Ice Maiden had finally cracked and how! He knew the rest of the boys were sick at the sight of him and Cara together, especially Pete Brennan. The look on his face alone had been worth it! Pete had everyone, including himself, convinced that Cara was mad after him, and he had a bet on with Mark Dignan that he would get off with her that same night. Well, Pete might be good with women, but he wasn't that good, Roan thought.

Everyone in the office had been surprised when she had joined them in the pub earlier that evening. Normally, Cara never deigned to go out with her workmates – she always made it seem as though she had something better to do. The other girls in the office thought she was a right stuck-up cow, and never stopped bitching about her behind her back.

"That Cara Stephens one thinks she's something special with her Prada suits and her Gucci shoes," the receptionist, Lynne Jenkins, had muttered one morning, after Cara had collected her messages from Lynne, without so much as a thank-you. She had been a little taken aback when Cara came back out to reception and, frowning, thrust a piece of paper at Lynne.

"This message is totally illegible," she said curtly. "There's not much point in taking messages for me if I can't tell who has actually left them. Oh – and by the way, Lynne, the suit is from Next and the shoes are from Dunnes, OK?"

Lynne's face and neck turned the colour of beetroot as Cara gave her a look that would cut diamonds. She couldn't think of anything in reply, and Cara turned on her Dunnes heels and walked off, head in the air.

Cara was equally cool and unfriendly towards the males in the office, with the notable exception of Pete Brennan, with whom she often worked directly. Roan had never worked alongside Cara on a project, and so had little to do with her, other than eye her long legs and super-fit body, whenever she walked past his desk.

Pete was always going on and on about how Cara fancied him, but Roan couldn't see it himself. Cara wasn't the type of girl to be making eyes and flirting in the office. She was much classier than that. She was a master at holding herself in check, and nothing ever seemed to faze her. Even when McNamara was putting pressure on her to finish a project, Cara always held her composure, and never seemed at all hassled by anything. Her constant and considerable frostiness towards the rest of her colleagues earned Cara the nickname 'Ice Maiden'.

Mark Dignan had explained this to Roan a few days after he joined their project team. She never socialised with them, he said, not even at the Christmas Party. "She stays for the meal, just to make an appearance, but as soon as the tables are cleared, she's off."

Roan had been intrigued by Cara from the very beginning – any red-blooded male would be attracted by her looks alone – not to mention the fact that she was cool, distant, and completely uninterested in him. And Roan wasn't used to not being noticed by women.

She had let her guard drop a little that evening in the pub. It had been a frantic week, and everyone on the team had worked like demons to get the Second Direct Insurance project completed on time. There had been jubilation in the office when Ross McNamara announced that he was taking them all out for drinks afterwards. "You too, Cara," he had said to her. "You're not getting out of it this time – we all deserve a little celebration after the terrific work we did this week."

To Roan's surprise, Cara had agreed, and had been knocking back glasses of wine in the pub like there was going to be a grape shortage.

Pete Brennan had bet Roan and Mark fifty quid that Cara would end up 'dragging him home' by the end of the night. That had been as good as a dare for Roan. He decided there and then that he would wipe the stupid grin off his workmate's face.

The likes of Pete Brennan was no match for him when it came to charming the birds. He'd wipe the floor with him.

Cara had been a little wary when Roan had first started chatting to her at the bar. He started out using his tried and trusted methods, like complimenting her on her appearance, and pretending to be deeply interested in everything she had to say. That usually made most birds weak at the knees. Not Cara, though. She had been very difficult to break down.

It was only when Roan began to talk to her about work that the conversation became at all animated. A definite gleam appeared in Cara's eye as she talked spiritedly about her job at Evanston Corporation. Then, little by little, as the evening went on, and the drinks kept flowing, Roan's compliments and loaded remarks finally began to hit the spot.

Pete had been livid when he copped on to what Roan was at. He tried on a number of occasions to join their conversation, but Roan, well-practised in monopolising a woman's attentions, was having none of it.

Even Roan had to admit he was surprised when Cara agreed to go clubbing with them. Mark had been insistent they all go on to Copper Faced Jack's – 'the best pulling joint in Dublin,' so that he could 'get some real action'.

Roan had taken Cara's hand and she hadn't pulled away, as they walked along behind the others towards Stephen's Green.

Before they reached the nightclub, Cara all of a sudden pulled Roan into a doorway, and kissed him urgently on the lips. He had been totally bowled over by the fact that she had made the first move. After all, he wasn't really sure that he *would* make a move on her – it was more a question of pissing off Pete Brennan, and messing up his precious bet, as well as bruising his ego.

He had Jenny to think of, after all. He had had enough close shaves to last him a lifetime.

Still, he debated with himself, the likes of Cara was enough to tempt any man, single or not. And Jenny wouldn't know the difference anyway. She was too caught up with work these days. She hardly paid him any attention at all. If she *did* find out that he had a bit of a snog, she couldn't really blame him for looking for a bit of affection elsewhere.

Anyway she wouldn't find out.

Jenny was probably tucked up at home, sitting in front of the telly, wrecked after a week's work. She had been going on and on at him all week about how tired she was lately. There was certainly no question of her going out on the razz tonight.

The nightclub was packed and as soon as they got inside, Roan realised that he wasn't really in the mood for clubbing.

"Do you want to get out of here?" he heard Cara ask him over the loud music. "It's getting too crowded."

Roan studied her face for a moment, a little unsure of what he wanted to do next. It would be the easiest thing in the world to go somewhere with Cara, have what he was certain would be amazing sex, and then go back to the flat he shared with Jenny. She'd probably be fast asleep, and wouldn't suspect a thing. But something inside Roan made him hesitate, and he didn't quite know what. After all, he thought, looking over his shoulder to where the others were standing at the bar, he would look like a right fool if he didn't follow through with Cara. But did it really matter?

Just then, one of Jenny's favourite songs blared from the loudspeakers. Cara, seemingly frustrated by the lack of a response to her question, lowered his face towards hers, and kissed him with a greater urgency, hoping to make up his mind for him.

Roan quickly pulled away from Cara. That was enough, he thought. He wasn't going any further with this – hearing that song was definitely some kind of sign.

He was just about to tell Cara that he was going home – without her, when he caught sight of Jenny, staring right at him, from where she stood shocked and bewildered on the dance floor.

Chapter 24

"He's the last person I want to see today," Jenny whispered into the telephone mouthpiece. She sincerely hoped that Barry Ferguson, who was going through a filing cabinet just outside her office, didn't overhear her conversation with Jackie, the receptionist. Barry certainly wouldn't approve of her refusing to meet with Robbie Courtney. Robbie was the son of Dan Courtney, a local hotelier, who held a variety of investment accounts at the branch. He was therefore a golf buddy and 'very close friend' of Barry's.

"Will you tell him to make an appointment in future, Jackie?" Jenny said quietly. "I'm up to my eyes at the moment, and with Conor out sick I haven't a spare minute."

"Right," Jackie said curtly, cutting her off.

Jenny shook her head as she replaced the receiver. Jackie was annoyed with her, because now *she'd* have to face the wrath of Robbie Courtney, once Jenny refused to see him. Well, there was nothing she could do about that, she thought, turning to her computer screen. She had enough on her plate at the moment without worrying about upsetting spoilt teenagers. Conor had been out sick for over a week, and without him, the work seemed never-ending.

She checked the time on the corner of her computer screen. It was nearly lunch-time. Karen was in Dun Laoghaire today, visiting a relative in St Michael's Hospital. They had arranged to meet for lunch in a small café on the seafront. Jenny was looking forward to it immensely. She didn't see her friend as often as she'd have liked, since moving out of Rathmines to Dun Laoghaire, almost six months before.

Karen had thought she was crazy to just pack up and leave all her friends, almost immediately after the break-up.

"You'll be all the way out there, on your own, Jen," she had said to her. "You need friends around you to help you get over this."

But Jenny had been insistent. She didn't want to stay on her own in the flat she had shared with Roan; there were just too many memories.

When the landlord increased the rent shortly afterwards, her mind was firmly made up. There was no point in her paying a huge amount for a two bedroomed flat, and she certainly didn't want to stay in a dingy student bed-sit. The spacious one-bed apartment overlooking the harbour that she rented in Dun Laoghaire was perfect for her and she had no regrets about leaving Rathmines. She needed solitude, and plenty of time to think things over. She couldn't have handled staying in Rathmines, and she knew that she was bound to run into Roan again, eventually. For her own sanity, and her own good, Jenny knew that she needed to stay as far away from Roan Williams as possible.

She had spent many evenings out on her balcony at first, looking out over the sea, watching the sailboats and ferries coming in and out of the harbour, and going over and over in her mind every word that Roan had said, and every lie he had told throughout their time together.

How could she have been so stupid for so long? Jenny had asked herself that question time and time again. She remembered all the times he had let her down in the past, and all the pathetic excuses he had given her.

Yet, even now, Jenny wished that Roan would put his arms around her, and tell her that he had made a dreadful mistake – that everything was a horrible lie, and that she was the one he wanted.

Not surprisingly, he *had* tried telling her all this, after she had finally caught him in the act with that girl. She had recognised her as one of his workmates from Evanston. They had met briefly at Roan's Christmas party. Jenny had found her very stand-offish at the time. Maybe that was the reason why. Maybe she and Roan had been carrying on behind her back for ages.

She hadn't realised that something could hurt so much until that night. It was as if Roan had reached right inside her, and grabbed her heart in a vice-like grip. She had felt dizzy and sick to her stomach as she watched them together, but yet still couldn't quite believe that it was actually Roan, until he looked up and saw her staring at them.

That was the very last time she saw him, Jenny thought, her eyes beginning to fill with tears as she typed. She had run straight out of the nightclub and all the way home, without stopping once to catch her breath.

Karen had been an absolute rock afterwards, making sure that Roan stayed away from the flat and away from Jenny, who flatly refused to see him, much as she wanted to. She knew that if she saw him face to face, there was a possibility that she might fall for his excuses all over again. For her own sake, she couldn't let that happen, not any more. Karen had made up a bed for Jenny in her own house, and supervised Roan when he came round to collect his things from the flat.

She hadn't pulled any punches in telling Jenny exactly what she thought of him either, she thought wryly, remembering one conversation where Karen had been particularly brutal in her assessment of the relationship. Roan had phoned her a number of times at work afterwards, trying to 'explain everything' and telling her that he loved her, but Jenny had been resolute. She had absolutely refused to meet with him, or listen to his explanations. In the end, she had asked the receptionist not to put his calls through to her.

It had been very difficult not to talk to him, and not let him explain himself, but Jenny knew that if she didn't hold her nerve then, she never would.

It had taken her months of introspection before she came to realise how wrong the relationship had been. Moving away from Rathmines, and putting a distance between her and Roan gave her the time and the space to look at it all clearly.

Yet, time hadn't quite diminished her love for him. That was something she couldn't run away from. Not yet.

She picked up a file and studied it absently. It was a miracle that she still had her job here at the bank, with the way she had carried on after the break-up. After a few weeks wandering around like a zombie, unable to concentrate on anything, Barry had one day called her into his office.

"You're an excellent worker, Jenny, but lately you've been making a lot of mistakes and Marion tells me you've been having trouble concentrating on the training," he had said in his best 'you can come to me' voice. "If you need to talk about anything, please don't hesitate to say something to either myself or Marion. We're not stupid, you know – it's obvious that there's something seriously bothering you, and we don't want it to affect your career with us." He had smiled and patted her hand paternally.

Jenny had been mortified. She had decided there and then to buck herself up, and contain her brooding to outside working hours. She knew Barry had meant well, but it had been terribly embarrassing nonetheless.

Marion's head appeared around the door of her office. "Jenny, it's just after one – you'd better go to lunch."

She looked up, startled for a moment. With all Jenny's musing, she hadn't realised that the half-hour had passed, and it was time to meet Karen.

She collected her bag and her coat, went downstairs, and out into the crisp September day with a slight spring in her step, anxious to hear her friend's news.

* * *

Karen groaned and pushed her plate away from her. She and Jenny were having lunch at Gino's, an Italian-style café/deli near the seafront. The place was surprisingly quiet, she noticed, considering the time of day and the quality of the menu. Karen, who had ordered bruschetta before Jenny arrived, struggled to finish her huge Italian salad.

"I bought a fabulously slinky Ben de Lisi dress for Tessa's wedding last week, but if I carry on like this, I'll never be able to fit into it! Did you get your invite?"

Jenny sipped her mineral water and nodded. "It came last week. Judging by the fancy invitation, I'd say it'll be a very lavish affair."

"Lavish is not the word for it!" Karen said. "I honestly think she's trying to outdo royalty with her designer wedding dress and her custom-made wedding rings, although I don't know where she's going to get the thrones from!"

Jenny smiled.

"You should see the amount of wedding magazines she has," Karen continued. "I'd say Gerry is sick to the teeth of the bloody weddings, at this stage. She's a woman possessed!"

"Oh, well, it'll be all over this time two months." Jenny popped a cherry tomato into her mouth. "I'm looking forward to it, actually. I haven't had a decent night out in ages."

Karen looked at her friend, worriedly. "You should meet up with us more often, you know. It can't be good for you, being all the way out here on your own."

"Karen, don't start – you'd swear I was a million miles

away. Anyway, I'm fine as I am, really. I'm pretty much over everything now, and I'm getting on with it."

Karen wasn't convinced. She couldn't believe the change in Jenny in the last few months. She was thin, and drawn-looking, and the clothes were practically hanging off her, she had lost so much weight. She had bags under her eyes, and didn't seem too bothered about concealing them with make-up. In fact, these days Jenny looked and behaved like a completely different person to the sunny, vibrant and glamorous young woman who had moved in with Karen nearly a year and a half ago. Once she moved away, into that big empty apartment, Jenny didn't keep in contact as much as Karen had hoped, either. She couldn't remember the last time the two of them had gone on a night out together. Maybe she should try and organise something.

Jenny seemed to read her thoughts and smiled softly.

"Don't give me that look, Karen. I'm fine, really."

"I know you are, Jen. I just wish you'd come and see us more often, that's all. Shane is always asking about you."

"I must call in and see what you've done with the house. Did you get the bedrooms finished yet?"

"What do *you* think?" Karen looked sheepish.

"Don't tell me you haven't done anything since?" Jenny said, her eyes widening in surprise.

Karen made a face. "You know what I'm like, Jen – I get stuck in big-time at the beginning of a project and then I just get bored."

"But it's your house, Karen – you can't have a load of unfinished rooms everywhere! What does Shane think?"

Karen snorted. "He's as bad. He got it into his head that he'd be able to change the tiles around the bath, and he borrowed one of those tile-cutters from some guy he knows from work." She rolled her eyes and sniggered. "You should hear the cursing and spluttering that was coming from the bathroom afterwards."

"So, did he finish it?" Jenny asked, unable to keep from smiling herself.

"Not at all! I made him get in a professional to tidy up after him. It cost a fortune, but you couldn't leave it like it was, one half dark blue and the other half yellow. It looked like a Tipperary GAA flag! At least no one else can tell that the bedroom is a half-assed job."

"I don't know," Jenny said, shaking her head in wonder. "The two of you are so well matched, you were bound to end up together."

"Yeah, shame about his family, though," Karen said sarcastically.

"What do you mean? I thought you and Mrs Quinn got on really well."

Karen shook her head. "No, Nellie's all right *sometimes* – it's the brother I can't stand. Remember the older one in England – the one that guaranteed the mortgage for us?"

Jenny nodded.

"Well, Jack – that's his name," she continued, "is acting the prat about it ever since. Shane is sorry he ever asked him."

"I don't understand. I thought he offered to do it for you," Jenny said, frowning.

"So did I. But apparently Nellie was the one who suggested it to Jack in the first place. Initially, he was against it, but I think she made him feel guilty about the fact that he had two properties and all this money, and here's poor old Shane, starting out with nothing."

She signalled to the waiter for a fresh pot of tea. "He was home a couple of weeks ago and we went up to Meath to see him. I hadn't seen him since that first time, and I wanted to thank him in person for what he did. Big mistake."

"Why, what happened?" Jenny said, leaning forward in her seat.

"He acted the absolute prat. Kept making sly comments about Shane, and his new job. He said that Shane would have been a hell of a lot better off working in Germany, more or less insinuating that the job he has now wasn't good enough, and he might have trouble making the repayments. You should have heard him, Jen. We went to the pub and he was watching Shane like a hawk every time he bought another pint. You'd swear Shane was out on the razz every night of the week, and didn't give a toss about his mortgage repayments!"

"That's awful!" Jenny said. "Poor Shane, he must feel terrible! As if either of you would default on the mortgage – you both have perfectly good jobs."

"Well, there's nothing we can do about it now. If I had my way, I'd tell your man to stuff his bloody guarantee and we'd go our own way. But, we have the mortgage and the house now, so . . . " She trailed off and spooned sugar into her tea.

"Have you made any plans for a wedding yourself?" Jenny asked, changing the subject.

"Well, remember I had that little chat with Shane about

it all before? He still doesn't understand exactly how I feel, but at least he's not pushing it as much these days to set a date. I'll see what happens after Tessa's wedding. Maybe it might get me in the mood!" She winked and raised the cup to her mouth.

"I take it that you won't be commissioning a wedding-gown designer for your big day!" Jenny said mischievously.

"No way!" Karen burst out laughing. "That kind of thing isn't my style at all!" She glanced at the clock above the deli counter. "I think I might do a bit of shopping after this. Might as well make the most of my day off."

"I need a day off myself soon if I want to get something to wear for Tessa's wedding," Jenny said. "I can't remember the last time I went shopping for clothes."

Karen noticed her staring into space, apparently lost in her own thoughts. Probably remembering the last time she could afford some new clothes, Karen thought sourly. She knew Jenny was tight for money after all the cash she had lent to Roan which had never been repaid. Not to mention the rent that had built up on the Rathmines flat, which Jenny had to pay in full before she left.

She sighed heavily. Sod it, she might as well say something.

"Jen, look, I don't know whether I should tell you this or not but . . . "

Jenny's head snapped up. "Tell me what?"

Karen took a deep breath. "I don't know if Roan's been in contact with you lately, or whether he's phoned you at work but . . ." She noticed Jenny's eyes cloud over at the mention of his name. She obviously knew nothing about it then. Maybe the rat was finally leaving her in peace.

"Well, it seems that he's moving to the States at the end of this month."

Karen watched Jenny flinch slightly at this.

"Oh . . . I see," Jenny said, her voice low. "How – how do you know that?"

"He met Shane in town a while ago. You know how the two of them always seemed to get along so well?" Karen had to resist the urge to add that she couldn't figure out how Shane could find anything in common with such a lying, cheating bastard.

"Anyway," she continued, "they went for a pint, and Roan told Shane that he and some others from the Dublin office were being voluntarily transferred to Evanston's parent company in New York, to work on something in-house."

"With *her*?" Jenny asked, in a small voice, still refusing to meet her eyes.

Karen understood. "No. He told Shane that that night was a big mistake, a once-off. I don't know if that was just for the cameras though, knowing that Shane would come back and tell me, and that I would no doubt tell you. Apparently, she has a two-year old son. Maybe Roan just didn't want to play daddy to him."

Karen could have kicked herself when she saw Jenny wince. "Ah, Jen, I'm sorry," she said softly. "I didn't mean to be so callous – I just can't help myself sometimes. Don't mind me."

Jenny brushed it off. "It's all right, I know how you feel about him, and you've got good reason. It still hurts to talk about it, though." Her eyes glistened brightly. "Did he tell Shane how long he'd be gone?"

"I'm not sure, but I got the impression from Shane that it'll be for a few months to start with, and maybe longer afterwards, depending on how it goes."

Karen looked across at her friend with concern. Jenny looked so sad, so broken. Despite her earlier protests about being fine, she could see that she wasn't fine at all, far from it. "I'm sorry, Jen. I had to tell you because I thought you should know. Believe me, I'd love to have kept it from you until he was well gone, but what kind of a friend would I be? It wouldn't have been fair of me to keep you in the dark. Just in case you want to –"

"What?" Jenny said sharply, "In case I wanted to say goodbye?" A fiercely determined look appeared on her face, and she sat up straight in her chair. "Karen, Roan Williams said goodbye to me a long time ago. Naturally, it's a shock knowing that now he's finally out of my life for good, but it shouldn't bother me that much and it doesn't. I'm over him now."

"Good, Jen, I'm glad about that," Karen said quietly, "but don't you think that it's about time you started living your life again? You don't have to hide away out here like this on your own, you know."

"I'm fine, Karen. I've already told you that. Look, I appreciate you telling me, you were right to do so, but I'm fine, really. It was a bit of a shock, but I'm fine." Jenny stood up from the table and rummaged under the seat for her handbag. "I'm due back at work in a few minutes so I'd better go," she said shortly.

"I'll walk you back."

Karen quickly drained her teacup, which was by then stone-cold. She picked up her bag and coat, and hurried out after Jenny, who was practically racing up the street.

"Hey, hold on will you? I can't walk that fast in these bloody heels!"

"Sorry." Jenny slowed her pace but, as Karen caught up with her, she turned her face away.

Karen could see immediately that her cheeks were drenched with tears. "Oh honey," she said sympathetically, "come here." Karen put her hands around Jenny, and held her close, while Jenny collapsed in tears against her shoulder. She shook her head from side to side. "It's all right, Jen – everything's going to be all right."

Chapter 25

Later that evening, Karen struggled to fit through the front door with all the shopping she had bought in Dun Laoghaire.

She stopped short when she saw the state of her living-room. Granted it was never tidy at the best of times, but today it looked as though at least twenty Andrex puppies had been let loose in the house. There was what looked like a complete roll of toilet paper – *wet* toilet paper – strewn across the coffee table, the Mexican pine coffee table that Jenny had given them as a housewarming present. That same Mexican pine coffee table now resembled one of Picasso's rejects, it was covered with so many multicoloured splashes of paint.

Green and blue-coloured handprints had been smeared on the wall beside the television and on the television screen itself. Karen noticed that they were small handprints – *children's* handprints. She was trying to make some sense of the situation when the realisation dawned on her. Keanu and bloody Pocahontas Byrne!

"Hi, hon!" A smiling Shane stuck his head around the kitchen door. "You're back early!"

"Shane – what the hell is going on here?" she asked in disbelief, surveying the devastation before her.

"Hi, Karen!" she heard his sister Marie's voice call out, from where she sat with Shane in the kitchen.

Karen was almost afraid to put her head around the door in case Shane's nieces and nephew had also targeted the kitchen with their guerrilla-warfare tactics. But the devastation had been somehow confined to the kitchen table, which was covered with semi-eaten chips, half-digested chips and squashed-into-the-kitchen-table chips. Not to mention the ketchup. If she didn't know better, Karen could have sworn that Keanu was performing open-heart surgery on his burger; there was so much red on his plate and on *her* table. And Honty was happily dipping the head of what looked like a brand new doll into a jar of Hellmann's. The little girl licked the mayonnaise from Barbie's hair before promptly lowering her doll back into the jar for a second helping. The baby, who for some reason was called by the relatively ordinary name of Mary – her mother must have run out of ideas, Karen thought – was sitting happily in Marie's lap. Shane sat chatting with his sister at the table, both seemingly oblivious to the devastation surrounding them. Marie looked up when Karen entered.

"Karen, I hope you don't mind, but Shane said that you'd baby-sit for us tonight. Me and Frank are going to a show in Dublin, and Nellie thought it might be nice for you and Shane to get in a bit of practice." She nudged Shane and winked. "You know, for when you get a move on with that niece or nephew I've been waiting for."

Oh-my-God! Unable to speak for shock, Karen kept repeating the words over and over again in her head. Baby-sit these three? What was Shane thinking?

"Shane – can I have a word please?" she said finally.

He looked up quickly at her sharp tone.

"What?" he asked, when they were in the next room and out of earshot.

"What? What do you mean – what?" Karen was red-faced. "Why did you tell her we'd baby-sit?"

Shane shrugged. "I thought it would be nice to give Marie and Frank a break for a night. They rarely get out on their own any more, and when Mam told me about the show out in the Red Cow Inn, and that Marie was anxious to go, I thought it would be the perfect opportunity for us to give a hand."

Karen now understood what it felt like to be a goldfish. She kept opening and closing her mouth but no words would come out. Shane seemed to have it all worked out.

"I've tidied up the spare room so Marie and Frank can spend the night here afterwards," he said, mistaking Karen's silence for assent. "Then they can both have a few drinks instead of having to travel back to Rathrigh. We can take the cushions off the couch and put Keanu and Honty on the floor in our room, and she brought a cot for Mary so there shouldn't be a problem ... what? Why are you looking at me like that?"

Karen was furious. "Shane – did you not think to check if *any* of this was OK with me? I live here too and I don't fancy spending my Friday night running around after three mad children!"

258

"Jeez, Karen, will you keep your voice down," Shane said, dropping his own voice to a whisper in case his sister might hear them. "I know they can be a bit boisterous, but –"

"A bit boisterous – *are you kidding me*?" Karen hissed. "Look at the state of the living- room – not to mention the kitchen!" She shook her head. "Did you even *think* to ask me what I thought?"

Shane looked hurt. "They're my family, Karen. Now that we have a place of our own, I can see them more often than when I lived in the flat. Obviously, I couldn't invite them there – you know yourself what a crummy place that was."

"So you decided to invite them here – to our house and let them loose on that instead? Shane, take a look around you! The place looks like a bomb hit it!"

"Look, it's not that bad," he said, following her gaze around the room. "The toilet roll can be picked up, and I'm pretty sure that the paint is only watercolour, so we can wash that off and –"

"Shane, it is – I mean it *was*, a Mexican pine coffee table," Karen interrupted. Despite her protestations to Jenny, she had worked very hard decorating her home, and was proud of the results. It was awful to just come home on a Friday evening and see it looking like that. "*We* won't be washing anything off. It's not varnished. The paint will never come off it – they might as well have used Ronseal Quick Drying Woodstain on the thing – beautiful but tough! Which is what your sister would be well advised to be with those kids – *tough*!"

Shane stepped back. "You're talking about my family Karen," he said, his voice hard.

Seeing his hurt expression, Karen immediately felt guilty. "You're right. You're right," she said wearily. "I'm sorry, but I'm just not used to having children around."

"I know that. But I like having them around. And as I said, I don't get much of a chance to spend time with them. I'd really like to do Marie the favour tonight, Karen."

She bit her lip. "Well, I suppose it might be OK but, it's just . . . well . . . I just don't really know what to do – I won't have to breastfeed any of them or anything, will I?" She had seen Marie do this once with Mary and it had terrified her.

Shane's eyes twinkled with amusement. "You really don't know much about children, do you? It's OK. They won't bite."

Karen smiled weakly. "Are you sure – that Keanu looks a little dangerous!"

Shane put an arm around her shoulders. "Go on into the kitchen and I'll make you a nice cup of tea. And maybe Marie can give you some child-minding tips," he added devilishly.

Karen followed him, her heart pounding. She knew then that, terrified or not, she'd have to go through with this. Maybe it wouldn't be too bad; maybe the kids might be worn out from all the running around. Maybe she wouldn't have to do anything. Karen smiled faintly at Marie who offered her the baby to hold. "Say hello to Auntie Karen!" she said, in a sing-song voice.

Karen's hands shook as she held the baby in her arms. Was she holding her the right way? She did seem to be squirming an awful lot – maybe she was hurting her. She sat down and awkwardly laid the child on her lap.

Karen looked up, feeling Shane watching her. Her fiancé's expression conveyed pure gratitude and seeing this, her heart melted.

She'd get through tonight, she decided – for Shane's sake.

* * *

"I was scared stiff," Karen said to Tessa, the following afternoon, "I didn't know what to do with them."

Tessa hid a grin. "What do you mean you were scared stiff? They're only kids, for goodness sake!"

They were sitting on Tessa's sofa, almost three-quarter ways through a bottle of wine, and most of the way through Tessa's bridal magazines.

"I don't know – it's hard to explain, really. I just – I just don't know what to say to them – or even how to *speak* to them. That baby voice that people use sometimes, with me it doesn't come out right, and I just feel silly – it's as though they know I'm faking it!"

Tessa laughed. "So you're not planning to have any of your own anytime soon, I take it?"

"Do you know something, Tessa? I really couldn't imagine myself with a child of my own. I think I'd be a terrible mother. I'm not used to dealing with them or having them around. Shane's nieces and nephews – well, it's all new to me. I'm a little scared, to be honest – not so much of the kids, just the idea of them."

Tessa waved her away. "Don't be silly. Everyone is different with their own children. And from what you said before, Shane's crowd aren't exactly well-behaved little angels, are they?"

"No, but," Karen exhaled deeply, "Tessa, to be perfectly honest, the thought of having children absolutely petrifies me and I don't know if that's ever going to change." She made a face. "And the way Shane's family are always going on dropping hints about our having a family, I don't know what I'll do."

"What does Shane think?"

"I really don't know. He knows that I don't exactly fall all over the kids whenever they visit but . . . " She shrugged.

Tessa looked thoughtful. "You said Shane's family are always dropping hints?"

"Yes, particularly his mother."

"And do you get on well with her – enough to maybe tell her how you feel?"

Karen shrugged. "Possibly. Nellie's OK. But she annoys me sometimes when she visits the house, in fact *every* time she visits the house. She always seems to find some fault with the place."

"What do you mean?"

Karen sat up in her chair. "Well, one day for instance, she picked up the sweeping brush and started poking around on the ceiling with it. She told me that she had spotted a few cobwebs up there."

"Oh?" Tessa arched an eyebrow.

"And another day, she came out of the bathroom and announced that the towels in there were beginning to smell. I wouldn't mind, but earlier that same day, I had been nagging Shane to pick up the towels he used for his shower. And sure enough, Mammy Dearest had to spot them."

Tessa made a face. "She had a bit of a cheek coming right out and saying it to you though, didn't she?"

"Yeah, but as it happened, she was right. Anyway, I don't think she means anything by it – she's just trying to help."

"Maybe, but I don't think I'd put up with Gerry's mother telling me what to do in my own house – whenever I finally get one, that is."

"Oh, how's the building going?" Karen asked.

"Not too bad, actually. The roof is on and Dad is waiting on the plasterer now."

Tessa and Gerry had decided that once they were married they would move to a village in West Cork, where Tessa was from originally. Tessa's dad was currently overseeing the construction of what would eventually become their new home. Gerry, who worked as a website designer, was planning to set up on his own and would run his business from the new house. Tessa hoped to secure a nursing position at a hospital close by and, with her widespread nursing experience, didn't anticipate any problems with getting a job.

Karen would miss her when she left. What with Jenny shutting herself away from the world out in Dun Laoghaire, and Tessa leaving for Cork, all of Karen's friends seemed to be disappearing from around her.

"Oh, I met Jenny yesterday," she said, changing the subject.

Tessa clapped her hands together. "I have to go out and see her myself. How is she these days?"

Karen grimaced. "Much improved, but I think it got to her a little when she heard about your man's impending departure."

"Oh, he hasn't contacted her then?"

Karen shook her head. "Thank God. Maybe he's developed a conscience and has decided to let her get on with her life. Or maybe he's just forgotten all about her. Rat!"

Tessa took a deep breath. "I met him one day in town," she said. "And he seemed really miserable."

"So he should be," Karen interjected. "She's been miserable for long enough, so why shouldn't he be? Anyway," she said, stealing a cigarette from Tessa, having forgotten to bring her own, "what was wrong with him? Feeling sorry for himself because he was caught out in his true colours, was it?"

Tessa paused. "Don't you think that sometimes you might have been just a little bit too hard on the guy?"

"What? You can't be serious! You were there that night; you saw what happened – what he did. You saw how devastated Jenny was – what do you mean I might have been too hard on the bastard?"

"Calm down, that's not what I meant. I know that Roan was wrong to do what he did to Jenny. But I think he knows that. And I think he really cares about her."

Karen set her glass down on the table and folded her arms across her chest.

"You're as bad as Shane – he thinks he's a great lad too. Tell me this, Tessa, would you be as forgiving towards Gerry if he treated *you* like Roan treated Jenny?"

"No, but . . . " Knowing she was fighting a losing battle, Tessa gave up. "You're probably right. It's just he seemed genuinely sorry for what had happened, and he was really anxious to find out how Jenny was doing."

Karen sniffed. "Probably wondering if she had calmed down enough for him to weasel his way into her affections again."

Tessa had to laugh. "Karen, do something for me, will you? Keep reminding me for the rest of my life that I should never, *ever* make an enemy out of you."

Karen giggled. "I know – I'm a cow. But Tessa, you didn't see half of what I saw throughout that relationship. When Jenny came back from Australia, she was so bubbly, and happy, and *confident*. When I saw her yesterday . . ." She shook her head. "I don't know – it was hard to believe I was talking to the same person. He shattered her, Tessa, really shattered her. I think she had put so much faith in *him*, and so much faith in that fortune-teller's prediction, that she just couldn't cope with finding out that it was all wrong."

"Do you think she'll be OK – eventually, I mean?" Tessa asked.

Karen gave a firm nod of the head. "She'll be OK – as long as that bastard stays out of her life and she never sees him again."

Chapter 26

Jenny couldn't believe it. How could she have been so careless?

It had happened the same day Karen had told her about Roan moving to New York. That was the last time she worked in the Commercial Cash, she was sure of it.

Barry paced up and down the office in front of her.

"I can't believe you could have done something like that, Jenny! What the hell has got into you lately? A bloody trainee wouldn't do something so stupid!"

"Barry, I don't know how it could have happened," Jenny, afraid to meet his eyes, stared down at her lap. "I just didn't realise."

She had never seen Barry so annoyed, and it was not a pretty sight. His face was bright red and screwed up in anger, and his eyes flashed dangerously.

"Just didn't realise! I should hope so, Jenny! After all, we wouldn't want you handing out dummy notes to all our customers just on a whim, would we?"

Jenny flinched at his words. She couldn't believe what she had done. The same afternoon after her lunch with Karen, Marion had asked her to step in and cover the Commercial Cash area for the afternoon, as one of the girls had gone home sick. Thursday was late opening, as well as being one of the busiest days of the week, so they needed extra cover there. It was the very last thing Jenny wanted to do, as her thoughts had been everywhere that afternoon. She remembered finding it very difficult to concentrate on anything after she had found out that Roan was leaving the country, possibly for good.

The Commercial Cash was a secure area, separate from the regular cashiers, and it usually dealt in large sums of money. The cashiers there took in substantial cash lodgements, and dispensed large amounts, generally to companies who paid their staff wages every week in cash. Jenny remembered that they had been especially busy that afternoon, and that she had been rapidly doling out more cash than she was taking in. She had forgotten to reset the timer on her safe and, as the safe was time-locked, she knew she had a few minutes to wait in order to replenish the notes in her drawer.

One of the directors from a local company had come up to her in a terrible hurry, looking to withdraw cash from the business account. She had been so harassed and harried by his impatience, that Jenny had mistakenly given him a wad of dummy notes, along with the rest of his cash.

The dummy notes were an Alliance Trust Bank security precaution, which usually resided in the cashier's drawer to be given out in the event of a hold-up. This cash was often referred to as the 'bomb' by some bank staff, and the reason for that was because, after a robbery, the fake wad of notes exploded a coloured dye onto the thief's hands, clothes, and (hopefully from the bank's point of view) onto the rest of the stolen notes, rendering them useless.

Jenny had given the bomb notes to an important customer of the bank. He had telephoned Barry the following morning, and had been absolutely livid. Jenny was only hearing about it now, because she had taken a sick day on Friday, and was out for two days the following week. The news of Roan's departure was an emotional setback for her, and she had felt she needed some uninterrupted time to decide whether or not she should get in contact with him before he left.

"What do you suppose I should do about this, Jenny?" Barry snapped. "How am I supposed to pacify a man that had one of his Armani suits ruined, as a result of your stupidity? Not to mention the fact that his hands are still covered in blue dye nearly a week later! He was on his way out of the country that same afternoon for a meeting, and he had to cancel it. He says he couldn't face anyone, not to mention an important client, in that state!"

"Barry, I don't know what to say. It was a mistake – I really am very, very sorry."

She *was* terribly sorry, but the image of this self-important businessman (as he undoubtedly was) covered in irremovable blue dye was comical. She could just imagine his face when the thing exploded all over him! Jenny bit her lip, trying to bite back a threatening smile. Barry was anything but amused.

The manager sat back in his chair, folded his arms

across his chest and exhaled loudly. Jenny noticed that the colour in his face had begun to recede a little.

"Well, I suppose what's done is done, at this stage," he said in a normal voice. "There's not a lot any of us can do now, except try to patch thing up as best we can. He's a decent enough customer, you know. The company's got an excellent credit grading, and Kennedy has investments, a pension and life assurance with us. We can't afford to lose him as a customer."

Jenny nodded. "I'll speak to him, Barry. Maybe now he'll have calmed down a little. He's the director of InTech, you say?"

"Michael Kennedy. I've never met him myself – he usually deals with the Assistant Manager."

Barry picked up the company file on the desk in front of him, studied it for a moment and then snapped it shut, before sliding it across to Jenny. "His contact details are all there. I suggest you write a personal letter of apology to him, and perhaps follow it up with a phone call to his office. Sweeten him up – send flowers or something – I don't know, just make sure he knows that this bank is not in the habit of putting imbeciles behind a cash desk." He dismissed her with a wave of his hand. "Go on, back to your office. I know you didn't do it on purpose – just try not to have an off-day from now on, OK?" He grimaced. "Now *I* have to try and sort him out with a replacement bloody suit. Unfortunately there's no dry cleaner on earth that can help him with that blue stuff."

Jenny said nothing more. She stood up and went towards the door, eager to get out of the office and away from Barry. When he was angry, it was as well to stay as far away from him as possible, particularly when she happened to be the cause of his anger in the first place.

However Jenny noticed a tiny glimmer of amusement in Barry's eyes when, on her way out the door, he suddenly asked her: "By the way, Jen, do you know if Arnott's do Armani suits these days, by any chance?"

* * *

One morning, nearly two weeks after she had sent him a ridiculously expensive gift basket, Jenny got a visit from Michael Kennedy.

The entire episode with 'the bomb' had made her famous throughout the Alliance Trust network. The story had been gleefully retold all over the district, not surprisingly becoming funnier and more exaggerated with each telling. Even the staff in some country branches had heard about it. Jenny's workmates in Dun Laoghaire had been teasing her unmercifully ever since.

"Feeling a bit *blue* today, Jenny?" Brendan had asked her cheekily one morning in the staff canteen, soon after the episode. Despite herself, Jenny couldn't help but giggle.

"I don't think *I'd* ever be able to afford an Armani suit," added Brian Keyes, getting into the swing of things. "Don't they cost an absolute *bomb*?"

Everyone roared with laughter as Brian and Declan gave one another a high five, delighted with their little act. Jenny enjoyed the banter; it took her mind off the fact that Roan had left for the States the previous weekend. Karen had been in contact, wondering if Jenny had heard from him before he went. Jenny hadn't, and was now resigned to the fact she was unlikely to ever see or hear from Roan Williams again.

The thought didn't disturb her as much as she thought it might. It merely meant that now, many months after the break-up, she could finally begin getting on with her life, instead of hiding away from it. It would be easier for her to do that now, without the risk of running into him again. Dublin was a relatively small city and chances were that their paths would certainly have crossed sometime in the future. Jenny didn't think she could handle that. This was the best way. Maybe now she could finally begin to let go.

Katrina, a young trainee from downstairs, had telephoned Jenny's office to warn of her of Kennedy's impending arrival.

"Jenny, Jenny, that fella that you gave the bomb-yoke to – he wanted to know where you were. I told him where your office is and he's gone upstairs and –"

"It's OK, Katrina. Thanks for letting me know," Jenny said quickly, trying to sound calmer than she felt. She had butterflies in her stomach as she put the phone down. Kennedy was here! What would he say to her?

She had sent him an impressively worded letter, and telephoned his office numerous times to apologise, but to her annoyance the pompous so-and-so hadn't even bothered to return her calls. His PA had seemed to know exactly who Jenny Hamilton was and obviously the reason for her call. The girl had been haughty and dismissive of her on the telephone. Jenny had got the distinct impression that an apologetic letter and a wine-and-chocolate gift basket would not nearly be enough to mollify the esteemed director of InTech.

She stood up and went out towards the waiting-area. A heavyset man in his late fifties sat on the sofa, flicking through *Banking News*. He looked up as Jenny approached. She tried to keep the nervousness out of her voice as she spoke.

"Mr Kennedy? Hello, I'm Jenny Hamilton, pleased to finally meet you." She smiled nervously and offered her hand.

He hesitated for a moment, and then shook her hand with a slightly confused expression. Jenny was surprised at his appearance. He didn't look like the executive type at all with his brown tweed ensemble. Where was the famous designer suit?

She certainly couldn't remember serving him that day. Then again, it had been so busy, she could have been serving George Clooney and she wouldn't have noticed.

"Did you get me box?" he asked, in a thick Wicklow accent. "I'm waitin' for me box."

Jenny looked at him, her mind blank. What was Kennedy on about? At that moment, Marion rushed upstairs towards the two of them, a safety-deposit box in her arms.

"Mr Kenny, you can use this room if you like." She indicated a room just behind Jenny. "Close the door for some privacy, and I'll be back to you in about ten minutes to put the box back in the safe, OK?"

The man looked from Marion to Jenny, then took the box into the room and closed the door behind him.

"Oh, thank God!" Jenny putting her hand to her throat. She gave Marion a relieved smile. "Katrina must have got it all wrong. She told me your man Kennedy from InTech was looking for me. She must have misheard the name! I didn't fancy meeting *him* face to face."

"No, your receptionist is quite correct, actually," said a deep voice from behind Marion.

They both turned to look as a tall, blond, and notably attractive younger man appeared at the top of the stairs. He stepped forward and offered his hand to Jenny.

"Mike Kennedy. I remember you now, Ms Hamilton," he said, a slight smile on his face. He nodded at Marion who smiled and nodded back at him.

"Oh . . . right. Pleased to meet you," Jenny stammered. "My office is just here. Please come in."

She followed him in, and grimaced at an amused Marion before closing the door behind them. Could it get any worse? Now Kennedy had caught her talking about him behind his back!

"First of all, Ms Hamilton, I have to say thank you for the fantastic gift basket you sent us. It was a lovely touch – we were all delighted with it."

"Um, you're welcome," Jenny said, unsure what to make of it all. She remembered serving *this* guy that day, but hadn't known who he was at the time. After all, he was so young! Barry had thrown her when he had said he was the InTech director. Jenny had been trying to place a much older man.

Kennedy sat down and put his briefcase on the floor in front of him.

"I understand that you telephoned the office a number of times, and I'm very sorry but I haven't had a chance to return your calls. I'm just back from the States yesterday morning."

"Oh!" His trusty PA hadn't bothered telling her *that*. She had wanted to get the apology over and done with, but now that he was here she didn't know what to say to him. Kennedy smiled across the table at her and, as he did, Jenny couldn't help thinking how very attractive he was. Stop it, she warned herself, this guy could get you fired yet!

"Ms Hamilton –" he began.

"Please, call me Jenny."

"OK then – Jenny. Look, the reason I came to see you today is because I wanted to put your mind at ease about the entire – 'situation'. I understand that it was a simple mistake, and I'm sure these things happen."

"But it shouldn't have happened," Jenny blurted, embarrassed. "A mistake like that should never have happened. I'm an experienced cashier – I wasn't concentrating and I should've been. If a junior staff member had done something like that, it would be bad enough but – "

"Look, let's just forget about it," he interjected softly. "I blew my top with your manager afterwards, but that was because I had to cancel my meeting, and it was really just heat-of-the-moment stuff. You must have got into terrible trouble."

Jenny managed to raise a smile, as she shook her head. "It wasn't a pretty sight in the manager's office, that's for sure."

"Neither was I afterwards, I can tell you that much," he said laughing. "That stuff went everywhere! I tried everything under the sun to try and get it off. Eventually it just wore off with washing – a week later, I might add."

Jenny grimaced. "It must have been dreadful. Oh, I really am sorry, Mr Kennedy. If there's anything at all I can say or do to make it up to you, please tell me."

"Honestly, Jenny, it's fine. I've got over it. There are worse things in life, I can tell you." He smiled at her again, his blue eyes alight with amusement.

Jenny couldn't believe how decent he was being about all this. No wonder she had been petrified about meeting him; Barry had made him out to be an awful monster. She wondered if he had spoken to the manager since. Kennedy appeared to read her thoughts and picked up his briefcase.

"Look, I popped in because I was in the area and I wanted to apologise for not returning your calls. I'm sure you're very busy, and I'm in a bit of a rush myself to be honest, but I wonder if your manager would be free to see me, just for a moment? I want to reassure him that I won't be moving the account, despite my earlier threats to the contrary." He chuckled and pushed his fair hair out of one eye. "I have to say, I did enjoy that telephone conversation. That's what you're supposed to do, isn't it? Frighten the life out of your bank manager, so that he'll be willing to give you whatever you want afterwards? You'd never know – this situation might work to my advantage, after all."

Jenny smiled and stood up to see him out.

He held out his hand to her again. "Jenny, it was a pleasure meeting you face to face. While I'm at it, I must also make sure Mr Ferguson doesn't make you pay for my replacement suit out of your own wages."

Jenny looked worried for a moment. She hadn't

thought about that. Shit, Barry wouldn't expect her to pay for it, would he?

She shook his hand and apologised all over again. Kennedy shrugged it off with a wave of his hand.

"Please, just forget about it now. It's over and done with. No harm done – really," he urged as he went towards the door.

Barry must have been trying to listen in on their conversation, because he was right outside her door when Jenny opened it. As soon as he saw Mike, he was all smiles.

"Michael Kennedy, how are you? Come in here and we'll have a chat! I hope Jenny explained everything to you! Jenny, why don't you get Mr Kennedy here a cup of coffee, and maybe pop down the road to the bakery for a few doughnuts or something while you're at it!" He pumped Mike's hand jovially.

"No, no," said Kennedy, with a smile to Jenny, "I don't have time for coffee unfortunately."

They disappeared into the office.

Jenny sat back down at her desk, and couldn't help letting out a huge sigh of relief. Thank goodness that was all over and done with! She had been dreading it. But he had been so nice about it all, apologising for not returning *her* calls!

She still couldn't believe how young Kennedy was. He was definitely mid-thirties, thirty-five at the most. Good for him, she thought. He was obviously very good at what he did; after all, InTech was one of the most dynamic, up-and-coming SME's in the software business. She had come across an article about them only last week in *Business and Finance* magazine.

Jenny had been amused to see him wink conspiratorially at her, before he disappeared into Barry's office. Mike Kennedy obviously knew well how to handle the likes of Barry Ferguson.

Chapter 27

It was a bright, pleasant and surprisingly sunny November day. Because the autumn had been relatively mild, many of the trees surrounding the tiny church still retained most of their golden leaves, adding a particularly autumnal feel to the quaint pastoral setting.

"I can't believe the weather she's getting," Karen said, struggling to appear ladylike while getting out of Shane's car in her high-heeled mules. She stood up straight, positioned her hat, and looked up at the sky in wonder. "You wouldn't get weather as good as this in June!"

"It's gorgeous here, isn't it?" Jenny agreed, taking in the surrounding area. The little village church was the smallest she had ever seen, and it looked even tinier beneath the surrounding oak and beech trees towering high above it. It was a beautiful place to get married, she decided.

Karen, Shane and Jenny had travelled from Dublin to West Cork earlier that morning. The rugged mountainous scenery they had passed on the journey down completely enthralled Shane, who had grown up in the relatively flat lands of County Meath, and had never travelled further south than Kildare.

During the journey Jenny wasn't sure which was worse, Shane driving without full concentration, or Karen driving as only she knew how. She was doing at least sixty miles an hour on the winding country by-roads like a woman possessed, beeping and honking at every tractor or slow driver who happened to get in her way. Jenny was sure the sides of the car must have scraped off the roadside walls; they were driving so close to them. She had spent the rest of the journey with her eyes closed, knowing she would definitely throw up if she looked out at the countryside whizzing past her window. She had been more than a little relieved when Karen finally pulled in to the church carpark, the Astra amazingly, still in one piece.

Slightly late, the three of them hurried into the church to take their seats. They were inside only a few minutes when the organist began the bridal march. Soon after, the bridesmaids began walking towards the altar, smirking at everyone and (very obviously Jenny thought) trying not to burst out laughing.

Tessa's sixteen-year-old twin sisters wore rust-red bridesmaid dresses, which looked particularly striking against their dusky complexions. The dresses were strapless and had satin, gold-embroidered bustiers fitted to the hip, and long satin skirts trained slightly on the ground behind them. They wore their long dark hair up, intertwined with gold-painted leaves and berries. Jenny thought the effect was especially stunning considering the time of year and the rural setting. Tessa followed close behind, a glorious vision in ivory satin, her father walking proudly alongside her.

"It's very posh, isn't it?" Karen whispered loudly over the music, so loudly in fact that some people sitting two of three pews in front of them turned around and stared at her. She giggled as Shane elbowed her roughly.

Jenny thought Tessa looked amazing in her Vera Wang wedding dress. Her hair had grown longer since Jenny had seen her last, and today she wore it curled and piled high on her head, a few tiny tendrils framing her face, and a gold tiara completing the overall 'fairy princess' effect. She inclined her head towards her father as he whispered something in her ear, and Jenny saw her eyes glisten as they walked towards the altar.

Mr Sullivan looked at his daughter with such pride and love that Jenny felt her own eyes smart with the beginning of tears. As she watched the two of them walk towards the altar, she felt she understood for the very first time why it was that so many people cried at weddings. The fairytale atmosphere in the tiny church was almost ethereal. Even Karen was softening a little, she thought, catching sight of her friend squeeze Shane's hand, as the bride and groom took their vows.

The reception was being held in a hotel not far from the village. When they got there, Shane spotted Aidan and his date – an old schoolfriend – sitting at the bar. Jenny hadn't noticed them at the church, and judging by the empty glasses in front of them, they had missed the ceremony.

"We couldn't find the bleedin' place," he said, throwing his hands up in despair. "I must have asked for directions from about ten different people but I couldn't understand a word any of them were saying! It's all 'boy' this and 'boy' that – I hadn't a clue! What's a boreen, by the way?" He winked at Shane.

"Nice try," Shane laughed. "It wasn't too bad though, only an hour long. I thought these things went on for ages."

"It was long enough for me!" Gerry exclaimed, coming up behind them, looking especially dashing in his morning-suit. "I thought your one would never stop singing there at the end."

"Gerry – congratulations, man!" Aidan stood up and clapped him on the back. "Where's the missus?"

"Running around chatting to everyone – you know yourself," Gerry beamed, as the barman handed him a pint. "I've been looking forward to this – cheers, lads!" Everyone raised their glasses in unison.

"It was a really lovely ceremony, wasn't it?" Jenny said, sitting at a window table beside Karen. "It must really get you thinking about your own wedding."

Karen shrugged her shoulders and poured diet Coke into her vodka. "I suppose so. But I thought that the horse and cart thing was a bit over the top!" She giggled. "Imagine myself and Shane going down the main street at home in a horse and cart? We'd be the talk of the place for months!"

Jenny laughed. "Poor old Nora Cronin would have a heart attack. Tessa seemed thrilled with it all, but I don't think Gerry enjoyed it too much. He looked a bit green when he got here."

"Yeah, and did you see him sink that pint of Guinness afterwards! I've never seen a man who needed a drink so badly!"

They were both laughing so much that they didn't notice someone come up beside their table.

"Hello, Jenny."

Jenny looked up, and when she saw who it was, she felt her cheeks redden. Mike Kennedy was standing there, looking very handsome in a black tuxedo. What was *he* doing at Tessa and Gerry's wedding? And why had his appearance made her feel tongue-tied all of a sudden?

"Mike, um, how are you?" she managed to say. Out of the corner of her eye, Jenny could see Karen watching her with interest.

"Great, thanks. This is a surprise – I didn't expect that I'd know anyone here. Hello!" He nodded at Karen.

"Oh, I'm sorry. Forgive my manners. Karen, this is Mike Kennedy. He's a customer of the bank. Mike – Karen Cassidy."

"Hello," Karen said coyly, extending her hand. "Pleased to meet you. How do you know Tessa and Gerry?" She beamed up at him.

Just then, a tall redhead wearing the shortest dress with the longest legs Jenny had ever seen, appeared at Mike's side. She tugged impatiently at his arm.

"Mike, I need a drink quick! I just met Sandra Thompson and she bored the face off me, telling me all about the feeding habits of her latest newborn. I thought I'd never get away from her." She turned and nudged through the crowd at the bar, nearly toppling Aidan off his barstool. Jenny noticed him give her an appreciative look as she ordered drinks from the barman. She didn't blame him. She was a stunning-looking girl.

"I'd better go," Mike said, nodding towards his companion. "Can I get you girls anything at the bar?"

Jenny shook her head and smiled. "We're fine. Thanks anyway."

Karen waited until he was a safe distance away, before turning to Jenny. "Who was *that*?" she asked, eyes wide with interest. "What a hunk! No wonder you were blushing so much!"

"Oh no, was I that bad?" Jenny said, mortified all over again. "I just got tongue tied – I couldn't think of anything to say to him. He's the one I told you about before, the one that was covered in blue dye."

"*That's* the guy!" Karen said, incredulously. "I got the impression he was one of those stuffed shirts, not an Adonis with a fine bod!"

Jenny laughed. "Well, his wife, or girlfriend, or whatever she might be, is more than a match for him – looks-wise, anyway." She watched his companion cross her long legs as she sat down at a table on the other side of the room. She noticed that every male in the room was practically drooling at the mouth as the girl leant forward to let Mike light her cigarette, exposing her ample cleavage.

"She's very good-looking all right," Karen agreed, following Jenny's gaze. "A bit obvious though in that get-up, isn't she?" She wrinkled her nose at the girl's flimsy hot-pink chiffon dress that clung to every curve.

An hour or so later they took their seats in the banqueting room.

Jenny looked around the room in wonder. Tessa had

really pulled out all the stops. A bouquet of heart-shaped helium balloons in red and gold had been placed in the centre of every round table, and two huge bride and groom air-walkers hovered behind Tessa and Gerry at the top table.

"I have to admit I really like the balloons," Karen said, taking a seat across from Jenny. "That's something I wouldn't mind doing for our wedding. What do you think?" She nudged Shane. "It takes the stuffy look away from everything, doesn't it?"

Shane nodded slightly and turned immediately back to Aidan, with whom he was in deep conversation.

"Do you mind if we join you?" said a voice from behind Jenny. "It's just that we don't really know anyone here, and I saw Mike talking to you two earlier." The girl looked around in alarm, and whispered conspiratorially to Karen. "I really don't want to get stuck with Miss Baby Talk again."

"Sure," Karen said automatically, pulling out a chair beside her for Mike Kennedy's companion.

The girl smiled and sat down, relieved. "Thanks. I'm Rachel, by the way."

She opened her handbag, and began to apply a thick coating of bright red lipstick.

Karen introduced Rachel to the others at their table. "Where *is* Mike?" she asked.

"He's still up at the bar, chatting to some oul' fella he met a few minutes ago." Rachel rolled her eyes. "I'm nearly sorry I brought him now – he's no good. I asked him to help find me the man of my dreams and what does he do? Chats to old-age pensioners!" She lowered her voice and looked around her. "Any decent single men at this table by any chance?"

Karen laughed. "Not this lot I'm afraid," she said. "Well, there is Aidan but I wouldn't wish him on my worst enemy! So, you're not with Mike then?"

Rachel looked at her as if she was mad. "Mike, yeuch! No, he's my brother! Oh, no, you didn't seriously think I was with him, did you?"

A few minutes later, Mike appeared at the table.

"I'm very sorry about this," he said, frowning at Rachel. "She tends to be a little . . . forward."

"Not at all," Jenny said, smiling as he took the seat beside her. "You're more than welcome to join us."

"How do you know the bride and groom?" Karen asked him. "Are you related?"

Mike shook his head. "I don't know them at all, actually," he said. "Rachel trained as a nurse with Tessa, and she asked me to come along with her today. She's determined to find a man, and has roped me in to help her out." He rolled his eyes at his sister.

"I haven't seen Tessa in about three years, but we keep in touch. I went to work in London after we qualified," Rachel explained, pushing her hair behind her ears as she buttered a bread roll. "I can't believe she's actually married though! It makes me feel ancient."

Jenny picked up her napkin, as a plate of egg mayonnaise was put on the table in front of her. "Ancient?" she said. "You couldn't be more than twenty-four or twenty-five, surely."

"Twenty-seven," Rachel answered glumly, "and unfortunately, still single." She shook her head dispiritedly, then added with a grin. "Your man over there is a bit of all right though. A bit old, but I'm sure we'd get around that!" She nodded in the direction of the top table.

Jenny followed her gaze and laughed out loud. "That's Tessa's father!"

"Oh! I didn't recognise him from the church," Rachel looked slightly bashful. "I don't suppose Mrs Sullivan would be too pleased if I made a play for her husband at her daughter's wedding!"

They all laughed.

"We're friends of Tessa's from Dublin," Karen informed her. "I used to share a flat with Gerry, before he and Tessa moved in together. This is my fiancé Shane," she added, nudging him. Shane nodded in their direction, his mouth full of salad.

"Good – another one spoken for, that means more men for me. What about you? Are you here with anyone?" Rachel asked, pointing towards Jenny with her fork.

She shifted in her seat uncomfortably. "Um, I've just come out of a relationship actually," she said, wishing Rachel hadn't asked. "He moved to America not so long ago."

"Rachel, don't be so bloody nosy," Mike admonished, sensing Jenny's obvious discomfort. "You can't go around asking personal questions of people you've just met."

Jenny smiled to defuse the tension. "No, it's fine, Rachel, really. It's just, it ended badly and sometimes I find it hard to talk about it."

"Sorry," Rachel looked embarrassed. "Mike's right. I shouldn't have been prying. It's just sometimes it feels like I'm the only single girl of my age left these days. It's a relief to find someone else who's not engaged, or married, or planning to do either." She giggled. "Maybe the two of us should go on a man-hunt together."

"I'm sure Jenny isn't as desperate as you are, Rachel," Mike said irritably. "Can't you leave the girl alone?"

Rachel made a face at him. "I don't know why I ask him to go anywhere with me," she said turning to Karen. "He's so dry –honestly! Wait until I tell you . . . "

Mike rolled his eyes apologetically at Jenny, as Rachel engaged Karen in conversation. "I'm really sorry if she embarrassed you. Sometimes she acts like a ten-year-old."

Jenny waved him away and took a sip of her wine. "It's fine honestly. She's a lovely girl – I'm glad you joined us. We thought you two were together actually, earlier on in the bar."

He laughed softly. "Please! She's my sister, and I love her dearly but someone like Rachel would be the complete opposite of my type!"

Jenny felt herself idly wondering what his type might be, and then she stopped. Was she mad? Mike was a customer, and she had already embarrassed herself enough with him.

"So, did Barry Ferguson organise a fitting for a new suit for you yet?" she asked, anxious to get the subject of their first meeting out of the way.

"Fitting?" Mike frowned. Then realisation dawned. "Ah, the famous Armani suit." He chuckled as if remembering something. "Promise me you won't say anything, but . . ." He beckoned Jenny forward, and the back of her neck tingled as she felt his warm breath against her ear. "My so-called designer suit cost a hundred and fifty quid from

Next," he whispered. He sat back, and laughed at Jenny's shocked expression. "Well, I have to keep up appearances with the bank manager, don't I? But, don't worry, I'll tell him the truth – eventually," he added with a grin. "I couldn't resist laying it on thick at the time. It was very funny, actually – I thought the poor guy would explode."

"It wasn't funny for me!" Jenny laughed. "I'll never be able to live it down – I'm the laughing-stock of the bank as it is!"

Jenny noticed Karen watching them closely from across the table, as she and Mike laughed together. When she went to the Ladies' just after they cleared the second course, Jenny knew if would only be a matter of seconds before Karen followed her. She was right.

"He's gorgeous," Karen giggled, the vodka and tonic having long since taken effect. "And he fancies you like mad!"

"He doesn't know anyone else here, that's all," Jenny said, dismissing the thought, as she reapplied her make-up in the mirror.

"Nope," Karen's words slurred slightly, as she spoke. "Rachel says that he couldn't stop talking about you earlier, after meeting you in the bar."

"That's because of what happened at work. I'm not surprised he told her about that. He probably said: 'There's that idiot from the bank' – nothing more."

"Mmm, whatever you say. But you like him too, don't you?" she challenged.

"Karen he's a customer!"

"Jen, you're not a doctor! Are there any rules about dating customers outside of working hours?"

Jenny shrugged her shoulders.

"I didn't think so," Karen said firmly. "Go and have a bit of fun, Jen – you deserve it. It's plain enough for all to see that he likes you – he hasn't been able to take his eyes off you all day, more's the pity," she added glancing at her reflection in the mirror. "I quite fancy him myself. Look at that! The bloody hat flattened my hair completely!" She took a brush out of her bag and began brushing her hair.

"Karen Cassidy – you're an engaged woman!"

"I'm only joking. I wouldn't change my Shane for anything. Seriously, though," she added sombrely, "maybe it's about time you started having fun again. You've locked yourself away from everything for months – it can't be good for you, you know. And *he's* ... well, Roan is out of the picture now, isn't he?"

Jenny nodded, the combination of the wine and Mike Kennedy's supposed interest in her making her euphoric. "You're right. And it's been a great day so far." She winked mischievously at Karen's reflection. "OK, you've convinced me. A little bit of flirting might be in order."

"Good girl!" Karen clapped both hands together. "That's more like the Jenny we know and love."

"Do I look all right though?"

"You look great," Karen enthused, not wanting to deflate her by admitting that the strappy, green dress Jenny wore was all wrong for her colouring. Nevertheless, her friend looked brighter and more confident than she had seen her in a long time. It had obviously done her to world of good to get out today and enjoy herself. "Your hair looks a lot thicker too, since you cut it."

Karen indicated Jenny's shorter, layered bob, which

her new hairdresser had styled and tinted just a few days beforehand.

"Anyway, we're running away with ourselves – Mike might already be involved with someone, for all we know," Jenny pondered.

Karen shook her head. "Rachel would have said something. Honestly, I haven't been able to get a word in with her! She's funny, isn't she?"

"Poor old Aidan hasn't stopped staring since she sat down at our table."

"Seriously? I hadn't noticed – I'll have to introduce them. Aidan could do with a woman in his life. It's been a long time since he's had a decent relationship, poor thing."

"Well, judging by her chat earlier, I'm sure Rachel would be pleased!".

"Then I'll put them both out of their misery and get them talking. Who knows?" Karen said, walking back out towards the banquet hall. "Tessa and Gerry's wedding might spawn a host of new romances!"

Soon after the main course had ended, the speeches began. Tessa's father, visibly nervous, gave a very short but loving speech about how proud and how happy he was for his eldest daughter and her new husband.

Soon after, a red-faced Gerry stood up and was greeted by whoops and jeers from around the room. The wedding speech had been a long-standing joke amongst Gerry and his mates, and they all knew that he was petrified at the thought of standing up in front of everyone on the day. His hands trembled as he clutched the microphone.

"Um, thank you all for coming here today," he began, his hands shaking as he tried to read his notes.

By the time Gerry had finished speaking, every single woman in the room including Tessa, was in tears. Even some of the men looked suitably moved by his words. It had been the most romantic and moving speech Jenny had ever heard, and as she watched Gerry sit down and reach for Tessa's hand, she envied her friend enormously.

"I didn't think Burkie had it in him," Shane said, his eyes watering suspiciously. He turned away from the table, and feigned blowing his nose. "Every woman in the place will wish they married him after that. Look, even that narky waitress from our table is all smiles at him now."

"It was incredible." Jenny dabbed at her eyes with a table napkin. "The things he said about Tessa – and the way he looked at her – the room might as well have been empty as far as the two of them were concerned."

And that was it in a nutshell, she thought. In all the time she and Roan had been together, he had never once looked at her like that and, she realised, he probably never would have. She found herself studying Tessa at the top table. The bride had been smiling contentedly all day long, and anyone could see how deliriously happy she was. With all her fussing beforehand, Jenny and Karen had expected the wedding to be more of a showpiece for Tessa, but now Jenny understood that wasn't the case. Her friend was simply trying to make the most memorable day in her life as special for everyone else as it was for her. As she watched Tessa glow with undisguised happiness, Jenny couldn't help feeling envious of her friend. It must be wonderful to be that happy, knowing that the person she loved returned that love, easily and without question. It must be the best feeling in the world, she decided, suddenly feeling terribly sad, and afraid that she might never experience it.

"Penny for your thoughts?" she heard Mike ask, as he returned from the bar.

She looked up and smiled, taking the glass of wine he offered her.

"I was just thinking about everything that Gerry was saying – about how he knew from day one that Tessa was the one for him, and how he knows without hesitation that he wants to be with her for the rest of his life. But how can he tell?" she pondered. "How can anyone tell?"

"I don't think anyone can tell – really." Mike sat down, and moved his chair closer. "Emotions always run high on the day, especially during the speeches. People tend to say a lot of things and make a lot of promises that they might not be able to keep." He shrugged dismissively.

"What do you mean?"

"Well, it's impossible to know how some things will pan out, that's all." He took a sip from his pint.

"Sounds to me like you've got a very poor view of marriage," Jenny said, a little taken aback at his cynical attitude. "I'm pretty sure that Gerry meant every word of what he said today."

"Of course, he meant it all – *today*," Mike said evenly. "It's all very well making promises on the day. It's what happens afterwards that counts and, believe me, words can be forgotten very easily."

He had such an edge to his tone that Jenny decided to drop the subject. She took a sip from her wine glass, and looked across the table at Rachel and Karen, who were chatting together easily.

"Does Rachel still work in London?" she asked casually.

Mike shook his head. "No, she moved back here a few months ago. Now she works in the Mater, and she's staying with me until she gets a place of her own." He rolled his eyes. "It can't come soon enough for me, I can tell you. Rachel has to be one of the most disorganised and untidy people in the world. Sometimes I find it difficult to believe that we were raised by the same parents." Then he laughed. "I still can't believe that Rachel ended up as a nurse. She's so ditsy, and I can't for the life of me understand how any intelligent person could put my little sister in charge of a hospital ward. Imagine relying on the likes of her to give out medication!"

Jenny laughed. "Typical! You probably still see her as your silly little sister, incapable of doing anything 'grown up'. I'm the same with my younger brothers. But Rachel couldn't have got through all those years of training if she was that bad. I'll bet she's brilliant at her job." She watched Rachel waving her arms animatedly as she chatted with Karen and Shane. "She seems like the type who would be excellent with patients – so friendly and chatty. They probably all adore her."

"Maybe. But I can tell you one thing – you won't ever catch me near the Mater Hospital if Rachel's on duty. I'd rather suffer than let her near me!"

They both laughed.

Eventually, each grew silent while the waitress cleared the table in front of them.

Jenny put her hands on her stomach and slumped into her seat. "Thank God – the sight of all that food was making me feel twice as full as I am already."

"Do you want to go for a walk?" Mike asked sitting back in his chair and stifling a yawn. "I'm stuffed after all that, and the grounds are beautiful here."

"Good idea." Jenny picked up her handbag and throw. "I could do with stretching the legs myself."

The air had grown colder as the evening began to draw in. Jenny wrapped the flimsy throw around her arms and hugged it tightly towards her. She shivered.

"It's a little chilly all the same," Mike said. "Do you want to leave it?"

"Not at all – I'll warm up as we walk," she said, waving away his concern. To her surprise, she found that, freezing or not, she wanted to spend time alone with him.

They walked together for a short while, chatting amiably about the day's events and Jenny wasn't quite sure why, but after a little while she found herself steering the conversation back to their earlier discussion about Gerry's speech.

"I'm curious about what you said before – about marriage. What do you have against it?" she asked simply.

She sensed Mike stiffen beside her and Jenny suspected that she had been too forward. She could have kicked herself. "I'm sorry, Mike – forget I said anything . . ." Then, remembering those comments and his reticence to discuss them, a sudden realisation dawned on her. "You're married, aren't you?" she said, looking straight at him.

Mike said nothing for a moment and, inexplicably, Jenny felt a rush of disappointment flood through her suspecting that she was correct.

"I *was* married," he confirmed, "but not any more."

"Oh!" She wanted to know more, but at the same time didn't want to pry. Was he a widower, separated – what had happened?

"I'm divorced," he said, answering her unspoken question. "I have been for over two years now."

"Oh!" Jenny repeated.

"It's no big deal," he said, noticing her discomfort. "It was a long time ago. But the experience has made me more than a little cynical about marriage, and so-called wedding vows."

Jenny nodded. His wife must have left or cheated on him, she thought. "I can imagine. I'm sorry. I feel really bad now. I didn't mean to pry. I mean I hardly know you . . . "

"Forget it, Jenny. Honestly."

She felt terrible. Why did she have to be so forward? He probably thought she was a right nosy cow.

"So?" Mike said, with a grin. "Tit for tat. You said earlier that you had just come out of a serious relationship. What's your story?"

Jenny was pleased that he didn't appear too annoyed with her for prying

"There is no story as such, and it wasn't that serious – not to him anyway," she added with a nervous laugh. "I caught him cheating on me at the end, but I'm pretty sure he was at it since the beginning, and all throughout our time together. I just wouldn't admit it." To her surprise, she felt liberated by her own words. Amazingly, she could finally admit out loud, not just to herself, but also to a complete stranger that their relationship had been a sham.

"I know this probably sounds clichéd," Mike said, giving her a sideways look, "but, he's a complete fool –

whoever he is. I can't imagine why anyone would feel the need to cheat, if they were in a relationship with someone like you."

She laughed. "You're right – it is terribly clichéd! But thank you. It's nice to hear it anyway."

They chatted for a while longer and Jenny discovered that she had been correct in guessing that his wife had left him.

"We'd been together for years before we married – I studied in London, and we met in college," he told her. "Rebecca was actually one of my lecturers, believe it or not!"

"We lived in London for the first few years of our marriage, and I set up InTech not long after our wedding. It was very difficult for a while – I was rarely home and under a lot of pressure with the business – and I suppose Becky was bored. She gave up her job when we married, and she seemed to have her heart set on starting a family immediately. It was silly, really – you'd imagine that something like that would be sorted out beforehand, but we had never really talked about it. I thought she knew that the business would be my main priority, for a while at least. We argued a lot, mostly about that . . . "

"You didn't want kids until the business was fully up and running?" Jenny finished. "That sounds reasonable enough."

Mike nodded. "I thought so too, but Rebecca is a few years older than I am, and her biological clock was ticking, as it were." He looked sadly into the distance for a moment and then continued. "She was determined to get pregnant, whether I liked it or not. One day I discovered accidentally that she had stopped taking the Pill. I went ballistic, Jenny. I just wasn't ready for a family. Having a child would have put me under twice as much pressure to make the business work, but Becky couldn't see that. We had it out again and again, and eventually she agreed to wait a few more years, or at least until I was sure InTech would be viable. When I say agreed, I mean very reluctantly," he added. "And then . . . then it wasn't long before things got very strained between us."

Jenny thought she could guess the end of the story. "She resented having to wait, and you grew apart?"

"Something like that," he said hoarsely. "Anyway, to cut a long story short, she ended up leaving me for someone else."

He said this in such a way that Jenny understood that Mike was still, despite his earlier protests, very hurt by it all.

"Were you married long?"

"Four years," he said. "It's strange, isn't it? We were together for ages before we married, and then it was all over, just like that."

"I'm sorry Mike," Jenny said, noticing his wounded expression. "I can only imagine how hard it must have been for you."

He said nothing and they walked on companionably together in silence, lost in their own thoughts.

"We'd better get back," he said eventually. "The band will be starting soon."

"Oh, I'd almost forgotten!" Jenny checked her watch, her eyes widening with mirth. "The big surprise!"

"What surprise?" Mike asked, slightly out of breath

trying to keep up with her, as she dragged him back towards the hotel.

"You'll never guess who Gerry got to play at this wedding tonight," she said excitedly. "I can't wait to see Tessa's face! Quick, quick before we miss it!"

There were no sooner back in the ballroom, when the hotel manager's voice boomed out of the loudspeaker. "We have a real entertainment treat for you all tonight, ladies and gentlemen. By all accounts, this is particularly unusual, but I understand Gerry Burke moved heaven and earth to organise it as a wedding gift for Mrs Burke!"

Jenny noticed Tessa suddenly look up from a conversation she was having with one of the guests. She glanced around in confusion, obviously unsure as to what was coming. As she caught sight of Gerry from across the room, he winked at her.

"Wait until she hears this!" Jenny said gleefully, returning to their table.

The hotel manager continued. "Without further ado, and by special request for the new Mrs Burke – who I understand is one of his biggest fans – I am delighted introduce to you tonight, the one, the *only* Mr Joe Dolan!"

Chapter 28

Shane nudged Karen's feet with the hoover, as he tried in vain to vacuum the mat beneath her. "Will you get a move on? They'll be here soon!"

Karen flipped across a page of the magazine she was reading, before looking up at him through narrowed eyes.

"Shane Quinn – if I'd known you were such a nag, I would never have moved in with you, not to mention agreed to marrying you. Honestly," she teased, "you're like a mother hen, going around with your polish and your duster. If I didn't know better, I'd swear you were gay." She slapped his thigh playfully.

"Ah, come on, Karen. Make a bit of an effort, will you? We're having visitors – I'm trying to make this place look a bit respectable, and all you do is sit there and get in my way." With feigned sternness, he handed her a cloth and a bottle of Mr Sheen. "Here – move your ass and your magazines, and get going on that coffee table."

"All right, Mammy!" Karen reluctantly got up from the couch. She looked at the clock on the mantelpiece.

Melissa Hill

"Shane, it's only two o'clock. Mike and Jenny won't be here for another hour at least, and you know what Tessa and Gerry are like for timekeeping. Relax."

Just then the doorbell rang on cue.

"Feck!" Shane shooed her out of his way and went to answer the door. "The traffic mustn't have been as bad as they thought."

Karen shook her head in amusement. Shane seemed really excited about Mike and Jenny's visit today. He was obviously trying to make some kind of impression on Mike Kennedy. Shane had really taken to him on the day of the wedding and, though he wouldn't admit it, Karen thought she knew exactly why. Mike was an avid Liverpool FC supporter and Shane, after years of ribbing from cocky Manchester United fans, had been thrilled to find a like-minded soul when it came to football. Not to mention the fact that Mike was a double season-ticket holder at Anfield.

Karen heard a shriek from the doorway

"Hi, guys!"

She went out to see a very tanned and overexcited Tessa engulf Shane in a bear-hug while Gerry looked on.

"Mr & Mrs Burke!" Karen said, kissing Gerry on the cheek. "Welcome home! How was Bali?"

"Oh Karen," Tessa said elated, "you wouldn't believe it! It was the most fantastic place I've ever seen. The hotel was fabulous and the weather – I thought I'd bake over there."

"Well, you got plenty of sunshine anyway. I thought honeymooners weren't supposed to be out in the sun long enough to get a tan like that!"

"Don't worry – there was plenty of that too," Tessa chuckled, walking towards the kitchen. "We have to make the most of it at the moment, don't we, Gerry?" she added, with a wink. Gerry blushed a deep shade of red and sat down at the kitchen table.

"I'll tell you later," she mouthed, as Karen looked at her questioningly.

"So – any news? What did we miss while we were away in Utopia?" Tessa asked, looking eagerly from Shane to Karen.

"Well, you know about Jenny and the delicious Mike Kennedy – I told you about that on the phone."

"Yes – but you didn't tell me any of the nitty-gritty. I only met him for a second or two at the wedding. I didn't even know he was Rachel's brother. What's he like?"

Shane groaned. "Here we go – gossip-time already. Come on, Gerry," he took a couple of beers from the fridge, "I think we'll go in and nab the comfortable seats and let these two natter in peace."

"Sounds good to me." Gerry followed him out of the kitchen.

Karen opened a bottle of chardonnay and took a pair of wineglasses from the cupboard. She handed a glass to Tessa.

"From what I can see he's an absolute dote. He seems mad about her, too."

"Is that a good or a bad thing?" Tessa said, with a frown. "I know it's been a while, but is our Jen ready to get involved with somebody else?"

Karen nodded. "I thought the same thing myself, to be honest. But, your wedding was exactly what she needed.

It was a good excuse for her to come out of herself and start living her life again."

"So what's his story? He's older than us, isn't he?"

"Thirty-five. He's divorced and his wife left him for someone else, apparently. I'd like to see the guy she's with now if she could leave a hunk like that."

Tessa giggled. "Maybe he's not great in the sack."

"Well, compared to that lump Roan Williams, I'd say he's a demon between the sheets," Karen said bitterly. "Jenny told me only recently that they hadn't had sex for ages before the end."

"What?" Tessa put down her glass. "With the way he carried on, you'd swear he was God's gift."

"He might have been God's gift, all right – but to everyone else but Jenny."

Tessa shook her head. "I felt so sorry for her that night. I didn't think she'd ever get over it. How did she stick with him for so long?"

Karen nodded. "I suppose it was harder for her to see it than it was for us. The simple fact was that she loved him, maybe she still loves him, in her own way. But the main thing is that he's out of her life now, and I think that this thing with Mike might be the best thing for her."

"Well, I suppose it's good that he's had some experience with bad relationships – with the divorce and everything," Tessa said. "Do you think it could get serious between them?"

"I don't know if there *is* anything between them. I do know that they've spent a lot of time together since your wedding, and they seem to get on very well." She took a sip from her wine glass. "I have to admit, I couldn't see

Jenny with anyone for a long time after Roan but, after meeting Mike, I can see why she likes him. He's a lovely guy – the complete opposite of Roan the Rat."

Tessa laughed at this. "You really hated him, didn't you?"

"From day one." Karen said firmly. "I tried my best, for Jenny's sake, but there was always something about him that really – I don't know – freaked me out. He was a lovely-looking guy, there's no denying that, but he was smarm personified as far as I'm concerned. I still can't figure out how he and Shane got on so well."

"Gerry didn't seem to mind him, either," Tessa said, "but when he did the dirt on Jenny, that was it. He wanted to go for Roan when I told him about it."

"Gerry's such a sweetheart – wasn't he the same about Shane and Lydia, that time?"

Tessa wrinkled her nose at the memory. "Yeah but that was different – Lydia was the culprit that time. Silly bitch."

"Agreed," Karen said vehemently, raising her glass and clinking it with Tessa's. She chuckled. "I heard that she was in a terrible snot when she didn't get an invite to the wedding."

"As if we'd invite that one. She'd probably end up causing a scene or something, anything to take the spotlight off me!"

Karen nearly choked on her wine. "God forbid that someone might take the spotlight off you, Tessa Sullivan!" she said, laughing.

"It's *Mrs* Tessa Burke now, thanks very much." Tessa feigned a snooty tone, her nose in the air, as she extended her wedding ring towards Karen.

"That sounds weird!" Karen said. "It'll be hard to get used to."

"Not as weird as Karen Quinn is going to sound – whenever that comes about!" She stopped laughing, when she saw Karen's face go serious, all of a sudden. "Hey, is everything OK?" she said, touching Karen's arm softly.

"Oh, I don't know, Tessa," Karen sighed, looking deep into her glass. "The thing with Shane's family just seems to be going from bad to worse lately."

"You mean the kids? Are they still driving you mad?"

"It's not just that, and believe me that's bad enough," she said, rolling her eyes. "Marie was here with her brood last weekend, and she didn't stop going on and on about us setting a date and 'doing the decent thing'. She kept saying how great it was to be young enough to enjoy your kids when they're young, and how Shane and I would want to 'get going' soon. Grrr! I felt like throttling her!" She saw Tessa watching her with amusement. "I know it might sound funny but it's not really. If you were in my position, you'd be exactly the same."

"What I can't understand is why you let them get away with it," Tessa said. "I can't imagine you being afraid to put them in their place. If that's the case, it's a first since I've known you."

"Yeah, but they're Shane's family, aren't they? I can't very well tell them where to go."

"Still," Tessa said, thoughtfully, "I have to admit I'm surprised that you're letting it get to you."

"It's not just that, Tess," Karen sighed again. "Remember I told you about Jack, the brother from England? Well, he's been spending a lot of time here lately. He's an architect and he's working on some development out in Sandymount."

"Right, and you don't think much of him?"

"I think he's a pompous prat, to put it mildly," Karen said. "Anyway, whenever he's in Dublin, he just turns up and expects to stay here, whether it suits us or not."

"I see," Tessa nodded, "and you're not particularly happy with that arrangement?"

"That's the problem," Karen moaned irritably. "It's never arranged. He just turns up on the doorstep with his suitcase, whenever the mood takes him. He never rings beforehand, and just takes it for granted that we'll be happy to put him up."

"And what does Shane think of that?"

Karen looked towards the kitchen door, keeping her voice low. "That's where the problems start. Shane won't say anything to him, because Jack's been 'so good to us'. He seems to think we owe him free room and board, because he helped us out with arranging our mortgage! Can you believe that?" He face was red with indignation. "The whole thing is driving me bloody mad! I like my privacy, Tessa, and I don't fancy having Shane's family appear on our doorstep, whenever they please. His mother did the same thing last weekend. Nellie decided she fancied a cup of tea after her shopping, so she just called in without letting us know, or finding out whether we were here or not! It frustrates me so much, because it's our house and our mortgage – we're the ones making the monthly repayments. I don't see old Jacko boy handing over the best part of a thousand euro to the bank every month! God, it's like being in the Mafia or something!"

"Sshh – calm down," Tessa said softly. "You don't want Shane to hear you."

"Do you know, I couldn't care less if he did or not at this stage." Karen refilled her wineglass, took a large mouthful and gulped it down. "He's too bloody placid for his own good."

"Have the two of you spoken about it? Have you told him that you're not comfortable having Jack stay here whenever he feels like it?"

"There's no point," Karen said flatly. "It wouldn't make the slightest bit of difference. As far as Shane's concerned, Jack is Big Brother Wonderful. What I think doesn't matter."

"Karen, you'll have to try and sort these things out soon. If you're unhappy now, what will you be like when you and Shane are married? I know they say that you marry him, and not his family, but in your case that doesn't appear to be true."

"I know," Karen said, standing up. "I keep threatening to sit him down and have it out – calmly. But you know what we're like – any problems we have are only ever sorted after a huge barney." She grimaced. "If we do end up fighting I'm afraid I might say some things I might regret – like insult that Quinn crowd."

"Well, make sure that it doesn't come to that. Go out to dinner some night, and bring it up then." She smiled. "Even the likes of you can't cause a scene in a 'civilised' setting. What do you think?"

"I suppose," Karen looked unconvinced. "Anyway I'm sick of talking about all my woes. I'm only depressing both myself and you."

"True," Tessa said, feigning a yawn. Then she smiled.

"Seriously, Karen, get it sorted. It won't do you any good to bottle it up – it'll end up getting a lot worse if you let it fester."

Karen saluted. "OK, Mrs Burke, I promise. I'll try and organise a night out for us next weekend or something." She looked at the clock and picked up her glass. "Come on, we'll go in and join the boys. Jenny and Mike should be here soon and you and Gerry can tell us all about beautiful Bali."

* * *

"There's something I've been dying to find out since the wedding," Mike said, turning to Gerry, who was sitting in the armchair opposite. "How on earth did you manage to get Joe Dolan to play at your wedding?"

"Don't you mean *why on earth*?" Karen laughed, the wine beginning to take effect.

She and Tessa – well, she seemed to be the one doing most of the drinking – had almost downed a second bottle of wine by the time Jenny and Mike arrived. Jenny looked absolutely radiant tonight, Karen thought. Obviously, spending time with Mike had done her the world of good. She hadn't stopped smiling since she walked in the door.

"*Why* – my thoughts exactly," Shane said, winking at Tessa.

"Oh come on!" Tessa gave Shane a sharp dig in his side. "Even you lot have to admit that he was absolutely brilliant that night. Everyone was shaking their stuff out on the dance floor."

"My aunt, Molly, is a huge fan," Gerry said, in response to Mike's question. "She knows Joe well, and she sorted it out for me."

"It must have cost you a fortune," Mike said, shaking his head in wonder.

"No, the date suited him as it happened. He had a gig in the city the same night, so he agreed to pop over for an hour, as a favour to Molly. I gave him a few quid though – and a slice of wedding cake," he added, with a wink.

"I thought it was brilliant," said Jenny, who was sitting comfortably beside Mike on the sofa. "You should have seen your face, Tessa – it was absolute picture! I don't think I've ever seen you look so surprised!"

Tessa looked lovingly over at Gerry. "I have to hand it to my hubby – he did everything right that day."

"Tell us about the honeymoon, Tessa," Jenny said. "Was it fantastic?"

"Oh, definitely!" Tessa gave a broad wink. "It was absolutely fantastic!"

"Oh, I don't mean *that*!" Jenny said, slightly pink-cheeked, as she realised her unintentional double-entendre, "I meant the place itself – what was it like?"

"Really amazing – wasn't it, Gerry? I have to admit when I got off the plane after a ten-hour flight to Bangkok, and another four hours again to Bali, I couldn't care less what the place was like, I just wanted to sleep for a week. And then . . . "

"Then we got to the hotel," Gerry finished.

"Girls, it was the most fantastic place I've ever seen!" Tessa exclaimed. "I said to myself, my God this is how the stars must live. I'll never forget that first look at it as we turned into the entrance."

"Where did you stay?" Mike asked, taking a handful of peanuts from a bowl on the coffee table.

"The Hilton," Gerry said. "It was all so exotic – Oriental statues and fountains everywhere – and inside the building was just as amazing. Gold and woodcarvings on the doors, the walls – everywhere."

"It was Paradise Found," Tessa added. "Bounty Ads, Robinson Crusoe – you name it. The hotel was on its own beach – there was hardly anyone else around."

"Sounds like paradise, all right," Shane said thoughtfully, and turned to Karen. "Where'll we go for our honeymoon, love?"

Jenny let out a little squeal of delight. "Does that mean what I think it means? Have you two finally set a date?"

Karen shook her head and caught Tessa's eye. "No, Jen," she said quietly, "we haven't – Shane is probably just thinking out loud. Aren't you?"

"I think she's having second thoughts about marrying me altogether," Shane joked, his smile not quite reaching his eyes.

"Pity. I wouldn't mind another day out. I really enjoyed your wedding."

"I'd say *you* did, all right," Tessa laughed, hoping to change the subject for Karen's sake.

Jenny caught her meaning and gave a little smile. "It was all right," she said, glancing sideways at Mike, "apart from this guy I met there who hasn't stopped tormenting me since. He just keeps following me everywhere, and won't leave me alone – ouch!" Mike pinched her thigh, and she grimaced.

Karen went out to the kitchen for more drinks, and Tessa followed her.

"Can you believe those two?" she asked, her eyes wide as she took another bottle of wine from the fridge.

Karen nodded smugly, folding her arms across her chest. "I told you, didn't I? They seem completely besotted with one another."

"But that's terrific," Tessa said. "It means that she's finally over Roan, doesn't it? Lucky thing – Mike's an absolute pet too! I have to admit, I didn't really believe it when you said she was back to herself."

"Did you notice how she hasn't stopped grinning since she walked in the door?" Karen was struggling with the bottle-opener.

"Who hasn't stopped grinning?" Jenny asked, entering the kitchen behind them.

"You – and the delicious Mr Kennedy." Karen handed her a newly opened bottle of wine. "Get another glass from the cupboard and sit down here for a minute. Tessa's dying to know all the gossip."

"There's no gossip," Jenny said, bashful. "We're just – friends, that's all."

"You lying madam, Jenny Hamilton!" Tessa said. "I've seen the looks the two of you are giving one another! Don't give me that 'just friends' rubbish!"

"Honestly – that's all it is. He's good fun, and I really enjoy spending time with him, but I'm not interested in Mike that way."

"Not interested . . . are you half-cracked, girl! What's not to like, for goodness sake? He's gorgeous!"

"It's just not like that between us, though. It's just a friendship thing."

"Are you sure that he feels the same way?" Karen

asked. "Because it looks to me as though he's more than a little interested in you."

Jenny shook her head. "Definitely not. We get on very well, but that's it. He's still in love with Rebecca – that's his wife – well, his ex-wife now. I think that's why we get on so well – there's no expectation, no pressure, nothing like that."

"And how do you feel about Roan now?" Tessa asked.

"To be honest, I've hardly even thought about him in the last few weeks – don't look at me like that – I mean it!" she said with a grin. "Thinking back over it now, Roan was completely wrong for me, and I'm finally beginning to realise that."

"Well, I think it's brilliant," Tessa said, patting her on the shoulder. "It can't have been easy for you these last few months."

"Agreed," Karen said. "Fair play to you, Jenny Hamilton – true to form, you're never without a good-looking man for long."

Jenny's eyes widened in disbelief. "Haven't you listened to a word I said, Karen? It's not like that with Mike."

"All right, we believe you," Tessa said, sardonically.

Karen raised her wine glass. "Girls, I think a toast is in order."

"To what?" Jenny asked.

"To us," she declared, "firstly to Tessa, the new Mrs Burke!"

The three girls clinked glasses.

"And to Jenny, and her new Mr Wonderful!"

Jenny smiled as they clinked again. She and Tessa were left with their glasses still in mid-air, when Karen had already taken a large gulp from her own.

"What about you?" Jenny asked in surprise, expecting Karen to toast her own forthcoming nuptials.

"Yes," Karen said, looking decidedly glum, as she set her glass down firmly on the table, "what about me, indeed?"

Chapter 29

Jenny studied the list of names on the report that Marion had given her earlier. The report listed personal accounts that were in excess of permitted overdraft limits, and Jenny shuddered when she realised that most of these customers had had their limits authorised by none other than herself.

Great, she thought. A stack of 'Account Overdrawn' letters to be dictated, as well as everything else she had to do today. She'd have to get tough on some of these guys, she thought, grimacing, as she looked through the list again. It wasn't the first time that these names had appeared on that report.

Jenny jumped as her extension buzzed.

"Jenny – line two."

"Thanks, Jackie. Who is –?" She broke off, realising the receptionist had already hung up. She shook her head as she picked up the receiver. The girl was so abrupt! She would never dream of letting Jenny know who her caller might be. Knowing Jackie, this call might not even be for her.

"Hello, Jenny Hamilton speaking," she said pleasantly.

A highly agitated voice came on the other end of the line. "I'd like someone there to *please* explain why my credit card was declined in Brown Thomas just now. I've been a customer of your bank for nearly thirty years, and I'm just not prepared to stand for this kind of carry-on! I was with my neighbour, and honestly – I've never been so embarrassed in front of anyone . . ."

Jenny grimaced, as the customer continued. She had been correct – the call shouldn't have been put through to her at all. Card authorisation was a matter for Credit Card Services, and Jackie should have referred the customer to them. She had no choice but to interrupt the woman in mid-flow. "I'm very sorry, madam – you've been put through to the wrong person – can you hold for a moment, please?"

"Hold? Hold? I've been holding for *the past ten minutes!*" The woman's already high-pitched voice threatened to become hysterical. "Now, you listen to me, young lady. I will not be fobbed off by you, and foisted onto somebody else, who doesn't know what they're doing. I want you to phone Brown Thomas right now, to explain the situation, *and* I want a very apologetic letter, signed personally by the bank manager, sent out to me before the end of the day. It's absolutely disgraceful! Maybe I was slightly overdrawn but . . ."

Jenny groaned inwardly as the woman droned on. From the sound of things, she'd have to try and sort the matter out here and now – the woman would be threatening to sue the bank soon. A quick call to Card Services soon established that the caller was considerably more than 'slightly overdrawn' and incidentally wasn't even a customer of Jenny's branch. After listening to a rant about bank policy, and how 'the dogs on the street can get credit these days,' Jenny finally managed to pacify the caller, with assurances that she would have the bank 're-evaluate her credit requirements'.

She groaned as she put the phone down. Honestly! She'd have to get Marion to have a word with Jackie. Goodness knows where her own calls were ending up. Seconds later, her extension buzzed again.

"Jenny, line three was holding for *ages*! He couldn't wait any longer for you, so I had to take a number in the end – can you phone him back?"

Jenny resisted the urge to tell Jackie where to go, but decided against it. There was just no point. As Jackie passed on the caller's number, she instantly recognised it as Mike's private line at InTech. He picked up after the second ring, and Jenny felt a flood of warmth rush through her, at the sound of his voice.

"Hi, Mike – it's me," she said.

"Hey – it's about time!" Jenny knew that he was smiling as he spoke. "I thought you were going to keep me on hold forever, back there."

"Sorry – not my fault," she said, settling back in her chair, ready for a bit of chat, "Jackie Super-Switch strikes again."

He laughed. "I thought that might have been it." He had heard her tales of woe about the bank's receptionist before. "What did you end up with?"

"You don't want to know," she said dryly. "Anyway, what's up? Are you just ringing for a chat, or does the high-and-mighty director of Ireland's most dynamic software company have a cash-flow problem?"

"Ha – very funny. But that may very well be the case after today. Listen, I can't talk long, but I need to ask you a favour."

"Fire away." As she listened, Jenny began to doodle on a pad of yellow Post-it notes.

"I'm going to view some houses in Blackrock this evening, and I wondered if you'd come out and have a look at them with me – tell me what you think."

Since moving to Ireland after the divorce Mike was living in what he called his 'bachelor pad' – a rented duplex in Shankill. He was anxious to move closer to the city, and to the company offices, which were located in the Sandyford Industrial Estate. With house prices rising at an alarming rate throughout the country, but especially so in Dublin, and with the growing success of the company, Mike felt that it was time for him to buy a place of his own. So far, he had seen houses around Cabinteely and Dun Laoghaire, but Jenny knew he was especially interested in Blackrock for its proximity to the city and the InTech offices.

"Great – I'd love to see how the other half live," Jenny teased, Blackrock being one of the more upmarket Dublin suburbs. "I'll be finished here around five – what time will I meet you?"

"Why don't I pick you up after work, and we'll go straight from there? We can go for a bite to eat somewhere afterwards. Unless you want to go back to the apartment beforehand?"

"No, that's fine. I'll see you outside later then."

"Great!" Mike was pleased. "You know how much I value your exquisite taste, and valued opinion, Jennifer," he went on, affecting a haughty South County Dublin accent which, Jenny thought, sounded totally at odds with his down-to-earth personality, and his northside upbringing.

"All right, all right – save it for later," she said, laughing as she put the phone down, already looking forward to their outing. After a day like this one, she thought, eyeing the stack of files on her desk that needed attention, she could do with some fun. And Mike was always great fun. Jenny picked up a file and switched on her Dictaphone, about to dictate the first of many 'Overdrawn Account' letters she needed to get out in the post today.

A little after five, Jenny exited the branch, and looked up and down the street. She smiled, as she caught sight of Mike's car across the road, a few cars down. It never failed to amuse her that Mike drove one of those tiny Smartcars, when he could easily afford an Audi, or a Mercedes. But, she thought, smiling as he waved across to her, that was pure Mike. He had told her that he had no interest in owning a huge car for the sake of it, and that he only needed 'enough room for himself and his laptop'. Jenny wondered idly, if he would apply the same criteria to buying a house.

She opened the car door, the scent of his aftershave assaulting her nostrils as she sat in.

"Phew! Do you have a date tonight, or something?" she teased, settling herself in the passenger seat. "What's the story with the full bottle of Brut?"

"Do you not like it?" He feigned a hurt look. "Your

woman in Arnotts told me that I'd have them falling at my feet, wearing this stuff. But it's not Brut – I can't remember the name on the bottle, but it's called after some fella called Packie."

"*Keeling* over with the fumes maybe," she said laughing, "and I think you mean Paco Rabanne?"

"Hmmm. Never trust a woman pointing a tester-bottle at you," he said, pulling out into the traffic.

"Where are these houses, then?" Jenny asked, straining to get an idea of the length of traffic ahead of them. "You said Blackrock, but you didn't say where, exactly."

"The estate agent is showing us two houses – one on Newtownpark Avenue, and another close to the seafront."

"The one on Newtownpark Avenue would be handy for the office," said Jenny, who was familiar with the area.

"True – but the one on the seafront sounds lovely. I had a look at it on the Internet, and I kind of fell in love with it."

"But you haven't even seen inside the house. It could be an awful kip."

"Which is why I'm bringing you along," he said simply. "I need you to keep me on the straight and narrow. I'm going to pretend that you're my missus, so that if I get too excited about either of them, you can pretend that you're not that interested. That way, the estate agent might haggle with me over the price. Otherwise, he'd probably convince me to sign there-and-then, and I couldn't trust myself not to. I'm useless when it comes to things like that. Rebecca ended up negotiating the sale of our house in England that time – I'd have taken the first offer we got for it."

"Mike Kennedy. I don't believe a word of it! The likes of you could buy and sell for Ireland, and you don't trust yourself to say no to a pushy estate agent!"

"I'm not joking – it's true. I'm useless at that kind of thing," he said, turning onto the Rock Road. "I fold completely under pressure. That's why I have Frank to look after the Sales and Marketing at InTech. I can design software for anything, but when it comes to promoting and selling it, I'm no good. Frank won't let me in the room when he's trying to negotiate a decent contract for us."

Jenny nodded, realising that he was actually serious. Who'd have thought it? Mike wanted her as backup, in case the estate agents railroaded him. "You take the job too personally – because you're so close to it all, I suppose."

"Exactly. Bet you never had me pegged as the emotional type, huh?"

"Nope – I always suspected you were a big baby, getting so upset over your precious suit being ruined."

He feigned an outraged expression. "You cheeky little brat! I have a good mind to turf you out on the road here and now, and get some other leggy blonde to come out here with me."

"Thanks – I've never been called a leggy blonde before," Jenny flicked her hair exaggeratedly, and grinned across at him.

"It was supposed to be an insult," he said, hitting the steering wheel in feigned frustration.

They eventually pulled up in front of a two-storey, red-brick house with a big 'For Sale' sign posted outside it.

"Is this it?" Jenny asked, getting out of the car. On first

impression, the house didn't look too appealing. The garden was overgrown and weeds ran along the edge of a broken path. It obviously hadn't been attended to in years, and it reminded Jenny of the houses in Rathmines converted into flats, the landlord's priority being only the collection of his rent each week.

A few minutes later, the estate agent confirmed her suspicions, by revealing to Mike that this was exactly the case. The house had been partitioned into four small studios, and the landlord had fallen behind on the upkeep. There hadn't been much effort put into it for quite some time but, he exclaimed eagerly, it had 'lots of potential'.

Potential for a wrecking-ball maybe, Jenny thought privately, taking in the patches of mildew along the dirty grey skirting, and walls the colour of diarrhoea in the kitchen. The place would need years of work to make it anyway livable. The windows were full of dry-rot, and the partition walls would have to be torn down. She couldn't see why anyone would want the hassle, irrespective of the price. Mike was looking for somewhere to live, after all, not a lifelong hobby.

It seemed that Mike was equally unimpressed with the place, and after visiting the second house in Blackrock with the same estate agent, he was no further forward in his quest for a new home.

"So much for my impressions from the Internet," he grimaced.

Afterwards, both ravenous, they went to dinner in Blake's in Stillorgan.

"So what do you think?" Mike asked, after ordering the biggest steak he could find in the menu.

"Mmm – I don't think I could manage a sixteen-ounce. I think I'll just have the pork instead," Jenny said, handing her menu to the waiter and relaxing in her seat.

"Not the food, you dope, I meant the houses – what did you think of the houses?"

Jenny gave a shrug of her shoulders. "I wasn't impressed with either, to be honest." She smiled at a waiter who had brought a glass of wine for her, and a bottle of Budweiser for Mike. "They both needed a lot of work – considering the asking price."

She had nearly fainted with shock when Mike had told her the guide price for the first house. It made Jenny wonder how on earth he could manage paying out what would undoubtedly be a huge mortgage repayment each month. Then again, with his money, and a successful company behind him, Mike probably wouldn't have any worries about something like that.

"I know what you mean," he said grimacing. "The living-room in the second one looked like something out of a bad sixties porn movie!" He laughed as Jenny raised an eyebrow. "Seriously, though – I don't want to buy something that needs a lot of work because I don't have the time, or more importantly, the inclination, for tearing down fireplaces and repainting walls." He traced a finger along his beer bottle, catching droplets of condensation as they fell.

"Isn't there anything you've seen so far that you like?"

He shook his head. "Nope – not so far, anyway. They're all either much too big or much too small."

"Nothing that's 'just right'?" Jenny teased. "I thought *I* was the only Goldilocks around here."

"Hey! You watch your cheek or you'll be paying for your own porridge this evening," he said, shaking a fork at her.

"Oh, I promise I'll be good, Daddy Bear," she countered, suddenly realising that she was thoroughly enjoying herself. In fact, Jenny thought, it was difficult *not* to enjoy being with Mike. Whenever they met up, which she admitted had been quite a bit lately, there was always something to talk about, and more often than not, something to laugh about. She pushed her salad around the plate, trying in vain to pick up pieces of shredded lettuce.

"Any plans for the weekend?" he asked nonchalantly.

Mouth full of salad, Jenny shook her head. "No, actually. I had been thinking of going home to Kilkenny for a visit, but Mum and Dad are away on a trip, and my younger brothers want the house to themselves." She rolled her eyes. "They're probably planning some mad party, and wouldn't want boring big sister cramping their style."

"Well, if you're not doing anything else –" Before he got a chance to finish, Mike's mobile phone began ringing loudly. Conscious of the disapproving stares he was getting from other diners, he answered on the second ring. "Hello? Oh, hi, Becky," he said easily, a smile breaking across his face as he realised who was on the other end.

Jenny's stomach did a little flip. Becky? She had known that they were still on good terms, but not that good! Mike seemed delighted with the call from his ex-wife. She made a great show of playing with her food, trying not to listen as Mike laughed heartily at something Rebecca was saying.

"I can imagine! Becky. That's just typical of you – the poor thing . . . " Mike chatted on for a few minutes more, before promising that he would 'sort it out', and speak to her tomorrow.

Jenny wished she could have heard both ends of the conversation. What was there to sort out? More to the point, why, if they were divorced, *was* there something to sort out? Right then, Jenny was aching with curiosity.

Mike put his phone back down on the table. "Sorry about that. I normally switch the damned thing off after hours. Anyway, what were we talking about?"

"You were asking about my weekend," she said quietly.

"Oh right – yes. Well, I've some more houses to see on Saturday, so if you're not doing anything, do you fancy coming house-hunting with me again?"

Jenny smiled across at him, childishly pleased at being the object of his attention once again. "OK – but only if you promise to come shopping with me afterwards! I need to get something for Karen – her birthday's coming up and she got me a gorgeous lamp for the apartment when I first moved in. Actually," she said, the thought of another outing with Mike cheering her more than she cared to admit, "*you* could come in very handy, now that I think of it."

"Handy," Mike said flatly, his chin resting on his hand as he looked across the table at her. "I've been described many ways in my life – intelligent, funny, sexy, gorgeous – but handy? Now *that's* a new one."

She giggled. "Sorry . . . no, seriously, I just thought I might get her a DVD player. Karen loves collecting movies and television shows. Something like that would be perfect for her. And you, being a technical whiz kid and all that, could help me pick it up . . . out – the DVD player I mean."

Jenny felt herself beginning to blush as she babbled out the rest of the sentence. Mike was smiling at her as if he knew exactly what she was up to. She must have been flirting too obviously with him, what with all that Goldilocks stuff and everything. She wouldn't normally behave like this, and it wasn't as if she was really sure she liked him as anything other than a friend but . . .

She glanced shyly across at Mike, who was now busily scraping the remainder of his food up onto his fork. He picked up the plate and for a moment it looked to Jenny as though he was going to lick it clean, but then thought the better of it.

"Now *that*," Mike said, signalling for the bill, "was absolutely fantastic. It was that good, I could eat the same again and still come back for more."

"Are you always this enthusiastic about your food?" Jenny asked, unable to stop herself from wondering, if he was that enthusiastic about food, what he would be like in bed. The women's magazines Karen used to buy were always going on about how the two were related. Jenny found she couldn't stop smiling at the thought, as they walked out towards the carpark.

A few minutes later, Mike pulled up outside Jenny's apartment block. As he stopped the car but left the engine running, Jenny felt almost lonely going back to her empty apartment. She wasn't sure exactly what, but she knew that something tonight had changed in the dynamic of their relationship. She still recalled quite clearly that sudden pang of jealousy she had felt when he chatted so amiably with his ex-wife on the phone. All of a sudden, Jenny felt quite possessive of Mike and didn't want the evening to end just yet. She wondered briefly whether she should ask him in for a while, but as they had already made arrangements for the following Saturday, there was no real reason for the invitation. Feeling stupid, and a little unnerved by her indecision, Jenny opened the car door and got out.

"See you Saturday then," she said cheerfully.

"Looking forward to it," he replied with grin, and he drove off, leaving Jenny smiling wistfully at his retreat.

Chapter 30

Karen hurried down the street in the pouring rain, battling against the wind with her umbrella, as the bus drove away from her stop. She put the key in the front door, dived inside and slammed the door behind her, relieved to be home at last. She removed her sopping wet jacket and wiped the dirty rain-spatters off the back of her tights. A bath – that's what she needed after the day she'd had today. A nice warm bath with some lavender oil and plenty of bubbles, she decided, the thought of it warming her up already.

But first, she needed something to eat. "Please, please, let there be something decent in the freezer," she said out loud to no one in particular. Luckily, there was a frozen lasagne at the very back of the icebox. Perfect! That would only take ten minutes in the microwave. She was absolutely starving, and definitely in no mood for cooking a culinary masterpiece at nearly eight o'clock on a Friday evening. What with Shane going out with his workmates tonight for some leaving do or other, Karen didn't need to. She switched on the microwave, and padded upstairs in her wet stocking-feet to check the immersion. Grabbing a towel from the rail, she went into her bedroom and changed into a T-shirt and her tracksuit bottoms, sorely tempted to put on her comfy bathrobe, but determined not to until after her bath.

A few minutes later, she went back downstairs to check on her lasagne. It was a little overdone and rubbery at the edges, but what the hell, she shrugged, plonking the lasagne unceremoniously out of its plastic tray onto a plate, tomato sauce and pasta running everywhere.

She went into the sitting-room, which was particularly untidy, even by her own standards. Yesterday's newspapers were strewn all over the sofa, and the coffee table was covered with overflowing ashtrays, empty glasses and crisp packets. A plate of dried-up noodles lay on the floor alongside Shane's armchair, along with a pair of trainers, a fleece top, and a copy of this month's *New Woman*.

She shook her head, moving aside the newspapers to find a space to sit down. Shane was usually great for tidying up after himself, but lately he had been working a lot of overtime and when he came home, was able for little else but flaking out on the sofa for an hour or so, and then off to bed. She couldn't blame him.

Anyway, she decided, she'd clean it up later – or, maybe it could wait until tomorrow. Tonight, all Karen felt like doing after her bath was flaking out on the sofa herself in a big fluffy bathrobe, with a bottle of wine, a big bag of crisps and Graham Norton on the telly. Anything but the *Late Late Show*.

She finished the last of her lasagne and, leaving the dirty plate on the coffee table, along with the rest of the previous night's debris, went upstairs to run her bath.

A few minutes later, she felt the weariness melt away as she closed her eyes and sank into the warm, frothy bubbles.

She was smiling happily to herself when she heard the telephone ring. She didn't bat an eyelid. Let it ring away, she thought, there was no way she was giving up her bath for anyone. Not after staying behind for two extra hours in the office on a Friday evening, trying to clean up the mess her assistant had made with the wages, *and* getting drenched trying to battle it home in the pouring wind and rain, standing on the bus for the entire journey. No way. She sank further and further into the water until her ears were covered and she could no longer hear the ringing.

Twenty minutes later, feeling rejuvenated and rather wrinkled, Karen dried off and stepped into her precious bathrobe; a fluffy, full-length chenille garment, with yellow stars and blue moons embroidered all over it. It had been a Christmas present from Shane one year, and Karen absolutely loved it. She wondered if he'd be late coming home tonight. It didn't matter, she thought, wrapping a towel around her head and rubbing moisturiser on her face. They could stay in bed for as long as they wanted in the morning. Karen loved Saturday mornings almost as much as quiet Friday nights in. She and Shane would wake up whenever they felt like it, maybe have some sleepy, lazy sex, before getting up and lounging around for the rest of the day, reading the newspapers and watching the football results come in on Sky Sports.

Karen walked back across the landing towards her bedroom to put on a pair of slippers, before going downstairs. As she did, she thought she heard rustling and movement downstairs. She checked the time on the alarm clock. The time read ten thirty, so that meant . . . Karen did a quick calculation in her head, being one of those people who tried to kid themselves into believing they would get up earlier if they put the time on the alarm clock forward. Her calculations told her that it wasn't even ten o'clock yet – Shane must have decided to come home early.

Coming back out of the bedroom, the pile of wet towels and underwear on the bathroom floor caught Karen's eye. She groaned. More mess! Well, that would have to be done tomorrow too, she decided firmly. They were all due a wash anyway, so it wouldn't matter at this stage whether they got damp on the floor, or damp in the laundry basket which at any rate was downstairs in the kitchen beside the washing machine.

Putting on her slippers and slipping a comb into her robe pocket, she went downstairs. She hoped Shane had had the intelligence to pick up a pizza or bag of chips on the way home from the pub. She certainly wasn't going to cook anything for him at this hour of the night, and he nearly always got the munchies after drink.

Then she did a double take.

There was – not Shane – but Nellie Quinn, happily pottering around the living-room, picking up newspapers and emptying ashtrays into a black refuse-sack.

"Nellie! What are you doing here?" she asked, incredulously. "Is Shane with you?"

"Oh, hello, Karen," Nellie said airily, scraping the remainder of Shane's noodles into the refuse sack. "I didn't think there was anyone here. I phoned about half an hour ago to let you know I was on my way over. I was in town for a bit of shopping earlier and with it being such a bad night, I thought I'd spend the night here."

She thought she'd spend the night . . . The cheek of the woman! Then Karen thought of something else.

"Nellie, how did you get in?" she asked, her voice rising in irritation, as she had visions of Nellie unceremoniously climbing in the back window.

"I have a key," Nellie said, reaching into her pocket and holding it up, as if Karen had never seen a key before. "I got Shane to cut one for me, in case any of us ever needed to get into the house when you're not home – like tonight, for instance. It came in very handy altogether. Otherwise I would've been stuck out in that rain."

Unperturbed by Karen's blatant annoyance, Nellie happily returned to tidying her son's living-room. "You really shouldn't leave these noodles dry overnight, you know," she said, seemingly unaware that Karen's insides were close to boiling point. "It's almost impossible to get them off the plate now. I'll have to soak them overnight."

"Nellie," Karen said, through gritted teeth, "I'll be tidying the place myself tomorrow. There's no need for you to be putting yourself to any bother."

"But why do it tomorrow, love, when you can do it today?" Nellie said sweetly enough, but with a slight edge to her voice.

Karen walked across the room and before she could stop herself, roughly wrenched the refuse-sack away from her future mother-in-law. "Nellie, don't take this the wrong way," she said, trying to keep her voice level, "but it's absolutely none of your business when, and *if*, I tidy my own house. If I want it tidy, it'll be tidy and if I want to leave it messy, then I'll bloody well leave it messy."

Nellie looked as if she had been slapped. "Well!" she said huffily. "If I'd known how strongly you feel about someone trying to help you out, Karen, I wouldn't have bothered." She perched on the edge of the sofa, as if afraid to sit down properly for fear of getting the remains of yesterday's dinner on her clothes.

Karen gritted her teeth as Nellie continued.

"There's a pile of washing-up in the sink that needs doing, and I thought I'd save you having to do it. After all, you obviously have some form of aversion towards housework. But," she continued, as Karen struggled with herself not to shake the woman hard, "it's not for me to decide how you want to keep your house – *or* live your life." She stared pointedly at the magazine on the ground in front of her.

Karen realised with horror that it lay open at an article Shane had been reading with great amusement the previous night, entitled 'Female Ejaculation – Can We Come Too?'

"However," Nellie said sharply, obviously not quite finished with Karen, "my son happens to live here too, and I'm not happy about *his* living amongst filth like this."

"Filth? *Filth?* You should pay a visit to Shane's old flat, and then you'd know all about filth, Nellie Quinn!" Karen said, her eyes flashing. "How dare you call me filthy! There's absolutely nothing wrong with the way I keep this house, considering that I work all day every day and don't have the time to be mopping up every little crumb that drops on the ground. *And* I very much resent your coming in here and trying to tell me what to do. The cheek of you!"

"If it wasn't for me, dear, you wouldn't even have a house to keep," Nellie countered, in an amazingly calm voice that added even more to Karen's annoyance. "Don't forget it was myself that arranged for Jack to help you with the mortgage for this very house."

Karen clenched her fists in anger. She couldn't believe what she was hearing! She tried to calm herself down before she said something to Nellie that she'd really regret. She could almost hear her father's voice in her head telling her to 'count to ten', like he always used to whenever he sensed her temper rising as a little girl. She felt her heartbeat quicken with rage, and she tried her best not to roar at the woman. This wasn't the first time that Nellie had tried to undermine Karen's housekeeping.

During one of her visits, Karen had found Nellie sweeping the kitchen floor, claiming that 'with that colour linoleum, it needed to be swept every day, and not just once a week'. And, on another visit, she had taken down the curtains from the spare room, telling Karen that she'd have them 'washed and ironed in no time'. Karen had been livid at the time, but for some reason hadn't mentioned either incident to Shane.

This time though, she knew that the swords were drawn as far as she and Nellie were concerned. Imagine letting herself into the house and taking over just like that? She'd murder Shane for giving her a key. There was no way she was going to have Shane's family crawling all over the place whenever they felt like it. Karen wouldn't have her own family do that!

Imagine if any of them walked in on her and Shane writhing on the floor some Sunday afternoon, she thought. Admittedly, it had been some time since they had done that, but that wasn't the point, was it? She'd never be able to relax in this house again, if she thought that Shane's crowd could arrive in at any minute. It was a crazy situation, and she'd be damned if she was going to put up with it for one minute longer. She'd have it out with Shane later when he got home.

In the meantime, she supposed she'd have to pacify Nellie; otherwise they'd soon be at one another's throats.

She tried to be amiable. "Nellie, look, I'm sorry. I know you're only trying to help. And the house isn't usually this untidy. But I've had a very hard week at work, I only just got home a while ago and, to be frank, the last thing I wanted was visitors tonight – you know what I mean," she added quickly, as Nellie looked huffy at being described as a visitor. "Look, all I wanted to do was relax for the evening, and not have to go on some cleaning frenzy. I was just surprised to find you here, that's all." Her voice softened. "Just forget about the plates and the washing-up – I'll get rid of the newspapers and we'll have a cup of tea, all right?"

Nellie nodded, saying nothing. Karen began picking up the magazines and newspapers and putting them into the refuse sack. Then she went into the kitchen to put on the kettle, noticing that all the cupboards were open and Nellie had put what looked like every dish, every plate and every piece of cutlery they owned soaking in piping hot water in the sink. A fresh burst of fury erupted inside Karen. The woman obviously thought she'd give the 'filthy' kitchen a good spring-clean while she had the place to herself. Karen fumed as she filled the kettle with water. Her kitchen was *not* filthy. Nor was she. Untidy maybe, but not dirty or filthy. She had lived away from home long enough at this stage, to be able to look after herself. If it wasn't good enough for Mrs Quinn or her darling son – tough! They'd just have to go take a running jump.

She felt an amazing surge of annoyance towards Shane, all of a sudden. Why couldn't he just tell his family to go and feck off for themselves, and leave the two of them alone? She felt tears smarting behind her eyes as she reached for the box of teabags she kept (in their own box, not in some fancy jar) in the cupboard. She had thought that owning their own home, and planning a future together would be fantastic, but so far it was turning into a complete disaster. The overbearing Quinn family's involvement in their relationship, what with any one of them arriving on the doorstep at any time, and the constant digs about them having children and setting a date for the wedding: the whole lot was bit by bit driving a wedge between her and Shane.

Karen knew for certain that she did not want to marry Shane if it meant sharing their lives with his family. They would need to sort that out before she'd ever dream of setting a date. Jenny and Tessa were absolutely right. She'd have to sit Shane down and talk to him about it, tell him exactly how she was feeling; otherwise their relationship would fall to pieces.

She went back into the living-room with a cup of tea for Nellie and a bottle of wine for herself, thinking that if Nellie said anything about her drinking, she'd have to throttle the woman. However, they appeared to have reached an impasse, because her future mother-in-law was sitting quite happily in front of the television, watching the *Late Late Show*.

Karen handed her a cup of tea and plastered a smile on her face. That put the kybosh on her plans for the evening then, she thought. There was no way she could watch *Graham Norton* with Nellie around. Knowing Karen's luck, tonight Graham would be featuring women peeing into brandy glasses and smoking cigarettes out of vaginas – or worse! She didn't think Nellie would be too impressed with that. She looked at her watch. Hopefully Shane wouldn't be out too late, and she wouldn't have to put up with the woman on her own for much longer.

"Do you have any nice biscuits to go with that, love?" Nellie asked, smiling beatifically. "It's good manners to offer a few biscuits with a cup of tea."

Blast the bloody woman, Karen said to herself, getting up again from the sofa. Was she ever going to get a chance to relax tonight?

Well, that was it. She'd get Nellie her precious biscuits and then she was going to bed. She'd talk to Shane in the morning. This time she'd definitely have it out with him. Definitely.

Without-a-Fucking-Doubt.

* * *

The next morning Karen awoke with a start, and opened

her eyes. What was Shane doing banging around in the kitchen, so early on a Saturday morning? She looked groggily at the alarm clock display. It was eight-thirty! Which actually meant eight o'clock – *a.m.!*

Then she felt movement beside her in the bed. It obviously wasn't Shane making all the noise – he was still asleep. Karen hadn't heard him come in the night before.

Then she sat up in the bed, remembering. Nellie!

"Shane! Wake up, will you?" she said, elbowing him none-too-gently in the ribs.

"Whah? What time is it?" Shane asked sleepily, through half-opened eyes.

"It's bloody eight o'clock, that's what time it is," Karen hissed. She couldn't believe that, not content with ruining her evening, now Nellie was trying to intrude on her precious Saturday mornings too. Why wouldn't the woman just go home?

"Aw, great – smells like she's making a fry-up," Shane said, now fully awake, sitting up in the bed and sniffing the air.

"Well, what in God's name is she doing making a fry-up in our house, at this hour on a Saturday morning?" Karen asked, incredulous at Nellie's behaviour. Did she not tell her to stop interfering last night?

"Calm down, Karen – it's no big deal. I know it's early – but Mam always gets up early, no matter what day it is." He threw back the duvet and got out of bed. "Aw – this is brilliant!" He pulled on a pair of jeans and a T-shirt. "I haven't had one of Mam's fry-ups in ages, and I'm absolutely starving!" Rubbing his hands with glee, off he went downstairs, completely oblivious to Karen's indignation.

336

She sank back down in the bed and pulled the covers over her head. Let Shane have breakfast with his mammy all he wanted, she fumed. But there was no way she was getting up at this unearthly hour. She closed her eyes and tried to get back to sleep.

A few minutes later, she heard Nellie shout loudly from downstairs.

"Karen, love – stop lolling around in bed, and hurry up! Your breakfast is nearly ready!"

Karen sat bolt upright on the bed. The cheek of Nellie Quinn, ordering her around like she was a ten-year-old – and in her own house too! Well, she could go sing – Karen would stay in bed for as long as she wanted. Then she heard footsteps on the stairs, and Shane stuck his head around the bedroom door.

"Karen," he said delightedly, "you should see the place downstairs – it's like a palace! She must have been up since six this morning, hoovering and polishing. Now neither of us have to do a tap over the weekend – isn't it brilliant?"

She resisted the urge to throw a pillow at his stupid, grinning face. Why didn't Nellie's actions bother him – or why couldn't he see that they were really bothering *her*? Didn't Shane feel any way possessive about his own home? Or was it perfectly reasonable to him that his mother could just arrive in, and change things around as she pleased?

"Shane, I'm not getting up until she's gone – all right?" she said sulkily, letting her head fall back hard on the pillow.

"What?" Shane looked puzzled. "But you're awake now – and she's cooked breakfast for us."

"I don't care." Karen turned her head away from him, towards the wall. "I don't think it's right that your mother is wandering around our house like it's her own, and I certainly don't think it's right that you gave her a key without consulting *me* first."

"What? But how else was she supposed to get in when none of us are here?" Shane asked, completely missing the point.

Karen sat up and turned around again to face him, her eyes flashing. "Why *should* she get in when none of us are here, Shane? This is *our* house – not a bloody stopover point for your family's little trips down to Dublin!" Her voice shook with fury.

"I don't know what you're getting so worked up about," Shane said, lowering his voice and looking towards the door, afraid that Nellie might hear them. "In fact, you seem to get worked up about everything these days, always giving out about something – what the hell is wrong with you?"

Karen was livid. She couldn't believe that he was trying to turn the tables on her, and make it seem as though *she* was the one that was being unreasonable.

"Just fuck off, Shane," was all she could think of in response. "Fuck off downstairs to your mother!"

"Fine! I will!" Shane said, turning back towards the door. "But whatever your problem is, Karen, you'd better sort it out soon. I don't know what's going on with you these days!"

He couldn't even bring himself to slam the door behind him, she thought sourly. He was too afraid that he might upset Mommy Dearest. Realising suddenly that she desperately needed to use the toilet, Karen got out of bed, opened the door and tiptoed across to the bathroom. She could hear Nellie telling Shane how she had to go out this morning to buy sausages and rashers, because there was nothing in the fridge. "Only a scrap of milk!" she trilled. "I can't understand how you young ones can live like this, Shane!"

Karen closed the bathroom door behind her, trying to shut out Nellie's annoying high-pitched laughter. Whilst sitting on the toilet, she noticed that the previous night's discarded wet towels and clothes had been picked up. The washbasin looked freshly scrubbed and the tap handles on the bath were gleaming. Nellie had been everywhere! What did she do, Karen wondered. Wait until I went to sleep so she could go over every room in the house with a J-cloth and a bottle of Cif?

But what should she do? She couldn't go downstairs and confront Nellie in front of Shane. That would only force him to take sides, and Karen couldn't be sure at this stage that he would take hers. Not that it would be fair to put him in a position where he would have to choose, she supposed, going back towards the bedroom, After all, he was very close to his mother – he had told her that often enough.

So what was she supposed to do? She couldn't let Nellie take over their lives like this. Glumly, Karen pulled on a pair of jeans and a fleece. There was no point in hiding up her room like this – she'd have to go down and make an attempt to be friendly – for Shane's sake, at least.

"Morning, Karen!" Nellie chirped brightly, as she joined the cosy scene at her kitchen table. "Or should I say 'good afternoon', at this stage?"

Shane looked up at her and winked, obviously pleased to see her up and about and making an effort. Nellie took a plate of food she had been keeping warm under the grill, and put it on the table, urging Karen to eat up.

This is bloody ridiculous, thought Karen to herself, trying not to show her annoyance. She was being ordered about in her own home and at the moment there was absolutely nothing she could do about it. She looked in dismay across the table at Shane, praying that he would notice that something was off, but no, Mammy's boy was happily munching on his third piece of toast. He really was completely unperturbed by how weird all of this was, she thought, pushing the food slowly around the plate.

When Nellie urged her again to 'eat up before it gets cold', Karen felt as though she were well and truly in some kind of Twilight Zone.

Chapter 31

Jenny critically examined her reflection and decided that today she looked good. She had been to hairdresser's the day before for a trim and to touch up her highlights, and her hair gleamed healthily. She wore a black T-shirt with a gold, oriental-type logo on the front, over a pair of light-coloured bootleg denims that she had picked up in Brown Thomas the previous week. A pair of black chunky high boots completed the outfit. The boots were new too, Jenny having only in recent weeks rediscovered her passion for shopping.

In fact, she thought, spraying *Contradiction* on her wrists; she had rediscovered her passion for a lot more than shopping. Although she hadn't relished the thought of it months earlier, Jenny found that she really enjoyed her independence. She had her own apartment, a good job and great friends. All she needed now was a man, she thought, giggling to herself as she put a hoop earring in each ear. She hadn't felt this good in ages, and was so looking forward to going out with Mike today. She had been looking forward to it all week.

As if on cue, the intercom buzzed and Jenny rushed to answer it.

"*Only me!*" Mike screeched, in his best Harry Enfield impression.

"You're early! I'm not ready yet – you'll have to come up and wait."

When she let him into the apartment, Mike stood back from her and wolf-whistled.

"Look at you, all rock-chick raunchy – do you have a date or something?" he teased.

Jenny made a face at him. She went back into her bedroom and continued getting ready, secretly delighted with the compliment. Mike didn't look too bad himself either, she thought. Today was the first time she had seen him without a suit, and the tan combats and navy rugby top he wore made him look a lot more approachable, easygoing, and Jenny had to admit, quite sexy.

"These apartments look deceptively small from outside," he said.

In her mirror Jenny watched him look around the living-room with interest. She remembered then that this was the first time he had been inside her apartment.

"Yes, it's a lot bigger than most of the places I've lived in – then again, it costs a lot more," she said, wondering if she should give him a guided tour, and then instantly deciding against it. That would mean going into her bedroom, and as soon as he saw the pile of clothes lying on the bed he would think that she had been making a concerted effort to impress him.

Which certainly wasn't the case, Jenny assured herself, while applying a slick of Vaseline on her lips. A few minutes later, she followed Mike downstairs and out into the bright morning sunshine. It was still quite cold, even for March but anyone could see that spring was definitely on the way. Daffodils and tulips blossomed from the flowerbeds alongside the apartment block entrance, reminding Jenny of her dad's flowerbeds at home, and of the fact that she hadn't paid her family a visit in weeks.

"What a fabulous day!" she said, following Mike's gaze out towards the pier. The water sparkled with reflected sunlight, as did the yachts and boats moored in the harbour.

"It is, isn't it?" he nodded, then turned and looked at her, a thoughtful expression on his face. "Do you know something – I think it's too nice a day to spend viewing dreary second-hand houses."

"What do you mean?" Jenny asked, feeling vaguely disappointed at the prospect of their outing being cancelled. "Do you want to call off the house-hunting altogether?"

"Most definitely," he said firmly, taking her by the arm. "I can do that any time – let's do something interesting instead, like take the Dart out to Howth, or walk along Killiney Hill – what do you think?"

"Well, yes, great – but haven't you already made an appointment to see the houses today?" Jenny said, in two minds; the first thrilled at the thoughts of doing something 'interesting' with Mike, and the second unsure as to whether or not she should show it. As for her shopping for Karen's birthday present, well, she could always go into town for late-night shopping during the week.

Mike was already on his mobile before she had time to think any more about it.

"Hello, Mr Peters? Hi, it's Mike Kennedy here. No, I can't make our appointment today, I'm afraid – something's come up. I'll have to arrange with you for another time . . . yes . . . OK, talk to you soon." He put the phone back in his pocket and grinned at her. "Right – that's that sorted! And I just had a brainwave while I was on the phone . . . have you ever been to Brittas Bay?"

Jenny hadn't, so they got into Mike's little yellow SmartCar, and headed towards the Wicklow coast, all thoughts of house-hunting forgotten. As it was still early enough for breakfast, they stopped off on the way at a cosy café in Ashford, for a big fry-up. Mike admitted that he rarely cooked for himself at his apartment. "It takes too much time and effort to cook for just one of me," he said, "although sometimes I do tend to eat enough for maybe two or three."

"I'd noticed," Jenny said dryly, watching him stuff two sausages and a piece of white pudding into his mouth all at once.

"Rebecca used to go mad," he said, taking a gulp of tea to wash it down. "She reckoned she always ended up making huge dinners for me, but ended eating a lot more herself as a result."

Watching him smile at the memory, Jenny felt a tinge of jealousy. Mike was always talking about Rebecca lately, commenting on things that Rebecca might do or Rebecca might like. It was fairly obvious by his behaviour that he still had strong feelings for his ex-wife. Still, she supposed, you don't forget someone to whom you were actually married that easily. In contrast, she rarely spoke about Roan to Mike other than that first night at Tessa's wedding. Mike knew that Jenny had been hurt by someone, and it seemed that that was all he needed to know. He had never pressed her for more information, and Jenny appreciated that. Although lessening as time went by, the pain was still there – admittedly not quite as sharp, but still there nonetheless.

Mike paid the bill and they continued their drive, reaching Brittas Bay within twenty minutes. Jenny gasped when she saw the spectacularly huge sand-dunes on the beach of powder-like white sand.

"Wow – this is fantastic!" she said in amazement, the cool breeze whipping through her blonde curls. "I hadn't expected anything like this, Mike. The beach is like something out of a Mediterranean holiday brochure." Jenny, more familiar with the dark and stony beaches of the south-east, couldn't believe that the east coast could be so different in appearance.

"Pity the temperatures don't fit that comparison," Mike laughed. He held out his hand. "Come on, let's go for a walk."

Giddy with delight, Jenny took his hand, and together they walked along the mostly deserted sea front, Mike unable to resist testing the water with his bare toes. Jenny wasn't quite so adventurous but regretted wearing her new chunky-heeled boots.

She watched Mike turn up the bottoms of his combats as far as his knees and wade further into the sea, urging her to join him. Jenny bent down to test the water.

"No way I'm getting my feet wet! This is bloody freezing!" she exclaimed, grimacing as the unexpected coldness of the water hit her fingers. Mike laughed and came back to join her. She walked along beside him happily, thinking that this had to be one of the nicest Saturday mornings she had ever spent. Although it was chilly on the beach, the sky was completely clear and she could feel the warmth of the early sun on her back.

"I can't believe I've never been here before," she said, looking around her in fresh wonder. "I've never been a big fan of the seaside, even when I was younger, but this is really fantastic."

"I'm glad you like it," Mike said, with a smile.

Jenny was very conscious of the fact that he was still holding her hand.

"But there are some gorgeous beaches down around Wexford direction that I'm sure you'd love as well," he continued. "We should continue driving down along that way, and make a day of it. What do you think?"

Jenny nodded vigorously – the thought of such an unplanned adventure delighting her tremendously.

Later that evening, having visited numerous beaches and beauty spots along the east coast, Mike suggested that they have dinner in Wexford town. "There's a lovely hotel just on the outskirts where I usually stay when I'm down here on business," he said, "or we could look for a nice restaurant in the town, if you like."

Jenny told him that she didn't care where they went, as long as they ate soon. She didn't know if it was the excitement of the day, or the sea-air in her lungs that was making her feel so hungry.

Mike opted for the hotel and soon they were comfortably seated, enjoying their starters.

"You'd better have some of this too," Jenny said, pushing a plate of garlic bread towards Mike, who had chosen a plate of deep-fried Brie. "Otherwise, you'll refuse to have me in the car with you on the way home."

"Agreed," he said, picking up a slice and popping it in his mouth, clearly delighted at the prospect of extra food.

"Pig!" she teased, highly amused at what had to be described as the passion Mike Kennedy had for his food. "Tell me, Mike," she said, taking a sip of what she thought was an especially delicious Californian Sauvignon. "Do you always eat this quickly?"

"Yep!" he said, taking another piece of her garlic bread as if to illustrate his point. "There were five in my family and it was every man for himself when it came to mealtimes. If you didn't eat quickly, you didn't eat. Simple as that."

Jenny chuckled. "You make it sound like something out of a Dickens novel."

"God no, I'm not trying to say that we were penniless, just that we're all savages when it comes to our food. Even now, when we all get together at Christmas or whatever, it's still the same, and Rachel is as bad as any of us." He sat back in his chair. "You should come along sometime – you'd see exactly what I'm talking about."

"Ah, no, thanks," Jenny said. "From what I've seen so far, one Kennedy is enough for me!" She indicated the empty plates in front of them. He'd even polished off the salad.

Mike shrugged. "I love my food and make no apology for it."

"What I can't understand is that you don't seem to show it – you're very trim."

"I think that all the running around and worrying I do every week at work is enough to keep it off, for the time being anyway. It'll probably catch up with me eventually. Ah, speaking of savages though," he indicated the almost empty wine bottle, "you're quite enjoying that, aren't you?"

Jenny took another sip and licked her lips. "It's a great wine. It's a pity you have to drive back, otherwise you could have some." She checked her watch and then looked across at him in surprise. "Mike – I hadn't realised the time! It's nearly nine o'clock! No wonder I was so hungry."

He nodded. "Hard to believe, isn't it? It'll be all hours by the time we get back to Dublin."

It must have been the wine because the words were out of her mouth before she could stop them. "Well, why don't we stay? I mean, we could both relax and have a few drinks, and you wouldn't have to worry about driving." She could feel her cheeks reddening as she spoke. Please don't let him take this the wrong way, she prayed silently.

"Great idea," Mike agreed happily. "When we're finished here, I'll ask for a couple of rooms at reception."

Jenny spread mint sauce over her Wicklow lamb, pleased with her suggestion, and the fact that Mike didn't seem to read anything into it. It had been a very long day and she was tired. The thought of spending the rest of the evening relaxing with a few drinks in the hotel bar, rather than facing the car trip back to Dublin, appealed to her a great deal.

As if to demonstrate his newfound freedom, Mike

poured a generous measure of wine into his glass, and ordered another bottle. The waiter was about to uncork the bottle, when Mike's mobile phone beeped loudly.

"Ah, a text message – somebody loves me!" he said, searching for the phone in the pockets of his jacket.

"I can never get the hang of those things," Jenny said. "All that word-shortening – it can't be good for the language. I'm pretty sure that eventually we won't be able to spell anything properly." She looked up when Mike didn't answer. He was laughing quietly at the contents of his message. "What's so funny?" she asked, feeling a bit put out about their cosy dinner being interrupted

"It's from Becky," he laughed, as he scrolled down through the message again. "She's just sent me the most stupid joke – here, take a look at it." He handed her the phone across the table.

Jenny read the message, reluctantly plastered a weak smile onto her face, and handed the phone back to him.

"Well?" said Mike good-humouredly. "Did you get it?"

Jenny didn't. She didn't get the joke and she certainly didn't get the seemingly close relationship Mike obviously still had with his ex-wife. She pushed her food around the plate, her appetite as well as her good mood having worn off all of a sudden.

"I didn't realise you and Rebecca got on so well, considering . . . " she said, unable to look at him.

"Considering?"

"Considering the reasons for your break-up, I mean," she stammered. "I mean – the way she left you for someone else and –" Seeing his expression darken, she broke off.

"Jenny," Mike said, a warning tone in his voice, "you and I have become good friends over the last few months. But you have no idea what you're talking about. The reasons for my marriage break-up weren't as straightforward as you might think."

He drank from his glass. "We each went through a lot of heartache towards the end. Believe me, I was no saint either. By throwing myself heavily into my work, I abandoned her too, in a way."

"Mike," Jenny interjected, annoyed with herself for saying anything, "I'm so sorry – it just came out. I really didn't mean to pry."

He shook his head. "It's probably my own fault for making it sound like I was the one hard done by. But you don't know how much it means to me that Rebecca and I are adult enough to stay friends, after everything we went through together. I have no animosity towards her, and she's always been, and still is, one of my closest friends. I even get on with Graham – that's her new man, by the way." He smiled. "I know what you're thinking," he went on, as Jenny struggled to keep the shock from registering on her face, "but there's no point in being bitter and twisted over it. I'm glad that she's found happiness with someone else, really I am. I still love her, but not in that way, not any more."

Jenny thought his eyes looked suspiciously bright and she resolved to change the subject. How could she have been so flippant about it? Mike and his ex-wife had probably been to hell and back together, yet still managed to maintain their friendship. It was a noble and very mature attitude – an adult attitude. Jenny thought she must have sounded like a spoilt teenager, going on about it like that. She shook her head. "Look, Mike, you don't know how sorry I am. I really didn't mean – "

His eyes twinkled with good humour. "Jenny – it's fine really. Just forget about it. Now," he said, pushing his empty plate away from him with a grin, "will we go for dessert or what?"

"No way," Jenny put a hand on her stomach, pleased that the uncomfortable moment had passed. "If I eat anything else, I'll explode."

"Not at all. If anything, you could do with a bit of meat on your bones. Ally McBeal has nothing on you, girl!"

Jenny laughed, her early good humour returning. "Don't try to justify your gluttony by forcing food on me! Seriously," she said, shaking her head at the waiter, who was waiting to take their order, "I really couldn't handle another bite."

"OK, OK. I won't have anything else either," he said, getting up from the table. "Why don't you go on into the bar, and I'll see if I can organise some rooms for the night?"

As Jenny watched him walk confidently through the double doors to reception, she again admonished herself for her behaviour earlier. What was wrong with her lately? Did she feel jealous of Rebecca and Mike's relationship? It wasn't as though she and Mike were anything more than friends, so what was the problem?

"Right – that's that sorted," he said, joining her at the bar. "We're on the third floor, across the hall from one another. I'll tell you though," he said, looking at his watch and yawning, "I'm fairly beat after today and after all that food. I don't think it'll be a late night for me."

"I know what you mean," Jenny agreed. "I feel like I've eaten enough to keep me going for a week!"

Mike sat down beside her on a comfy sofa against the wall. For a Saturday night, the place seemed very quiet. Apart from a small group sitting up at the bar watching *Match of the Day* and some couples sitting at tables dotted around the room, the place was practically empty. Jenny sat back almost horizontally on the sofa. The combination of the food, the wine and the day's driving was making her feel very drowsy. Mike was sitting so close to her; she'd only have to lift her head slightly to lay it on his chest. She longed for sleep.

Mike smiled lazily across at her. "Are you thinking what I'm thinking?"

Jenny nodded, with heavy-lidded eyes. "If it involves a bed, most definitely yes."

Mike sat up. "Jenny Hamilton! Are you propositioning me?"

Looking up, Jenny saw his eyes twinkling with humour. Then his expression changed and become very serious. He must have seen it in her eyes, because she couldn't help what she did next. Putting an arm around his neck, Jenny pulled his head towards hers and planted a gentle kiss on his mouth. He pulled back slightly, looking at her questioningly for a moment, but then she reached up for another kiss, answering his question without saying a word. This time the kiss wasn't as one-sided, and as it deepened, a massive longing swept through Jenny like a thunderbolt. Then she remembered where they were. "Mike," she said, opening her eyes and looking around her with embarrassment.

"You're right," he said breathlessly, sitting up straight, "I'm sorry – it was all my fault, I shouldn't have – "

"No, silly," she said with a grin, tightening her arms around him. "I meant that I have no intention of providing unexpected entertainment in this place."

They were upstairs and inside his room within minutes.

Jenny didn't quite know why she had done what she did just then in the bar, but she knew without hesitation that she wanted Mike Kennedy. There was no point in trying to kid herself any longer. There was, and probably had been from the beginning, she admitted, a lot more between the two of them than friendship.

Mike was passionate and extremely skilful. They made love the first time with a ferocity that surprised them both, Jenny slightly overwhelmed at the depth of her longing for him. The second time was gentler, more loving and, Jenny thought, for the very first time with anyone – a lot more fun. With Mike, it was all about touching and teasing, and laughing, not about racing to the finishing line, which is how it had been with Roan.

Afterwards, she nestled easily into the crook of his arm and fell fast asleep, waking only when she felt him kiss the tip of her nose the next morning.

She looked up and him and smiled. "Morning," she said shyly.

"Hi," he grinned, kissing her gently on the mouth and then proceeding to make love to her slowly and sensuously.

They dozed happily in bed for the remainder of the morning, until around eleven o'clock when Mike declared that he was ravenous, and couldn't wait a minute longer for breakfast, even if he had to go into town to get it.

"Typical!" Jenny said, sitting up in the bed and crossing her arms in mock petulance. "You and your bloody stomach!"

Mike laughed and kicked her under the sheets. "Come on, woman! You don't think a man can carry on like that all night, *and* the next morning without the need for some form of sustenance, do you?"

"Well, I suppose you *do* deserve something for that performance," she teased

"You'd better believe it!" Mike dragged her back down beside him, and kissed her deeply. "And," he added, with a serious look in his eyes, "you'd better get used to it."

Jenny looked up at him, not sure what to say. She hoped that he meant it. It certainly seemed like this could be the beginning of something good between them, but she wasn't quite sure about how Mike felt about getting involved in another relationship. She hoped that things wouldn't become strange between them if he decided he didn't want that. Although, thought Jenny, she wasn't quite sure about it herself. All along she had protested to anyone that asked that she didn't feel that way about Mike, but lately, her feelings had changed. If he was willing, she certainly wouldn't mind giving it a shot. Mike seemed to read her thoughts.

"I'm really glad this happened, Jenny," he said, searching for his boxers at the end of the bed. "You probably know well that I've fancied you for ages."

Jenny burst out laughing. Putting it like that, Mike sounded like a school-kid, not a thirty-five-year-old divorcee! She realised then that his childlike honesty and unyielding good nature were the things she liked most about him. She need not have worried about any discomfort between them afterwards. There would be no game-playing where Mike was concerned.

"I'm glad too," she said, "but it was certainly unexpected. I don't know what came over me in the bar last night."

"You wanton woman, pulling and dragging at me in front of a room full of people." He ducked as she tried to whack him with a pillow.

"I'll show you a wanton woman," Jenny said, dragging him back down on the bed and kissing him decisively.

Chapter 32

Karen sat staring at the monitor in front of her eyes. Try as she might, she just couldn't concentrate on anything today. Her weekend had been disastrous and she and Shane were hardly speaking. Nellie Quinn hadn't left the house until late Saturday evening, and by then Karen had had more than enough.

She had let rip at Shane as soon as Nellie was out the door, not caring whether or not the woman heard her. But he just couldn't seem to understand her point of view.

"What's the big deal about giving her a key? She's my mother, for God's sake – I can't have her standing outside in the wind and the rain."

"Shane, this is our house! I'm a private person – I can't handle all this interfering and criticism about my housekeeping, my decorating *or* my procreating for that matter!"

"What in God's name are you talking about now?" Shane asked, his voice slow and deliberate.

"Oh come on!" she shouted. "Don't tell me you haven't noticed it! All this 'when are you setting a date, Karen – you don't want to be too old for your first, Karen – your biological clock is ticking, Karen'? Jesus Christ, I feel like some kind of brood mare these days!" She sat down at the kitchen table, her face red with exasperation.

"Well – maybe they have a point," he said carefully. "When *are* we going to set a date? I've mentioned it a million times since we moved in here, and you keep avoiding the subject. What's going on?"

She said nothing.

"I asked you a question," Shane said, his voice getting angry. "What's going on?"

She couldn't look at him. She didn't know what to say. Shane didn't understand, couldn't understand how much she resented his family's involvement in their life together. They were trying to control everything, from the mortgage, to the house and the wedding – everything. Naturally, she wanted to make plans for their future, but just the two of them – just her and Shane. No one else had any right to interfere.

"I'm sorry, Shane," was all she could say. "I'm just not sure any more."

She regretted the words as soon as they were out of her mouth. The look on his face was pure hurt. Karen didn't think she had ever seen him look so wounded.

He had walked out of the kitchen, and a few minutes later she heard the front door slam.

Karen jumped when the telephone on her desk rang suddenly. It was Mark King from Head Office, wanting to know if she had yet found a suitable temporary replacement for his PA. Melanie, his existing assistant, was going on maternity leave next month. The girl was only twenty-three, Karen thought, pulling the personnel file from a drawer beside her desk. Did she have any idea how much her life would change once she had this baby? Karen thought that it was highly unlikely that Melanie would return to work afterwards, and she had interviewed prospective candidates with this in mind. It would save her extra work in having to find someone permanent, once Melanie finally made up her mind, and announced that she wasn't coming back. It was assuming a lot, Karen knew, but she was pretty confident in her assumption, having seen it happen time and time again within the company. She discovered that many careers and ambitions were often hastily discarded once a child appeared on the scene. Sure, many woman returned to work, but Karen couldn't see how they could possibly have the same drive and energy to succeed. Work became just a necessity, a means to an end – a way of paying the mortgage, not to mention the childminder. Years of effort sacrificed, gone straight out the window, or to the next bright young thing that came in to take your place.

Karen was not going to let that happen to her. She loved this job, had worked hard to get where she was, and she wasn't going to let Shane and his interfering family put pressure on her to start a family and throw it all away. Maybe they might have children eventually, but not until they were both ready. After all, money would be more than tight if one of them was absent from work for any length of time. Nellie Quinn would just have to wait a little longer for her precious first Quinn grandchild. What a pity old Jackie boy wouldn't find a woman for himself, and take some of the heat off her and Shane.

Karen sighed. She was tired of feeling morose and depressed lately. She couldn't remember the last time she had been able to really relax and have a bit of fun. The situation with Shane's family consumed her thoughts from the moment she woke up each morning to the hours it took her to get to sleep each night. Lying in the dark beside a snoring Shane, she just couldn't stop her mind racing, as she had imaginary conversations and arguments with Nellie for hours on end. She could actually feel a knot of anxiety and frustration forming within her. She couldn't go on like this.

Karen picked up the handset and dialled Jenny's work number.

* * *

The following Thursday evening after work, Karen took a bus as far as Dawson Street, and walked the rest of the way to Pearse Street station. As she approached the building from across the road, she saw Jenny waiting outside for her.

"Wow, you look fantastic!" Karen said, when Jenny skipped across the pedestrian crossing to join her. "You've put on some weight, haven't you?"

"Karen, do you honestly think that's some kind of compliment?" Jenny said, trying to look insulted, but the glint in her eye suggesting she was not at all put out by the comment.

"It is when it comes to you. You lost a lot of weight over the last few months, so it's nice to see you looking normal, and with a bit of colour in your cheeks again."

Jenny grimaced. "So what's up?" she asked, watching her friend with some concern. She might have noticed a change in Jenny's appearance, but there was no mistaking the strained look on Karen's face. The heavy make-up she wore couldn't conceal the dark circles under her eyes, and the blemishes on her skin. Karen looked as though she hadn't slept for a week.

"I'll tell you later," Karen said glumly, not wanting to go into the gory details with Jenny while walking down the street. "Let's go somewhere nice for food – I had an early lunch today and I'm pretty famished."

They decided on Pasta Fresca, a little Italian pizzeria just off Grafton Street.

"So, tell me your news," Karen urged, as soon as they were comfortably settled at a table for two, a bottle of the house white cooling on the table between them. "You mentioned on the phone that you had a bit of gossip, and you haven't been able to stop smiling since I met you at the station."

Jenny smiled broadly, as if she had been waiting for Karen to ask that very question.

"Well," she clasped her fingers together, "it's Mike, well, me and Mike really –"

Karen, grinned, understanding perfectly. "You and Mike Kennedy finally got it together – that's terrific news, Jenny! Tell me how, when, where, everything!"

"Well . . . I was supposed to be helping him look for a new house this weekend and . . . "

Karen leaned in closer, as Jenny recalled the previous weekend's events. She was thrilled for her friend but at the same time felt a little more deflated about her own situation with Shane. Why was it that when she had been at her happiest, Jenny had been going through hell with Roan, and now that Jenny had found happiness with someone, Karen was the one in trouble? It seemed cruel.

While Jenny had had what sounded like a fantastic weekend with Mike, Karen and Shane had slept in completely separate rooms and had done so since. Shane hadn't got home from work until after ten the previous evening. He had barely uttered a word when he came in, had gone straight to the kitchen to make himself a cup of tea and a sandwich, and soon after went straight to bed – in the cluttered spare room. Karen had hoped that they might discuss the situation without it turning into a screaming match, but so far there hadn't been an opportunity. They had had some stupid fights throughout their relationship, she thought, but this one was without doubt the worst ever. Shane could never hold out in an argument for long and was usually the one to break the ice. This time though he seemed to be sticking to his guns. This time, *she* might just have to make the effort.

"I'm so pleased for you, Jen," she said. "You know I've always thought that Mike was a lovely guy. From that first time I met him at the wedding, I knew he had a bit of a thing for you."

"That's what he said too!" Jenny said, as if the thought had never crossed her mind before. "I'm just trying not to get too excited about it though, in case it all goes pear-shaped, you know? He sent me two dozen roses at work yesterday." She giggled excitedly. Then her faced changed. "The only thing is . . ." she winced.

"What?"

"Well, I came off the Pill ages ago – you know how much I hate it, and it always makes me feel bloated . . . "

Karen fixed her with a hard stare. "Please tell me that you used some form of contraception that night."

"I just didn't think – "

"Oh Jenny!"

"I know, I know I'm stupid – me of all people. But I took the morning-after pill as soon as I could get it, so I should be OK." She grimaced. "I'll go mad if I've messed this up even before it's started. I mean, I'm not fully sure how he feels about it all."

"Jen, Mike's a lovely guy. From what I know of him so far, he's not the type to get into something he's not sure of, not after the divorce anyway. And he's not at all like the other fella – if that's what you're afraid of."

Jenny looked away at the mention of Roan. "It's not that, although I suppose it did cross my mind. I know now that Roan was an immature brat who probably didn't give a shit about me, but I didn't know that at the beginning, did I?"

"The rest of us had a good idea though," Karen said quietly.

Jenny nodded. "You're right. My gut instinct is telling me that Mike's a good guy, and that he's nothing at all like Roan. But at the same time, you can't get too carried away."

"Certainly. But Jen, don't let that stop you. It sounds as though Mike is absolutely crazy about you. Enjoy it while it lasts."

She sat back as the waitress brought a plate of spaghetti bolognese for Jenny and a Hawaiian pizza for herself.

"I will," Jenny grinned, as she made a poor attempt of winding strings of spaghetti onto her fork. "I couldn't wait to tell you all about it. I feel like I'm walking on air since the weekend!"

"Have you seen him since?"

"No, but he's constantly on the phone, and he's coming over to the apartment for dinner tomorrow night. It'll be weird, you know? I had myself convinced that I didn't see him as anything other than a friend. Then the other night, everything changed."

Karen smiled half-heartedly. She wished she could feel more enthusiastic, but with Jenny's every word, she was feeling more and more despondent about Shane.

Jenny put down her fork. "Karen, I'm sorry. Here I am rabbiting on and on about Mike and me and how wonderful everything is. I've never even asked you about Shane. Did you get everything sorted out?" Karen had told her on the phone that she and Shane had an argument.

"Not really." The tears started to trickle down her face before Karen even knew they were there. Furious with herself, she hurriedly dried them with her napkin.

"Oh, Karen – what is it?" Jenny asked, raging at herself for not noticing her friend's distress sooner.

"I don't know what's happening between us." Karen sniffed and took a mouthful of wine. "We haven't spoken in days. He's mad at me because I dared to question why he gave his mother a key to our house and she came in on Friday while I was in the bath and started cleaning up and criticising me and – oh, I'm just so sick of them all, Jenny!" The tears were flowing freely now. Karen gripped her napkin so hard that her knuckles were white.

"Shush, shush, relax," Jenny soothed. "Look, why don't we finish up here and go somewhere quiet for a drink – then you can tell me all about it."

Karen nodded. A few minutes later, seated in a quiet corner of a nearby pub, Karen retold the weekend's events along with all the other instances of Nellie Quinn's interference. "The thing is, Jen, sometimes I'm not sure whether it's just me getting all worked up about nothing. Shane certainly thinks that that's the case, and I know I can get a bit wound up now and again, but I can't handle it! I really can't!"

"Of course it's not just you," Jenny said. "There's no woman on earth that would put up with that kind of thing. Shane was terribly wrong to think that he could give his mother a key without asking you first. She could walk in on you at any time."

"That's exactly what I was thinking," Karen agreed, "but Shane seems to think it's all perfectly reasonable. What I think doesn't seem to matter at all."

Jenny shook her head. "It doesn't sound like Shane to be that inconsiderate of your feelings. Have you two been arguing a lot lately?"

"That's an understatement," Karen said dryly, "but then, it's always about the same thing, his bloody family! I really wish we had never got them so involved in the first place. I told you before what Jack was like and now the rest of them seem to be getting in on the act too."

"Well, I noticed that something was a little off, that day at the house with Tessa and Gerry – it was pretty hard not to."

Karen hung her head. "There's more. He keeps

pushing me to set a date for the wedding. Like I told you before, I have no intention of getting married so that all the Quinns can start annoying me about having kids. Nellie is determined to get a Quinn grandchild out of me!" She laughed bitterly. "Can you believe it? In this day and age? Well, I've told Shane that we'll get married when we're good and ready, and not before – but certainly not just to suit the Quinns."

Jenny looked perplexed. "Karen, can I ask you a question?"

"Sure, what?"

"Well, you keep talking about what the Quinns want, and what you're determined you don't want. Have you actually asked Shane how he feels about it all?"

"What do you mean?"

"Well, correct me if I'm wrong, but last year Shane asked you to marry him. He said, 'Will you marry me?' He did not say, 'Will you marry me and instantly become my baby-machine', did he?"

"But the two are connected, Jenny. As far as Nellie Quinn is concerned, I should be giving birth exactly nine months after my wedding night!"

"That's exactly what I mean. You keep saying, 'Nellie Quinn says this and she thinks that'. Has Shane actually told you that he expects you to give up your career, and start mothering a huge brood, after you two get married?"

"No but – "

"But nothing, Karen. You can't think straight, so you're confusing the two. I've known Shane for a while now, and he's a sensible guy. I can't imagine that he'd expect you to give up your job and have children once you're married.

For one thing, you could hardly afford it with a new mortgage." She sat up and looked Karen straight in the eye. "I'll be willing to bet that you've never ever asked him about it."

"Obviously, I've asked him!" Karen answered indignantly, "I've told him there's no way I'm giving up my job and everything I've worked for, to stay at home changing dirty nappies and watching Jerry Springer. He knows that!"

"Karen, would you listen to yourself!" Jenny said, getting annoyed. "You keep going on and on about how you won't do this, and you won't give up that! Did you ever think for a second that Shane might just want to *marry* you? Has he ever actually told you that he expects to 'get a Quinn grandchild out of you' as you so eloquently put it yourself? Be honest with me, has he?"

Karen thought for a moment. "No, he hasn't actually said anything like that out straight. But I *know* that it's what he wants, Jenny. He loves kids. He's always messing around with his nephews and nieces and –"

"Karen, I know I'm no one to talk about relationships, but you won't have much of a marriage if you can't talk about things like that. Look, the way I see it, Shane can't understand your resentment towards his family because he doesn't realise the pressure you're putting yourself under. Yes," she added vehemently, seeing Karen's expression tighten, "you're your own worst enemy. If you just sit down calmly and explain to him exactly how you're feeling, I'll bet that he'll be absolutely shocked."

"I don't think so, Jenny. He knows how I feel – "

"Karen," Jenny interrupted calmly, "promise me."

"What?"

"Please, just promise me. Promise me that you'll go home now and talk to Shane about it. Forget about Nellie and the Quinns; just find out exactly what *he* thinks about it. It's the only way you'll sort it out, once and for all."

Karen gave a slow shake of her head. She could understand in a way where Jenny was coming from. After all, she and Shane had never actually discussed whether or when they would have children after the wedding. Jenny was right. His feelings on the subject always seemed to get lost in the arguments about his family. Maybe, as Jenny said, she should find out once and for all what he thought about it. But what if he said yes, that he *did* expect to start a family straight away? What would she do then? Would it mean the end of their relationship?

* * *

Shane was half asleep on the sofa when she got back to the house, having seen Jenny safely as far as Pearse Street station, before getting a taxi home.

His eyes refused to budge from the television screen when she walked in. Karen took off her jacket, and hung it in the hallway. She sat beside him on the sofa.

"Shane, we have to talk."

"I know," he said, his eyes glued to the television screen.

Karen turned to face him, not sure how she would begin. "Look, Shane, I've been worrying about a lot of things lately and, to be honest, I've been taking all of it out on you."

"You can say that again." Still, he didn't look at her.

Right, Karen told herself. Keep calm – don't rise to it. "I know and I'm sorry. It's not your fault, and you shouldn't have to deal with it. The thing is, when you keep talking about our setting a date for the wedding, well – I freeze."

"Doesn't matter," Shane said, picking up a newspaper from the coffee table, and flicking idly through it. "I think we're finished, Karen."

Karen felt as though she had been kicked hard in the stomach. "What do you mean?"

"What I *mean*," he said mimicking her tone, "is that we're finished, over, Kaput – whatever way you want to put it."

"Shane – " Karen reached across to touch him.

"Forget it." He stood up, his face filled with emotion. "I've had just about enough of this, Karen. When we got engaged and then we got this place, I was the happiest man alive. But you've changed! You're not happy with anything any more. Lately, I've been working my ass off on overtime whenever I can get it. I was planning to surprise you, bring you off on holiday somewhere – anything that might cheer you up. But I'm wasting my time, aren't I? You have no intention of marrying me. Did you think I wouldn't notice that every time I, or anyone else, brings up the subject, you react as though you've been burnt?"

Karen felt very afraid. "Shane, I'm sorry. But if you'd just let me explain –"

"Look, as far as I'm concerned, there can only be one explanation. You obviously don't love me any more, Karen. Not to mention the fact that you seem to hold some kind of vendetta against my family."

"Oh, for God's sake, Shane, what do you expect?" She couldn't hold it in any longer. "How would you feel if my father was constantly on and on at you about how you paint the doors, or fit the carpets in this place? Nothing I do is good enough for your mother. I don't know what she has against me but –"

"Can you not hear yourself?" Shane said, putting a hand to his head in exasperation. "What does my mother have to do with any of this?"

Karen took a deep breath, sat back down and clasped her hands together. "Look, I know you're angry with me and in a way, I can understand why. But you don't know what's been going on in my head, lately. I've been worried and –"

"Too right, I don't know what's going on in your head. Well, come on then, tell me – why don't you just get it all out in the open, and tell me exactly what is going on, because I know I can't carry on like this any more – all this fighting, and silences, and sleeping in separate rooms is driving me crazy!"

"Will you sit down – please?" She motioned towards the space beside her.

Shane relented.

She took a deep breath. "You mightn't like what I'm going to say but please, Shane, don't interrupt. If I don't get this out now, I never will."

"OK, shoot."

She saw that he was still very angry, but seemed have calmed down a little.

"Right. When we got engaged and after we went to your mum's house – I think it might have been a couple

369

of weeks afterwards – I had a conversation with Marie. I didn't think much of it at the time, but it just seemed to come up time and time again."

Shane looked at her, puzzled, but didn't say anything.

"She was telling me how much they were all looking forward to another grandchild, how your mother had been saying she thought neither you nor Jack would ever get married. She asked when we were planning to get married and start a family. As you know, we were holding off on the wedding until we got the house sorted, and I told her that." She shrugged. "After that, it seemed like no time at all until Jack announced that he'd help us out securing the mortgage for this place. It just seemed to me as though your family were trying to smooth things along, so that we would hurry up and get married."

"But it wasn't like that all!" Shane said, unable to keep his promise not to interrupt. "Jack did us a huge favour – why can't you see that?"

"Please, Shane, just let me speak, will you?"

"Fine, go on," he said wearily.

"Anyway, soon after we got settled in here, we seemed to see a lot more of your mum and the rest of your family. They always seemed to be popping in and out for some reason or another. And to me it was like, 'Well, you've got your house sorted – now get a move on with my grandson'. Don't look at me like that, Shane, I'm just telling you how I felt." She saw him shake his head from side to side, but he didn't speak.

"Then you kept talking about setting a date, and I was thinking 'Woah, I'm not about to give up my job – which I love, by the way – just to keep the Quinn family stocked with grandchildren. To me, getting married became equated to giving up a life that I love, and starting a new one."

"I'm sorry, Karen, but I have to interrupt," Shane said sternly. "Why didn't you ever ask me what I thought about all of this? OK, I know Marie can be a bit painful when it comes to her kids – after all she's got three of them – but what made you think that I would expect you to give up your job once we were married?"

Karen felt slightly elated. Was it possible that Jenny could be right?

"I'm working hard enough as it is, love. We couldn't possibly manage to keep the proverbial roof over our heads if only one of us were working, could we?"

He moved closer to her and put an arm around her. "Karen, I really wish you could have told me this before. I had no idea you were feeling like this. I thought that you had changed your mind about the wedding, and didn't want to tell me."

"Well, I suppose I had changed my mind about it – in a way," she said, relief flooding through her body, as she felt his arms around her.

"Karen, having a family is *not* something that's foremost in my mind, I can assure you of that. I just want to us to get married, and enjoy our life together first. If, and when, we do decide to have children, it'll be *our* decision, nobody else's."

"Are you sure?" Karen asked, hardly daring to believe him.

"Definitely," he said, planting a kiss on the top of her forehead. "Don't mind Mam and Marie – they've never known anything other than getting married and having children rolled into one. Marie has never worked, apart from on the farm and neither has Mam. You should never have let them get to you like that."

"I suppose so," Karen said, biting her lip. "And I'm sorry about all the arguments about your family, Shane. I don't want you to think that I have a vendetta against them because I don't. But I've always felt that they disapproved of me, somehow."

"Look, I'll have a word with Mam – tell her to make sure Marie lays off on the baby-talk, OK?"

Karen nodded, relieved. She couldn't believe that she had let this go on for so long, let it drive a wedge between her and Shane, without even finding out how he really felt about it.

Shane gathered in his arms and hugged her tightly. "I love you, and nothing, or no one is going to change that. Do you believe me?"

She nodded into his shoulder.

"OK. So, I'm asking you again – for the *third* time, Karen Cassidy, will you marry me?"

Chapter 33

Tessa squealed down the phone excitedly. "So you've got it all booked – the church, the flowers, the dress, everything?"

"Everything except the dress," Karen said proudly. She was started to look forward to this wedding, now that everything had been arranged. She had spent the last half hour on the phone to Tessa, filling her in on all that had happened, and to let her know that she and Shane had confirmed a date.

"June 15th – put it in your diary. And it's not at the church, by the way, but at the register office."

"Oh," Tessa was taken aback. "But what about your dress, flowers and bridesmaids and everything? Won't you miss having all that?"

Karen laughed. "Tessa, the register office can be decorated with flowers too, you know – we're not getting married in The Temple of Doom!"

"Oh right." Tessa considered this. "It's just that I've

never been to a register office wedding before. I haven't a clue what to expect, that's all."

"It'll be fine. I can assure you that Shane and I will not be dancing around an open fire, our faces painted in pagan blood. And don't worry, you can still dress up to the nines in some slinky figure-hugging outfit, if that's what you're worried about."

Tessa gave a little giggle. "At that stage, I won't get an ordinary dress to fit me, let alone a slinky one."

Karen shook her head in amusement. "Why, have you put on weight? I didn't notice anything when you were here last." Knowing Tessa, she would undoubtedly turn up at the wedding, wearing some kind of show-stopping, super-sexy outfit that would make Liz Hurley look frumpy.

"Not exactly," Tessa sounded coy.

"Not exactly? What do you mean by that?" Then it hit her. "Oh my God! Tessa – you're not telling me what I think you're telling me, are you?"

Tessa laughed. "I'm nearly five months gone."

"Five months! But you must have known that time you and Gerry were here after the honeymoon – why didn't you tell me?"

She could sense Tessa shrug on the other end of the line. "If you think back, you were upset at the time about all the baby-talk you were getting from the Quinns. You might have exploded if I landed that on you, and I didn't think it'd be fair to tell you then, so I told Gerry to keep his mouth shut too."

"Oh no, I feel awful now! You must have been dying to tell us." Now that she thought of it, Karen remembered that she herself had drunk most of the wine on the day of their visit.

"Well, as you know, I was never a great one for keeping secrets. We worked out the dates and it seems that we conceived just a few weeks before the wedding – can you believe it?"

"So, it wasn't exactly planned then?"

"Not at all! I went to the doctor not long after the honeymoon, not suspecting a thing. I got some shock, I can tell you! But we're both thrilled about it now that we've had the chance to get used to it."

"Oh, I'm so pleased for you. Wait until I tell Jenny – she'll be delighted!"

"How is she anyway? The big romance still going well, I hope?"

"Seems to be," Karen nodded, forgetting that Tessa couldn't see her. "You should see her – she's going around these last few weeks positively beaming."

"And she's thrilled about being your bridesmaid too, I suppose?"

Karen paused. She had wondered whether Tessa might not be a bit put out by the fact that she was having only one bridesmaid. She had no sisters and, as her oldest friend, Jenny was the obvious choice.

"Yeah. I hope you don't mind me asking her, Tessa. It's just that she's been my friend since we were kids and –"

"Will you get away out of that, girl?" Tessa was having none of it. "I wouldn't expect you to have anyone else. Anyway," she groaned, "come June I'll be the size of a house, and ready to drop any minute."

"When *are* you due?" Karen asked, momentarily

afraid that that very thing might happen. Imagine Tessa going into labour on her and Shane's wedding day!

"Not until July so you're safe enough yet."

"Good. I have to admit I was a bit worried there for a minute."

"I kind of gathered that," Tessa said, and they both laughed. "I'm glad you rang. God knows I needed to hear a bit of good news. We went home last week and there's another delay on the house, apparently, so we won't be moving for a while yet."

"Sounds like it's taking a lot longer than you expected," Karen said, remembering that she and Gerry had told them their new house should be completed early in the New Year, and it was now late March.

"Don't talk to me," Tessa moaned. "We're having terrible trouble with planning permission, and I think we might have to change the plans for the house. I'm raging, because I had my heart set on Liscannor stone-facing, you know, to give it a rustic look, but now it seems that the planning board won't allow it. Not in 'keeping with existing surroundings' or some other rubbish like that."

"That's a pity," Jenny said, "Still, I'm sure it'll be fabulous when it's finished and decorated."

"I don't know about that. Money will be tight enough when junior comes along, and with my having to give up work."

"Will you give up for good when you move home?" Karen asked, wondering how on earth Tessa would manage at home with just a baby for company.

"Not at all – are you mad? A few months of nappies and bottles will be more than enough for me – after that, he can go to Granny Sullivan. Luckily, I don't have to worry about finding a childminder down there."

"I suppose it's good your mum is willing to help out."

"Mmm – take over, more like. Anyway, speaking of parents, how are things with you and Nasty Nellie?"

Karen rolled her eyes. "Well, since Shane and I had our little chat, I haven't seen her half as much lately." *Thank God*, she added silently to herself. "Jack is still hanging around, though."

"I thought he was based in London," Tessa mused. "Why is he spending so much time over here?"

"Good question. I know he has business contacts in the city but honestly, he's back and forth nearly every second week."

"Maybe he's seeing someone and doesn't want anyone to know yet," Tessa said reasonably. "You said before that he didn't have a girlfriend."

Karen sat up in her chair in surprise. "You could have something there, you know – it would certainly explain why he doesn't stay up in Meath with Nellie."

"He's what – thirty-three or something?" Tessa asked. "Surely he's a bit old to be hiding his girlfriends from Mammy."

"Depends on whether or not it *is* a girlfriend."

"Oh." Tessa understood immediately. "You think he might be the other way inclined?"

"It had crossed my mind, although I'm not quite sure why. It's just something about him. And the fact that he's never had a serious relationship, as far as Shane knows. The family seem to have given up on Jack producing the heir to the Quinn empire."

"Empire?"

"Well – the ten-acre farm, anyway," Karen laughed. "I don't think Nellie would be too impressed if it turned out that one of her little darlings was gay."

"Not in this day and age surely?" Tessa sounded appalled at the idea.

"We're talking a sixty-odd-year-old farmer's wife from the wilds of Meath, Tessa. She's not exactly a regular in The George, you know." Karen laughed out loud at the notion of Nellie Quinn having a drink in one of Dublin's best-known gay bars.

"Poor old Jack," Tessa said, sympathetically.

"Poor old Jack nothing – if he wants to conduct an illicit affair, let him do it somewhere else."

"You don't think he'd bring anyone back to your house, surely?"

"I should bloody hope not – male or female," Karen exclaimed, "but obviously if he's seeing someone, he'll be in Dublin more often. Anyway, I'm not going to rock the boat by saying anything to Shane. He and I are getting on brilliantly at the moment, so I'm just going to mind my own business."

"For a change!" Tessa laughed.

It was true though, Karen thought, after she and Tessa had said their goodbyes. As far as she was concerned Jack could do whatever he liked, as long as it didn't interfere with her and Shane. She had just put the phone back in its cradle when it rang again.

"Karen? It's Nellie Quinn," said a prim voice at the other end.

Karen cursed silently to herself. Speak of the bloody

devil! "Hello, Nellie – how are you?" she said pleasantly, trying her best to be civil. "Shane's not back from work yet if you're hoping to speak to him."

"It's you I wanted to speak to, actually," she sniffed.

Karen groaned inwardly. *What was it this time?*

"Shane told me at the weekend that you've set a date for the wedding, and I might add that it's about time. But he says the ceremony will be taking place in some kind of – of council office in Kilkenny. Is that right?"

"Quite right, Nellie." She had expected that Nellie would disapprove of a register-office wedding, but by her tone you'd swear that the place was on equal par with a lap-dancing club, or a brothel.

Nellie sniffed again. "Karen, far be it from me to interfere, but I don't think that such a place is at all suitable for a wedding. Why can't you have a normal church wedding, like everyone else? I don't know if you were reared as a child of the Lord, but Shane certainly was and –"

"Really?" Karen interjected, stung by the remark about her upbringing, "and when was the last time Shane was inside a church, Nellie?"

"But you could ask that of every couple your age these days, dear," pleaded the other woman, "and it doesn't stop any of them getting married in the Lord's house. After all, where else would you get such beautiful surroundings? The photographs would be no good otherwise."

"Nellie, with all due respect, Shane and I aren't getting married so that we can look pretty in our wedding photographs." Karen's voice was steely. "Nor have we any interest in lighting a rake of candles up at the altar, and rattling off prayers for the sake of it." She had been through this a dozen times already with the girls at work, today with Tessa, and even with Jenny. Everyone, with the exception of her own parents, had seemed almost appalled at the idea of a civil wedding ceremony. They couldn't understand that she and Shane had absolutely no interest in a church wedding. Karen could almost picture Nellie's apoplectic expression down the telephone line.

"Well, I simply won't have it!" Nellie cried, her earlier calm deserting her. "I do not like being stopped on the street, by people wondering why my youngest can't get married in the Lord's house. Will you please tell Shane to telephone me, when he gets home from work?"

"Fine," Karen answered shortly, and without another word, hung up on her mother-in-law-to-be.

When Shane arrived home later, she passed on the message for him to ring Nellie, giving him no hint of their earlier conversation. Dutiful son that he was, Shane returned the call after dinner.

She looked up from scraping the plates in surprise when, minutes later, Shane returned to the kitchen guffawing loudly.

"Mam's hopping mad," he said with a grin. "Some oul' wan from the Legion of Mary stopped her in the street today, and asked her if it was true that her youngest was marrying a refugee or something, seeing that he couldn't get married in the church. I nearly wet myself when she told me."

"Oh dear," Karen said, a smile crossing her features as she filled the kettle. "I wondered what she meant earlier about people stopping her in the street about it. What did you say to her?"

"Well," he said, coming up behind Karen, and putting both arms around her, "I told her to tell people that it was no business of theirs, but if they really wanted to know, she should tell them that I'm getting hitched to a rich American who's had so many husbands they wouldn't let her within a shadow of the church – a woman that would make Liz Taylor blush! That should give them all something to talk about."

"Shane, you're OK with all of this, aren't you? I mean, you're sure that we're doing the right thing here?" Karen was feeling guilty all of a sudden. Maybe they should just go with the flow, and do what everyone else expected them to do, rather than having to put up with all this hassle.

Shane was having none of it. "What did I say to you before, love? It's our wedding, and as long as we're happy Mam can say what she likes. It's nothing to do with her."

"But what if she ends up boycotting in protest, or something? None of us would want that."

"Let her," Shane said firmly. "If she's more worried about what the neighbours think than being happy for us, then that's her look-out." He kissed her softly on the forehead. "Look, it took me long enough to convince you to set a date, I've no intention of changing anything, just to keep my mother happy."

"You're positive?" Karen said, a little unsurely. She just hoped that the woman would leave them alone to get on with the wedding plans, without whining and complaining about every detail. Knowing Nellie, she'd develop a severe allergy to orchids (Karen's choice for the flower arrangements) or have some aversion to Wicklow lamb for the banquet. She'd already expressed her opinion on the venue. Goodness knows it was hard enough as it was, trying to organise the entire thing, without the added strain of a finicky in-law. She and Shane had just come through a difficult patch, and now was certainly not the time for his mother to try and throw a spanner in the works.

But unfortunately, Karen had already experienced that Nellie Quinn could be terribly persuasive in trying to get her own way.

Chapter 34

"Cheers!" Jenny smiled at Mike as they clinked glasses. She had cooked him dinner at her apartment, to celebrate the fact that a bid he had placed for a house in Blackrock had been accepted earlier that day. Jenny had gone with him to see the house some time before, and had agreed that the four-bed 1930's bungalow suited Mike perfectly. The house had been only recently renovated with an attic conversion; the owners keeping the original streamlined look on the outside, but to Mike's delight, had favoured a stylish and modern interior. The house itself was situated off the busy roadway, and not far from Blackrock village. The fact that it was surrounded by its own garden and hidden behind mature elms and beech trees, gave the property extra privacy. Mike had instantly fallen in love with it; so much so that he had engaged in a bidding war with other interested parties, and had paid well over the asking price. He was hoping to have everything finalised within a few weeks.

"I can't wait to move in," he said dreamily, sitting back on the couch, and putting a hand behind his head, "I was sure that English couple were going to bid higher again. Thank God they didn't; I would have to have got a second job to afford that house."

Jenny laughed. "Hey – cut the poor boy crap! Remember where you keep your bank accounts."

Mike grimaced. "I'd forgotten you know my net worth. Mmm – maybe I should move to another bank."

"Don't you dare," Jenny exclaimed. "I'm already getting weird vibes from Barry. I have a feeling he thinks my seeing you is some kind of conflict of interest."

"And is it?" Mike looked momentarily concerned.

"Nah!" She refilled her glass with Moet. "As far as I know, there's nothing in my contract that says I can't date rich and powerful customers. Anyway," she added with a wicked grin, "it's never stopped me before." She ducked just in time to miss the cushion he threw at her. "Hey, watch it – you nearly knocked over my glass."

"Sorry." Mike tried to look ashamed. He sat up suddenly. "Are you doing anything this weekend?"

Jenny shook her head. "Why – were you thinking of whisking me away somewhere romantic?"

"Not exactly," Mike said, the expression on his face becoming serious. "It's just . . . " He hesitated. "Well, Rebecca's in town, and I've told her about us, and – well she'd really like to meet you."

"Oh." Jenny couldn't think of anything else to say. Rebecca. For all her curiosity about Mike's ex, the last thing Jenny wanted to do was meet the woman face-to-face. What on earth would they have to say to one another? And why was Rebecca so anxious to meet her? Was she checking her out?

Since that time in Wexford, she and Mike had hardly spent a night apart. They had been on a night out with the InTech crowd only recently and he had introduced her to his colleagues and staff as his 'partner'. Jenny had been a little taken aback by this at first, but gradually found that she was very much excited by the prospect of a real relationship with Mike and being considered important in his life. And it was wonderful not to have to worry about whether or not he was really interested in her, or whether or not he was going to get bored with her and leave, as she had always felt in the relationship with Roan. With Mike, everything, including his feelings, was totally transparent, and he expected the same from Jenny.

And now, he wanted her to meet his ex-wife. How very civilised. Jenny wasn't quite sure why but she already disliked this woman. After all, the way she saw it, Rebecca had up and left Mike when he didn't agree to her demands for a family, instead of supporting him in setting up his business. And then afterwards, to rub salt in the wounds, she had gone on to have two children with this other guy Graham.

Again, Jenny wondered why on earth Mike stayed friendly with the woman after everything she had done to him. But then again, that was the kind of guy he was. She couldn't imagine him being angry with anyone, at least not for very long, although she had heard from Ken, who managed his accounts at the branch, that he was as hard as nails when it came to his business.

"Well, what do you think?" Mike asked, bringing her

back to the present. "Graham is Welsh, and they're coming over here for the rugby match at Lansdowne. Rebecca thought it would be a perfect opportunity for us all to meet up."

"At a rugby match? Wouldn't it be a little noisy?"

Mike laughed. "No, we could meet them somewhere in town afterwards."

"OK." Jenny thought she'd better agree before Mike picked up on her hesitancy.

"Great! You'll like her, Jen. I think the two of you will get on really well, actually. Becky is very easy-going."

Jenny forced a smile as she took a mouthful of her now-tepid dregs of champagne, remembering an article she had read only recently in *Cosmo* about so-called 'ex-etiquette'. The moral of the story seemed to be that there *was* none – it was claws out for the majority of women, regardless of the personalities involved. Jenny wished she had paid more attention. Because soon she'd get to experience some 'ex-etiquette' of her very own.

* * *

Jenny spent most of Saturday afternoon in front of the mirror in her bedroom, trying to decide upon an outfit for that evening. She had absolutely no idea what to wear for this outing. She wanted to look stylish but at the same time not too vampish. She didn't want to wear anything too fashionable, because it would undoubtedly highlight the fact that she was a good ten years younger than Mike's ex-wife and she didn't want to be come across as a silly teenager. She didn't want to wear high heels because Mike wasn't sure whether or not they would be going out on the town – and there was no way she would be able to wait in heels for up to two hours in the taxi queue to get back home. Jenny had never felt this self-conscious in her life – had never agonised over an outfit for so long! She was completely unsure of the image she was supposed to project. Normally, she knew instinctively what to wear – tailored trouser-suits to the office, funky casuals for a night out in the pub, elegant but fashionable party-wear for special occasions. Then there was the problem of what to do with her hair. She had let it grow much longer lately, and it now reached well below shoulder-length.

If she wore her hair down, Rebecca's first impression of her might be that she was the stereotypical blonde bimbo hoping to nab herself a rich divorcé. If she wore it up, she might look too severe or too dressy, depending on her choice of outfit. Which brought Jenny back to square one.

She needed some advice with this one, she thought, discarding a bias-cut chiffon skirt on top of at least twenty other prospects on her bed. Jenny walked barefoot and bra-less out into the front room towards the telephone.

"Tessa – it's Jenny. I need your advice and I need it fast!"

Later that evening, when Mike picked her up in the taxi, Jenny was feeling a lot more confident. Taking Tessa's advice, she had worn her black sleeveless cashmere turtleneck, her red cropped leather jacket over a pair of black wide-leg trousers, and a pair of black, strappy, highish sandals. Tessa had been adamant that she should step out in nothing less than a three-inch heel.

"It'll give you confidence," she had insisted. "There's

nothing better than the clicking of high heels on the ground to make you feel great about what you're wearing. But you can't go wrong with black – and there's no harm in showing a bit of flesh, either."

Jenny had felt much better after that telephone call and, as it turned out, Tessa was right. No one could fault her with this outfit. Her blonde hair always looked particularly dramatic against darker colours. She had worn it down but, as Tessa suggested, had tucked a few strands casually behind her ears.

Mike had seemed happy enough with her anyway, she thought, recalling his appreciative wolf-whistle when she got into the taxi. But that wasn't even half the battle. Despite Tessa's assurances that she'd 'blow them all away', Jenny wasn't feeling at all confident about tonight. What if Rebecca was the highbrow intellectual type and they all started discussing politics? Jenny was no fool but current politics didn't interest her one whit, nor did she have particularly strong opinions about the coalition government or the opposition parties. She could hold her own well in a discussion on economics or business but after that . . .

"Are you OK? You're very quiet." Mike stroked her arm.

Jenny smiled. "I suppose I'm feeling a little nervous about this – I don't exactly know what to expect."

"Honestly, Jen, it'll be fine. Rebecca and Graham are totally down-to-earth. I know you'll all get on really well."

"I hope so. Where are we meeting them anyway?"

"They're staying at Jury's in Christchurch – I told them

we'd meet them in the bar and we can decide where to go from there."

"Oh, we'll probably end up somewhere in Temple Bar, seeing as it's only down the road."

"Maybe – but I should warn you. Becky and Graham aren't exactly the pub-crawling types."

"Oh." He was obviously pointing out the age difference between herself and the others. All of a sudden Jenny felt very foolish. She sat back in the seat and said little else for the rest of the journey. Mike was also uncharacteristically quiet, she noticed. Maybe he was nervous too. Nervous about parading his younger new woman.

A while later, the taxi pulled up outside Jury's Inn. As Mike walked in front of her through the sliding doors, Jenny took a deep breath. She looked to her left towards the bar, and saw a smiling, slightly plump woman wave out at them – Rebecca? Jenny took another deep breath, this one coming out as a sigh of relief. This woman looked totally non-threatening. But Mike continued walking straight past her, and into the bar towards an elegant-looking redhead who was sitting at the bar.

"Becky, hello, you look fabulous!" Mike stepped forward and hugged her, kissing her lightly on both cheeks.

Rebecca eagerly returned his hug. "And you must be Jenny," she said a husky voice. "I'm Rebecca – it's lovely to meet you finally." She was smiled warmly as she shook Jenny's hand.

"Where's Graham?" Mike asked, looking around the room.

"Never far," said a lilting, Welsh voice from behind them. He walked up and slapped Mike hard on the back. "How are things, man?"

"Fine, fine. You're looking very well – all those hours on the golf course are doing you the world of good."

"Well, as you well know – any excuse to get away from Becky is a good one!"

"Thanks very much," Rebecca said incredulously. "You're giving Jenny here a terrible impression of me already."

"Only joking." Graham put an arm around her waist. He smiled at Jenny. "Hello, my lovely," he said. "Jenny, isn't it? I'm Graham – nice to meet you."

Jenny shook his hand, warming to him instantly. It was probably the accent, she thought, or the fact that he reminded her a little of a young Kevin Keegan. She shouldn't forget, of course, that this was the guy who ran away with Mike's wife. Although Mike certainly seemed to have forgotten it. The two of them were chatting away as if they were the best of friends.

Mike ordered drinks and the four of them sat down at a quiet table in the small but cosy hotel bar. As the other three chatted amongst themselves, Jenny noticed that although Rebecca wasn't conventionally beautiful she had an effortless sexiness about her. In other words, she could see why Mike had fallen for her.

At least she herself was holding her own in the outfit stakes, she thought, regarding Rebecca's outfit with a slight feeling of triumph. The older woman was wearing a long fitted black skirt and a cerise polo-neck, the colour clashing dreadfully with her hair. Yet she had an air about her that suggested she didn't give a damn about what she wore. Jenny decided she'd better make some effort to join in the conversation.

"So, you two live in Wales, is it?" she asked.

Rebecca laughed. "God, no – we live in the centre of London! I couldn't live all that way out in the country."

Graham rolled his eyes. "She makes the place sound like it was the back of beyond! Poor old Becky couldn't function if she didn't have Chelsea High-street shopping, within walking distance of her front door – isn't that right, my love?"

"Well, for grocery-shopping at least," she said grimacing. "Unfortunately, Jenny, I'm a terrible cook."

"I can certainly vouch for that," Mike piped up and they all laughed.

"Help! They're ganging up on me now!" Rebecca gave Jenny a desperate look.

Jenny laughed, still a little in awe of the easygoing relationship Mike enjoyed with them, but feeling, to her surprise, that she was becoming more and more relaxed in their company. She certainly hadn't expected them to be so nice. Rebecca and Graham were full of chat – in fact, between the two of them, it was difficult for Jenny to get a word in.

It appeared that Graham was also involved in the software industry, and it wasn't long before he and Mike were deep in conversation about business. Rebecca rolled her eyes and leaned towards Jenny conspiratorially. "They're off – Jenny, is it just me or does all that computer-talk bore you senseless too? Anyway, enough about work," she said before Jenny could answer. She rubbed her hands together with glee. "You just won't believe the stuff I picked up in town today – I'll have to take you up to the room and show you. I had forgotten how great the shopping is in Dublin – you've even got Debenhams here!"

* * *

Later that night, lying in the darkness beside Mike, Jenny went over the evening's events in her head. She was so pleased that the meeting with Rebecca had gone well. Mike had been right – both she and Graham were terribly down-to-earth. Rebecca, obviously sensing Jenny's nervousness, had made every effort to make her feel comfortable.

"I know you probably think it's strange that Mike and I have such a good relationship," she had said, when he and Graham were out of earshot, "but we've known one another for a long, long time and have been through a lot together.'

She smiled and put a hand on Jenny's arm. "It was very hard but thankfully we sorted everything out and managed to stay friends after the divorce. It took a while though!"

Jenny nodded, unsure how to respond.

"I think what I'm trying to say, and please don't take this the wrong way . . . " She looked at Jenny kindly. "I can only imagine how hard it must have been for you to come here tonight. I'd be the same way myself, meeting the dreaded ex-wife."

She looked across the table at Mike and Graham, who were engrossed in the rugby highlights on the television. "Things went wrong for us early in the marriage. At the very end, although I can't say it was easy, we were more like brother and sister than husband and wife, and I'm certain Mike would agree with that. Then I met Graham and –"

"It's OK," Jenny interjected. "Please don't feel that you have to tell me this, Rebecca. It's none of my business, after all."

"I think it is," Rebecca said firmly. "I know Mike feels very strongly about you and I'm afraid that my friendship with him might make you uncomfortable. I just want you to know that I'm not a threat to you, and I never will be. I still love Mike, but only as a friend, and I know he feels the same way about me. We both have our own lives now – you know that Graham and I have two little girls?" Her face lit up when she mentioned her children, and Jenny realised then how important having a family must have been to Rebecca – so important that it ruined her marriage.

"Yes. Mike mentioned that."

"And we're hoping to get married next year – if we can find the time, that is! It's so difficult to organise a wedding when you've got two little madams like ours. Rosie and Robyn are still only toddlers but sometimes . . . !" She rolled her eyes.

"Anyway, I was absolutely thrilled when Mike told me that you and he had finally got it together." She nudged Jenny softly. "I hope you don't mind, but he had told me all about you long before you two began seeing one another."

Jenny smiled at this.

"Anyway – you'll have to come over to London for a visit sometime. I could take you down to Fulham – there's some fantastic shopping there and . . . "

Jenny smiled to herself in the darkness. Rebecca was quite a woman. She herself didn't know how she would react to meeting an ex's new girlfriend. She rarely stayed friends with her exes; after all, look at what had happened to her and Roan.

She hadn't seen him for over a year now. It was hard to believe that this time last year she had been an absolute wreck, pining over the silly bastard. She didn't know how she'd react if she met him now. It would certainly be a little bit scary, not to mention extremely uncomfortable!

Still, she thought, rolling over on her side and snuggling close to Mike. She was in Dublin and Roan was in New York. She wouldn't have to worry about bumping into him on the street anytime soon.

Chapter 35

Karen glared at her reflection with absolute horror. She frowned at Jenny, who was beside herself with laughter outside the fitting room.

"It's bloody hideous!" she said, trying to lift the heavy skirt over her head, but to no avail. They were shopping for Karen's wedding dress, and Jenny had persuaded her to try on what could only be described as the biggest, flounciest, fluffiest 'meringue' Karen had ever seen.

"You'll look gorgeous in it," she had insisted. Karen wasn't convinced but tried the dress on just to pacify her. Otherwise, Jenny would be on at her all day. She hated this, hated having to trawl the shops looking for the 'perfect dress'. She had hoped just to walk into a bridal shop and pick one up from the rack. One shop assistant had nearly choked with shock when Karen had told her the date of her wedding.

"June? You mean June – as in twelve months?" she had said, her eyes wide with surprise.

"No," Karen told her flatly. "I mean June – as six weeks' time."

"But . . . but," the sales assistant spluttered, "our dresses need to be ordered at least a year in advance! You'll need to first make your choice – and of course this takes time in order to ensure it really is the *perfect* dress for you," she added reverently, as if the decision was on par with choosing your husband. "Then you'll need a fitting, the dress will need to be ordered and of course adjustments will need to be made and . . . "

Karen hadn't stayed to hear the rest of the assistant's bluster. She was down the escalator and out of the shop as fast as the steps would carry her, Jenny following close behind.

"Honest to God – it's only a dress! You'd swear it was a bloody work of art, the way they go on about it! Jen, what am I going to do? I'll never find a decent dress at this stage!"

It was only through sheer desperation that Karen had been persuaded to deviate from her search for a plain and straight wedding dress, hence the meringue.

"You're right. It's absolutely horrendous!" Jenny said, a hand over her mouth to try and stop the laughter. With her top-heavy chest, that particular dress made her look like an advertisement for a new brand of marshmallow. "You look like a . . . a . . . "

"She looks like a *princess*! My dear, that has to be the one! It looks amazing on you! Oh, wait, I'll go and get a veil. Now stay right where you are – don't move for one second!" The elderly sales assistant scuttled off eagerly.

"Jenny!" Karen hissed. "Get me out of this thing – *quick*!"

Jenny was laughing so much she could hardly get the zip undone. Karen roughly dragged the dress over her head, put her own clothes back on and ran out of the cubicle, nearly knocking over another bride-to-be, who was preening in front of the mirror outside the changing rooms, and wearing an equally hideous dress. An older woman, obviously the girl's mother was placing a tiara carefully on her daughter's head, the two of them in floods of tears, obviously moved by the glorious vision in satin and lace.

"I'd be crying too if I had to wear a dress like that to *my* wedding," Karen said under her breath, as she and Jenny sped past them and out of the shop, laughing uproariously.

Almost two hours later, exhausted from battling the Saturday crowds and still without Karen's perfect dress, the two girls grabbed a precious free table in a packed Bewley's.

"Look, don't worry about it," Jenny said, stirring a marshmallow into her hot chocolate. "You've still got plenty of time to get something before the wedding."

"Jen, it's hopeless. I haven't seen anything that might even be a prospect, and we haven't even started on a bridesmaid dress for you. What if I don't find anything in time?"

"Of course you will! And I'll help you as much as I can." She put her mug down and looked at Karen thoughtfully. "I've just had a brainwave . . . we've been looking in the same shops, and the same places all the time. Why don't we go somewhere different – like Belfast, for instance?"

"Belfast? You mean Northern Ireland Belfast?"

Jenny nodded eagerly. "Why not? The shopping is supposed to be excellent up there, as good as any English city. Rebecca said – "

"Rebecca? The famous ex?" Karen asked, looking startled.

"Oh, I didn't tell you, did I?" Jenny grinned. "We all met up last weekend. She's great."

"She's great? What do you mean she's great? She's his ex, for goodness sake!"

"I know, that's what I thought too," Jenny said, leaning her elbows on the table, "but she's really, really, nice – couldn't be nicer, in fact."

Karen shook her head in wonder. "That's terrific Jen. To be honest, I was a bit worried about all that. I don't how I'd be able to handle it myself, if I was in your position."

"I'll admit I was more than a little worried at first, but having met Rebecca face to face, it's pretty obvious that she and Mike have moved on completely. We got on really well."

"You know, I have to say, I'm very proud of you, Jen – you've really come a long way since this time last year."

Jenny shrugged, her face slightly flushed. "I suppose I have, haven't I?"

"Most definitely," Karen said, draining her mug of hot chocolate. "Anyway, I think Belfast is a great idea. What about next weekend? I could drive." She missed Jenny's petrified look. "Oh no – I can't, actually. Shane has to leave the car in for the NCT, and you haven't been driving long enough to take the Punto. I suppose we'll have to take the train then?"

"The train would be perfect!" Jenny agreed, trying not to let the relief show on her face. Luckily for her, she'd got away with not having to sit in a car with Karen for the almost three-hour trip to the North. Although the way Karen drove, they'd probably have made it within two. Jenny had recently bought a car of her own – a three-year-old Fiat Punto, and was currently taking driving lessons in it. While she was happy to drive in and around Dun Laoghaire, and maybe into the city centre once in a while, Jenny knew that she wouldn't be able for such a long trip. It was a blessing in disguise that Shane's car was due for its NCT, she thought, negotiating her way through the crowds, and out behind Karen out into the sunlight.

Chapter 36

Karen checked her watch. She couldn't wait to leave the office. Today had seemed like the longest day she had even put down at work. Still, only a few weeks to go until the wedding, and then she and Shane were flying out to Thailand for two blissful weeks in the (hopefully) blistering sunshine. They both needed the break, actually. Shane had been really putting in the hours at work these days. Sometimes he didn't get home until well after she had gone to bed. He was often quite irritable as a result too. Their wedding was going to be quite small, but Shane was insistent that they pay for everything themselves – hotel, flowers, honeymoon etc, without having to resort to borrowing. Which was why he was working all that overtime.

Karen checked her watch again, hoping that by some miracle the hands might read five o'clock. No such luck. She was looking forward to this shopping trip to Belfast with Jenny at the weekend. Hopefully, there she'd find something half-decent for her own wedding. Surely there was something that would do? Karen was afraid that if she didn't get a dress in Belfast, she might have to think about wearing a suit to the register office. She didn't want to resort to that. She would hate it if she weren't looking her best in her wedding photographs. Still, with her build, it was proving increasingly difficult to find a dress that would do the trick. Such were the delights of having a big chest. She couldn't understand why so many women were obsessed with having bigger breasts. In Karen's experience, it caused nothing but trouble. From her leotard-wearing schooldays, to the search for the ultimate white dress, Karen's boobs were, quite literally, getting in her way.

Anyway, Shane seemed to love her just the way she was and that was the main thing. Although, with his being away so much, there hadn't been much loving lately. Karen wondered if getting married would have much of an effect on their sex life. She must ask Tessa, although maybe she wasn't the right person to ask at the moment. Tessa was getting bigger by the minute, and the last time Karen had spoken with her, her friend had been terribly depressed.

"What if I can't lose all this weight afterwards?" she had said tearfully. "I'll never go outside the front door again!"

Karen hadn't been able to persuade her otherwise. She smiled to herself as she tried hard to imagine what Tessa would be like as a mother. She would probably be brilliant, and needless to say her nursing experience would stand to her. Karen wondered if she would ever be able to think seriously about having children herself. It just didn't appeal to her in the slightest, and listening to Tessa recount tales of 'all day and all night' sickness ('whoever called it morning sickness was having a laugh') didn't at all endear her to the possibility. There was no way Karen would have taken a chance like Jenny did, that time with Mike. She was absolutely crazy to have unprotected sex with him in Wexford and *very* lucky to have got away with it!

She decided to make a quick phone call to Shane, before leaving the office. No doubt he would still be at his desk, slogging away on the plans for that new toll bridge, or something similar. Karen tapped her fingernails on the desktop as she waited to be put through to his department.

"I'm sorry, Karen – he left about half an hour ago. Will I take a message or . . . ?" the receptionist asked.

Karen frowned. She was sure Shane had told her he was working late tonight. She shrugged. Must have been a change of plan.

"No, thanks, Stephanie. I'll catch him at home. Thanks – bye."

What an unexpected bonus, Karen thought, smiling to herself as she shut down her PC. A quiet night relaxing in front of the telly tonight, just the two of them, was exactly what she and Shane needed. They hadn't had time to themselves in ages.

* * *

Shortly after five thirty pm, Aidan heard the alarm go off. He jumped up quickly, casting aside the playing cards he had been using for a poker game with Donal Ryan, his fellow fire-officer.

Noel Flanagan came running out of the Watchroom waving a white telex in his hand.

"RTA on the M50 southbound," he shouted above the heads of the other fire officers, who raced to the dressing room, "person's trapped, person's reported, two vehicles – get a move on, lads!"

An RTA, Aidan said to himself, as he quickly changed into uniform. Road Traffic Accidents were the worst. And from the sounds of the report, this accident was a serious one. He lifted his helmet from where it hung on the wall, and followed the others towards the fire trucks.

"Aidan, take the second appliance, will you?" said John Cullinane, the Station Officer. "We've already got six men in here."

Aidan nodded and dutifully rushed towards the second truck and, passing the Jaws of Life hanging on the side of the unit, his stomach turned. He hated the very sight of that machine and everything it stood for. He hated the sounds of screeching metal piercing his eardrums, whenever they used it to prise open a space wide enough, and safe enough, to remove a crash victim. It was this part of his job that Aidan hated the most.

The two fire appliances hurtled out of the station, sirens screaming, past the rush-hour traffic, as they raced towards the scene of the accident on the M50. The station officer radioed instructions to Aidan's unit, from his position on the appliance up ahead.

"Colin and Tony – fend off position. Aidan and Donal – airbags."

As the instruction suggested, Colin and Tony would be responsible for sectioning off the crash scene, ensuring that the rescue team and the paramedics would have enough room in which to carry out their duties. As he and Donal had been given airbag duties, Aidan knew that at least one of the cars had been tipped over onto the driver's side, during, or after the crash. The airbags would be used to lift the car back up, so that the rescue team could get access to the victim.

The ambulance and the Garda Siochana had already reached the scene. When the truck stopped, Aidan and Donal jumped out, and immediately grabbed the air bags, deploying them as the Senior Fire Officer directed them towards the first vehicle. Aidan raced towards the mangled vehicle and, as he did, his breath caught in his throat.

"Jesus Christ," he whispered hoarsely to Donal, "I know that car."

* * *

Tessa decided to check on Mrs Cleary once more, before going off duty.

"How are you feeling now?" she asked the older woman, who had been complaining all day of a ferocious headache.

"Not too bad," Mrs Cleary said hoarsely, "I think those tablets you gave me did the trick."

Tessa patted her hand. "Oh, look at those fabulous flowers. Who sent you those?"

Ms Cleary sniffed. "That rap of a daughter of mine. It'd be more in her line to call in and see how I was, but sure that would be too much trouble for her."

Tessa nodded sympathetically. She had met Mrs Cleary's daughter once before, and once had been enough. The woman had treated the hospital staff as though they were skivvies, hired only to look after her mother. Mrs Cleary had broken her hip, after falling from her chair while trying to replace a light bulb. If her own daughter hadn't been too self-absorbed to pay her regular visits in the first place, the incident would never have happened. Yet she treated the nurses as though they had been the ones that had broken the light bulb in the first place.

"I'll miss you when you're gone," the older woman said to her. "When are you moving down to Cork?"

"Next week," Tessa confirmed. She was looking forward to it. New house, new job and new baby. And the beginnings of a new life for herself and Gerry.

Tessa said goodbye to the Ward Sister and switched on her Walkman as she turned out of St Vincent's Hospital, and headed towards her bus stop on the Donnybrook Road. She fiddled with the dial for a few moments, trying to find a clear signal for *Today FM*. It was bloody cold out this evening, she thought, shivering as she wrapped a light cardigan around her midriff. She had planned on walking home, but she'd freeze if she stayed out in this much longer. Typical Irish summer. As she waited idly at the bus stop she listened to the five-thirty news bulletin. Apparently, there had been a very bad car crash out on the motorway a little while ago. Tessa shivered again, but not from the cold. She hated hearing things like that, and always wondered whether anyone she knew was involved.

And Gerry travelled on the M50 on his way home.

Tessa retrieved her mobile phone from her handbag, and quickly dialled her husband's number.

* * *

Jenny saw Barry switch off the light in his office. She checked her watch. It was just after five-forty-five. Time for her to finish what she was doing and head home.

Home. She recalled a recent conversation with Mike when she had been moaning about the rent on her apartment, and how the landlord had informed her that he was increasing the rent, and did she want to renew her lease?

Things were going well for her at the bank. There was an Officer post coming up in the district within the next few weeks, and Marion had already suggested her to Barry as an ideal candidate. Sometimes Jenny thought Marion was more anxious to keep her moving up the corporate ladder than she was in climbing it herself. But the Administration Manager thought she deserved it. If she was promoted again, Jenny knew that she would hardly notice the rent increase. In fact, she thought, she could start thinking about buying a place of her own. But she liked living out here in Dun Laoghaire, liked living on the southside. There was no way she'd be able to do what Mike had done and buy a house out here. Even with her job in the Bank, she would never qualify for such a mortgage. When discussing all of this with Mike, Jenny had got the impression – although he hadn't exactly said anything – that he would like her to move in with him.

The thought of it didn't frighten her to death, but yet Jenny was loath to give up her independence, and her new-found sense of freedom, so soon after achieving it. Was she ready for this? Was she ready to commit herself to someone again, and commit freely, without any baggage from her previous relationship, or *relationships* even?

Was Mike supposed to be The One?

Jenny laughed softly to herself as she recalled Mrs Crowley's prediction all that time ago. This time it fitted.

Maybe she and Mike should talk seriously about where the relationship was going. She'd give him a ring and see if it was OK to call over to his house later that evening. She hadn't seen him since the middle of last week. She had warned him to stay away from her until she rid herself of a stomach bug that had finally abated at the weekend. For a while, she had been afraid she wouldn't get over it in time for her shopping trip with Karen. She dialled his private number at the office, heard it ring for a moment, and then her call was diverted to reception.

"Hi Ciara, it's Jenny Hamilton here. I was looking for Mike," she said when her call was answered.

"Mr Kennedy isn't working from here today," the receptionist said snootily. "I thought he would have told *you* that."

"Well, he didn't," Jenny said simply. "Where *is* he working from then?"

"At a client's office," Alison said, "in one of the business parks off the M50 somewhere."

Chapter 37

Karen sat in front of the TV, languidly flicking from *Coronation Street* to *EastEnders* with the remote control. She didn't follow either soap, and tonight couldn't find any particular reason to start. Most of the characters seemed to spend all their time in the local pub, throwing dirty looks at everyone else.

She felt a low rumble in her stomach and wondered what on earth was keeping Shane. He had since left a message on her mobile phone, telling her that he'd pick up a Chinese takeaway for dinner on the way home from work. Karen wished he'd hurry up, because she was so hungry she didn't think she'd be able to hold out much longer. The thoughts of chicken with green peppers and black bean sauce was making her mouth water. She hoped he'd got the message she'd left on his message-minder asking him to get some spring rolls and prawn crackers.

EastEnders ended with yet another resident upset or annoyed about something.

Oh, sod it, she thought, she might as well get something to eat. A slice of bread would keep her going until Shane got back, she thought, wandering into the kitchen. She winced when she saw the contents of the bread bin. A Brennan's sliced pan had been there for so long that any bread that might once have existed was now completely indistinguishable under the mildew.

A few minutes later Karen was still searching for something edible at the back of her never-defrosted-freezer, when she heard the front doorbell ring. Great, she thought glumly. Only one of the bloody Quinns would arrive at her doorstep unannounced on a weeknight. Either that, or it was someone looking for directions – again. Living at the corner of a busy junction brought its own problems, and she couldn't count the number of times she and Shane had been disturbed in the evening by some lost soul trying to find his way to Terenure. Karen padded out towards the door in her stocking-feet.

An ashen-faced Aidan stood in her doorway.

"Aidan – hi!" she said good-humouredly. "I haven't seen you for a while. If you're looking for Shane, he's not home yet –"

"Karen . . . love," Aidan cut her off. He came into the hallway and took both of her hands in his. "Karen . . . there's been an accident."

"An accident? Where – at the crossroads?" she said, looking past him to the street.

"Please, love – just sit down for a moment," Aidan said, and Karen felt a rod of panic shoot through her, as she realised that there was another person standing outside her door – in uniform.

The garda car was parked a little way down from her house, its blue overhead lights flashing wildly and illuminating the expectant faces of the small crowd gathering around it on the path, hoping to catch a little drama. The panic began to travel from her toes to the top of her throat, and back down again. Her stomach constricted with fear, and her heart hammered loudly against her chest.

"An accident? Well, I don't know what *I* can do for you, Aidan – are you hurt? I don't have any bandages here, or anything if that's what you want, but – "

"Karen – "

"I mean, I'm not a nurse or anything, I don't even know first aid. Tessa's the one you want, really, but she's not here though, is she? Of course not, she's probably at work – oh well, I suppose you'd better call an ambulance."

"Karen, please . . . sit down." Tears streamed down Aidan's face as he reached for her.

She stepped back from him as if electrocuted.

"Aidan – stop it, please! I don't know why you're doing this! If this is your idea of a joke, it's not funny! It's not bloody funny, OK? Why are you trying to scare me like this? Oh, God!" Suddenly, dizzy with panic, Karen lost her balance and slumped heavily against the front door.

She knew what he was here to tell her – knew it before Aidan had even opened his mouth. His expression told her everything – he didn't have to say it. She hoped he wouldn't, because she didn't think she could bear to hear the words out loud.

"He didn't suffer, love," Aidan said, his voice

constricted with grief. He reached for her again, and this time Karen let him guide her back towards the sofa. He sat down next to her, holding her gently in his arms. "It was a head-on collision. He was coming back from a site inspection, and a driver going north on the motorway at ninety miles an hour had a tyre blow-out. He skidded across the reservation, straight into Shane. He was killed instantly – there was no pain."

Karen said nothing.

"I'm so, so sorry, love," he said, resting his head on top of hers, his tears dropping onto her hair, as she rocked back and forth in his arms, staring into space.

"No," she said finally, her face fixed in a mask of defiance, "no, Aidan, you're wrong. You have to be wrong – he couldn't be – it mustn't have been Shane."

Aidan turned to face her. "Karen – "

"No, seriously, think about it," she said, her voice rising as she shook her head from side to side. "He was picking up a takeaway – he's probably in the Jasmine Palace even as we speak! It wasn't Shane – I'm telling you!"

"Karen – "

"Aidan, don't you think you should have got your bloody facts right, before you came waltzing in here and upsetting me? The least you could have done is found out for sure!"

Aidan shook his head, tear after tear rolling down his face, as he looked back towards the garda for some assistance.

The garda went up to Karen, and put his hand on her shoulder. "I'm sorry, Ms Cassidy. I know how difficult

411

this is for you, but your fiancé has already been identified by Fireman Reilly."

"What do you mean?" Karen implored in a small voice. "What does he mean 'identified', Aidan – what?"

Aidan wiped the tears from his eyes. "My unit was called to the scene of the accident – I've seen him, Karen. It is Shane, and he's gone. I'm so, so sorry, but he's gone." With this he broke down in tears again.

* * *

He's gone . . . he's gone . . . he's gone. For the next few hours, Aidan's words echoed through Karen's brain like some crazy mantra. She could barely remember what happened next – she vaguely remembered picking up the phone and calmly telling Nellie that her youngest son had today died in a head-on collision on the M50, at the same time that Nellie and the rest of the country were happily tucking into their supper, couldn't remember Nellie's racking sobs on the other end, and hysterical accusations of Karen forcing him to work so many extra hours, that Shane was so tired he mustn't have been concentrating on his driving, couldn't remember Jenny and Mike getting here, couldn't understand why they all wouldn't just leave her alone.

He's gone.

Shane was gone.

Her Shane.

Why him? Why not her?*She* was the one that deserved to die in that crash – not Shane. Shane wouldn't harm a fly. All that time they had spent arguing over the wedding, all the time they had spent arguing over stupid things, all the time she had spent resenting his family – Karen would have given anything in the world to have all that time back. She would give anything just for someone to wave a magic wand, and take it all back, take the nightmare away.

Why? Why would someone let this happen?

Was God punishing her because she hadn't been to Mass in over twelve years? Was He punishing her because she had been so determined not to get married in His church? Or was it simply because she was a twisted, bitter, resentful bitch who didn't want to share Shane with anyone else? She had made no secret of her dislike and resentment towards his family. Was this her punishment for trying to keep him to herself?

Karen couldn't find any answers. All she knew now was that she would never again feel Shane's arms around her, never wake up beside him in the bed, and never feel his kisses on her lips. They would never again laugh together, never share a moment of happiness or share another moment of sadness. They would never be able to do all the things they had planned to do after the wedding, like visit Las Vegas or New York like Shane always wanted, or Rome and Paris, like Karen did.

There would be no wedding, no new life together, no nothing.

Nothing.

He was gone.

Chapter 38

From across the room, and with growing concern, Jenny watched Karen. She cut a very lonely figure slumped in the armchair, directly in front of the TV. She had barely uttered two words to anyone since the gardai left the house, and seemed not to notice the arrival of more and more sympathisers as the night went on.

A still-devastated Aidan was sitting in the kitchen with Gerry, deeply affected by the evening's events. Jenny knew that Karen was undoubtedly in shock, but she was becoming more and more frightened by how terribly introverted, and isolated she was at the moment. She took a tissue from a box on the table, and blew her nose into it, all the time watching Karen, who was still staring at the television, seemingly oblivious to everyone around her.

Jenny hoped that Nellie Quinn would stay away at least for a night, and give Karen some time to herself before the funeral. She had to take the telephone away from Karen earlier, upon hearing Nellie's sobbing and ranting on the other end. Jenny knew it was just a shock reaction to the news of her son's death, but the last thing Karen needed right now was recrimination and conflict with Shane's family. Karen had said nothing afterwards; she had just taken to the armchair – Shane's armchair – and wrapped her cardigan tightly around her. Offers of coffee, tea and invitations to talk had been rejected with a slow shake of the head.

Jenny had never felt so helpless in her entire life. How could she possibly even imagine how Karen must be feeling at the moment? The sheer magnitude of the day's events must be completely overwhelming, and Karen's way of coping, at least for the moment, was to shut down and pretend that it all wasn't happening, that it wasn't real.

Karen stood up from her chair. "I'm going to bed," she said softly, heading towards the stairs.

"Do you want me to . . . ?" Jenny's words trailed off as Mike shook his head

"Leave her, Jen. She probably needs time on her own."

Jenny felt her eyes quicken with tears. "I don't know what to say to her, Mike. I don't know what to do. How can I help her?"

"You can't," Mike said simply. "Just leave her be, let her grieve in peace."

Jenny nodded. "I just can't believe that all of this has happened. I mean, they were getting married next month. How could this happen? It's not fair."

"I don't know. It's never fair in any circumstance, love," Mike said, sighing as he took her hand in his. "All you can do now is be there for Karen and be her friend, same as always."

"My heart is breaking for her, though – and for Aidan. Imagine him being called to the accident that resulted in the death of his best friend . . ."

Upon discovering Shane's demise, Aidan had insisted on accompanying his senior fire officer and the garda to the house on Harold's Cross. Although his own heart was breaking, he knew that he didn't want anyone else to break the news to Karen. Although protocol demanded that a senior fire officer, or a member of the gardai should inform family members, Aidan's colleague had bent the rules in view of the circumstances. The driver of the car that caused the accident had also been killed. Jenny knew that there was no doubt but that another household somewhere in the country was equally as shattered as this one.

"I know it was tough on Aidan, but at least Karen had someone she knew with her at the time," Mike said. "Wouldn't it have been a lot worse if the gardai had turned up on their own with the news, and asked Karen to identify the body?"

"Maybe," Jenny sniffed. "Mike, this is such a nightmare, and all so sudden. How can she possibly ever get over this?"

"It won't be easy, and she'll need people around her. What about her parents? You said before that they lived abroad?"

"In Tenerife, yes. I wonder has anyone told them yet? They'll need to come back for the funeral." As far as Jenny was aware, the only people Karen had spoken to tonight were the Quinns. Aidan had telephoned her and the others soon after he had broken the news to Karen. Jenny resolved to contact Jonathan and Clara Cassidy first thing the following morning, as they would no doubt need to make flight arrangements to come back for Shane's funeral.

"Look, I know it's probably not the best time to be thinking like this, but what will happen to Karen now – with this house, I mean?" Mike asked.

"Well, it's her house now, isn't it?"

"I don't think so, Jen. She and Shane were never married. Remember they used to joke about the fact that the mortgage was solely in his name? And because his brother guaranteed the debt, and everything was arranged by him and Shane, then as far as I know, Karen has little or no rights over the house, in the event of Shane's death."

"What? Then who does?" Jenny was puzzled.

Mike sighed deeply. "Shane's next of kin."

* * *

That same night they sat up with Aidan, and Shane's workmate Tony – a distraught Aidan trying to make some sense of the sudden death of his closest friend. Jenny stayed on the next morning to be with Karen, should her friend need her.

She hadn't reappeared from her bedroom since retiring the night before, and Jenny hoped that she'd been able to get some sleep. She'd managed to catch a few hours herself on the sofa when Aidan and the others had gone home, and Mike had left for the office, despite his protests to stay with her. It didn't seem at all real to Jenny, not at least until Tessa called and produced a copy of the morning paper. A huge banner headline proclaimed that Shane and the other driver were the eighty-sixth and eighty-seventh victims of road accidents in Ireland that year. Displayed underneath the headline was a huge colour photograph of the car in which Shane had died, the silver Astra's chassis bent and twisted beyond recognition.

"How is she?" Tessa asked, enveloping Jenny in a huge hug.

Jenny shook her head. "I'm worried about her. She hasn't come out of her bedroom, or spoken a word since last night."

"God love her, she's probably still in shock."

"I know, but I wish she'd do something – cry, scream, kick the walls, just *something*!"

"She probably has – in her own mind, at least," Gerry said softly, from behind his wife. "Everyone copes differently when faced with news like that, Jenny. Some of us grieve openly, sobbing and crying like you'd expect; others like Karen just want to be away from everything and everyone else. And who'd blame her?"

"I know, I know. I just wish I could do something for her," Jenny said, filling the kettle. "I don't know how many times I've been up to the bedroom today, but she still doesn't want to talk."

She heard the telephone ring and went out to the hallway to answer it, leaving Tessa and Gerry sitting in silence at the kitchen table. The caller was Nellie Quinn letting them know that arrangements had been made for the removal from the hospital that same evening, and the burial to take place in Rathrigh the following morning. Apparently Jack had organised everything. Jenny smarted at the fact that they hadn't consulted or included Karen in the arrangements, but judging from what she had heard about the Quinns, it didn't surprise her. And maybe Karen didn't want to be included. She telephoned the others to let them know and then went upstairs to break the news to Karen.

She knocked softly on the door. There was no answer, and she could hear no movement inside. She tried the door handle and walked in to find the room in darkness, and Karen lying on the bed with her eyes wide open, staring at the ceiling.

"I'm not going to the funeral," was all she said.

"Karen, honey – "

"I'm not going, Jenny," she repeated, an edge to her tone. "I heard you on the phone downstairs. I know that it's tomorrow and I'm not going. Don't try to change my mind because you'll be wasting your time." With this she turned onto her side, facing away from Jenny.

Jenny sat down and put a hand on her friend's shoulder. "I have no idea how you're feeling, Karen. I can't even begin to imagine it, and it's up to you to decide what you want to do. But don't you think that Shane would think it's important that you go?"

"No," she answered simply.

"I know it's been a terrible shock, but –"

"No, you don't know!" Karen shrieked, turning back to face her, her eyes flashing with anger. "You haven't got a clue, Jenny! Do you know what I did yesterday morning, when Shane was leaving for work? I was still in bed when he was leaving, and he called in to give me a kiss goodbye. I groaned and turned away from him, annoyed because he had woken me up. Imagine! It was the last time he would ever kiss me and I turned away, because I was too damned lazy to bother with him! *The very last time.*"

"But you couldn't possibly have known . . ." Jenny knew it was a waste of time trying to soothe her – Karen was in full flight now.

"And then – yesterday evening, I left a message on his mobile phone. I said, 'Hurry up – I'm starving – don't forget the spring rolls.' Can you believe that? *Don't forget the fucking spring rolls*! That was very last thing I said to him! I didn't tell him I loved him, or that I missed him, or that he was the most important thing in the world to me! I just said something so bloody trivial!" Karen thrashed on the bed, thumping her fists on the covers.

"Karen, you didn't know what would happen – "

"And when he was sitting mangled in that crash, maybe even still alive and crying out for help, I was sitting here annoyed with him for being late, and worrying about my bloody dinner! What sort of a person does that make me, Jenny? What? Why am I the one that's still here, and he's the one that's gone? What's the point of that?"

"That's not the way it works, love," Jenny said eventually.

Karen was crying now, the tears falling rapidly down her cheeks.

"To think that I spent all that time trying to delay our wedding, resenting his family, and making him miserable. Well, I got what I wanted, didn't I? Now there'll be no wedding, they'll never be a wedding, because I was too damned selfish!"

"You never made him miserable, Karen – you're being too hard on yourself. It could just as easily been you or

me in that crash. Don't eat yourself up with guilt over this
– you've enough to deal with now. If you start blaming
yourself for what happened, then you might as well have
died in the crash with him."

"I wish I had." Karen sank back heavily on the pillows
and again turned away, wiping her eyes with the quilt
cover. "I have nothing now, Jenny, nothing or nobody.
Shane was my life, my entire future. Where do I go from
here?"

"The first thing you can do is go to the funeral. I'm
sure – no, I'm certain that Shane wouldn't want you
sitting here miserable, on your own. You need people
around you, Karen. That's all part of it. It's the right thing
to do."

As she listened to her own words of supposed advice,
Jenny wondered if she believed them herself. She couldn't
even begin to imagine how she herself would feel, if
someone she loved had been taken from her like this.
Maybe Karen was right to shut herself away from the
empty platitudes, and tired comforting clichés, that
would be no doubt offered at the funeral. Who knew
whether going to the funeral and facing everyone was the
right thing to do?

"Look," she said softly, "if you really don't want to go,
then I'll stay here with you. Don't argue," she said, seeing
Karen stir, "I'm not leaving you on your own. I'll stay
downstairs, and if you want to talk, then talk, but no one
will force you to do anything you don't want to."

Karen nodded, her eyes brimming with fresh tears.
"Thanks. I just can't face getting dressed up and facing all
these people, most of whom I don't know. I don't want to

have to face the Quinns. They hate me enough as it is –
don't tell me otherwise, I heard every word Nellie said
last night."

"Don't forget that she was in shock too, Karen. He was
her son."

"Maybe she was right about a few things. I did give
him a hard time, you know that."

"Karen, you and Shane were two of a kind. You argued
more than any other couple I've ever come across, but it
was obvious to all and sundry that you loved one other
deeply. I'm sorry, but you shouldn't turn yourself into a
martyr over this. You didn't force Shane to work late, or
to do anything he didn't want to. Anyway he was coming
home early, wasn't he?"

Karen winced.

"Look, if it had happened on the road to Kilrigh, do
you think that Nellie Quinn would have blamed herself
because Shane was coming to visit her? Don't take to
heart what she said yesterday, Karen. She was upset, in
the same way that you are now. She probably has her own
regrets too, you know. Everyone does when they don't get
the chance to say goodbye properly."

Karen sat up against the pillow, her face red and
tearstained.

"Will you stay with me tomorrow, Jen?" she asked in a
child-like voice.

Jenny laid a hand on top of Karen's. "I'll stay here for
as long as you need me."

Chapter 39

It was to be the warmest May day in Ireland for over fifteen years, and midday temperatures were predicted to rise to above twenty-five degrees in the midlands.

That was according to the weather forecast coming from his radio, but as the taxi driver reiterated to his passenger, Met office predictions – particularly in this country – couldn't always be trusted.

The sun had not yet begun to burn through the early-morning blanket of haze that obstructed Roan's first view of his homeland. He thought that the pilot had made an excellent landing, considering the fact that, to him, Dublin Airport seemed completely invisible from the sky.

An old road sign told Roan that Rathrigh was another twenty miles away. It was odd, but strangely comforting to him, that the old black-and-white road signs, which showed distance in miles, and not kilometres, were still prevalent throughout the Irish countryside. He hadn't seen any green-and-white kilometre signs since they turned off the N3. Not that he had travelled on too many roadways, or freeways as they were called in the States – in fact, he had barely ventured out of the city since arriving nearly a year ago. As thrilling as the city had been, when he caught his first glimpse of the famous Manhattan skyline on the journey in from JFK, Roan soon decided that living in New York with a crowd of Irish lads in Yonkers wasn't that different from living in Rathmines. His goal was to make enough money to afford a place of his own in Manhattan, Chinatown, The Village – anywhere would do.

He was on his way to achieving that goal too; in fact, he was still at the office when he opened the email from Aidan at 9.30 New York time, telling him about Shane's accident.

He had been in the process of debugging a computerised filing system the company had designed for a New York publishing company. It was a huge undertaking, and Roan had been originally transferred from the Dublin office to oversee the project in its final stages, and ensure that the system was completed on schedule. There had been a few hiccups along the way, but Roan knew that a good job on this would be an almost guaranteed stepping-stone to greater things. He was determined to stay on in the New York office after the project, and if things went according to plan, he'd be first in line for a promotion. For the first time in his life, Roan knew exactly what he wanted.

Despite himself, the news of Shane's death had shaken him. It wasn't that the two of them were particularly close. Roan had never been that close to anyone in his life but, to his surprise, Shane and Aidan had made a particular effort to stay in constant contact with him since he left Dublin. Never a week went by when he didn't get a chatty email or corny joke from one or the other of them. None of his other so-called mates had ever bothered even telephoning to see how he was. For some reason, he had expected them all to be madly envious of his big-city job, expecting to be bombarded with requests to come and visit. To be honest, he had been looking forward to a little showing-off. But no visits had ever materialised. Roan hadn't thought that something like that would ever have bothered him and, in fairness, he wasn't the best himself for keeping in contact, but after a while he found that he appreciated the interest and effort from Aidan and Shane. It was important to him that somebody back home gave a shit about what happened in his life.

And now poor old Shane was gone.

Reeling with shock after opening Aidan's email, he had phoned to enquire about the funeral. He knew that Aidan had been a little surprised about his coming home for the service, but when Roan heard the news, there was never a question that he might not attend. He had always had terrific respect for Shane, and from the sounds of it; poor Aidan was absolutely devastated. The very least he could do was go home and pay his respects to the family. He felt sorry for Karen too. God knows the two of them had never got on, but it must've been very hard for the girl to lose her fiancé like that.

"Any idea where we go from here, buck?" the taxi driver asked, interrupting Roan's train of thought. They had stopped at a T-junction and there didn't appear to be a road sign for Kilrigh, or indeed, for anywhere else. Like Roan, the taxi driver wasn't familiar with the back roads and by-roads of County Meath.

"I'm not sure myself." Roan shifted in his seat to get a better look out the window.

The tarmac road on which they were travelling seemed to lead left onto a narrow, heavily, overgrown by-road, which to him looked no more than a cattle trail. The alternative was a similarly narrow roadway, this one with tall grass growing directly down the middle, and gravelled on either side. Both roads looked particularly daunting, not seeming to lead to anywhere near civilisation.

The sun had risen much higher in the sky, and Roan guessed that the time must now be close to ten o'clock or half-past. Aidan had told him that the funeral Mass was at eleven o'clock. At this stage, it looked as though he was going to be late.

* * *

Tessa took Gerry's hand and squeezed it tightly, as the smell of incense filled the air, a signal that it was time to bring the coffin out of the small church to the graveyard. They waited for Shane's family to exit the pews, then the small group of friends followed the priest, altar boys, and other mourners down the aisle, and out the door into the bright sunlight.

It was a glorious day, Tessa noted. It had been a mild few weeks, but considering that the country had been pelted with wind and rain all over the previous week and weekend, the sun shining happily in a cloudless sky just didn't fit. In fact, it almost seemed to mock the tragic circumstances that brought them all here. Then again, she thought, there was probably a delighted bride-to-be somewhere else in the country, that had spent all week hoping and praying for that same sky. Walking slowly through the graveyard, she caught Mike's eye and gave him a little smile. He had come to the funeral without Jenny, and seemed a bit lost in the middle of it all. Tessa thought she could understand why Karen couldn't bring herself to attend the funeral, but she wasn't sure if her friend was doing the right thing. Laying a loved one to rest was an important part of the grieving process; this she understood from her own experience with grieving relatives at the hospital. By trying to shut it all out, Karen was simply delaying the inevitable. She knew that her friend's decision had been unpopular with the Quinn family. Upon hearing that Karen wouldn't be attending the funeral, Barbara Quinn – Shane's elder sister – had been totally scandalised. Temporarily putting aside her grief, she had launched an all-out-attack on Karen.

"I don't know why I'm even surprised," she had said, when Jenny had phoned the Quinn household to inform them of Karen's decision. "It's just typical of that girl – selfish to the end! God forgive me, but the only good thing that's come out of this is that she'll never be part of this family!"

She was an odious woman, Tessa thought. At the removal the night before, Barbara had been close to disrespectful towards her brother with the way she carried on – chatting and gossiping with the other women as if they were attending a country fair – then turning on the tears, and wailing like a banshee as soon as the priest arrived for the blessing. Tessa didn't doubt that she had loved her brother, but to Barbara, the funeral seemed more of an excuse for a social outing at which she was the centre of attention, rather than the tragic and poignant occasion that it was. It was a terrible thing to be thinking, especially in present circumstances, but Tessa felt that Karen was well rid of the Quinns.

The funeral procession stopped, and the crowd began to gather in small groups beside the grave. Nellie, looking deeply saddened, was supported on one side by Shane's sisters, and on the other by a tall, wirily built man with a moustache, whom Tessa recognised as Jack, the older brother. The wreaths had been laid alongside the coffin and the priest had just begun a decade of the Rosary when Tessa noticed some movement amongst the crowd. With Jenny a couple of steps behind her, a terribly frail-looking Karen – her face pallid, and tears streaming down her cheeks – walked through the crowd. When she reached the graveside, she bent down at the head of the coffin, and briefly touched the brass plate on the lid. Then, crouched at the graveside, Karen lowered her head and began to sob quietly. It was a heartbreaking sight, and Tessa's tears flowed freely as she felt her friend's pain.

Chapter 40

After the service, the funeral party went to Mulligan's – Rathrigh's only pub – where drinks and refreshments were served.

"I'm delighted that you managed to convince her," Aidan said to Jenny. "We were all so sure that she wouldn't come."

"I didn't have to," she said. "Nothing would have dragged Karen here last night, but when she got up this morning, something had changed. She told me that she had spent all night thinking it over, and that this time she *would* say goodbye to him properly." She glanced towards Karen, who was sitting in another corner of the pub, in gentle conversation with Gerry.

"Mike's gone back then," Tessa said, sipping her mineral water and at the same time, trying to dodge Aidan's cigarette smoke. "I noticed him leave earlier."

Jenny nodded. "He feels so guilty about having to rush off to London like that. But there's no point in his being here – it's all over now."

Tessa followed Jenny's gaze across the room towards her husband.

"He's been terrific with Gerry, you know. I don't know how he does it, but Mike has this knack of saying the right thing to people, especially at times like this."

It was true, Jenny thought. Mike had a wonderful manner about him. Most people outside a close circle of friends had absolutely no idea how to react to such a tragedy, and generally resorted to supposedly comforting but mostly meaningless clichés.

Mike was no such person, however. He had been a rock to them all throughout these last few days, but particularly to the men: spending hours talking with Aidan, who was still trying to take some meaning from the death of his closest friend. The night before, he had sat up talking with Gerry until the early hours of this morning.

He would be absolutely shattered by the time he got to London. Jenny hoped that he'd have the chance to catch a few hours' sleep before the meeting.

Since she decided to attend the funeral this morning, Karen had bucked up a little but Jenny could see from her friend's face that the strain of it all was starting to get to her. She'd drive her back to Dublin as soon as an opportunity presented itself, but in the meantime, it was good to have Karen up out of bed, and sharing her grief with her friends. Especially since she couldn't rely on either Shane's family or her own. Jenny was still smarting from her conversation with Mrs Cassidy the previous day.

"I'm sorry dear, but it will be just *impossible* for us to get back in time for this funeral. Jonathan has a huge

American booking this week and well, we had to keep June free for the wedding, and all that. We couldn't possibly rearrange everything so quickly. Karen will understand. She knows how it is. Tell her we love her very much and we'll send some flowers."

Send some flowers indeed! Now she knew why her own mother never had any time for Clara and Jonathan Cassidy. Jenny knew that Karen's parents were busy people, but what kind of parents would desert their only child at a time like this?

"I'm getting another Coke. Does anyone want anything?" she asked, draining her glass. Tessa and Aidan shook their heads.

She looked up as Jack Quinn waylaid her on her way to the bar.

"Jenny, isn't it?" he said. "I'd just like to apologise for my sister's behaviour on the phone last night. She was upset – we all were."

Jenny nodded. "I understand. I'm sure Karen will too."

"Barbara can be a little," he searched for the right word, "'difficult' sometimes. But it's nothing personal."

"It's fine, honestly. I'm sure Karen won't take it that way," Jenny said with a placating smile. At least Jack had the decency to apologise, knowing full well that his sister was out of order in blasting Karen for her decision not to attend the removal. Out of the corner of her eye, she saw Nellie Quinn approach Karen at her table.

"Well, thank you for coming Jenny," Jack continued. "I've often heard Shane speak about you, and I know you were a good friend."

Jack walked away and as he moved, Jenny's breath caught in her throat. Her head started spinning while the rest of the world stood still.

Roan Williams was leaning casually alongside the bar counter to her left, chatting with a dark-suited man that Jenny didn't recognise. Her stomach constricted and her heart started pounding at the rate of what seemed like a thousand beats per minute. What was he doing here? No, it couldn't be him – it was just someone who looked like Roan. She was tired and her mind was just playing tricks on her. Jenny looked, away, shook her head slightly and then looked back again. No, it was definitely him!

She heard the barman ask for her order, and Jenny had no choice but to collect herself, while still reeling with the shock of it.

Oh, stop being so silly, she told herself. So what if Roan was here? It was no big deal, was it? But it was just so unexpected to see him in the flesh after such a long time. She paid the barman, and shakily made her way back to the table, taking such a huge gulp from her glass that she ended up with a mouthful of ice.

"You've seen Roan, I take it," whispered Tessa, just out of earshot from the others.

Jenny nodded, trying to her best to appear nonchalant. "I didn't know he was back from the States, did you?"

Tessa shook her head. "No, but I saw him earlier standing at the back of the church on our way out." She leaned forward and whispered, "How are you feeling?"

"Me? Oh, I'm fine, absolutely fine. It was a bit unexpected but . . ."

She stopped short as Roan approached the table and

nodded briefly towards the others. Aidan, who was sitting with his back to the bar, turned around in surprise when Roan tapped him on the shoulder. He stood up and the two men clapped one another on the back.

"Mate – how are you? Thanks for coming," Aidan said warmly.

Jenny tried to avert her eyes, but didn't succeed. Over Aidan's shoulder, Roan was staring right at her, with those deep, dark eyes she had once known so well.

"Hi guys, how are you all?" He pulled up a stool and sat down in the space between Jenny and Aidan. She shuffled uncomfortably in her seat. "Jenny – it's been a long time. How have you been?" he asked, smiling as he took a drink from his pint.

Jenny bristled at his casualness. How could he speak to her as if she were just another one of the gang, as if nothing had ever happened between them? She wanted to scream at him. *How have I been? Oh I've been just fine, Roan! By the way, you broke my heart and practically ruined my life, but I'm just fine and dandy now. Thanks for asking!*

"Very well thanks, and you?" was all she said, her voice even, although her heart was racing a mile a second. *Two can play at that game, buster!*

"Great, great. I've no complaints."

Good for you!

Noticing Jenny's obvious discomfort, Tessa swiftly changed the direction of the conversation, by asking Roan how long he had been back in Ireland. Jenny tried to appear uninterested when he told them that he had flown in to Dublin earlier that same day for the funeral; and was going back to the States the following day. It was simply a flying visit, he explained, and he probably wouldn't even get the chance to visit his family.

Jenny digested this information with a mixture of relief and disappointment.

She had tried so long to pretend she didn't care, had *told* herself she didn't care, but seeing Roan here now, and after so long, brought everything back. All those lonely months of heartbreak and self-doubt, wondering why he found it necessary to deceive her for so long, wondering why she hadn't been enough for him. Jenny needed to know. She *had* to know why.

She knew she shouldn't be feeling like this, not when she had got her life back on track. And then there was Mike. Mike, who she knew would do anything for her, who trusted her implicitly, and would never treat her as Roan had.

Anyway, she thought, seeing Karen walk towards them, today was not the day to be revisiting the past.

"Jen, I hope you don't mind, but the Quinns have asked me to come back to the house. They have some things of Shane's that Nellie wants me to have."

"OK, do you want me to come with you?"

She sank down on the seat beside her. "No, you go on home if you like. I don't really want to go, but I probably won't get the chance again. After all, I have no ties with them now, do I?" Eyes glistening, she looked away for a moment. "I might end up staying the night, but if not, I'm sure Jack or one of the others will drop me home later. You go on back to Dublin after this. You haven't been home for days, and I know you've had even less sleep than I've had."

Jenny smiled and patted her friend's hand. "Are you sure?" she asked, not too happy about leaving her alone with the Quinns. She hoped Barbara Quinn would behave herself, because at this stage, poor Karen had been through enough. Then again, maybe this would be the opportunity she and Nellie needed to put the past behind them.

"I am. I think everyone will be heading back soon, anyway, although Gerry looks like he's enjoying his few pints," she said to Tessa.

Tessa looked across the room to where her husband was sitting, with a half-finished pint of Guinness in his hand, and a fresh one on the table in front of him.

"I don't mind," said Tessa. "I think we all deserve to relax after this. You know, I used to hate the way everyone in this country always seemed to rush straight into the pub after a funeral. I always thought it was disrespectful. But after everything that's happened over these last few days, I can see why people need to feel someway close to normal again." She saw Karen wince and Tessa could have kicked herself. "Oh, I'm sorry love. I know it'll be a very long time before you feel anyway close to normal again. I just didn't think."

"No, it's fine," Karen said, getting up from the stool. "To be honest, today has been a lot easier than I expected. I know it sounds weird, but I'm sort of glad I decided to come. Thanks, you two. I appreciate you being there for me."

"Karen, you know we'll still be here whenever you need us," said Tessa, embracing her fondly. "By the looks of things, we'll be staying on here for a while longer. I'll see you tomorrow." Tessa and Gerry had planned to stay the night at Harold's Cross, so that Karen wouldn't be on her own.

"You have a key?" Karen asked.

"Yes, now don't you worry about us. I see Nellie Quinn is waving at you – she must be ready to leave."

"I'd better go, then. Thanks for everything."

Karen hugged Jenny and Tessa again and went to join the Quinns, who were waiting for her by the door.

"I'm going to go too," said Jenny with a yawn. "Karen was right. I've hardly had any sleep and I'm absolutely whacked."

"Are you sure that you'll be OK to drive, then?" Tessa asked.

"I'll be fine, honestly. Say goodbye to Gerry for me, will you?" She looked around to say goodbye to the others but in the meantime everyone seemed to have moved. And she couldn't see Roan anywhere.

Feeling strangely empty, Jenny left the small pub, and walked outside towards the tiny carpark, at the rear of the building. For some reason, she had always expected that when she finally came face-to-face with Roan again, it would be different to this. She had spent so many nights playing a variety of scenes over and over in her head.

In one, Roan would be full of remorse, and maybe plead with her to take him back, realising how much he loved her, and how much he had lost. In another, she would scream at him, asking him why – why he had hurt her the way he did? And then, maybe they would fall into one another arms, or maybe they would go their separate ways. But today, there had been nothing like that. Roan had barely even acknowledged her. Jenny switched on the ignition; her vision blurred and her eyes filled with tears, as she made her way out of the carpark, and away from Rathrigh.

She had reached the carpark exit, when she noticed a tall figure run up beside the car.

"What do you want?" She rolled down the window, but wasn't able to look at him.

Roan began to say something, then stopped, putting both hands in his trouser pockets. Then he said, "I saw you leave and I just wanted to –" At that moment, Aidan came out the side door of the pub and wandered towards the carpark.

"For goodness sake, get in, will you?" Jenny said impatiently. She wasn't quite sure why, but she didn't want anyone to see them together. Roan obliged and Jenny put the Punto into gear and sped down the main street, her own thoughts going much faster than the car's speedometer.

Neither of them said anything until they were outside the village.

"Where are you staying? Can I give you a lift?" Jenny said, anxious to break the silence, and unnerved by his close proximity.

"I'm staying at the Skylon, near the airport. I'd appreciate you dropping me back. I had to get a taxi out here."

"No problem."

They drove for what seemed like ages, without saying another word. Spurred by nervousness and anticipation, Jenny drove much faster than she would normally allow herself, especially on such narrow and winding roads.

She was so aware of him, so conscious of the familiar scent of him. He looked good, she thought.

When they reached the main Dublin road, Roan finally said something.

"How have you been?" he asked, as he had back in Rathrigh, though this time gentler, with a little more feeling.

"Fine," Jenny said, trying to keep her voice even. "I didn't expect you to be here today. I knew that you and Shane had kept in touch, but I didn't think you were that close."

"Shane was a good guy," said Roan, with a slight American twang. "He gave me his email address before I left, and for some reason, we just kept corresponding – Aidan too. It was pretty lonely out there at the beginning. New York is such a huge place. I didn't know many others in the office, and the company put me in a hotel for the first few weeks, until I could sort out a place of my own."

"Didn't Cara Stephens go out there too?" Jenny asked bitterly, before she could stop herself. "I'm sure she would have kept you company." Shit – why had she said that? Now he would know she still cared.

Roan took a deep breath. "It wasn't like that, Jenny. There was never anything between Cara and I."

"Oh, I see, I just imagined that night, did I? I just imagined seeing you wrapped around her in the corner of some nightclub." Jenny noticed that her hands were sweating badly, as she grasped the gear-stick to move the Punto into fifth gear.

"Jen, this is why I caught up with you back there. I know you're still angry with me, and you've every right to be. Look, pull in and we'll go somewhere where we can talk properly – not like this. You're getting yourself all worked up. Please – you'll have us both killed otherwise," he added, trying to make light of the situation and instantly realising that, in view of the day that was in it, the comment was in very bad taste.

Satisfied at the realisation that after all this time she was the one making *him* feel uncomfortable; Jenny had slowed off the accelerator and brought her speed back down to fifty. He was right. They needed to talk. Properly. Maybe then, Jenny thought, she could get some answers but then, a part of her wasn't quite sure whether or not she wanted to hear them.

A few miles further down, close to Balbriggan, Jenny pulled in and parked the car at a small picnic area, situated in a lay-by just off the main road. Although it was heading towards teatime, some picnicking families were still present amongst the small wooden tables, undoubtedly taking advantage of the day's unexpected fine weather, and the gorgeous view out towards Dublin Bay.

Jenny and Roan sat side by side at the nearest vacant bench.

"Now that you're here, I'm not sure what to say to you," he said quietly. "I've rehearsed this conversation a thousand times in my head, but now I just don't know where to start."

For once, Roan actually looked a little unsure of himself, she thought. But she wasn't going to be taken in by his little-boy-lost attitude. Not this time.

"How about, 'Jenny, I'm sorry for lying to you. I'm

sorry for cheating on you, and I'm sorry for treating you like shit throughout the entirety of our relationship?' That would be a good start, Roan." She noticed that her voice sounded bitter, more so than she would have imagined.

"You're right, you know. I won't argue with that." He turned to face her, but Jenny concentrated her stare away from his, and out towards the sea. "I *am* sorry, Jenny. I'm sorry for everything. You deserved better."

"Yes," she said simply. "I did. You told me you loved me; we were living together, for goodness sake! And yet you still cheated on me, and lied to me all the way through. Why? If you didn't love me, why not just finish it?"

He shook his head. "Jenny, I honestly don't know why. When I said I loved you, I thought I meant it – at the time I meant it, but I suppose back then I had absolutely no idea what I was really saying."

"Oh." So he didn't love her then. He had never really loved her after all. At least now, Jenny knew for sure.

"Look Jen, you were right when you said that I lied and cheated my way through our relationship. And to this day, I don't know why I did that. It's just that girls always seemed to really like me, and I just couldn't help myself sometimes. I know that sounds pathetic, but it was true."

"Like Cara, I suppose," Jenny said, numbness spreading through her. Even though she had realised all of this a long time ago, and had come to terms with it in a way, it was still very difficult to hear him say it. Roan had never really loved her.

"Yes, like Cara. But that night didn't happen like you

thought it did. I know you won't believe me, but that night, I actually had a crisis of conscience. I knew that Cara was up for it, and I thought to myself 'Why am I doing this? What's the point?' I didn't really care about Cara; I didn't really care about any of them. All I was doing was hurting myself and hurting you, not to mention ruining any chance of our having a half-decent relationship."

Jenny could feel the tears starting from behind her eyes, and she willed herself not to cry. They were all coming back now, all the old feelings of hurt, betrayal, and humiliation. Back then, she had fooled herself into thinking that they had more than a half-decent relationship. While she had put her very heart and soul into making it work, Roan had done everything to tear it asunder – tearing Jenny asunder in the process.

"I'm sorry, Jenny," he said finally. "Really I am. I know you did your best and I didn't know at the time how lucky I was to have someone like you. It was only when I moved away that I realised how few people really cared about me. I quickly found that I had nobody to rely on, that through my own selfishness I had driven everyone away. I thought that everyone, all my so-called friends back here, would be really impressed by my big-shot Manhattan lifestyle. I thought they'd all be clambering for invitations to visit, and I was looking forward to showing off. But after a few months, I realised that nobody gave a shit. I ring my mother once a month and once in a blue moon, if she wants something, she might ring me. But that's it. I could be lying dead in the Bronx somewhere, for all they care."

"What about the people you work with?" asked Jenny. "Surely you made some friends at Evanston?"

Roan shook his head. "I work with them, Jenny, but I don't really know them. Americans are different from us – they're much more independent. They don't find it absolutely necessary to know everything about everyone else. They have their own lives outside work and they just get on with it. Look, I'm not trying to make you feel sorry for me. It's just, I had a lot of time on my hands and I got to thinking a lot about my behaviour, not just towards you, but also towards everyone else. And I soon realised that I didn't have anyone I could turn to. There was absolutely no one I could confide in. I couldn't admit to anyone that I was finding it hard over there.

Then one day, I came across Shane's email address in my wallet and I sent him a quick note, asking how things were. He replied the next day." He looked sadly out towards the sea. "I've always had great time for Aidan and after a while, I wrote to him too. Hardly a week went by when we didn't correspond. And it seemed easier to admit to them both that I was having a hard time, although I knew Shane had long since read between the lines, so to speak."

"And that's why you came back for the funeral?"

Roan nodded. "I had to pay my respects. He and I had got quite close, closer than you might expect. I confided in him, and in return he confided in me. I knew he had been under a lot of strain there for a while, before he and Karen decided upon a date for the wedding. I think he felt that she was getting cold feet, and might call the whole thing off."

Jenny was shocked upon hearing this. She was sure too, that Karen would have had no idea that Roan and Shane had been communicating like that. She was certain that her friend would have mentioned it.

"Were you really that miserable?" Jenny asked, wondering why he had stayed in New York if things had been that bad.

"At the beginning, yes, but after a while I got a place of my own – well, a house-share in Yonkers with a crowd of Dublin lads." He shook his head in wonder. "Talk about living home away from home, Jen. Out there it's much the same as living in Rathmines. Yonkers is where most of the Irish live in New York, and at the shop near my place you can buy Galtee sausages for your breakfast and Jacob's Cream Crackers for your lunch. They even stock all the regional Irish newspapers. I buy the *Leinster Post* in there every week." He laughed, relaxing a little. "I suppose all of this helped me settle. Then I met someone."

Jenny said nothing. She'd had a feeling that this was coming.

"Her name's Kelly," Roan went on. "She's American but tells everyone she's Irish-American, even though she's never even been outside the city! She works as a radio dispatcher for the NYPD." He smiled at Jenny's expression, before he continued.

"I know what you're thinking, but that's not how we met. I haven't been in any trouble over there – quite the opposite actually. The job is going really well and I'm next in line for promotion."

Jenny listened in silence as he told her all this. It was incredible, she thought. Roan had another life now, a completely different life from the one they had shared. And he sounded happy with his new life, and his new love. He had moved on.

And now he was here, apologising, trying to explain, and asking for forgiveness, so that he could go back with a clear conscience to his nice new life, with his nice new girlfriend.

"I met someone too," Jenny said, suddenly aware that she was using her words as both a shield against her own feelings, and as weapon towards his. She wanted him to be affected by this, maybe even a little jealous.

"I'm glad. You deserve it, Jen," he said, and then he smiled that amazing smile, that genuine smile, the one that showed up the tiny dimples on each side of his mouth. It had been a long time since Jenny had seen that smile. Towards the end, Roan had rarely smiled at her, had rarely smiled at anything. Had she made him that unhappy, she wondered.

He gave a short laugh. "You won't believe me, but I spoke to Shane about you shortly before I left, and I asked him to keep an eye on you." He shrugged. "Arrogant of me, I know – because I should have realised you'd bounce back without help from anyone else."

"It wasn't that easy, Roan."

"I don't think that for second," he said. "I wanted to tell you I was leaving for good, but by then it had been what – five, six months since we'd seen one another? Shane advised me against it, said that you'd moved on and it would be better if I just left you alone."

"He was right, as it happened," she said with a smile.

"I wanted to pick up the phone to you so many times,

Jenny. I was such a bastard – I know that now. But believe me when I tell you that my stupid behaviour back then was absolutely no reflection on you. I had always been exactly the same – with Siobhan, with everyone else."

"Tell me about Siobhan," Jenny said bravely, even thought she didn't really want to hear what she knew he was going to tell her.

He sighed. "I suppose if we're being honest, I might as well tell you everything. That night in the pub, Lydia Reilly wasn't lying about Siobhan and I being engaged."

Jenny's heart sank. She had thought that she couldn't possibly feel any worse, but at this, she felt as though Roan had taken her heart and given it to a pair of Chinese ping-pong world champions to use in a final. She let him continue.

"We were together for a long time after that, right up until after the Venice trip. She was the daughter of a one-hundred-acre stud-owner, and we had been going out since secondary school." He said this ashamedly, looking down at the grass. "She was the one I thought I'd eventually marry but, after Venice, I think she saw through me, realised that I'd been doing the dirt on her in Dublin, that I'd been doing the dirt all along."

"And you were doing the same to me. Why? What was the point? Doing something like that was just plain cruel – to both of us!"

Jenny remembered only too clearly the naked pain she had felt the day she discovered he had gone to Venice with Siobhan. Still, she had suspected that they were still together, that they had never broken up as Roan had told her they had. In her heart of hearts, Jenny had known the truth all along.

"I know, and I'm sorry. Siobhan was supposed to have been away on a modelling shoot that weekend, and wouldn't have been able to go. So I asked you. Then she heard about my winning the competition, and cancelled the shoot to go with me. I didn't know what to do. Then we had the fight and . . . "

"Competition? *You won the trip in a bloody competition?*" Jenny cried. Enraged, she jumped off the wooden bench, not caring one whit about what the other picnickers thought of her. This revelation was way too much for her. By his own admission Roan was a lying conniving, cheating little rat, but *this!* How could anyone be so deceitful?

"Jenny – "

"Forget it!" she said, rummaging in her handbag for the car keys. "I've had enough, Roan. I don't want to hear another word!" She raged past the group of teenagers on the next bench, who for the last couple of minutes had been watching the scene with interest, pleased with the unexpected entertainment this madwoman and her poor hen-pecked boyfriend were providing. "I'm out of here, and don't think you're coming with me! You can crawl your way back to Dublin. It's the least you deserve, you fucking creep!"

Roan stood up in shock. He couldn't remember ever hearing Jenny use such bad language. He followed her back to the car where she stood in tears, struggling to get the key in the driver door.

"Jenny I'm sorry. I really am," he said softly, coming up beside her, and putting an arm around her.

She whirled around to face him, tears flooding down her cheeks.

"Do you know how much shit I went through last year, trying to figure it all out, wondering what I did wrong? Thinking that it was me, that it had to be me, that I wasn't attractive enough for you, that I was too fat, that I was crap in bed, that I wasn't enough! I wasn't enough! Did you have any idea?"

"Sssh, Jen, it's OK."

"And all that time, after wondering whether or not you were cheating on me, after trying my utmost to keep you happy, you turn around and tell me that I wasn't the one who was being cheated on. I wasn't even number one! I was just the other woman. She had dumped you so you had to settle for second best!"

"It wasn't like that, Jenny. I cared about you a lot – I still do." Clearly disturbed, Roan ran a hand through his hair. "Look, when Siobhan and I broke up, I was determined to give things a decent shot with you and for a while there, things were going well and we were happy. But I don't know, I think we got into some kind of rut – *I* got into some kind of rut. I wasn't happy with my life, Jen, and I didn't know why. But now I do – now I realise that I'd spent most of my life using other people, expecting them to keep *me* happy, while I gave nothing in return." He walked closer to her. "Come here – please."

He reached for Jenny and held her close to him.

Inside, Jenny felt that her heart was breaking all over again. "Did you have any idea Roan," she said, sobbing miserably into his chest, "ever have any idea how much I loved you?"

Chapter 41

Much later, Jenny drove Roan back to his hotel. They were both silent for most of the journey, and the atmosphere hung heavily between them. He had changed, she thought, glancing sideways at him as they approached the entrance to the Skylon hotel.

Breaking down in front of him like that had been incredibly embarrassing. He seemed to understand though, and had held her in his arms for a long time afterwards, saying nothing while she cried. He openly accepted complete responsibility for the failure of their relationship, and had admitted that he had been ruthless with her feelings, not to mention her health. For that, he said, he was truly sorry.

It had been a new departure for Jenny. Never once, throughout the course of their relationship, had he taken the blame for anything. She appreciated his sincerity, but still wasn't sure how she felt about this new, improved, and obviously much more mature Roan Williams.

There had been a moment back there at the picnic area, a moment that Jenny was finding, now driving towards his hotel, very difficult to put out of her mind. When he had put his arms around her as she cried, Jenny had felt the almost unreal sensation of being in his arms again, immersed in the familiar scent of him. Then Roan had stared into her eyes with such a strange look on his face that Jenny was almost certain that he was about to kiss her. They stayed like that, eyes locked together, for what seemed like an age. Then Jenny looked away, the moment passed, and shortly afterwards, the two of them returned to the car.

Now she didn't know what to think.

All she knew was that she had never felt so exhausted in her life, the hours of heavy, emotive conversation with him draining her entire being. Not to mention the fact that she hadn't had a decent night's sleep in days. She pulled up outside the hotel entrance, kept the engine running, and put the car back into first gear. Roan got out.

"It's close to seven o'clock," he said, glancing at his watch, which Jenny noticed was an expensive looking Tag Heuer. He obviously hadn't been lying about doing well in New York. "Do you want to come in for a while? We could maybe get something to eat? I know I'm pretty hungry after all that, and I'm sure you must be too."

He cleared his throat. He was nervous, she realised.

Jenny looked up into those intense brown eyes, and once more saw something in them, something she wasn't sure she wanted to see. Was it just nostalgia, this strange feeling between them now? Jenny was no longer sure. After today, the rules had changed. She had thought that knowing and understanding Roan's motives for hurting her back then would have been enough. Afterwards, she could move on and put all that hurt and longing behind her. But, she realised, there was something unfinished hanging in the air between them. She could feel it, and she was certain he could too. Jenny's heart began to pound, and she felt beads of moisture form on her forehead.

"I'm – I'm very tired," she said quickly, afraid to meet his eyes.

"Yes . . . I suppose you want to be getting back home. Do you still live in Dun Laoghaire?"

She nodded, unable to take her eyes off the dashboard, wanting to look at him, to touch him, but not daring to.

There was a heavy pause.

"Um, thanks for the lift," Roan said. Out of the corner of her eye, Jenny could see him watching her, almost willing her to look up. But if she looked into his eyes again, she didn't know what might happen. Jenny felt a sense of panic envelop her.

"You're welcome." She grasped the steering wheel as tightly as she could.

"Well, I guess I'll see you around then." Roan swallowed hard.

She nodded, still afraid to look at him, afraid to say anything more. She could feel the tension simmer between them. She put the car into first gear for the second time, as if to convince herself that she was leaving soon – needed to leave soon. Roan hesitated for what seemed like forever, but was actually only a couple of seconds, and then softly closed the passenger door.

Jenny sped off without checking her rear-view mirror, afraid that if she looked back and saw his face, she would almost certainly falter. She had to get out of here – quickly.

Thumpety-thump, thumpety-thump – Jenny's heart raced. *Don't look back. Don't look back,* she kept repeating to herself. But, when she stopped the car at the hotel exit onto the Drumcondra Road, she couldn't help it. It was as though some strange invisible force had taken control of her responses. She looked back and saw Roan still standing, still watching her outside the hotel – a strange expression on his face.

That was it, she thought – she couldn't stand it any longer.

Jenny put the car into reverse and sped backwards towards the hotel, her sense of orientation all over the place. She had just narrowly missed bumping into a parked Mondeo reversing around a corner when she saw Roan run towards her. She parked the car in what was probably a reserved staff space, but Jenny didn't care, she was far beyond caring. She got out of the car and, slamming shut the driver's door, flung herself into Roan's arms, holding on to him as if her life depended on it.

They kissed hungrily, not caring who saw them, not caring what the consequences might be. Jenny knew that she wanted, no, *needed* to be with him once more, just one more time.

Roan broke away for a moment. He cupped her upturned face between both hands and looked directly into her eyes. Jenny could see her own passion mirrored in his. "Are you sure about this?" he asked.

She nodded, not saying a single word, not wanting to break the spell.

Just one more time.

Chapter 42

Karen's Kitchen – Present Day

"So you were with Roan again – all that time ago, and you never said anything?" Karen asked.

Having reached the end of her tale, Jenny watched her friend's expression with nervous anticipation, praying that Karen would understand. She picked the chocolate chips off her untouched muffin.

"For goodness sake, Jenny! Why didn't you tell me?"

Jenny dropped her hands in her lap. "I tried to tell you, but there was never a right time. You had just buried Shane; and I was ashamed of myself. It was an emotional day, and to be honest, at the time I felt as though I was betraying you. I was afraid you'd think that all I cared about was myself. But it wasn't like that, Karen. I didn't expect him to come back."

"It doesn't matter *what* day it was, Jenny. I'm just annoyed at you for letting him get away with everything, all over again. To think of the way he treated you – "

"That was another reason why I didn't say anything. I

didn't want to have to go through it all again with you or Tessa. And I was afraid that Mike would find out. But this time, it was different – *he* was different. We thrashed everything out between us, and afterwards Roan went back to New York, and I was finally ready to move on with my life. As far as we were concerned it was unlikely we would ever see one another again."

"So you decided to have a little snogging session, for old time's sake?" Karen said sarcastically. Seeing that the remark had stung, she relented. "I'm sorry, Jen – it's just a bit of a shock, hearing all of this now, when none of us had any idea that the two of you had been alone together."

"But you're right, in a way," Jenny said. "After that day, I no longer had any doubts. I realised that Mike was the one I wanted, the one I really loved. Until then, I hadn't been sure; I was still caught in the past. But once I had seen Roan again, I could finally let go. I hadn't been able to before then, not completely." She bit her lip. "I know it's difficult for you to understand but afterwards, I knew for certain that I wanted to spend the rest of my life with Mike. I still do."

"Which is why you two got engaged so soon afterwards." Karen said.

"Partly, yes. There were other things, but afterwards I put my heart and soul into making our relationship work. I think Mike realised that something had changed. He knew that Roan had been at the funeral that day, although he didn't know the whole story, obviously. Maybe he sensed that finally I was ready to move on and that's why he proposed. And he was right. I *was* ready to move on and relegate Roan to the past."

Karen was silent for a moment. "Things haven't turned

out that way though, have they?" she said. "There's more, isn't there? Otherwise, you wouldn't be upset – you wouldn't be here." She watched Jenny closely for a reaction, and her friend's haunted expression told her all she needed to know. "I'm right, aren't I?"

Jenny nodded, her eyes betraying her feelings as her eyelids battled hard to keep away the tears.

"Oh Jenny. Is there any doubt?" Karen asked softly.

"No, at least I don't think so."

"Are you going to tell him?"

"I'm not sure. But now that Roan is back, and he's going to be working closely with Mike, one of them is bound to make the connection. And you know how often we socialise with the InTech crowd. I'm almost certain to bump into him sometime."

Karen shook her head. "Jenny, do you realise the significance of what you've done? You should have said something back then – if not to Mike, then at least to me."

"I know, and believe me I had planned to, but with everything happening back then, there was never an opportunity. You had enough on your plate without me burdening you with my problems."

Karen exhaled loudly. She couldn't believe that once again, after all that time, Jenny had again fallen under Roan William's spell, just when she was beginning to get her life back together. Mike was a good person; he didn't deserve any of this and obviously Jenny hadn't told him a thing, otherwise she wouldn't have been so concerned about Roan's return to Dublin. She herself had never suspected anything, had never known that Jenny and Roan had even spoken that day.

She had been so out of it that she hadn't even seen him at the funeral, and wouldn't have known whether or not he had been there at all; had Tessa not told her afterwards. But according to Tessa, Roan hadn't stayed long before heading back to Dublin for the night. Obviously, she had had absolutely no idea, either.

And needless to say, Karen had had her own upheavals back then. Jenny was right – there would never have been a good time. Because a few weeks after Shane's funeral, just when Karen was trying to get her life back in order, something else had happened to turn her entire world upside-down again.

She had got a call from their solicitor, Shane's solicitor, asking her to come in to his office for 'a discussion' about Shane's assets. Karen had intended to pay a quick visit to the Quinns on her way to the office of Kearney & Associates in Navan, but when she called to the door, there had been no answer at the farmhouse. She soon found out why.

Upon her arrival at the solicitor's office, and to Karen's surprise, Jack and Nellie Quinn were sitting together in the plush carpeted waiting-room. Nellie had made small-talk while they waited – stiff, awkward and meaningless small-talk – Jack sitting stony-faced throughout and barely acknowledging Karen's presence. She should have suspected something then, should have known that something was wrong.

But Karen could never have imagined in her wildest dreams what she would hear that day. She could still hear Jim Kearney's soft voice explaining that, because Shane had left no Will, and because he and Karen weren't married, that Shane's share of the house in Harold's Cross now legally belonged to his next of kin – his mother. She listened in disbelief, as the solicitor kindly told her that the property had been registered solely in Shane's name, and would now be registered in Nellie Quinn's. As Jack was acting as guarantor for the mortgage, he also had a legal interest in the property. Would Karen like to make arrangements to sell the remainder of her share to the Quinns?

It had all been surreal, Nellie patting her hand and telling her that they wouldn't expect her to decide straightaway, that she should go home and have a think about it. Home? Hadn't they just told Karen she no longer had a home?

She had never even considered the legal implications of Shane's death, never had considered anything more than overcoming the huge emotional void left in her life after the accident. She had briefly wondered how she might continue paying the mortgage on her own, but had assumed that whatever life assurance Shane had would cover his share of the repayments. She then briefly remembered Aidan advising her to contact a solicitor to find out about such things, but Karen had been too wrapped up in trying to survive each day without Shane that she hadn't thought about it for longer than a second.

It had all come tumbling down on top of her, in the same way that a huge pile of Shane's clothes had come tumbling out of the wardrobe one day, when Karen had felt well enough to go through his things – the smell of him still painfully evident on the jumpers and T-shirts that fell to the ground and bringing about another intense wave of grief. She had been angry then, and she was equally angry sitting in that office, wanting to scream at them all, wishing that he didn't have to die, wishing that he was still here, and that she didn't have to suffer this pain all over again.

But the suffering had only just begun. Jack Quinn had told her some time later in no uncertain terms that they had every intention of selling the house in Harold's Cross. He would give Karen a couple of months to sort herself out and her contributions towards the mortgage would be repaid in full. He hadn't bargained on Karen's resilience. It had been the proverbial kick up the backside that she needed. Since then, Karen had temporarily laid aside her grief, and set about making an absolute mission of saving her home. Suddenly she had something to fight for. There was no way she was going to pack her bags and just up and leave her home, the home she had shared with Shane. Not without a fight. After a few false starts, her dad had put her in touch with a good solicitor in Dublin and as she had learnt only that morning, she and Jack Quinn were going to battle it out in court.

No, Karen thought, bringing her thoughts back to the present, there had been no opportunity for Jenny to tell her about that time with Roan, had she wanted to.

"You'll have to tell Mike, Jen. It could be very embarrassing for him if he finds out any other way. You were a fool to think that you could get away with saying nothing."

"I know. But, Karen, I just didn't think. I tried to convince myself it wouldn't matter. And anyway, with the way everything happened . . . there wasn't an opportunity.

Mike and I were happy, we were getting on with our lives, and there wasn't any point. And I was almost certain that I would never see Roan again. Mike wouldn't have understood if I had told him back then."

"And what makes you think that he would understand now?"

Jenny buried her face in her hands. "I'll just have to take that chance, won't I?"

* * *

Much later, Jenny drove along the seafront towards Blackrock, barely noticing the activity and traffic around her. It had turned out to be a much drearier day than the earlier bright skies had suggested, which she thought was fitting to her mood.

As she passed through Booterstown she looked out over Dublin Bay, and remembered the evening that Mike had proposed. It wasn't long after Shane's funeral and they had gone for a walk along Sandymount Strand, Mike teasing her relentlessly about that day they had spent in Brittas Bay, the day that she wouldn't get her feet wet, that very first day they kissed. Jenny had taken off her shoes and socks, and rushed straight into the water as if to prove him wrong and show him that, this time, she had no problems at all with getting her feet wet.

Mike had followed her, and the two of them spent ages jumping around and splashing one another until they were soaked. Afterwards, they both collapsed laughing and exhausted onto the beach. Mike had sat up with his head on one elbow, looked down seriously at Jenny's upturned face, and suddenly asked her to marry him. It had been so unexpected, and yet it had felt so right. Jenny had said yes without any hesitation whatsoever. Roan had since ceased to exist in her thoughts.

Mike was the one she wanted, pure and simple. She knew his love for her was implicit, had long known it. He had nothing to fear from her past, and Jenny knew unreservedly that she had nothing to fear from his.

When they telephoned Rebecca a few days later to announce that they were getting married, she and Graham had been absolutely thrilled. As had everyone else, Jenny's parents, Mike's parents, and all their friends, including Tessa and Gerry, who had their own reasons to celebrate a few weeks later when Tessa gave birth to a baby boy.

Jenny had hesitated before telling Karen, fully aware that the news would no doubt resurrect her friend's memories of her own engagement. But Karen had been equally delighted for them, aware that Shane's death had had a profound effect on Jenny and Mike's relationship, although not for the reason she suspected.

Mike had admitted as much to Jenny the day they picked out the ring.

"I knew that I would marry again, eventually," he said afterwards over dinner, his expression unusually serious, "but I had every intention of taking it slowly and not rushing into anything. After the accident, though, everything changed. Suddenly I put myself in Karen's shoes and wondered how I would feel if I lost you. And I decided that I wasn't going to waste any more time, Jenny; I decided that if I wanted you to be part of my life, if I wanted to be with you for the rest of my life, that now was as good a time as any to start. Because none of us ever know how long that might be. The rest of our lives – it could mean anything. Do you understand that?"

Jenny did. Shortly after their engagement she gave up her apartment, and moved into Mike's house in Blackrock.

In the meantime, she was promoted to Senior Lender at the Bank, and she and Mike spent most of their time and money redecorating the house, and making it their own. They began making plans for the wedding, and provisionally set the date for the following spring. Life was going as well as it ever had for her, and Jenny didn't think anything could spoil her happiness. She had well and truly moved on.

Indicating right, Jenny crossed the main road and turned into her driveway. She got out of the car, and paused for a moment before putting her key in the front door.

What was it they said about the best-laid plans?

Chapter 43

"We're back!" Mike called happily into the kitchen where Jenny had sat for the last hour, nervously awaiting his return. She looked up as he came through the doorway and despite her heavy heart, couldn't help but smile.

"Look, Holly, there's Mummy!" Mike said to the toddler in his arms. The child's face lit up at the sight of her mother, and she stretched both arms out, wanting to be held.

"Hello, darling!" Jenny said, taking her daughter in her arms. "Did you have a good time at Auntie Rachel's last night? I hope she wasn't too much trouble, Mike – did Rachel say anything?"

"She was fine," Mike soothed. "She said she slept 'til nearly lunch-time today, and spent the rest of the afternoon watching the *Teletubbies*. I'm not quite sure if I'm happy about our daughter watching television at such a young age, but I didn't say anything to Rach. She'd probably be offended and never offer to baby-sit again."

Mike removed Holly's bag, which hung on one shoulder and his laptop bag, which hung on the other, before bending down to kiss Jenny on the lips.

"Did you get all you wanted done today?" he asked.

For a brief moment, Jenny didn't understand what he was talking about. Then she remembered – the exam, she was supposed to have spent today studying for her Mortgage Practice exam. Mike's sister, Rachel, had offered to baby-sit her niece, and had brought Holly directly to the childminder's that morning, in order to give Jenny a full day to herself.

"I did as much as I could," Jenny answered. At least it was something that resembled the truth. Since this morning, she hadn't been able to do a thing, hadn't been able to concentrate on anything other than what Mike had told her over breakfast.

"You must be wrecked, you poor thing," Mike said. "I used to hate studying. I was always so drained after hours of trying to take it all in. Why don't you go and sit down in front of the telly for a while? I'll look after Holly, and organise something for dinner." He removed the child's coat and sat her in her play-chair, before taking Holly's favourite teddy-bear out of the bag and handing it to her. The little girl began playing happily with the toy, banging it up and down on the plastic table in front of her.

"No, it's fine, really. I was just about to start dinner." Jenny said. She got up from the table and took some carrots from the vegetable trolley beside the sink. "You go on and have your shower."

"Are you sure?" Mike said gratefully, taking a carton of orange juice out of the fridge and drinking it directly from the carton. "It was a tough day, to be honest. And battling the traffic all the way from the other side of town wasn't much fun either. I don't know how people put up with having to do that even one day a week, not to mention every single day!"

Rachel lived in Phibsboro, close to the Mater Hospital where she worked as a nurse. Mike had had to make the trip from his office in Sandyford and through the city centre to collect Holly from Rachel's flat in Phibsboro, and then back to their house in Blackrock. He had left the office early, but because of the city's almost guaranteed traffic congestion, the journey had taken him nearly two hours.

"Anyway," Mike continued, "I tried ringing earlier to see how you were getting on, but you must have been so immersed in your books that you didn't get up to answer it."

Jenny thought quickly. She couldn't tell him she had spent the day at Karen's.

"I know," she lied. "I heard it ringing, but by the time I got up to answer, it had rung off. Sorry." Jenny hated herself for lying to him, hated herself even more for deceiving him. Mike noticed nothing amiss, though. He tickled Holly in her play-chair, and she chuckled happily, enjoying the attention she was getting from her dad.

"Oh," he said, looking up as if remembering something, "I've booked a table for four at that new Oriental restaurant in Killiney for tomorrow night. I asked Rachel and she said she'd be delighted to come over and baby-sit her favourite niece again. Remember I told you this morning that I was planning to bring the new guy, Roan Williams, out to dinner?"

Jenny nodded, wondering why he didn't ask her what was wrong, certain that he could hear the blood gushing quickly through her veins.

"I think he's bringing his girlfriend – or is it his wife?" Mike pondered. "I'm not really sure. It should be a good night, Jen. I haven't really had a chance to get to know him since he started, and I'm anxious for all of us to start off on the right foot. After all, he'll be the one running the show when I'm on leave for the wedding."

He grinned. "Anyway, I think the two of us could do with the night out. I know you've been under a lot of pressure with the exams, so we should really let our hair down."

Jenny tried to relax as he came up and put his arms around her, nuzzling her neck.

"You should wear that gorgeous outfit you got for the Christening that time. I'm sure your man would be impressed as hell if he saw you in that!" Mistaking her silence as tiredness from her tough day with the books, Mike gave Jenny a quick kiss on the cheek, and then hummed a little tune on his way upstairs.

She shuddered. She couldn't do it, couldn't pretend any longer. She had to tell Mike – tonight.

* * *

Jenny swallowed hard, and took both of his hands in hers.

"Firstly, I want you to know that I never planned this . . . I never planned to lie to you, I never ever planned to deceive you. It was just the way things happened."

"Deceive me?" Mike laughed nervously, "Jen, what are

you talking about? Hey, you're shaking like a leaf, what's wrong?"

Later that evening, after they had put Holly to bed, Jenny decided that now would be as good a time as any to tell Mike. The eventual contact with Roan couldn't be avoided for much longer, and she knew now that she could no longer live with the guilt.

"Mike, what I'm about to tell is going to hurt you terribly, and will probably mean the end of any respect you have for me, but nevertheless it's something you should know." Jenny clasped her hands tightly around his, willing herself to tell him, hoping that she would have enough strength to do so, wishing that she hadn't lied to him in the first place. "The new guy you've taken on at InTech – Roan Williams? He was my – my ex, Mike, the one who had moved to America, the one that I was getting over when I met you." She waited anxiously for Mike's response.

"OK," he said cautiously, "and how is that significant? It was such a long time ago, Jen. Surely you're not still carrying a torch for him?"

She swallowed hard. "There's more. I told you that we met again last year when Roan turned up unexpectedly at Shane's funeral. We hadn't seen one another since. . . well, since before he left for the States."

"I remember," he said, waiting for her to continue.

"As you can imagine, it was difficult seeing him again and it sent me into a tailspin," she said, watching Mike closely for a reaction. "There had been so much left unsaid since the last time we met." Again Mike said nothing, and Jenny continued. "I left the pub shortly after Karen went away with the Quinns, because I was exhausted. It had been an emotional time, and I felt as though I hadn't slept in days. And, I admit that I was hurt by the fact that Roan didn't seem as disturbed about seeing me again, as I was about seeing him."

Mike nodded slowly. "Well, I can understand that. It must have been a sort of an anticlimax, meeting him again, and getting little or no reaction when you had spent so much time getting over him. I had thought that myself when you told me he had been there."

"Exactly," Jenny said, relieved that at least he could identify with her state of mind at the time. "I don't quite know what I had expected, but I suppose I thought that he might at least try and speak to me about it, rather than behave as though nothing had ever happened between us. I was angry with him, and even angrier with myself for expecting him to be any different, or at all sorry for what he had done to me. But I had been wrong about that. I didn't tell you this, but after I left the pub, Roan followed me out to the car." She told Mike about what had happened afterwards; about Roan's apologies and explanations and about how upset she had been afterwards.

"But I already know most of this," Mike said. "I mean, I knew you had spoken to him, and you told me you'd laid the ghost to rest, as it were. I admit that I hadn't realised how affected you had been by it all, and you hadn't told me that you had given him a lift back to Dublin, but what does it matter now? I'm not the kind of guy that would hold a grudge against Roan, if that's what you're thinking. OK, I'll admit that it might be a little awkward from a social point of view, but we can get over that surely?" When Jenny wouldn't meet his eyes, he realised that there was more to the story. "What? Oh, please don't tell me that you're still in love with him, Jenny! Is that what all this is about?"

Still she said nothing, unable to come up with the right words.

Mike looked totally bewildered. "Jesus, Jenny! We're getting married soon – we have a daughter. We're happy, aren't we? Aren't we?"

Jenny watched his expression change from initial concern, to confusion, bewilderment and finally, pure hurt. She ached to touch him but was afraid to in case she would lose her nerve.

"Why didn't you tell me?" Mike continued hoarsely. "I had no idea that you still loved him." He shook his head to try and stop his eyes filling with tears. "If he was the one you always wanted, if you had never got over him, why on earth did you agree to marry me? Say something, for God's sake!"

Jenny's voice shook as she spoke. She tried to battle with her tears as they spilled out a lot faster than the words, but at the same time resigned herself to the fact that there would be more tears, many more after tonight.

"No, Mike, it wasn't that. I wasn't . . . I'm not in love with him. It's you that I love, more than anything else, and you have to believe that. It's just . . . I should never . . . oh Mike, I've ruined everything!" Jenny put her head in her hands and sobbed, afraid to continue, afraid to tell him the rest, knowing that the truth would destroy them both.

"What? What have you ruined? Please, Jenny, tell me!"

Mike sounded panicked, wanting to know, but at the same time not.

Jenny couldn't look at his face, knowing that his eyes would reflect her own pain.

"Mike, I'm so, so sorry," she said softly. "I made a terrible mistake, and I should have never have done this to you – to *us*. But by the time I found out, by the time I even suspected anything, it was much too late. Anyway, I never thought that I'd see him again. But now that he's back, and part of our lives again, you have to know the truth – you deserve to know the truth."

Mike entwined her fingers in his. "Jen, whatever it is, we'll work through it. We've been through a lot together already, haven't we? Maybe it's just cold feet, after all the wedding is not that far away and – "

"Stop it, you don't understand!" Jenny's voice raised an octave as she became frustrated. She was desperate to get it all out now, as if saying it out loud would unburden the guilt of knowing the truth. "I'm sorry, Mike." Jenny met his eyes for the very first time since the beginning of the conversation. "I wanted to tell you this before, and you don't know how many times I tried to tell you beforehand but . . . oh God." Jenny paused and took a deep breath. Her voice quivered as she said the words. "Holly . . . she isn't your daughter, Mike . . . she's Roan's."

Chapter 44

Holly sat contentedly in her play-chair, while her mother made her favourite breakfast of Rice Krispies with hot milk.

Thankfully, Jenny thought, watching her daughter gurgle merrily to herself, Holly seemed unaware of the controversy surrounding her, unaware that Mike, the man she had called Daddy for the duration of her short life, had days before packed his bags and walked out of the house and out of their lives.

"If it wasn't for the love I have for our daughter, I mean *your* daughter," he had said, his eyes brimming with hurt as he corrected himself, "it would be you packing your bags tonight. You can stay here until you find somewhere else, somewhere decent for you and Holly to live. It's the very least you can do for the child after lying to her since the day she was born."

"Mike, please," she had said, panic consuming her as she realised that he wasn't going to give her a chance to explain, "you can't just leave like this."

"And why not? It seems to me that I can do what I damn well like in this relationship. God knows you did!" he said, eyes flashing angrily.

Jenny hung her head. "We have to talk about it. You need to know that what I did that night was nothing to do with you and me, nothing to do with my love for you – it just was something I needed to get out of my system."

Mike looked at her, outraged by this. "Well, good for you, Jenny! I'm so glad you got it out of your system! Maybe the next time you have something to get out of your system, we'll end up with a little boy!"

The comment stung and Jenny felt ashamed of herself. She had been so consumed with her own guilt, and so anxious to unburden the truth, that she hadn't thought properly about how Mike would react and what would happen next.

"Mike, please try and understand – "

"Understand!" he almost shouted, and then remembered that Holly was sleeping in the room across the hallway. "Understand?" he said again, his voice dropping to a whisper. "What I don't understand is why, after all this time, you decided to tell me the truth?"

"I had to," she said simply. "The guilt has been eating me up inside, ever since I first realised she wasn't yours. I love you too much to lie to you any longer."

Mike winced as he heard this. He looked old and weary as he sat down onto the bed, keeping his back to Jenny, unable to look at her.

"How could you have done it? How could you have lied like that, pretending you were happy, pretending you were as delighted as I was when Holly was born? How could you have done that, when you knew all along that we were living a lie!"

"It wasn't like that. I didn't know – the thought had never even crossed my mind at the beginning. I did think she was yours but by the time I realised, it was too late. We were both in the surgery when Dr Clohessy told me I was pregnant, remember?" she said, trying to make him understand, to let him know that she had never planned to deceive him, that there hadn't been any alternative to doing what she did.

Mike nodded slowly. He had been ecstatic that day. Her own reaction had been a little less assured. How could she be pregnant? Jenny had asked her doctor upon discovering the news, just a few weeks after she and Mike announced their engagement. She'd been taking the Pill religiously every day since she and Mike had begun sleeping together. The doctor began to trot out statistics about the Pill's effectiveness, before a beaming Mike reminded Jenny that she'd had a stomach bug that time shortly before Shane's accident. Dr Clohessy confirmed that the illness was likely to have interfered with her contraception, especially if she had been vomiting.

It was only at that moment, sitting in the doctor's surgery alongside Mike, that the realisation dawned on Jenny that there was a very real possibility Mike might not be the father of her baby. Panic enveloped her, and Jenny remembered that she had never felt so petrified as she had at that moment.

"I promise you, Mike, I promise you that it had never crossed my mind before then that the baby might not be yours. Remember you mentioned how quiet I was being afterwards, and I told you that I was just letting it all sink in? That was true. I *was* letting it all sink in, and trying to come to terms with it. But what could I do? I had never seen you so excited about anything in all my life. There was no way I could tell you then."

"You could have said something," Mike said gruffly.

"Mike, I didn't have a chance! And before long, they all knew, your mother, my parents – everyone. You told them all before I had a chance to think. How could I have said anything then?" Her own parents had been thrilled; Mike's mother had been shocked at first to hear that her son was to be a father so soon after getting engaged, but then equally as thrilled. "I promise you that I had no idea, I had absolutely no idea. It was a shock, hearing I was pregnant when it had been the very last thing on my mind. OK, I hadn't been well, but I didn't even consider the possibility. And with my period being so irregular, I just didn't realise."

She should have realised though. Of course she should have known. But there was so much happening in her life back then. She and Mike had just begun planning the wedding, and she had got her promotion and was working flat out to prove she deserved it. Jenny had thought then that if anything she was simply run-down. Mike had been worried about her frequent headaches, pallid complexion and continual lack of energy, having seen similar symptoms in his father, who had died of brain cancer years before. He had insisted she 'get herself checked out' and one day the two of them went to see Dr Clohessy.

Had she discovered the news by herself, Jenny told

herself that she would have undoubtedly admitted her infidelity to Mike, and made him aware of the possibility that he wasn't the father. Ironically enough, she had never been a good liar, had never been able to sit comfortably with deception. Without doubt, Jenny thought, she would have told Mike the truth and faced the accusations and admonitions. The very least she could have done was let him be the one to decide whether or not he wished to continue with their relationship. And if he had left her then, she would have brought up Holly on her own.

It would have broken her heart to do it, but afterwards, Jenny convinced herself time and time again, that she would have done just that, had she had the chance.

"Anyway," she said to Mike, "it was very possible that you *were* the father. I had slept with Roan once, just once, whereas you and I had been sleeping together all along." She spoke softly, aware of the effect her words must be having on him. "Mike, it was highly unlikely that that one night with someone else had resulted in my becoming pregnant. What were the odds on that?" Although she couldn't see his face, Jenny heard him sob quietly. She moved to sit beside him on the bed. "I'm so sorry, Mike. I made some stupid decisions – decisions that I can't go back on, and you don't know how much I wish that I could. But, believe me when I tell you that none of this was intentional. Try and put yourself in my shoes back then. There was nothing else I could have done. I never, ever meant to hurt you or intended to deceive you about Holly. You have to believe me."

Mike said nothing; he just kept both eyes fixed on the carpet. "I was so happy," he whispered.

"I know."

"No, you don't know, Jenny. You don't know anything!" He raised his voice and his entire body shook as he spoke. "You've made me look like a dumb fool, and all you can say is that you never meant to! Tell me this – why now, after all this time, did you decide to tell me? Why decide to turn what I thought was our happy little world upside down? Why rock the boat?"

Jenny looked away. "Because he's come back," she replied eventually, "and I think that I had always known, deep down, that the truth would come out. When you told me this morning that he would be working with you, it made me realise that there was no hiding from it any more. It was too much of a coincidence. Think about it – it must be some kind of sick fate or something. It's my punishment, Mike. Somebody somewhere is making me pay for what I did to you – and to Holly."

Mike wiped his eyes. "So I suppose now the plan is to go off and play happy families with *him*, is it?"

"It's not like that. I haven't decided whether or not I'll tell him."

"Oh I see," he said, his knuckles white as he clenched both hands into fists. "Somehow, you felt obliged to tell *me* the truth, and turn *my* life upside down, but you're going to go easy on him, is it? Well, fuck that, Jenny!"

He stood up and angrily resumed flinging his clothes into his suitcase, rumpling and creasing his shirts as he did. "He deserves to know the truth too, don't you think? After all, he *is* Holly's father!" And with this, unable to hold back his feelings any longer, Mike broke down and began sobbing uncontrollably.

Jenny went to him, anxious to hold him in her arms, to apologise, to try and make everything OK again. But as he turned away from her, she knew deep down that for Mike things would never be OK again.

What she had said to him was true: she *hadn't* yet decided whether or not to tell Roan. But it wasn't about that. His return had simply been the catalyst for Jenny to rid herself of the guilt that consumed her every day, since she discovered her fears about Holly's parentage had been realised.

It had hit her suddenly not long after her daughter was born, when one day she noticed Holly watching a baby-mobile dangling above her cot, puzzled by it. She had been staring at it with the same expression that Jenny had often seen Roan use, when he was perplexed about something. Additionally, as she got older, Holly's complexion and hair colour became darker, whereas Mike and Jenny were both fair. She had inherited her mother's pale blue eyes and this it seemed was enough to deflect comment or suspicion from anyone, including Mike.

But strangely enough, Holly appeared to possess Mike's temperament. She was rarely grumpy or troublesome, and if anything, Jenny thought, she was an unusually good-natured child, always smiling and laughing at anyone who noticed her. She adored attention but unlike most other toddlers Jenny had come across, didn't roar or sulk if it wasn't forthcoming. Often, she had been stopped on the street while talking Holly for a walk, complete strangers captivated by her daughter's beaming smile and happy giggle.

"She's got the cutest little dimples," an older woman

had said to her one day, while bending down to admire Holly in her buggy. Jenny had been so upset by this that she had rushed off without a word, leaving the woman staring after her in surprise and remarking sadly that if the mother had no manners, then there wasn't any hope at all for the poor child.

Jenny stood watching in silence, as Mike finished collecting his things. Picking up his suitcase, and without looking at her, he walked through their bedroom doorway and out into the hallway. Then he hesitated a moment, dropped his bags and went into Holly's room, planting a little kiss on her forehead as she lay sleeping soundly. When he came back out and Jenny saw the pain etched on his face, she thought at that moment her heart would surely break.

"I'll – I'll try and be out of here as soon as I can," she said, afraid to look at him, aching to touch him.

Mike picked up his suitcase and head towards the front door.

"Take your time. I wouldn't want Holly ending up in a dingy flat somewhere," he said, his eyes hard as flints. He looked through Jenny as though she wasn't even there, his mind elsewhere.

She asked him where he would go. Mike told her nothing, other than she should leave a message at the office, as soon as she and Holly found somewhere else to live.

He had walked out the front door without another word and without looking back.

Jenny stood there with the door open for a long time afterwards, trying to pretend it wasn't real, hoping that it wasn't happening. She hadn't heard a word from him since. It was over, and both of them knew it.

But had she really expected anything else?

The smell of burning milk brought Jenny sharply back to the present. She looked over at the cooker and noticed to her dismay that the pot of milk she had been warming for Holly's breakfast had boiled over and congealed all over the hob. Feeling well and truly defeated, Jenny sank down at the kitchen table and put her head in her hands.

Mike was gone. It was all over. With her lies, Jenny had ruined everything. She had hoped that after he calmed down and had a chance to think about everything, that he might reconsider, he might be able to forgive her, he might even try and understand. But she knew that she didn't even have the luxury of clinging to a false hope. There was simply no hope to cling to.

She would ring him tomorrow and let him know that she and Holly would be out of house by the weekend. Despite Jenny's protests that her friend had enough to contend with, with her court case on the horizon, Karen had insisted that they come live with her until Jenny found something else.

"Anyway," Karen had said good-humouredly, "the more of us there are living there, the harder it is for them to kick us out!"

Jenny had reluctantly agreed, but only because she wanted to get away from Mike's house. She had felt guilty enough staying there after he left. Soon, she would have to find a place of her own and begin a new life, life as a single mother.

But despite the hurt, the pain and the desperation she

felt since losing Mike, Jenny felt a clear sense of relief, relief at the proverbial weight having been lifted from her shoulders, relief at the fact that she no longer had to live a lie. At least now, although uncertain about what life had in store for her and her daughter, Jenny could finally live with herself, and this thought brought her some comfort.

Ill at ease, little Holly watched her mother from across the room, upset by her melancholy demeanour and the tears running down Jenny's face.

"Da-Da!" she said, banging her spoon happily on the plastic play-chair, trying to cheer up her mother, by reciting the only word that her thirteen-month-old vocal chords could manage. "Da-Da! Da-Da! Da-Da!"

Chapter 45

Karen looked around her living-room and tried to view it through fresh eyes, prospective buyers' eyes. Inviting and homely, the warm gold walls, terracotta curtains and suite complemented the pine wooden floor perfectly.

Shane had been so proud of the house, but Karen knew that this room in particular had been his favourite. She remembered him cursing wildly the day he tried laying the wooden floor, determined that he could do it without any help. It had taken him much longer to complete it than the 'couple of hours' the sales assistant at Woodies had advised, not to mention the additional hours of repeated sanding and varnishing, but to Shane it had all been worth the satisfaction of being able to tell everyone that he had done it all himself 'no problem'.

Karen had been surprised that Shane enjoyed DIY as much as he had. He had tackled the kitchen units with gusto, albeit with a little help from Aidan, whose father was a carpenter by trade. Between them, they had ripped down the dreary wine-coloured painted doors and white frames, and had modernised the room instantly by replacing the units with bright maple doors, modern chrome handles and a solid granite worktop.

Room by room, and with infectious enthusiasm, Shane had transformed the dull décor of 22a Harolds Cross Crescent. Gone was the jaded floral wallpaper, the swirling patterned carpets and the off-white doors and skirting. Instead, he and Karen had opted for wooden fixtures and warm colours, deep reds, warm gold and terracotta.

The results had been stunning. Karen knew that if this house were to be offered on the market, it would be snapped up within days and for a grossly inflated price, netting the seller something reasonably close to a fortune.

But the house would not be going on the market anytime soon, not if Karen could help it. There was no way the Quinns were getting their grubby, selfish little hands on Shane's home, not without one hell of a fight.

Or, Karen thought, to put it less dramatically, a court battle. The solicitor had telephoned that morning to tell her that a court date had been agreed. She and Jack Quinn were to come before a judge on February 18th

Karen was determined to fight and to win.

People that she didn't even know very well, work colleagues, her boss, her next door neighbour – a snobbish woman who had never deigned to speak to either Karen or Shane before his death – had been telling her that she was coping well, that she was doing the right thing by going back to work so soon after the funeral, that she was managing 'admirably'. Even her own mother had complimented her on her ability to 'bounce back'. Mrs Cassidy had said this a few weeks after the funeral, when her parents had finally been able to tear themselves away from business, to pay her a visit – the same weekend they had scheduled to come home for the wedding.

Karen had sent them back to Tenerife early, frustrated with her mother's constant jabbering about how living in a sunny climate had done untold damage to her skin, and couldn't Karen see all the wrinkles that had suddenly appeared on her face? Clara Cassidy could never have been described as maternal, and Karen didn't expect her to be any different, but she wondered how any mother could be so self-absorbed and seemingly oblivious to her child's pain. After spending a couple of days with her mother, Karen literally had to stop herself from hitting the woman, and she was pretty sure she would have done so had Aidan not been at the house with them.

He had been wonderful, especially in the months afterwards, when everyone else, unable to be of any help, had left her alone, and got on with their own lives, hoping to regain some sense of normality. He had been the one to cancel the wedding and honeymoon arrangements, ensuring Karen would not have to make the heartbreaking calls to the register office and the hotel. Jenny and Mike had been there whenever Karen needed someone to talk to, or a shoulder to cry on, and Tessa was never off the phone asking her to come and visit her and Gerry in Cork.

On the day that was to be Karen and Shane's wedding day, both couples insisted that she come and stay with them, hoping to keep her mind occupied, but Karen couldn't bring herself to spend the day pretending. She knew that June 15th, which should have been the happiest day of her life, would now always be associated with sadness, loss, and regret. She and Jenny had never made it to Belfast for their shopping trip, so at least she didn't have a wedding dress to mock and remind her of everything she had lost.

Maybe it would get easier as time went by. People kept telling her it would, but how did they know?

Aidan was the only one who seemed to understand, the only one who didn't tell Karen that she would get over it, that it would get easier, that she had to get on with her life. United by their mutual loss, she and Aidan shared the understanding that it would be a very long time before either of them managed to do that, if ever. It was this shared understanding, and unified sorrow, that enabled Aidan and Karen to comfort one another. For this Karen had been grateful. She had been grateful that Aidan understood every time she rang him crying, lonely and vulnerable in the middle of the night, after waking up from a nightmare. She had been grateful that, unlike everyone else, he had respected her wishes to be left alone on her wedding day, but had dropped everything when she phoned that evening, and let her cry silently in his arms for a very long time. Karen knew that each would have been lost without the other's support.

However, Aidan was in serious disagreement with Karen over her decision to fight the Quinn family for possession of her house.

"Karen, I've checked it out, and in cases like this the law is absolutely clear. You are not Shane's next-of-kin; you were never his next-of-kin. You can't fight the wording on it," he had said one day, after Karen had been turned down again by yet another solicitor, unwilling to take the case.

But nothing anyone could say would stop her. Karen was going to fight Jack Quinn and she was going to win.

* * *

That evening Jenny arrived, anxious, tired, and straining with the weight of her problems, and the bags containing Holly's things.

"I didn't want to leave anything behind," she explained, seeing Karen eyeing the Punto's open boot, which contained a stack of suitcases and a pile of black refuse sacks, ostensibly containing everything Jenny had ever owned.

"Did you tell Mike you were coming here?" Karen asked her, trying to ignore Holly holding her arms out towards her, obviously wanting to be untied from her car seat. Holly was one of the few children that Karen wasn't afraid of, but she wouldn't go as far as picking her up and cuddling her.

"Here, I'll get the bags – why don't you organise Holly first?" she said.

Jenny handed her the bags with a grateful look. She mopped her sweating brow and then went about the not-inconsiderable task of settling Holly.

"He was in a meeting when I called, so I left a message on his voice-mail," Jenny said, referring to Mike. "I was glad in a way, because then I didn't have to speak to him directly – Holly, stop whingeing! But," she continued, "Alison the receptionist, who obviously didn't recognise my voice – and I didn't introduce myself – told me that Mr Williams was available to take Mike's calls and would I like to speak to him?" She rolled her eyes. "I would have laughed, only it's not one bit funny."

Karen nodded sympathetically, understanding that things were difficult for Jenny, but they must be equally as difficult for Mike, who had to continue working with Roan since discovering who he was, and what he stood for.

Later, after Jenny had settled her things in the spare room, and Holly was sleeping peacefully in her carry-cot, Karen opened a bottle of wine, and the two of them sat companionably in her living-room.

"So, how are you feeling?" Karen asked, pouring her friend a glass of Chablis.

"Better than I expected, to be honest," she answered. "I was just so anxious to get out of there. Thanks so much for letting us stay here."

Karen waved her away. "You're welcome, but unfortunately I can't add that you can stay as long as you like! I told you that a date has been set for the case, didn't I?"

Jenny nodded. "You're definitely going to go through with it, then?"

"Absolutely," Karen said in a tone that brooked no argument. "I told you before, even if I haven't a chance in hell, I'm not letting the Quinns think they can walk all over me like that."

"But what happens if the courts side with Jack Quinn? That's the general consensus, isn't it, that as a common-law wife you have effectively no rights?"

Karen sighed. "Jenny, please don't try and talk me out of this. I didn't take the decision lightly, you know. It took me long enough to get this thing into the courts as it is."

"I know that. And I know how important the house is to you. But don't you think that this whole thing is . . ." She broke off, thinking that if she continued with what she was going to say, her friend would go ballistic. "I'm just afraid that you'll get hurt," she said softly. "There's no love lost between you and the Quinns and you never know what they might say about you, what kind of things they might drag up. Character assassination is a great way to lose any sympathy you might get."

Karen gave a short laugh. "You've been watching too much Judge Judy. I know what I'm doing, Jen."

Jenny shifted uncomfortably in her seat. She and Karen had had this conversation many times before, and she knew by now that Karen would never yield to anyone else's point of view. She feared that her friend was making a big mistake taking on Shane's family over an already established point of law. She couldn't possibly win and the Quinns knew it, their solicitor knew it, and Karen's solicitor knew it. The only person that didn't know it – or at least wouldn't admit to it – was Karen.

Jenny believed that the entire situation would end not only in tears, but also with a fat expenses bill from both solicitors. And Karen certainly couldn't afford that; she could barely afford the mortgage. As things stood, practically all of her salary went towards the repayments.

"What does Aidan think?" she asked carefully.

Karen sniffed. "He wants me to give it up, forget about it, – same as you do."

"Karen, it's not like that. You know full well that I'll support you, *we'll* support you every step of the way – we're just not as convinced as you are that this is the best way forward."

"And what am I supposed to do, Jenny?" Karen said, cheeks reddening with annoyance. "Where am I supposed to go? This is my home, our home, Shane's and mine. He worked himself to the bone to get the deposit, sacrificed a lot to keep up the repayments. You know how tight things were for us. It can't be all for nothing!"

Her eyes flashed angrily as she spoke. "You saw it yourself the other day when the estate agent called here. Jack Quinn wants to sell this place off – he doesn't care about me, doesn't care about Shane and what he might have wanted. He just wants to make a profit, another few quid to add to the thousands of euros he already has in the bank! He doesn't give a shit, Jenny!" She wiped her eyes viciously and in such a way that, if any tears even thought about appearing, they would disappear just as quickly if they knew what was good for them.

Jenny wished she hadn't said anything. It was, and had always been a very sore subject, since they first learnt of the Quinn's intention to sell the house and Karen's decision to fight them.

Mike had told Jenny privately on more than one occasion that Karen 'hadn't a chance in hell'. Since the house and the mortgage had never been in her name, she had absolutely no rights over the property, other than what she had paid towards the mortgage. She could certainly argue that she had contributed towards furnishings and improvements which consequently increased the value of the house, but with the way house prices were rising in Dublin these days, it would be difficult to prove this or put any kind of figure on it. And as Jack Quinn had guaranteed the mortgage in the first place, everything was in his favour.

Saying nothing more, and allowing Karen to calm down a little, Jenny reached for the bottle of wine and refilled their glasses.

"I'm sorry," Karen said softly.

Jenny smiled. "Don't be silly. You're entitled to get upset, you know. We all do it, believe me," she added wryly.

Karen picked up a strand of her dark hair and began twisting it between her fingers.

"I know you're only trying to help, Jen, but can we change the subject?"

Jenny knew better than to say any more. She had thought, *hoped* that just for a minute back there, she was getting through to Karen. But she had forgotten how solidly stubborn her friend could be.

The telephone rang in the hallway and Karen got up to answer it. Seconds later, she took the portable handset back into the living-room with her, raising an eyebrow at Jenny, as she listened to whatever the person on the other end was saying.

"Here she is now," she said, eyeing Jenny who gave her a curious look, wanting to know who the caller was. Karen shrugged as she handed her the handset.

"Hello?" Jenny said curiously.

"Jenny – hi, it's Rebecca. I hope you don't mind me ringing you here. I got the number from Rachel."

"Rebecca . . . um, hi, how are you?" Jenny was shocked. Why was Mike's ex phoning her at Karen's? And, more importantly, how did Rebecca know she was here?

Jenny's tone must have betrayed her, because straightaway Rebecca answered her unspoken questions. "Look, Jenny, Mike told me what happened."

Mortification burned through Jenny like fire through crepe paper. How could he have told Rebecca about the break-up – and so soon?

"He told you?" she said, her voice high with emotion.

"Yes, but that's not the reason I rang. I'm not trying to judge you, or take sides or anything – believe me I probably would have done the same thing in your position – after all, you weren't to know but –"

"You would have done the same thing in my position – you mean he told you *everything*?" Jenny felt the blood rush to her head so quickly; she thought she would faint there and then. Betrayal, anger and disappointment coursed simultaneously through her, as she tried to take in what Mike had done. How *dare* he? How dare he humiliate her and Holly like that? She knew that Mike had been shocked and betrayed, but did he have to exasperate those feeling by telling everyone else? It didn't sound like the Mike she knew.

The worst feeling of all though, was the realisation that Mike was obviously determined to cut both of them – not just herself but Holly too – out of his life completely. She hoped that maybe he might continue to see Holly, just for the child's sake. It had been a slim hope, but a hope nonetheless. After all, he had been a father to Holly since the day she was born, had been beside Jenny throughout her fifteen hours of labour, and had even cut the umbilical cord. She knew that she was being selfish in assuming that he might be able to come to terms with it, but Holly had been Mike's world. He couldn't have loved her any more than he did, or so she had thought. But he was obviously going to let Holly suffer for what Jenny had done, by revealing the truth about her father to anyone that might be interested. This showed a cruel and unforgiving side of him that Jenny hadn't thought existed.

Rebecca continued. "I only rang because I thought you must be wondering where Mike is staying and if he's OK. I know he probably didn't even ring to tell you where he went, but he was staying with Rachel these last few days. Don't worry," she added, correctly reading Jenny's thoughts. "He hasn't told her anything, but you know Rachel, she'll be digging like crazy to find out what's going on, and he's sworn me to secrecy. Anyway, love, I just wanted to let you know that I'm thinking of you and don't worry – it'll all work out in the end."

Jenny barely remembered saying goodbye to the other woman and her head was spinning as she put down the phone.

"What did she want?" Karen asked, intrigued by the one side of the conversation she had heard.

"I don't honestly know," Jenny said, wide-eyed with mystification. "It was one of the strangest conversations I have ever had. From what I can make out, Mike told Rebecca that we had broken up and she just phoned to tell me that he's fine and that everything will work out in the end. What do you think of that? The woman must be on drugs, or something!"

Chapter 46

It was a mild day, but the sun was nowhere to be seen. A dense blanket of dark, angry cloud that threatened rain had hidden it well.

As she continued walking up the hill, Karen found the air becoming thicker as it passed through her lungs. It was especially humid today, she noticed, although maybe it was just that she was here again. She didn't visit very often, didn't feel the need to, because she knew that Shane was always with her.

But today, Karen needed to ask him something.

She noticed that the Quinns had erected a mammoth black marble headstone at the head of the grave. Shane's name, date of birth and date of death had been etched in gold underneath a similar inscription bearing the name of Patrick Quinn, Shane's father. Karen had only been at the graveside twice, once at the funeral and again last year for Shane's first anniversary, but judging by the headstone's pristine appearance and the fresh-looking etchings, it had been a recent addition to the hundreds, maybe thousands of other memorials in the graveyard.

She took the gift she had brought him – a small teddy bear dressed in a miniature Liverpool football jersey – out of its bag, and sat it against the headstone. She smiled. Shane would get a laugh out of that.

"They still haven't won anything, love, not this year, but supposedly they're getting better and better," she said conversationally. "Mike says they're got some great players, so it's only a matter of time. Michael Owen is back from injury and scoring mad, but unfortunately that Manchester crowd are still doing it better than everyone else. Maybe next year." Karen gave a little laugh and then her expression grew serious. She swallowed hard. "Shane, I'm in a bit of a quandary and I need your advice. This court case between your brother and me is coming up next week. I know I told you before that I was going to keep going, that I was going to fight to the end but, love, I don't know if I'm doing the right thing any more." She bit her lip. "I'm tired. I mean, sometimes I can barely sleep at night for thinking about it. And I feel angry all the time, not just angry at your mam and Jack, but angry at everyone! I get so wound up these days by everything, even the simplest little things. And I know that people think I'm crazy and obsessive about this, so much so that they can't even talk about it any more, without me flying into a rage. They all think I'm going to lose, that I haven't a hope of winning but they just can't understand that I have to try – for your sake I have to try, don't I?"

She tried to imagine his face in front of her, but Karen found that as time went on, this was becoming more and more difficult. It wasn't as though she had forgotten him, it was just getting harder to picture Shane exactly how he had been. The thought terrified her.

"It's just – God, this is hard – it's just that I don't know if I'm doing the right thing any more, love. I'm finding it hard trying to make ends meet, and you know I've never *ever* been the best with money, but it's so difficult to keep paying this mortgage on my own. I know how important that house was to you, and it's important to me too but, Shane, I don't know if I have the strength left in me to fight for it any more."

Karen stooped low beside the grave, and leaned her head on the headstone, tears dropping quickly onto cold marble. "I know that you'd have wanted me to try, and I will if you want me to. But if you could just let me know, somehow, what you think I should do. Please Shane, could you? Because I just don't know any more. I'm doing my best to keep your memory alive, but it's just so hard!"

Hearing a sound behind her, Karen jumped up with fright. She looked behind her and saw a woman wearing a headscarf standing at the foot of another grave about ten yards away. The woman sneezed again and, head bent low; she held a handkerchief up to her mouth, appearing not to have noticed Karen.

Karen exhaled a long breath, the unexpected interruption calming her a little. She turned back to the grave.

"I'd better go, love," she said softly. "It looks like it's about to rain." She gazed up at the by-now almost black clouds above them, clouds about to let loose a torrent of rain that would fall as quickly as balloons at midnight on New Year's Eve.

Karen gathered her jacket tightly around her shoulders, and walked quickly back towards the car. She had just reached it and was struggling to find her keys, when she felt heavy drops of rain on her head. She was soaked within seconds, having been unable to locate the offending keys, and then swore under her breath as she realised they had been in the ignition all along.

The car wasn't locked and a drenched Karen removed her sopping leather jacket and flung it behind onto the back seat. Luckily, there was a fleece in the car. In an attempt to get dry, Karen put it on, then looked up miserably at the seemingly endless rain clouds. There wasn't a streak of blue in sight.

Despite herself, Karen chuckled. If this is supposed to be a sign from Shane, she thought, starting the ignition, she was more confused now than ever before.

* * *

'Thanks, Marion, I really appreciate that – see you soon." Jenny replaced the phone in its receiver. "She said I can take as much time off as I need, and I can take the exam at the repeats in a few months' time," she told Karen, who was trying her best not to look uncomfortable, having been given the job of feeding Holly while Jenny telephoned the office. Holly, aware of Karen's discomfort, and clearly enjoying it, giggled and shook her head from side-to-side whenever a spoonful of food approached her mouth.

"Um, Jen – I don't think she's hungry," Karen said, hoping to be relieved of her duties.

Jenny looked distracted. "What? Oh, she can be a bi

fussy sometimes. Just keep trying. She'll eat it eventually."

Karen couldn't be sure, but she was almost positive that just then she saw Holly wink at her. Encouraged by this, she tried feeding her again but to no avail. Eventually, Karen put the food back down on the kitchen table and folded her arms across her chest. As soon as she did this, Holly began to cry.

"Oh, I get it," Karen said with a sardonic smile. "You don't like it when the shoe's on the other foot, do you? Well, missy, what's good for the goose is good for the gander, and you won't get it until I'm good and ready to give it to you."

Holly gave her a look that conveyed utter disbelief.

"Karen! She's only a baby – she doesn't understand!"

"Ah, you see that's what they want, Jen – they want us all to think that they're helpless and innocent so they can get away with murder. I'll bet you anything that it's only an act, and they all know exactly what's going on all the time. We're the ones that are the fools."

"Oh, give it here, you idiot," Jenny said, a smile playing about her lips. "God help us all if you ever have children."

"Well, if I do, they won't get much past me,' Karen said. "I won't stand for any of this helpless nonsense."

Jenny nodded sagely. "Oh, I'm sure that they'll be perfectly behaved children – model children. And before the age of two they'll probably be able to hold full conversations, change their own nappies, and feed themselves, because Mommy won't let them get away with 'the innocent act'. I tell you, Karen, I can't wait to meet these kids."

Karen laughed. "Well, you'll have a long wait. There isn't even a daddy on the horizon yet."

"What about Aidan?" Jenny asked carefully. "You two have got very close."

Karen felt herself redden slightly. "Aidan's been a good friend to me."

"And?"

"And what? It wouldn't be right. I'd feel as though I was betraying Shane."

Jenny was about to start a spiel about him wanting her to be happy, but she had put her foot in it too many times before. She didn't want to risk upsetting Karen, who seemed in much better form since visiting Shane's grave the other day.

"I know what you're thinking," Karen said, "and there's a side of me that knows full well that I should move on, that way. But there's a lot that needs sorting out. I wouldn't be able to deal with seeing someone new, and all the complications associated with it."

"And what does Aidan think?"

Karen blushed. "I know he has feelings for me, but I'm not sure. We'll see what happens. There might not be anything real there; maybe we've just become artificially close because of everything we've gone through."

"It's a good a reason as any," Jenny said, thinking it would be wonderful for Karen to start living a normal life again. As far as she was concerned, her friend had grieved long enough. She would never stop loving Shane and she would never forget him, but that didn't mean that she should hide away from life and love forever. Aidan was probably the one person that would be able to understa that while Karen could never quite let go, at least she could move on. What a pity, Jenny thought, that she couldn't move on from her obsession with keeping the house.

Karen resumed feeding Holly who, this time, took the food from her without complaint. "See? I told you I'd sort her out," she said to Jenny with a grin. "Your little girl is a fast learner. She knows now that she can't mess with the likes of Karen Cassidy – Toddler Trainer Extraordinaire!"

"You idiot," Jenny said, filling a basin for the washing-up. "Now – as soon as we're finished here, I'm going to take Holly for a spin out to Dun Laoghaire to meet with this estate agent. It's the same guy that sold Mike our house in Blackrock so I hope he doesn't recognise me! Anyway, if all goes well we'll be out of your hair soon."

"I told you before that it's not a problem," Karen said with a smile. "I like having you two around. After all, I wouldn't know myself if I didn't fall over one of Holly's toys on the stairs at least once a day, and I *definitely* couldn't live without regular doses of *Bananas in Pyjamas* – hey, I'm only joking!" She ducked laughing, as Jenny tried to shower her with washing-up suds. Holly let out a shriek of delight, obviously pleased to see her mother being playful. "Seriously, you can stay as long as you like – well, as long as I'm here anyway," she added quickly.

Jenny hugged her warmly. "Thanks. I don't know what I would have done without you. I couldn't have stayed at our – at Mike's house for much longer."

Karen stood up and took a tea towel from a cupboard beneath the sink.

"How do you feel about everything now?" she asked,

picking up a bundle of cutlery and drying each piece separately, before replacing them in a drawer.

Jenny shrugged. "It's kind of strange, really, but I feel – and I'm sure that this is hard for you to understand – kind of liberated, I suppose. I couldn't ever say that I'm glad about what happened, but I'm kind of glad that I was forced into being honest."

"Have you decided whether or not you're going to tell Roan?"

Jenny stopped what she was doing for a moment and looked up. "I haven't fully decided yet but no, I don't think I'll tell him. It was never about that, really. It was more about freeing myself, if you like."

Karen hesitated. "Jen, I hope you don't mind my saying so, but I think then that it was a little unfair of you to tell Mike the truth. It all seems a little bit pointless if you don't follow it up by telling Roan. I mean, why hurt Mike and deprive Holly of a father? Why say anything at all?"

Jenny shrugged. "I had to – I just had to tell him. What kind of relationship could Mike and I have had if I didn't?"

"Yes, but you've got no relationship at all now, do you? You've sacrificed everything for the sake of one little detail."

"It's not a little detail to me, though – it never has been. I couldn't have gone on the way I had for much longer, constantly afraid that somebody might notice something. You can see for yourself how different she is from Mike and me. It would have come out sooner or later, Karen. Roan's return gave me the push I needed.'

"And none of this was about Roan at all? Not even a teeny-tiny bit?" asked Karen, anxious for Jenny's response to this particular question.

Jenny shook her head firmly from side to side, and smiled as she noticed Holly imitating her from where she sat across the room.

"Not even a teeny-tiny bit. I got over Roan a long time ago. He means nothing to me now. And any love I had for him doesn't even come close to what I feel for Mike. He is, well, he *was*, the only one for me. I don't think it's possible for me to love him any more than I do, Karen." Her eyes brimmed with unshed tears. "And it is for exactly that reason that I had to tell him. I know that he's hurting terribly now, but I think that in the long run, he'll be glad that he knows the truth. At least now he has the choice of either walking away, or living with the consequences. Imagine if he found out after we were married? Wouldn't that be a lot worse?"

Karen nodded. "Maybe you're right. But I feel sorry for him, though. He loves you two so much."

"Not any longer, but we'll have to live with it," said Jenny. "Anyway, we'll be OK, won't we Holly?"

Holly responded by grinning and waving her hands happily in the air.

Karen finished putting away the delph and boiled more water in the kettle for a pot of tea. Then she stopped and put her hand on her hips. "OK," she began, exhaling loudly, "I have to tell you something."

"What?" Jenny looked up sharply from across the room, where she had been disentangling Holly from her ~rty dinner bib.

Karen remained standing at the sink. "Aidan's met up with Roan a few times since he came back from America."

"Oh! He hasn't said anything, has he?"

"No, I don't think Aidan even has a clue that Mike and Roan are in the same line of work, let alone the same company. Anyway, Jen, after all this time, Aidan probably wouldn't even remember that you and Roan were ever going out together. You know what guys are like."

Jenny nodded silently, wondering what was coming next.

Karen took a deep breath. "Apparently, Roan got married sometime last year to an American girl that he met over there. They have a seven-month-old baby, a boy I think." She waited for a reaction from Jenny but there was none. "They moved to Ireland for a couple of reasons, one because the economy is on the slide in the States, and two, because your woman didn't want to bring up the child in the big city. Roan put out a few feelers back here, and somehow ended up at InTech."

"Wow," was all Jenny could say. Roan married – and with a baby!

"Doesn't this make you wonder whether or not you should have rushed into telling Mike?"

"Nope." Jenny said, with a definite shake of the head.

"Nope?" Karen repeated. "What do you mean 'nope'? All of this could have been avoided if you'd known about Roan's little family, surely? I mean, he's no threat to you now."

"I told you before – it was never about Roan; it was about me. Me, and *my* guilt. What you've just told me has simply made my mind up never to tell him anythin about Holly. I'll admit I mulled over it, but now he has his own life, and a wife and a child who need him. I'm sure they could do without the complication."

"Jenny, you're a strange girl. I still don't understand why you did what you did but you seem to have come to terms with it all anyway."

Jenny shrugged. "I wouldn't say that yet. But I'll get there, eventually."

Chapter 47

After lunch, when Jenny had set out for Dun Laoghaire, Karen decided to make the most of a quiet afternoon to herself by catching up on her reading. She was sitting comfortably on the couch in her tracksuit bottoms with the latest John Grisham – legs sprawled across the table, and a packet of half-eaten Boasters biscuits alongside her – when she heard the doorbell ring. Thinking it was Jenny returning early from a cancelled appointment, or an unsuccessful viewing, Karen let out a loud exaggerated sigh, hoping her friend would hear and be amused by it.

But when she opened the door Karen got the shock of her life.

There, standing in her doorway and looking oddly uncomfortable, was none other than Nellie Quinn.

"Hello, Karen," Nellie said quietly and, Karen noticed, almost shyly. "Can I come in for a minute?"

"Um, yeah, sure." Karen was so surprised to see he‘ there that she forgot to affect the menacing manner s‘

normally used for dealing with any member of the Quinn family. She and Nellie Quinn hadn't spoken to one another face-to-face for well over a year. She stood back to let Nellie pass her and instantly wished she hadn't. As usual, whenever a member of the Quinn family came within ten yards of her, the house was like the aftermath of a hurricane. Jenny had left a pile of Holly's freshly-washed baby clothes on one arm of the couch, a pair of dirty mugs sat on the coffee table, and the floor was littered with children's toys – toys that Jenny had insisted Karen leave for her to tidy when she got back from Dun Laoghaire.

Nellie, for once, didn't comment on the mess and Karen thought she seemed too preoccupied with whatever was on her mind to even notice that the dust was nearly an inch thick on top of the television.

"Karen, about this 'thing' on Wednesday," Nellie began, referring to the court case. "I'd like to talk to you about it."

Karen instantly felt her instincts sharpen and her hackles rise. "Fire away," she said, folding her arms defensively across her chest.

"Look, do you mind if I sit down?" Nellie asked, looking wearily towards the couch.

Karen sat across from her in the armchair and waited, arms still folded.

"I don't know how to begin, really," Nellie said. "I suppose I just want to tell you that I'm sorry."

Sorry? The word echoed in Karen's brain. The very last thing she expected to hear from Nellie Quinn was 'sorry'.

"I'm sorry for the way we've treated you since . . . well, ce we lost poor Shane."

Karen's mind began to race, and her brain clicked into overtime. What was Nellie trying to do? Was this some kind of trick to try and get her to back down?

"You see, Karen, we didn't – well, I suppose I didn't really understand what you were going through back then. You and I never really got along, even when Shane was still alive. Somehow I always saw you as a spoilt little girl trying to play house with my son."

"Now, hold on a minute . . ." Karen began but Nellie interrupted her with a quick shake of the head.

"I'm sorry, that's not the way I meant it to sound. What I mean is that back then I could see only what I wanted to see. Shane was my youngest and – I suppose I might as well admit it – my favourite. Jack was, and still is, very independent and the girls – well, you know yourself, girls are different." Nellie removed her glasses and smiled then – a real smile that softened her features and displaced the older woman's normally brittle countenance. "It wasn't that Shane was a Mammy's boy," she continued. "It's just that I could never quite picture him all grown-up and with a wife. I knew he had lots of girlfriends growing up, like any normal young fella, but when he met you, I knew things were different. You were the one he wanted for the long haul, and it broke my heart, to be honest."

She gave a short laugh, and Karen didn't know whether to be insulted or touched by this last remark.

"Karen, I know this will be hard for you to understand, but I would never have imagined Shane with a girl like you – now don't take that the wrong way," she said, putting a hand up to prevent Karen from speaking. "What I mean is that I always imagined Shane with a quiet little thing who was afraid to say boo to a goose – or to me. But you were nothing like that. You were never afraid to speak your mind, and you never left us in any doubt about your feelings on marriage, children or otherwise. You had everything, a good education, your own career and a strong mind and to be perfectly honest, I felt threatened by you. And after a while, everything became a battle between us. It was always you versus ourselves – Shane's family. I've thought about this before, and I've told myself that I don't really know how it happened – but now I think I do. You won't like to hear this, Karen, but you remind me of myself when I was a young one."

Without meaning to, Karen snorted.

"Oh, I know what you're thinking," Nellie said, "but I'm not wrong, you know. You and I are so stubborn that between the two of us we could make the Dalai Lama look fidgety." She laughed and Karen had to smile. "And I couldn't tolerate it. I couldn't tolerate someone getting the better of me, particularly when it came to Shane. And I know I'm not the only mother who doesn't see eye-to-eye with her daughter-in-law – sure, there have been many books written about that very struggle." Nellie paused. "But when Shane died, I didn't reach out to you and, Karen, I should have. For some reason, I was never able to imagine that you were grieving as much as I was, maybe more so because you had lost the man you were supposed to marry, whereas I had lost my son. I never pictured you grieving for him the way I did, and I was angry and upset when I heard you weren't going to the funeral. I wasn't able to put myself in your shoes, but I should have been able, because I knew what it was like to lose my Patrick." Her eyes glistened, as she stared across the room at nothing in particular.

"When Patrick died, he took a big piece of me with him. If he were here now he would probably tell you that he wished the piece he had taken was my sharp tongue!" She chuckled softly. "Anyway, over time, you and I built up a wall between us, and after Shane's death and all this business with this house, it became thicker and stronger."

Karen nodded wordlessly, still wondering where this was going.

"Karen, I was in the cemetery the other day when you were visiting Shane's grave," Nellie said slowly. She saw a shadow cross Karen's face, but continued when the other woman said nothing. "I go up there a lot. It's a nice walk and it's very peaceful – a welcome break from the farmhouse, especially if Keanu is around."

She chuckled at Karen's surprised expression. "Sure, don't I know he's a little brat, and he's only getting worse as time goes by? Anyway, a good friend of mine is buried across the way, and I said I'd pay her a quick visit before heading over to Patrick and Shane. I was in the middle of a decade of the rosary when I saw you come up. I knew you hadn't seen me, and I made my way over to you, fully intending to give you a piece of my mind for deigning to visit then, when I knew that you rarely did."

"But it isn't that I don't care!" Karen blurted out, unable to hold her counsel any longer.

"I know that, pet," Nellie soothed. "I discovered that when I overheard you talking to him. I didn't intend to eavesdrop but I was glad I did, because it was only then that I could get it into my thick skull that you had loved

Shane just as much, if not more, than any of the rest of us."
Nellie removed her glasses again and dabbed her eyes
with a handkerchief.

Karen fixed her with a look of utter disbelief. "How
could you *not* know that!" she almost shouted. "How
could you *not* know that I was hurting as much as the rest
of you, that I'm *still* hurting?"

"Shush, child, let me finish, please."

Karen sat back rigidly in her seat.

"All this time, I thought that you were fighting to keep
this house simply to try and get one over on us – on me
even. That you were determined to fight to the death for
the house, just to prevent us from getting our hands on it.
It was only when I heard you talking the other day that I
realised exactly why you're doing what you're doing.
You're trying to hold onto him, aren't you Karen? You're
simply trying to preserve all that you have left – your
memories."

Nellie leant over and took one of Karen's hands in
hers. Karen looked away from her; her eyes brimming
with unshed tears. "But, love, that won't work – Shane is
gone. There's only one place where you can keep those
memories safe, and that's there, in your heart." She
grasped Karen's hand tightly. "When Patrick died, at first
I wouldn't let anyone near anything belonging to him. I
wouldn't let them get rid of his things – you know the
way people always force you to do that afterwards? They
tell you that it's for the best, that it'll be easier, but how do
they know? How do they know that it'll be easier? They
don't know how it feels – how you feel, when it's like
someone has sliced you in two, taken away one half and

told you to fend for yourself with the half that's left. Karen, I did you a great disservice when Shane died, because I left *you* to fend for yourself. I should have helped you. I should have known what you were going through, because I went through it too."

Karen sat quietly on the couch; her entire body heaving with sobs that wouldn't come. When eventually they did, Nellie went to her and held her close, and the two women wept together for a long time – at last sharing one another's grief.

"I'm sorry," Karen said, after a little while. "What you said there was true for me too. To be honest, when Shane died, I didn't give a toss about what you were feeling. I was too wrapped up in myself and so determined to keep you away from the house."

Nellie waved her away. "There's two of us in it, and we're as bad as one another. At this stage, there's no point in going back over it. What's done is done, and we've both made some stupid mistakes."

They sat in silence and then, after a while, Nellie smiled and patted Karen's hand. "Go in there and make us an oul' cuppa, and the two of us will have a chat about the house, and see if we can sort something out between us."

Karen stood up and did as she was bid. Then, as she walked towards the kitchen, she heard Nellie give one of her trademark sniffs. "Now are you going to tidy this place up," she asked, "or will it be left to me, as usual?"

Karen looked back sharply, and then let out a sigh of relief when she saw the twinkle in Nellie's eyes, and the smile playing about her lips.

Chapter 48

Jenny struggled with her City of Dublin map, while trying to block out the sound of Holly *la-la-la-ing* to the Steps song playing on the radio. Holly was a huge Steps fan and by the sounds of it, Jenny thought, she had serious aspirations towards becoming a pop star herself once she was old enough.

"King's Green, King's Lawn – where the bloody hell is King's Terrace?" she asked out loud impatiently, and then instantly put a hand to her mouth. She was a very bad mother. If Holly's next words were 'bloody' or 'feck'; then Jenny had only herself to blame.

She finally located King's Terrace, which was, from what Jenny could make out on the map, a lot closer to Seapoint than to Dun Laoghaire.

It was here that she was to meet the estate agent to view the two-bedroom apartment that might possibly end up as her and Holly's new home. She drove expertly along the narrow streets, turned left where the map indicated, and a few minutes later spied a row of run-down three-storey terraced houses. The faded green and white sign fixed to the red-brick wall of the end house confirmed to Jenny that she had reached King's Terrace. She checked her watch. It was two-forty, she was ten minutes late and there was no sign of the estate agent.

"Terrific," Jenny said out loud, to no one in particular. Holly chuckled contentedly behind her in the car seat. "Oh, you might think it's funny now, missy, but if Mummy doesn't find anywhere for us to live soon, we might have to give away all your toys to the St Vincent de Paul."

Holly was silent on cue, and Jenny searched in her handbag for the estate agent's telephone number. She was certain that she had the number in her wallet. Or had she put it in the glove compartment, just in case?

"Da-Da! Da-Da!" Holly cried, waving her arms up and down. "Da-Da!"

"Daddy's not here, honey," Jenny said, absentmindedly continuing her search. Frustrated, she struggled out of her seatbelt to allow herself room to search underneath the passenger seat. When she heard a knock on the driver's side window, Jenny jumped up with a start, and bumped her head on the inside of the car roof.

"Jesus!" she said, when she realised who was there. She rolled down the driver's window.

"No, it's not Jesus," Mike said. "Sorry to disappoint you." He shifted his gaze towards the back seat. "Hello, baby. Aren't you the pretty girl today?"

Jenny thoughts raced through her mind like a horse on the first day of Cheltenham. What was Mike doing? How had he known they were here? What did he want?

Then for one terrible second the thought crept into her mind that he might attempt to snatch Holly.

"This is a coincidence," Jenny said to him, as calmly as she could muster. "Are you visiting a client around this area, or something?" It looked unlikely, but some of Mike's clients had offices tucked away in housing estates worse than this one.

"No, I came here to meet you two, actually," he said, resting one arm on the roof of the car. "I think we need to talk."

"Oh." Jenny couldn't think of anything to say as Mike opened the passenger door, and sat in beside her. He turned back again towards Holly and caught her by the hand. Panicked by his interest in the child, Jenny asked him, "What's all this about?"

Mike took a deep breath. "Can we go somewhere else? I don't really want to talk about it here. Maybe we can take a walk down by the pier – do you have the buggy with you?"

That was it, Jenny thought. He was going to trick her into bringing Holly down to the harbour and then he would run off with the buggy and grab the ferry to England!

"I don't have the buggy with me," she lied.

"What's wrong, Jenny – don't you trust me?" Mike said with a menacing smile, and all of a sudden Jenny felt terrified by him. But then his face changed, and he laughed.

"I'm sorry," he snorted, "but it's so obvious from your face what's going on in that imaginative little head of yours. You thought I was about to run off somewhere with Holly, didn't you?"

"No, I did not," Jenny said, her red cheeks betraying her. "I'm just trying to figure out what you're doing here, that's all. You have to admit Mike, it's a bit strange our meeting here like this."

"It's not strange at all. I arranged it that way."

"You what?"

"I arranged it. The estate agent had to cancel today. He had lost your number apparently, but recognised you from that time he sold us the house. He had my mobile number on file, so he rang me instead and I told him I'd let you know. So here I am."

"You came all the way out here on a Friday evening to pass on the message face-to-face. Why didn't you ring me at Karen's?"

"Because I wanted to see you," he said seriously. "We have some things to discuss. I thought this would be the perfect opportunity."

Jenny said nothing.

"Look, let's go for a walk somewhere with Holly, maybe not the pier but somewhere quiet. What do you think?"

She nodded, wondering what was to come. She drove away from shabby King's Terrace and drove for a few minutes until she reached The People's Park, not far from the centre of Dun Laoghaire. With Holly strapped safely into her buggy, and Jenny at the helm, the threesome walked companionably through the park.

"When you first told me about you and Roan, I didn't understand," Mike began. "I didn't understand why you had lied to me for so long, and then shattered all we had built by admitting the truth. I don't know how ma" times I repeated that conversation over and over in my head these last few weeks." He paused for a moment. "But there was one thing you said that stuck out in my mind. *'I love you too much to lie to you any longer.'* At the time Jen, that didn't make any sense to me. I mean, how could you say you love me in one breath, and yet destroy everything that was precious to me in the next?"

"I had to," she said simply. "The guilt had been killing me, eating me up inside for so long, that I knew I couldn't go on any longer. I should have told you at the beginning I know that, but it just went on and on, and then I wasn't even sure if Roan was the father and – "

"There was never any question that Roan might not be the father," Mike said, stopping and turning to look at her. "I should have realised that, and I should have told you that, a long time ago."

Jenny's eyes widened. "What? You should have told me what? What are you talking about, Mike?"

He sat down wearily on a bench nearby and Jenny stayed standing beside him.

"I could have saved you all that worry, all that guilt, and all that confusion if I had been honest with you from the very beginning," he said.

"What do you mean?" she asked again, nervously.

Mike exhaled. "When we found out that you were pregnant and I started jumping around like some demented kangaroo, remember you asked me why I was so happy about it, when I never wanted to have kids with Rebecca?"

Jenny nodded.

Mike hung his head. "That wasn't it. It was never that ʾidn't want to, Jenny. The simple truth is that I couldn't."

Jenny's mouth dropped open in surprise.

"I couldn't . . . *can't* have children," Mike continued, his voice low. "It was true that I wanted to wait until InTech was up and running, and Rebecca agreed that we should wait until I thought the time was right. Eventually, we decided to give it a go. We tried for over a year and a half, and when nothing was happening we both went for fertility testing. The doctors soon discovered that I have an abnormally low sperm count, and low sperm motility. They told me that the chances of my fathering a child were extremely low, even with IVF. Rebecca was devastated. As you know she's older than I am, and the doctors told us that her age would probably work against us if we tried IVF. We tried anyway, but nothing happened." Mike paused for a moment and then continued, his voice hoarse. "At first Rebecca was fine. She was supportive of my 'problem' and we decided that we'd do whatever we could, try whatever we could to help us conceive. But eventually, the strain of it all got to both of us, and Rebecca began to blame me for not wanting to try for a baby sooner. Her thinking was that if I hadn't wanted to wait, then she would have been that bit younger, and our chances would have been better with IVF. Eventually her bitterness and my guilt drove us apart."

Jenny listened silently, tears running slowly down both cheeks.

"If I had told you that at the beginning when we got engaged, if I had been honest with you back then, you wouldn't have had to lie to me, and when you became pregnant the truth would have been there for all to see. But I was so thrilled when I heard you were pregnant,

Jenny. I thought that by some miracle, or freak of nature I had managed to do what the doctors thought I never could."

"Oh, Mike . . . "

"I'm sorry," he said. "I'm sorry that I didn't tell you. You deserved to know that, as much as I deserved to know the truth about Holly. Rebecca went on and on at me from the very beginning of our relationship to get everything out in the open with you. You remember she reacted strangely when she heard about your pregnancy? That's because she knew that there was no way I could be the father. She'd researched these things, she knew what the percentages were, and she knew what the doctors had told us. She realised straight away that something was amiss. But I foolishly believed that some kind of miracle had happened."

"So Rebecca knew all along that you weren't Holly's father?"

What Rebecca had said on the phone the other night now made sense to Jenny. *'I'm not judging you. I probably would have done the same thing in your position . . . '*

Jenny felt her insides spin, felt as though the ground was rising up to meet her. Rebecca had known all along.

"She wanted to speak to you then, to ask you if there was anything funny going on but I wouldn't let her. I was angry with her for even thinking that you might have done anything wrong, and I wouldn't let myself believe that such a thing could have happened. As far as I was concerned, I was Mr Supersperm – defying all the odds, a medical miracle!" He gave a wry smile and looked out towards the sea.

Jenny stared at Holly, her thoughts going a mile a minute. She tried to comprehend what she was feeling – anger, hurt, disappointment, what? But Jenny knew that she felt none of those things.

They were both silent for what seemed like a very long time, and then Mike tentatively took her hand. Holly gurgled up at them both and he looked at the child tenderly.

"We haven't given her a very good start, have we?" Mike said softly. "The very foundation of our relationship was built on lies."

"That's not true," Jenny shook her head. "We loved one another, didn't we? I made one very stupid mistake, and by some cruel twist of fate it turned back on itself and against me. You wanted to believe something so much that you were afraid to face the truth. There's nothing wrong with that, Mike."

"Yes, there is," he said firmly. "I should never have asked you to marry me without telling you beforehand. That was my first mistake. God knows I should have learnt how something like that could kill a marriage before it's even begun."

"You thought you were doing the right thing, I suppose."

"And I understand that you thought you were doing the right thing too."

She nodded and again they grew quiet.

"What are we like – the two of us?" Jenny said, after a little while.

He sighed. "I take it that you haven't told Roan."

She shook her head.

"He hasn't been acting anyway out of the ordinary at work, and he's still anxious to meet you, so he obviously has no idea who you are. I didn't tell him that he's already met you, so to speak." Despite himself, Mike managed a tiny grin.

Jenny shrugged. "There was no point. From what I understand he has his own life now."

"Ah, I take it you've heard about Kelly?"

"Karen told me. Have you met her?"

He nodded. "She seems like a nice girl, but is very obviously a ball-breaker who keeps Roan on his toes. I pity him, actually."

"Imagine?" Jenny smiled.

Mike began caressing her hand with his thumb. "Look, Jen, I don't know how you feel about what I've told you today, and I'm not asking you to make any snap decision but – "

Jenny's expression grew serious. "Mike, Holly needs people around her that she can trust."

"Yes." He looked away glumly.

"People she can rely on."

"Of course." He took his hand away and hung his head.

"I suppose," Jenny said, with a twinkle in her eye, "I suppose we could always put her up for auction on the Internet, and see if we could find such people for her."

Mike's eyes widened for a second, and then his face broke into a wide smile. "You brat – you frightened me there for a minute."

"Are you mad? I couldn't frighten you."

"Come here."

"Where?"

"Here." Mike encircled Jenny's waist with his arms and pulled her close to him.

"OK." She leaned forward, waiting for his kiss.

"OK!"

Startled, they both looked up and Holly chuckled happily, pleased to have had the final say on the matter.

THE END

Jenny stared at Holly, her thoughts going a mile a minute. She tried to comprehend what she was feeling – anger, hurt, disappointment, what? But Jenny knew that she felt none of those things.

They were both silent for what seemed like a very long time, and then Mike tentatively took her hand. Holly gurgled up at them both and he looked at the child tenderly.

"We haven't given her a very good start, have we?" Mike said softly. "The very foundation of our relationship was built on lies."

"That's not true," Jenny shook her head. "We loved one another, didn't we? I made one very stupid mistake, and by some cruel twist of fate it turned back on itself and against me. You wanted to believe something so much that you were afraid to face the truth. There's nothing wrong with that, Mike."

"Yes, there is," he said firmly. "I should never have asked you to marry me without telling you beforehand. That was my first mistake. God knows I should have learnt how something like that could kill a marriage before it's even begun."

"You thought you were doing the right thing, I suppose."

"And I understand that you thought you were doing the right thing too."

She nodded and again they grew quiet.

"What are we like – the two of us?" Jenny said, after a little while.

He sighed. "I take it that you haven't told Roan."

She shook her head.

"He hasn't been acting anyway out of the ordinary at work, and he's still anxious to meet you, so he obviously has no idea who you are. I didn't tell him that he's already met you, so to speak." Despite himself, Mike managed a tiny grin.

Jenny shrugged. "There was no point. From what I understand he has his own life now."

"Ah, I take it you've heard about Kelly?"

"Karen told me. Have you met her?"

He nodded. "She seems like a nice girl, but is very obviously a ball-breaker who keeps Roan on his toes. I pity him, actually."

"Imagine?" Jenny smiled.

Mike began caressing her hand with his thumb. "Look, Jen, I don't know how you feel about what I've told you today, and I'm not asking you to make any snap decision but – "

Jenny's expression grew serious. "Mike, Holly needs people around her that she can trust."

"Yes." He looked away glumly.

"People she can rely on."

"Of course." He took his hand away and hung his head.

"I suppose," Jenny said, with a twinkle in her eye, "I suppose we could always put her up for auction on the Internet, and see if we could find such people for her."

Mike's eyes widened for a second, and then his face broke into a wide smile. "You brat – you frightened me there for a minute."

"Are you mad? I couldn't frighten you."

"Come here."